KEEPING SECRETS

Sarah Shankman

SIMON AND SCHUSTER
NEW YORK • LONDON • TORONTO • SYDNEY • TOKYO

SIMON AND SCHUSTER
Simon & Schuster Building
Rockefeller Center
1230 Avenue of the Americas
New York, New York 10020

10 9 8 7 6 5 4 3 2 1

Library of Congress Cataloging in Publication Data

Shankman, Sarah.
    Keeping secrets.
    I. Title.
PS3569.H3327K44   1988   813'.54   88-4485
ISBN 0-671-66057-8

There are many people I would like to thank for their generosity, love and support during the writing of this book. The Virginia Center for the Creative Arts and its director, William Smart, and staff have four times given me a room and a studio of my own, gifts beyond measure. Tom Smythe read the first words and said yes. Rita Sitnick and Vin Gizzi, Laura and Vin Gizzi, Sr., Karen and Gary Bradley are always home. Harvey Klinger, my agent, is also a wonderful editor who keeps me on track even when I don't want to be there. Trish Lande, my editor, and Cheryl Weinstein, her assistant, have been grand. And many thanks and much love to all the other friends in New York, Atlanta and California who cheer me on, who put me up to it.

This book is dedicated with love to the memory of Robert M. Daniels—Southern gentleman, gifted artist, uncommon friend and the dearest of dearhearts.

1

Los Gatos, California
1974

THE RAIN pattered on the rooftop of the house in which Emma and Jesse Tree lay sleeping. Emma's dream shifted; someone was tap-dancing. Clickety, clickety, click—her unconscious heard the rain as time-steps.

In the small yard, squirrels chittered to one another about the falling water. Would it wash away the nuts they'd hidden so carefully in the redwood siding that covered the small two-story house? They'd tucked reserves into its red shutters too, and around the edges of the now screened-in carport where in summer the Trees potted begonias and barbequed. Would it wash away the ivy they'd watched Emma plant beneath the back of the house where the house stood on stilts?

The rain ran in torrents down the single-lane twisting road that led to the house. It wiped out the tracks of pickup trucks lugging in cords of wood for the canyon's fireplaces. It washed them down into the creek which flowed out of the canyon, under the highway, into the reservoir.

It scrubbed the large windows that paraded across the back of the Trees' bedroom, cleaning the outside where Emma couldn't reach, for the land dropped off there and she'd need a ladder fifty feet tall.

Emma was dreaming of sailing now, sailing in rough seas. Salty water was splashing in her face, roiling in bigger and even bigger waves. She was going to drown. Someone had been in the boat with her, but now he had disappeared. She was all alone, terrified, and there was water, rising water, everywhere.

Then she jolted awake to the taste of salt in her mouth. She was drinking her own tears.

She wiped her bright-blue eyes open. Then Emma, a long, pretty blonde woman, smiled. She wasn't drowning after all. She was safe, well, as safe as she could be, in bed with her husband, Jesse. It was only the first rain, early this season, only the rainfall of which she was dreaming.

Thank God, the rain was back from wherever it had spent its summer vacation. Emma hated the long annual drought that spread from May to October, sometimes November, the endless golden days when nothing changed, as if the weather wore a permanent smile and she felt that she should, too. If the weather was this good, shouldn't she be deliriously happy? Instead, she waited for the rain as if she were waiting for her period, holding her breath, teetering on the edge of good news or bad.

Slyly, slowly then, Emma pulled her long blonde hair across her face like a curtain. She peeked through it to see whether Jesse was awake.

She hoped not. She wanted to lie here for a while alone.

She didn't want to answer Jesse's questions about the weekend she'd just spent in Berkeley. She didn't want him to reach over and tweak her nipple like the switch on the automatic coffeemaker, as if he could turn her on just like that. She wanted to simply wallow in the glory, like the first taste of a lemon-meringue pie, of this first day of rain—and she had the time to do that.

Emma had never had free time in the fall before—teachers didn't. But this year she'd taken a leave from the junior college where she taught literature and composition. In another month she'd be leaving for Italy, then France.

She stretched her arms, but carefully so as not to awaken Jesse. Oh, she was in hog heaven, happy—as they would say back home, her home, in Louisiana—as a pig in shit on this rainy October Monday morning. Nowhere to be, nothing pressing. How she adored rainy days with no have-tos. They were like Saturday mornings when she was a child, a little bit too comfortable to rise and shine with Big John and Sparky on the radio who couldn't see her anyway—so she'd told herself in West Cypress. How would they know if she didn't march around her room when Sparky sang their theme song? "If you go down in the woods today, you'd better not go alone."

But this morning she was already in the woods in her California mountain home, and she most certainly was not alone.

She sneaked another blue-eyed look at Jesse, listened to his steady breathing and his little whistling snore.

Then, propped on one elbow, she studied his lovely paper-bag-brown face, the full lips, the slight tilt of his closed lids. The springy curls of his short black hair and beard were sprigged just here and there with white. He was holding his own. Jesse, she thought, you're going to be gorgeous forever. Who would guess that you're thirty-six? But then his brown skin was never going to tell tales on him as her complexion, translucent as a fine china cup, was beginning to.

Emma ran her eyes over her husband's naked body. Always hotter than she, he had tossed the covers down.

His broad brown chest, shoulders and arms were thick with muscle. His stomach was flat. At six feet he was a big man, but not nearly as big as people thought.

"It's the combination of things, darling, that builds the illusion," Emma had once told him, ticking off as if they were building blocks his bull-like neck, the surname Tree, his rich deep bass-baritone.

"They think you're the Jolly Black Giant," she had teased. "If it weren't for that laugh of yours you'd be downright scary." For Jesse did have the most wonderful laugh, though on this rainy morning she couldn't remember having heard it in a very long time.

"That ain't why, honey," he'd gone along with the joke, imitating a Deep South (where he'd never been) black. "It's 'cause I'm a darky is why they thinks I'se big. Big *everywhere!*"

Then he'd leered like a lunatic, wet his lips, jutted his pelvis and reached for her rear end.

"Ain't that right, Miss Emma, ain't that what you white folks think?"

They'd fallen onto the bed laughing then, Jesse rolling over her, or was it she who was on top? It hadn't mattered in those good old days, at first.

A while later, he'd breathed into her ear, "Miss Anne, Miss Anne," still teasing her with the black slang for a high and mighty white lady, "I'm coming, I'm coming." Then the joke had stopped. "Jesus, Emma," he'd gasped. She'd smiled and held him tight. But she didn't want to think about that now.

Then Miss Emma, Miss Anne, Miss Scarlett, she said to herself, staring out the windows at the rain, what are you going to think about? The rain, perhaps?

I will. I'll do just that. She closed her eyes again, and time fell back.

She was in a steamy delta summer of her childhood, flopped out in the side yard watching the thunderheads gather. The hot heavy sky darkened, and the mile-high cumulus clouds that had grown gigantic out over the Gulf piled one on top of another like meringue on a banana pudding.

Something about the waiting for them to collide and then explode made her itch. Then there was a CRASH! and the smell of ozone just as the drops began to fall was quick and sharp, a rush of aphrodisiac—though she hadn't put a name to it as a little girl. She had known only that the flash of lightning, the roll of thunder, the sudden dizziness in the sultry summer air made her want to run around the yard like a crazy person, rubbing her legs together very fast until she was tingly all over.

Now Emma sneaked another glance at her sleeping husband. Her lust for Jesse—the most handsome man she had ever known, whose sexuality practically glowed in the dark—used to strike her like lightning, stun her with its force. Where had that passion run away to now? Why did she never smell the heat, the ozone, the musk?

There *had* been a time when the rain outside drip-dripping made her grin and roll against him, tickling him awake. Then they would pull the covers over their heads and play with each other till they couldn't anymore.

"No need to rise and shine if there's no shine," Jesse had said, his fingers exploring all the while.

Where had all that loving gone?

Was it up in the beams of Skytop, the old hotel that he'd been renovating for all of their four years together?

Had their heat been transmogrified into the lodge's joists and ceilings, studs and posts, the mile after mile of cabinetry—all of which Jesse insisted on doing by hand, alone? Jesse, trained as a sculptor, was a cabinetmaker, a fine-furniture maker, an artist in wood.

When Emma met Jesse his work had already been in a host of museums, including the de Young, MOMA, the Metropolitan, and the Boston Museum of Fine Arts. He was a success—approaching fame.

But, Emma thought, nobody was ever going to see another of Jesse's massive desks of ebony, delicate tables of tulipwood, cherry jewelry boxes, signed and dated on bottoms that were finished as finely as if they were the tops. If you wanted to see Jesse's work now, you'd have to drive up and see Skytop.

THEIR conversations went like this: "Jesse, you're obsessing. You're not a carpenter, you're not an innkeeper, you're an artist. You've taken a wrong turn. You can't see the forest for the tree."

"Mixed metaphors and a bad pun, love."

"What about the New York Contemporary Crafts Show? You're going to let that opportunity pass you by?"

"How many times have I told you, Skytop *is* my work now. Every foot of it is part of one gigantic show!"

Emma changed her tack. "I never see you."

"You never saw me in the studio."

"That's not true. All I had to do was walk out the back door and up the steps. I don't know what you're doing anymore."

Jesse raised one eyebrow, cocked it like a pistol. "And you've always been an open book. Right, Emma? Always laid out every little part of yourself for me?"

"Oh, please, let's don't go over that. Jesse, come with me off this mountain. Come with me to Italy."

She could see them in her mind's eye, in a little inn, still slightly drunk on the rough red wine they'd drunk before bedding down for the night.

"Run away with me," she had begged. "Come to Europe for a while. We'll eat ourselves silly, drink buckets of good wine."

For Emma, who had been hungry for a multitude of things for most of her life, had discovered that more than anything what she wanted to do was cook, not just cook but *cook*. Her dream was to leave her junior-college English post forever, to do more than her part-time catering, to do it right: apprentice in restaurants in Italy and France and return home a chef. And now she was standing on the edge of her dream. She had finished summer school. In a few weeks she'd be cooking in a kitchen in Rome, then Provence.

"No," he said, "I have to stay here. Then we'll talk about traveling, before I go back to furniture again."

"It's not that easy to go back," she had answered.

"No," he had said, giving her a long look, "not for some things."

JESSE stirred again, murmured, groaned. He smiled, still asleep, dreaming as the rain raged.

Emma watched his face. And about whom, my good man, my dear husband, are you dreaming? Who makes you stiffen and grow erect? Your ever-loving wife, Emma Fine Tree? Or Caroline, your lover, that bitch?

I'm getting out of here, she said to herself then, easing up and reaching for her robe. Lying here lonely but not alone is no way to spend a perfectly good rainy morning.

As Emma shut the bedroom door behind her, Jesse Tree opened one brown eye and grinned. He wore a very amused expression for a man whose wife had just left him in bed with a magnificent erection.

EMMA reached out of the tub to tune the bright-red radio. Her favorite country-and-western station was fading. She couldn't make out which it was, his busted tires, busted wallet or busted heart, that was causing the singer such pain.

She wondered: If the portable radio fell into the tub, would she fry? Would her silver fillings bounce radio waves off the mountains over to the Pacific thirty miles away? Would her lover, for, yes, she too had one, though Jesse didn't know it, would her lover on his sailboat bouncing on the waves read her last electric gasps on his radio: *Mayday, Mayday?*

Suddenly the bathroom door flew open and in strode Jesse wrapped in the paisley silk robe she'd given him for Christmas. Circling around his head as he whistled were the tinkling notes of a Vivaldi melody.

Jesse loved baroque music. It wound Emma up tighter than a tick.

She splashed one hand in the water and waited for the question he would ask in his ever-so-polite classical-radio-announcer voice, his tones plummy and full as if the words Neville Marriner and St. Martin-in-the-Fields wouldn't melt in his mouth: "You don't mind if I turn this down, do you?"

But this time he didn't say that. Instead his full lips, pursed into a sweet brownness like a fig, changed their tune, segueing neatly into the lament of being busted flat in New Orleans that was playing on the radio.

Emma narrowed her eyes at his wide silken back, the interlocking figures of the paisley fitting together like pieces of a puzzle or gourds making love. What was up with him this morning? Jesse, who was whistling harmony now, hated country music.

"Excuse me," he said, lifting the toilet seat and relieving himself in a hot, splashing stream. He dropped the seat again before running cold water in the sink. One thing for which she was grateful—growing up with two sisters, Jesse did know that the proper position of the toilet seat was *down*.

He brushed his perfect teeth, then patted hot water on his cheeks and neck, on the parts where he shaved around and under his beard.

Emma stared at his reflection in the mirror.

She loved the ritual of shaving; it was a peek behind the door marked MEN. That intense act with a deadly sharp razor on the face, so close to the jugular, how did it feel, that singular act reeking of soap and testosterone? How did it feel, pitching instead of catching? Flexing muscles, slapping towels in locker rooms, all that bullshit and bravado, how did it feel?

Then his brown eyes caught her blue ones on the shiny face of the mirror. Her gaze could run, slipping off the edges, but it was already too late to hide. She knew that he knew what she was thinking.

Suddenly she was aware of her nakedness—covered only with a thin blanket of iridescent and now cooling bubbles. It reminded her of her other nakednesses, stolen embraces, things she didn't want Jesse to look into her eyes and know.

Play busy, she thought, falling back on the posturing that came naturally to a Southern girl. A study in nonchalance, she turned on the hot water and switched on the Jacuzzi.

"So, how were Clifton and Maria?"

Emma's answer, just as she'd practiced it, was cool as lemonade on a summer afternoon. "Just great. Maria and I took a drive up into the hills, found a little vineyard we'd never seen before."

"Do some tasting? Anything good?"

Emma nodded. "A dessert wine I loved."

"Since when do you like sweet wines?" He paused a beat. "But your tastes have changed so, I don't know what you like anymore."

Emma opened her mouth and closed it again. Be careful, she warned herself. This bathroom is laced with mines. Watch where you step.

Jesse turned back to the mirror now. He was letting the moment go. She couldn't believe that—Jesse retreating, Jesse who was so clever at closing in for the kill. What did he suspect about the weekend she told him she'd spent in Berkeley? What did he know? But he was concentrating now on his neck, the silvery razor flashing. Then once again he caught her reflected eye. He grinned and touched his nose.

"Wanna trade?"

It was an old joke.

Jesse's nose was almost as broad as it was long, with a rounded Santa Claus tip. Hers, like her father Jake's, was long and thin with a little hump. Night and day, black and white, they had chosen their noses to joke about.

"Sure, I'll trade." She kept it light. What did he have on his mind or up his gold-and-red-paisleyed sleeve?

She watched her husband pat himself dry, and then he turned to face her. He leaned back on the redwood vanity of his creation; in its doors graceful irises supported milk-glass dragonflies. She escaped his gaze and fiddled for a moment, letting a little of the water out of the tub. Yes, two could play this game. In fact, two were. Except that Jesse's affair with Caroline had been on the table for a while. She was still holding her lover hidden in her hand, a trump card whose value she was unsure of. She reached for a can of shaving cream, shook it and pressed the button, releasing a cloud of foam onto her fingertips. Then she lifted her long right leg and began to paint it soft white.

Jesse was leaning over her. "Here," he said, taking the razor from her, "let me do that."

Emma looked up at her husband standing over her. The sharp steel glittered. A shadow crossed her clear blue eyes.

"I'm not going to cut you, woman." He chuckled and reached for her calf. "Now give me that long pretty leg."

Her grin looked silly as she did as she was told.

Jesse pulled his robe around his middle and settled on the

edge of the tub. Then in slow careful strokes he pulled the razor
up and up again, pausing to dunk it now and then, leaving little
foam islands in the warm bubbles.

He stroked gingerly over the dead-white scar on her left shin,
a testament to the first time she had locked herself in the bathroom to scrape away her adolescent fuzz. "Emma, you open this
door this minute, do you hear?" Rosalie Fine had cried. When
she finally did, she'd left behind a bathtub full of bloody water
and a six-inch piece of shin skin curled up just like a potato peel.

"Would you relax?" Jesse goosed her in the ribs beneath the
water.

Gradually she did. She leaned back against the end of the tub
and closed her eyes. She listened to the man on the radio sing of
old love and new tricks and wondered what Jesse was up to.

When he finished with her legs, he started on her toes, lather-
ing them with soap and kneading, massaging, finding tender
places he hadn't explored in ages.

She wondered, as she stretched even longer, her limbs liquid
like warm maple syrup, what had happened to the times when
they used to play like this before making love.

Now he was sucking her toes. Nibbling. Tickling. Licking in
between. A hotline of electricity zapped straight up her legs,
making her damp in a way that the tubful of water couldn't.

The next thing she knew, he had lifted her up and out and
had wrapped a blue bath sheet around her. He was rubbing
softly through the nubby cotton, drying and warming her at the
same time. But gently, judiciously, thinking about what he was
doing. He concentrated on the hollow just above the flare of her
hips, the tender spots behind her knees. Now he was rubbing her
temples, the top of her head as if she were a pup. She tried to
fight it, wanting to stay in that distant place from Jesse where
she'd been so long, that place which neither gave her pleasure
nor caused her pain, but the momentum had already carried her
too far to catch herself. She was falling. She was done for. She
was gone.

Emma turned and pressed herself full against him. She smelled
the minty fragrance the shaving cream had left on his warm neck.
She nuzzled there, her tongue tracing the contours of the little
scoop beneath his Adam's apple.

"Jesse," she breathed.

"Yes, babe," he answered and lifted her once more. He carried her quickly past the bright-blue lacquered stairs, through the long living room, back into their bedroom, where he gently lowered her to the now-cold bed.

Outside, the rain had revved up, gathered force and speed. This was a storm now, banking against the tall windows that looked out across the valley to the tops of the mountains on the other side. But the mountains were invisible as gray sheets of rain filled the air. Naked, Emma shivered.

Heat was only a touch away. Jesse threw aside his robe and pulled her to him. He gently stretched her out full length. Nose to nose, her feet atop his, their toes pumped up/down, up/down, in a love calisthenic from the good old days, now almost forgotten.

He nibbled at her bottom lip, then let her suck his in. How long had it been, she couldn't remember, since he had moved over and let her do what she did so well? Best kisser in her class, even when she'd been caught by Rosalie practicing her technique in a church park the summer after the sixth grade. Kissing was an art, she thought, a talent. It could be developed, but you had to have a God-given gift for it, like painting, or sculpting, or writing, or music, to understand all its shades and nuances and do it well.

Which she did, but Jesse hardly ever let her. In that, as in all things, he wanted to direct. It was his mouth over hers setting the rhythm, his tongue pushing hers back. Why could she never convince him that the appeal was in the play: *Your turn, kiss, mine, I'll raise you, suck, I'll see you, rub, ours.*

But this time his mouth was listening, attentive. He let her lead, and then he answered. Once again, his mouth received. Then as she began to rock her full length against his, slowly looking for the places that felt the best, he followed. He was letting her dance.

Around and around they whirled, twirling in tandem, the rhythm and the posture ever changing. The motion and the heat grew and grew and grew, and then he found her center, and he nuzzled there, suckled there, drew it all out of her, pulled as if he were a magician, pulled all the vibrating light right out from between her legs. He dangled everything she'd ever been or wanted to be on the tip of his tongue. Then he raised his head for a moment and lowered his wet mouth on hers. She could smell her heat and taste it. He whispered, teased as his fingers replaced his mouth, then the insinuating question, "Now? Now?"

When finally she could resist no longer, she grasped him, pulled him down into her, and answered, "Yes, damnit, now!"

It was good, oh God, it was *so* good. She couldn't remember when it had last been like this.

She was soaring, lights and colors flashing behind her lids. The rain outside was pummeling, falling so hard she couldn't hear Jesse. She knew he was speaking, but she couldn't make out his meaning.

And then she did.

"Is this how he does it to you? Huh? Is this the way you like it with him?"

Her blue gaze snapped open into his brown one. His face was contorted with rage.

"Jesse?" She heard her voice, soft and small, coming from the far-off place where she'd been. She sounded like a little girl.

"Yes, bitch?"

He wasn't kidding. Something had gone very wrong. She tried to turn, to lift herself out from under him, but his big hands, strong, beautifully articulated sculptor's hands, grabbed her by the shoulders and pinned her down.

The long slow stroking had become a whole different thing. He pumped raggedly into her now. Their pelvic bones clashed and pounded. Her pale skin was going to be marked black, purple and blue.

"Jesse, you're hurting me!" she yelled right into his face.

"I know." An ugly grin pulled his lips tight, showing his ever-so-perfect teeth. "Like you hurt me, babe, fucking with that son-of-a-bitch."

She twisted, but he followed. She pushed with her hips, but his determination was too strong.

"Oh, no, you're not getting away. I'm having you this time, Miss High and Mighty, my way." He drove again and again and again inside her. "Isn't this the way you like it, you and your boyfriend?"

"Jesse," she gasped, "what the hell are you talking about?"

Lie, lie like a rug, she said to herself. Don't admit a thing until you see how far he's caught you out.

He laughed. It was a very nasty sound, the laugh that boiled up out of him when he was angry. She had never believed the laugh before, had thought it a stagey bit of business, his James Earl Jones in *The Great White Hope* routine. But this time she was a believer. He'd scare her pants off, if she were wearing any.

"Don't play coy with me, you whore," he snarled, and then he pulled himself out of her so quickly it was like a slap in reverse.

Before she could move away, he grabbed her and flipped her over. Her hands scrabbled to hold on to the side of the bed. He held one hand on the back of her neck, shoved her face deep into the pillow. The other hand was beneath her belly, lifting her up. He plunged into her again.

"Jesse, stop! I don't want to!"

"I don't give a shit what you want. What you want is that prick Tony, isn't it?" He punctuated each phrase with his cock.

Who the hell was he talking about? Tony Boccia, the restauranteur who'd hired her to cook in his kitchen from time to time, who'd helped arrange her cooking abroad, was a beautiful and charming man, but was also as queer as they come. She almost wanted to laugh. Jesse, oh Jesse, how could you be so wrong? I told you you should have met him.

He was still pumping. She'd never felt him this hard before. She was going to die before he came.

"Do you think I'm a fool?" Behind her his voice was ice. "Did you think you could flaunt it in my face and I'd never know?"

He slid a hand up under her, searching for a nipple he found, and squeezed.

"Jesse!" she grimaced.

His mouth was on her ear. "Don't you like it, my precious? A little pain? You could have used a bit of this years ago."

Was that true? She felt dizzy, sick to her stomach. The tub, the warm bubbles, the slow stroking, the excitement, the aphrodisiac of guilt, the fear, the pain: she wasn't sure where one left off and another began.

"I never slept with Tony." Her words slurred against the pillow.

He ripped himself out of her once more and flipped her over again, slamming his body down flat atop hers. His face was inches away. On her wrists, his hands were steel bands.

The question came slowly, his beautiful voice insinuating, coaxing, almost sexy, almost to the end. "Well, if you didn't fuck Tony and you didn't fuck me, and I know *damn* well I haven't been getting any, *then who the hell were you fucking this weekend?*"

His gaze drilled hers. Did he think if he looked hard enough he could read the answer printed in scarlet letters on her brain?

"Answer me." He shook her wrists, and her hands flapped as if she were a chicken. "If not Boccia, then who?"

Emma had thought about the possibility of this moment for months now. She had carefully turned it this way and that as if it were a miniature, like the tiny moment frozen on the cameo she wore on a gold chain around her neck. And she had decided that when the moment came, *if* the moment came, she'd never say her lover's name. No matter what, she'd lie. No matter whether Jesse thought it was Tony while the correct answer lay, probably still sleeping now, right up the hill.

"*Nobody*, that's who." Emma spat out the words while she screwed her eyes shut to hide their lie.

Jesse collapsed then. All the air sputtered out of him as if he were a great dirigible and her words had perforated his silver skin. He let go of her wrists, rolled off her and flopped over on his back.

"You make me crazy, do you know that?" His voice was weary. It sounded as if it came from far, far away. "You never fight fair, Em."

"What's fair?" she spat. "That you have a lover and so you wish I did, too? Would that make you feel better?"

Besides, I fight any way I can, she thought. And now I'm going to run while I can still get out of here.

She sat up slowly, testing the waters. Jesse didn't move.

She edged off the bed and gingerly stood as if she expected the floor to slip away. Her robe was hanging on the doorknob.

Jesse rolled his great bearlike head and looked at her. "Where are you going?"

"To make some coffee."

He sighed, but he didn't move to stop her. His head rolled back and he stared at the ceiling.

Then she got while the getting was good.

STANDING in the kitchen now, Emma carefully ground, then measured French dark roast coffee into a paper filter and poured boiling water over it. There was no sense in depriving herself of a good cup of coffee, she thought, just because her marriage was crumbling into ruins.

Jesse stepped into the room. He leaned against the countertop. "Em, I'm not letting this go. You have to tell me what you've been doing."

"I don't have to tell you anything, my man." She was sloshing hot water now in her growing anger. He'd been cheating on her for months now. Who the hell did he think he was?

"Tell me!" The escalation was quick. Again Jesse was approaching fury, hot rage this time, different from his bedroom ice.

"Why? You want to swap war stories? You want me to tell you all about my lover, Jesse, and you'll tell me what you and that tramp do in bed? Want to compare notes?"

At that Jesse slammed down his empty coffee mug so hard that it shattered, leaving only the handle on his forefinger.

"Leave Caroline out of this!"

"Why? Doesn't she count? I mean, I know she's not much, but we ought to at least consider her in the game."

And then she stepped back. Both lightning and tears flashed in Jesse's eyes. Oh, the histrionics, Emma thought. Talk about who doesn't play fair.

Hot and cold, cold and hot, Jesse's voice now came from an underground cave. "Caroline counts all right. She keeps me sane. If it weren't for her I'd have gone crazy already, living with you!"

Emma leaned her chin into the cup of one hand and smiled. It was not a very nice smile.

"Does she like to do it every day, Jesse? Or does she fake the desire—" and now her voice began to rise as she lost control— "does she fake it like anybody would have to to keep you happy, keep you feeling like a man?"

"Fuck you, Emma!" And his hand, empty now, slammed again on the counter. Veins stood out on his neck. He had never hit her. He had never laid a finger on her. Yet she wondered if this time maybe she hadn't gone too far.

But his explosion had given him a little distance. Just enough to grasp again the real, real for him at least, issue at hand.

He plopped down heavily on a stool. "But we're not talking

about me here, my lovely. What we're talking about is *you*. And
where you really spent this past weekend."

Emma's heart hesitated and her blood pooled. Keep it going,
she said to herself. And keep it simple.

"You know where I was—with Maria and Clifton."

"Yes." The *s* hissed like a snake. Ah. *Now* he was closing in for
the kill.

"Yes. That's true. Almost. But I called yesterday noon, and
Clifton fumbled around, then said you had already left. Six
hours before you got home." He dangled the next words slowly,
as if *he* were the one with the secret. "What did you do with
those six hours, Emma? Hmmmmmm? Or were you ever really
there at all?"

How could she have been so careless? But she'd been furious
when she left for the weekend with her lover, so angry she had
grabbed at any story as if it were a sweater, a last-minute after-
thought. She should have known Clifton would never get it
right. After all, Clifton was *Jesse's* friend. Well, it didn't matter now. What mattered was that she be nimble, that she be
quick. You can do it, Emma, you can tap-dance. You can dazzle
him with the flashy spangles of your virtuosity as you lie through
your teeth.

"I drove. I cruised around the hills. I picked up two sixteen-
year-old boys and fucked them silly. It's none of your damn business what I did."

WHAT she did. What she really did. Even as she said those words,
she warmed inside, she tingled, just as she did under her lover's
stroking fingers.

She could lie forever in his arms on that boat bouncing out in
the blue Pacific. He waited for her there, his patience endless, he
had waited and taken her for a ride, out across the waves, out toward the sunset, out beyond the three-mile limit. Away from the
pain of Jesse and his Caroline.

But no, that wasn't right. Or was it? Was Jesse right when he
said that Caroline was just a symptom? That he hadn't stopped
loving Emma, that she had pushed him away, that she'd never
really wanted him?

"You let me get this close, Emma." He had held up a thumb
and forefinger, almost touching, but you could see light between

them. "But never any closer. Do you think I'm going to steal your soul? Find out all your secrets and then run away?"

"I don't have any secrets," she'd said.

"I think you're the biggest secret of all, Emma, from yourself. A goddamned mystery. You don't know what the fuck you want. Or you do, and you lie about it."

"You think *fucking* means being close, Jesse?'"

For, even when he was angry with her, cold and distant, even after Caroline, he still demanded her flesh, all too often, as if coupling meant coupled.

"You never get it, do you, Emma? I still love you. Fucking you is the only way I have of getting inside you anymore."

"No, that's the only way you can control me anymore—with your dick."

It was different with her lover. In his arms, it just flowed, she was free.

But Emma, a voice whispered, it isn't for real, is it? He's not free, you're not free. You *can't* be tied together. Or is that the real freedom?

"Oh yes, it is my business," Jesse was saying, pulling her mind back into the kitchen. The rain was still pounding outside. It poured off the redwoods onto the deck like torrents of mountain tears. "It is most definitely my business and you're going to tell me." She could feel his breath on her face.

The coffee had dripped through. She reached for a mug and poured herself a cup. She stared at her hand, waiting for it to shake. It didn't.

"I went for a long drive, Jesse. I wanted to think. Now, that's the truth, and that's the end of this stupid conversation."

If he ground them any harder, she thought, his front teeth were going to snap.

"Then get out."

She turned from the refrigerator, where she was looking for the cream.

"I beg your pardon."

"I said get out."

"Get out where, Jesse? Where would you have me go?" Her words were slow and deliberate, her blue eyes cool as a High Sierra lake. She stared at him until his gaze broke. Then his body followed, crumbling bit by bit like a china doll that had been dropped. He leaned forward as if his stomach hurt, his chin tucked. His right arm and leg pumped in unison, knee toward elbow. Tears poured down his face like the rain rivuletting on the kitchen windows. This didn't look like acting anymore. This was for real, for, more than anything, though he didn't know what to do about the mess they'd gotten themselves into, Jesse loved Emma to death.

His voice sounded like breaking glass as he cried, "I can't stand this anymore!"

Emma stood staring at him for moments that seemed hours long, holding the cream in one hand, her pink-and-blue mug in the other. Everything inside her was stopped. There was a dazzling white quiet in her head.

Then something clicked. Finally, after months of indecision, Emma knew what she was doing.

"Jesse," her voice so soft he could hardly hear her, "you're right. I need twenty-four hours. I'll be gone after coffee tomorrow morning."

HE stood naked in the doorway, early-morning bleary-eyed, watching as she slammed the trunk of her little blue sedan. Even the rumple of pillow prints on his face couldn't hide his disbelief.

Had he thought she was joking?

"Where are you going?" he called into the bright air washed fresh by the rains the day before.

"Home."

"To Louisiana?"

"No, to Alaska. Where do you think?"

"You *hate* it in Louisiana."

"So what?"

"So why are you going there?"

"You know, Jesse," she smiled her not-very-nice smile, "one of the nice things about leaving is that we don't have to have these stupid conversations anymore."

At that he turned on his heel with as much dignity as his nakedness would allow and slammed the door behind him.

She was almost out of the driveway when he reappeared, partially covered by his robe, followed by Elmer, their collie. Emma's heart lurched. No problem leaving Jesse, she thought, but you're sure as hell going to miss the dog.

"When are you coming back?"

"I don't know," she called over the revving engine.
"You'd better be back in time for dinner."
"I wouldn't count on it."
She stepped on the gas and was gone.

THE miles had flown by. Leaving California was easy, zipping down Highway 5, the straight six-lane north–south red line through the middle of the state. There was nothing to see and nothing to do but drive.

Emma kept waiting for the bottom of her stomach to drop, for a cold hand to clutch it and make her tremble. Instead, she was grinning into the wind. She felt like Elmer with his head hanging out the car window, ears flying.

She fiddled with the radio, finding more and more honest-to-God country-and-western stations as she drove into the Big Valley.

Why didn't she feel scared, sad, brokenhearted like the good old boys singing on the radio? All she seemed to feel was relief.

Maybe it was because this wasn't really running away from home—if she was also running *to* home on the other end. Except Louisiana hadn't been home for many years, and she really didn't know why she was going there. To see Rosalie and Jake? That was a joke.

Maybe she'd told Jesse she was going home to make him mad, because she knew he hated the South.

Let's think about this a minute, Emma. No need to cut off your nose to spite your face. You don't *have* to go to Louisiana just because you told Jesse you were going to. That's even more reason *not* to. Why don't you go back, pack your stuff, and leave early for Italy?

It was too complicated, the travel arrangements, they wouldn't be expecting her.

Emma kept driving south.

THERE was Bakersfield, quick, she missed it. Then she hung a left and headed east across the Mojave Desert as the sun set behind her back. She stopped with a toe still in California, pulled up in front of a motel in Needles. Just across the dotted blue line on the map was Nevada.

Dinner was a hamburger. Not bad. Maybe she'd eat nothing

but hamburgers all the way. "The Definitive Emma Rochelle Fine Tree Survey of the American Hamburger." Back in her room, she took a long hot shower, pulled back the swirly orange-and-brown bedspread and collapsed.

She stretched and rooted. For the first time in four years she was truly alone again. She could read in bed all night long if she wanted to. She could call room service, if there were room service. She could eat nothing but Mallomars, drink a fifth of Southern Comfort, *bathe* in it if she wanted. She could do anything she was big enough to, when she got around to it.

For now, she reached into her zippered bag and pulled out the new paperback she'd been waiting to have a chance to read.

She held the book up and stared at its cover. *Even Cowgirls Get the Blues*. Well, she'd just see about that.

But Emma and the cowgirls didn't ride very far together. Four pages down the road, she began to fade. It had been a hell of a forty-eight hours.

She switched out the light, snuggled down and began to drift, when a thought lit her mind like Las Vegas neon.

Goddamn Jesse to hell! Why did he have to remind her, with his soft sweet insidious seduction, that lovely fucking, before he'd gone insane and pounded into her as if she were a piece of liver, that he remembered exactly what would sweet-feel her into boneless, mindless lust?

Come, now, Emma, she asked herself, did you really think that he'd forgotten?

Then why didn't he ever do it? she argued with herself. Why had it been so long that she'd forgotten that he knew?

Because he's an ornery, manipulative six-plus son-of-a-bitch, that's why.

That settled, she closed her eyes and relaxed—for a moment.

Is that what you're going to tell them when you get to West Cypress? Are you going to tell on Jesse? Tell them that he'd been fucking around instead of sweet-fucking you until you decided to do the same?

Of course not.

There would be cold comfort indeed in spilling out all her troubles to Rosalie and Jake. She wasn't quite sure why she was headed south, but it sure as hell wasn't for that.

They weren't that kind of Southern parents. And she wasn't that kind of Southern girl.

Southern girl . . . she was drifting again. Words played hide-and-seek on a drive-in movie screen in her mind.

Hell, what was a Southern girl? After all those years away, was she one anymore?

Jesse had always teased her—*You can take the girl out of the South, but you can't* . . . And what was it about Southern girls? She remembered a childhood singsong.

Nice Southern girls don't drink or smoke or go with boys who do.

Southern girls don't say shit even if they have a mouth full of it.

Southern girls *definitely* don't screw.

And Southern girls don't go out in the sun.

Emma drifted further and further, then her body jolted. She balanced on the knife edge of sleep.

Don't go out in the sun 'cause it's bad for your complexion, makes your skin all dark and wrinkly like a prune. Then who will want to marry you? And if you're not married, honey, where are you? You're alone in the world, with nobody to love or take care of you.

The way she was right now.

At least, that's what most folks would say.

Except Rosalie.

She wouldn't say that at all.

She'd say, had always said since Emma was a little girl, "Emma, don't you ever depend on a man. Most of them are no good, even if they look it at first. Girl, you better learn to take care of yourself."

Emma *had* taken care of herself. She always had. Even when she didn't want to.

And years later, when she was grown up, long after all the others in West Cypress had written her off as an old maid, Rosalie Fine had never asked that terribly rude question that others posed: "Why's a good-looking girl like you not married?"

Though when Emma finally did meet and marry Jesse Tree, she hadn't bothered to tell her parents.

As she'd said to Jesse and herself, there were lots of things Jake and Rosalie hadn't told *her*.

Keeping secrets ran in the family.

2

West Cypress, Louisiana
1944

IT WAS LATE in the evening of Jake Fine's third night on the road when the bus driver announced, "Next stop, Cypress, Louisiana."

Jake stretched and yawned, as much to relieve his nervousness as his fatigue. What was he doing here?

Then the baby in the seat beside him whimpered. He looked down at her and remembered. Emma, she was the reason he was three days and nights and fifteen hundred miles from New York City, Emma and the promise he'd made to Helen.

"If anything happens," she had said, somber-faced, four months pregnant, "promise me you'll never give up the baby, Jake. Find it another mother, but don't ever let it go."

So Jake was on this bus, changing diapers, changing his life as the miles rolled on, setting out on his second giant migration. And though the distance of the first, from Minsk to New York City, was greater than that from New York to West Cypress, he had a feeling that the changes were going to be just as momentous.

Jake leaned his bald head back against the prickly brown cushion once more. His hazel eyes closed. He didn't want to think about what might lie ahead for him. It was too terrifying. The past was safer. The memories of his first trip were like sepia photos, crackled and faded, but nonetheless preserved.

HE could see himself as a tiny boy in short pants holding on to his mother, Riva's, hand. They were in a tremendous open hall jammed with thousands of people all jabbering in languages he couldn't understand.

A fat woman on the bench next to them whispered rumors into his mother's ear.

"They won't admit you if you have more than four children. . . . They send you back if you have lice. . . . You have to have a job . . . a relative who can vouch for you."

Then, finally, up the long stairs they marched, his father, Isidore, straight-backed and stern, his mother Riva, with Rhoda, Moe and Jake holding hands between them.

"Hurry," Isidore urged them. "Take the stairs in big steps and don't stumble. It's a test, to see if you're strong enough to make it."

They'd streaked up the steps and soon were on the ferry headed toward buildings taller than he'd ever imagined, even in his dreams.

As the breezes blew his hair, Jake looked up at his stern-faced father with pride. Isidore was a *macher,* a *mensch.* He knew his way around. Two years earlier, he'd made the journey alone. Now in this place called Battery Park he waved away the flailing arms of men shouting their offers: "Rooms . . ." "Over here, jobs . . ." "Work papers, I'll get you work papers . . ." "Trains, where do you want to go?"

Isidore knew where he was going. The first time, a greenhorn, he had almost ended up on a train for Houston, Texas, rather than on a trolley for Houston Street and the Lower East Side. But he had found his way, had worked in a kitchen, behind a pushcart, in a boiler room, to earn the dollars with which to bring over his family.

This time, with them firmly in tow, he stayed on the trolley until it reached Grand Central Station. He had moved up and out of the city already. There was an apartment waiting for them, six rooms at a respectable address in New Haven, Connecticut. There the family would live and three more children, Joseph, Ruth and Sidney, would be born.

Jake smiled as he thought of that first apartment's kitchen, the kosher meals his short, round mother prepared, the kasha, the borscht, the chickens yellow with fat. What kind of food was there going to be in West Cypress?

Outside the bus windows, the lights of Cypress were beginning to flare through the flat blackness like Friday-night candles. Jake could see himself in the mirror of remembrance in a yarmulke, serious-faced among the children as they watched Riva light the Sabbath candles. Were there synagogues in the South? Were there even any Jews?

The city lights grew brighter, and his pulse quickened. It wouldn't be long now. He thought about friends he'd left behind: the Goldbergs, who had lived next door in New Haven. They'd come over a couple of years earlier, and their kids were already as proud and as street-smart as the natives. They taught the Fines more English than the Cedar Street School. And they taught them stickball, how to order in the candy store, how to fit in.

It was their father, Nathan Goldberg, who taught Isidore the fine arts of distilling and bottling. The smell of their homemade hooch, rich and ripe and yeasty, filled the whole neighborhood until Riva put her foot down.

"What are we going to do, Isidore, when they lock you in prison and send you back to the other side for this little bit of extra money? Are you going to be happy then, when the children and I starve to death?"

Where was Jake going to find another friend like Herb Goldberg, who had stood under the wedding tent with his sister Rhoda? Rhoda and Herb—they had been the first, when the family had started to grow smaller, yet larger; Rhoda, then Ruth, then Moe, and on down the line, the children had married and left. Except for Jake. Jake had stayed at home.

"You'll find someone, Jakey," his mother hugged him and said. "The right girl will come along."

But Jake knew that she wouldn't.

He was the one who had dropped out of the Cedar Street School the earliest, after the sixth grade when he couldn't take the taunting anymore: "J-J-J-Jake, wh-wh-what's the matter, cat got your tongue?"

He could rattle on in Yiddish just as well as the next one, but when he had tried to wrap his tongue around this new language it twisted and turned.

At home he told tales about the weekend trip to Coney Island, the rides, the roller coaster, the beach, the daring with which he had jumped into the mammoth waves—*that* big. He bragged in the kitchen to his mother and his favorite redheaded sister Ruth until they threatened to toss him out.

But his father insisted. "He's got to speak English, Riva, if he wants to get ahead." So his mother tried her best to practice the little English she had with Jake, but late at night, after Isidore had gone to bed, it was in Yiddish that they whispered.

Those nights couldn't last forever, though, and as Jake grew and the family shrank, he became more silent. As long as he said nothing, no one could laugh. He sought out jobs in the back of a grocery store, in a cannery, a cleaner's, jobs that he could hold with no education, jobs where he could keep his mouth shut.

Long days of work ran one into the other until one of the Goldberg boys said, "Come on, Jake, let's go see the world." Why not? That's what the Navy promised. And for three years he was a real man, a sailor in San Diego. He went home with tattoos blue as the Pacific on both his forearms. The heart, the flowers, the cowgirl, Mom—they were on special, he told his mother proudly, a bargain twenty-five cents apiece. Back home in New Haven, Isidore frowned: Jews don't have tattoos.

Isidore had frowned at him more and more after his return, so he hadn't settled back into the family house but moved into Manhattan. There eight, ten, twelve years had slipped by, the days all the same at one job or another, the evenings brightened by picture shows and vaudeville.

Al Jolson, Burns and Allen, and Jack Benny were on stages just minutes away on Broadway. The movies were a quarter, and dime novels, especially his favorite detectives, filled the stands. These were enough for Jake. So the twenties, the thirties, his twenties and thirties, passed; except for the visits to his family's homes, he lived his life quietly and alone.

Until Helen. At first he hadn't seen her in the dark hallway of his rooming house on upper Broadway and had bumped into her coming out of the room next door.

"Sorry," he'd muttered and then flushed. He was always bumbling, he thought, always putting his foot in it.

"Oh no," she'd said in a soft Southern drawl that prolonged and multiplied every word until it sounded like three. "It's my fault. I should have looked where I was going."

And then he looked at her. She was tall for a woman, an armful, with soft brown hair and a pretty smile.

He'd thought about her for days after, listening in hopes of hearing her through the wall. He found himself racing home from work in the evenings, taking a quick shower in the bathroom down the hall and dressing in his best pleated pants, a fresh shirt. Then he sat and listened. When he heard her radio go off, he grabbed his coat and ran out the door. They almost collided once again.

She'd smiled. "Well, isn't this a coincidence? Neighbors back home run into each other all the time, but here in New York it seems like everyone's just strangers. Doesn't it?"

Jake nodded and ducked his head. He wanted to talk to her. Oh, how he wanted to talk with her. But what to say? And how to make his tongue do his bidding?

Goddamn you, stutter, behave! he shouted inside his head.

"Yes, b-b-b-bu . . ." He couldn't get it out. Goddammit, he couldn't. He wheeled away.

"But what?" she asked softly. Was she laughing at him? "But you aren't a stranger, are you, even though I don't know your name."

"Jake," he'd managed. Quick, he'd outtricked his tongue. "Jake Fine."

"Helen Kaplan." She'd stuck out her hand. Jake couldn't believe it—a Jew with a Southern accent. "'I'm on my way to get some Chinese food for supper. Would you like to join me?"

Over chow mein she told him she'd been in New York a year. She was from Georgia, from a small town. She was working as a clerk and seeing doctors at Mount Zion. Something about her heart. Two weeks later they had married at City Hall. Helen was lovely in a pale-blue gabardine dress. Jake's vanilla-colored suit looked like ice cream. The next day they moved to Baltimore. The jobs were better there, Helen had said, shipbuilding for the war. It was early spring 1943.

"Will you have to go into the service again?" Helen asked Jake while sweeping the steps of their little row house, its red-brick face like that of a hundred thousand others.

"I served my time. And until they call me again, I'm not volunteering." They didn't call, and Jake went to the shipyard every day and stayed home evenings with Helen, listening to the radio. They had just settled in, new curtains just hung, when she told him about the baby. At first he thought she was joking.

But she wasn't joking when she extracted the promise from

Jake. "If anything happens, you never give our baby up. Do
you hear?"

"Don't be silly," he'd answered, when he'd gotten used to the
idea, patting her stomach beneath a brown-and-white polka-
dotted dress. "Nothing's going to happen." He'd reached across
their kitchen table and touched her light-brown hair. "You'll
see."

But he'd promised.

Had she known then that they would never cuddle a child
together, watch her grow into a long-legged little girl? Had she
always known that her heart wasn't up to it?

"Don't make me laugh so hard." (Or love so hard, she'd
whisper.)

"Jake, if you tickle me anymore, I swear I'm going to have
an attack."

"Honey, would you carry this sack for me? I can't walk up
these stairs as fast as you."

Then she'd grown pale, and a little clammy, but what did he
know? What did a Yankee Russian Jew know about a Southern
lady and her games? All he knew was that he loved her. Nothing
else mattered.

And for a brief time, all was golden. They named the beautiful blue-eyed baby Emma after Helen's mother. Then came that
afternoon just nineteen days after Emma was born, when Jake
came home from work to a house that was too still.

He had raced the last few blocks from the trolley down Independence Avenue, hurried so that the roses wouldn't wilt and
the milk wouldn't grow warm. He'd made it. The milk was still
cold when he walked in the door, the cream separated, rich and
thick in the bottle's neck.

"Helen," Jake had called.

He waited for her answer from the bedroom, but none came.

Then there was a whimper which swelled into a wail. He
dropped the roses and the milk on the table and stepped to the
bedroom door.

"Helen?"

Emma was in her crib, her little pink mouth wide with rage.

Helen was lying face down on the floor on the far side of the
bed. She was marble pale, marble cold and very still.

"Probably heart failure," said the white-coated doctor sum-
moned by the frantic call on a neighbor's phone.

It didn't matter what the doctor thought was probable, what he guessed. No matter what he called it, Helen was dead.

Just the day before they had eaten half a cake decorated with little pink roses, thirty-seven candles, and "Happy Birthday, Jake" spelled out in blue icing.

Jake sat in their quiet kitchen, with the cake on the cabinet growing stale, for what might have been hours, could have been days. Emma never left his arms. She was all he had left.

Then as if waking from a dream he asked himself, What next?

His mother, Riva, had been gone for several years. His older sister, Rhoda Goldberg, rambled through her big house carrying pictures of her son Marty, the bravest little boy in New Jersey, as if she could find him again if only she opened the right door. Her husband, Herb, said she looked through their other two children as if they were ghosts, as if they too had been snatched away by rheumatic fever.

His brothers had families, problems, of their own.

"Ruth," he cried into the phone, "Helen's gone."

The next day his redhaired baby sister was at his side, Ruth who had slapped the faces of boys who teased him about his stutter, the one who could always make him laugh, dancing a jig, striking a pose.

"Oh, Jake." She stroked the top of his balding head. "Poor, Jake, I'll take her home to raise with my little Ed."

"No!" The word had burst out. But then he wrapped Emma in the blanket embroidered with pink and blue cat faces that Helen had stitched with her slender hands. He had to move back to New York and let Ruth keep Emma. This wasn't breaking his promise to Helen. This wasn't letting Emma go.

He took the train Saturdays at noon after his job at a Manhattan cleaner's. It was only an hour to Connecticut, where Ruth lived while her husband George built destroyers in New London.

Ruth met him at the door with Emma, handing the bundled baby to him before she even kissed him hello. They they sat in her front room, their feet resting on an Oriental carpet, and sipped hot tea through lumps of sugar held in their mouths as Riva had taught them. Ruth served a pot roast, purchased with the coupons Jake had saved, and her famous pilaff with noodles, tomatoes and green beans.

"She's a precious baby, Jake. Helen would have been so proud. I just wish I'd known her."

Jake's eyes filled with tears and he nodded.

No one had known Helen except him.

"Why didn't you ever bring her around, Jake? Just that once, to Rhoda's house, that one afternoon."

Jake stared into his hands. He couldn't explain to Ruth that he'd always felt himself a failure, that his father favored the other brothers, the ones who never stopped talking, talking, talking with glib tongues that made deals, made money, made friends, while he sat silent on the sofa and watched his life drift by. Finally, when he had found Helen, the things he felt were too complicated to even begin to explain.

Perhaps he had feared that they would disapprove. And if his father had said a single harsh word, he would have . . . well, he wouldn't have been responsible.

Or was he afraid his brothers would tease him, marrying so quickly and so late, as if to seize romance, under any circumstances, before it got away?

He only knew that it felt safer just keeping to themselves. Helen hadn't asked any questions about his family. And he didn't ask any about hers. They had each other. The past didn't matter. What they had was enough.

"I don't know, Ruth," he finally answered.

"Well, that's okay. We'll just raise her as a Fine. Nothing wrong with that." Jake agreed, nothing wrong at all.

But it wasn't long after that—Emma was just beginning to creep across Ruth's red-and-blue Oriental carpet—when a middle-of-the-night desperate call had come the other way, from Ruth's house to his.

God, if anything's happened to my baby I'll curse your name and die, Jake thought as he squeezed the receiver in his hand.

"It's George," Ruth cried on the other end of the line. "He's been burned—in an accident in New London. They don't expect him to live the night."

George did live, with Ruth at his side changing his dressings, slipping ice through his parched lips.

And Jake stood, once again, alone with the infant Emma in his arms.

Then his old friend and brother-in-law Herb called. "My sister Shirley is living out in Brooklyn, in Flatbush. Her husband is overseas. She'll take care of Emma."

"But I can't . . ."

"Can't what, Jake?"

Shirley's family, Helen. I'm not letting her go.

"THERE are lots of women in this neighborhood giving you the eye, Jake," Shirley said. They were walking to the candy store for an egg cream on a steamy Brooklyn afternoon.

"Don't be silly."

Emma, dressed only in a diaper against the August heat, gurgled in his arms.

"You listen to me, Jake. It's been eight months now. You know I love Emma and if you'd let me I'd keep her forever."

Yes, he did know that, and it was beginning to worry him. Shirley was growing too attached.

"But there are plenty of widows here, nice women whose husbands aren't coming home from the war, and you ought to start thinking about settling down with one."

How was he going to do that? He worked five and a half days a week stocking and sweeping a grocery store nearby. He picked up Emma Saturday noon and kept her all day Sunday. He couldn't court someone with his baby in his arms.

"Well, if you don't want to remarry, there are lots of women who would love to have this precious little girl. Why, just the other day Mrs. Rosenberg asked me—she and her husband can't have any—"

"No!"

"Shhhh! You're shouting. Here, I'll hold her while you go in and get the egg creams. Watch out for those little boys. They'll mow you down."

They walked with their sodas toward Prospect Park, where it was cooler. "But you know what I'm saying, Jake. You need to find a wife."

He knew Shirley was right. And that had been part of the promise to Helen, too, hadn't it? Never give her away. But find her a mother.

Helen, it took me thirty-six years to find you, he said to her before he went to sleep that night. How am I ever going to find another?

"WELL," said Herb, spreading the paper out in front of him. "I don't think it's a bad idea at all."

Jake shook his head.

"Wait, Jake, before you say no. Mrs. Rodolitz in our neighborhood found a new husband this way, and she's not half as good-looking as you. You both have the same nose, and I guess she's got more hair than you."

Jake laughed. Herb had always been able to make him laugh.

"Look at all these ads—women who are looking for husbands. You just pick one, or more, hell, play the field, write them letters, and see what you get. Or, if you want to, you place a listing, and they'll write you. It's all by mail, Jake. And it doesn't cost much."

"I'll see. I'll see." Who knew, Jake thought, what such a thing might cost?

"CYPRESS," the bus driver called again, and Jake started. The bus pulled into the terminal and the door opened. His journey was over.

Jake let all the other passengers go by before he rose stiffly from his seat, bundled up the sleeping Emma, his coat and hat, and gingerly picked his way down the aisle, then down the bus's steps. He didn't want to fall on his face before the waiting Rosalie, his mail-order bride.

3

NOTHING moves very fast in West Cypress. And nothing ever changes—not even the inferiority complex the town, situated across the Coupitaw River from its richer and larger twin city, Cypress, has suffered from its very beginnings.

In 1792, when Cypress was a fort established by the French and continued by the Spanish, a pair of wild and boisterous soldiering brothers, the Laplante boys, were told by the Fort Cypress commandant that he'd just as soon they moved out of the compound and made other arrangements.

In a huff, the Laplantes took the few shreds of blankets they owned and their horses and forded the river to the uninhabited side. Within a few hot months—for their resettlement occurred in the trough of a Louisiana mosquito-plagued summer—they had built six huts along a dirt path and had established themselves as entrepreneurs of a particular kind, filling the lean-tos with liquor and women and gambling, the likes of which had not been seen before within the boundaries of what was to be the Louisiana Purchase.

Now, about one hundred and fifty years after the Laplante boys had been run off by the proper citizens of Cypress, the only emporium for sin in West Cypress was the Ritz Bar located on one end of the town's main street, which was still no more than two blocks long. And that sinning was mild, in the form of dominoes and beer, for this was the intense Bible Belt, where sugared iced tea, white bread, and churchgoing were the accepted standards of consumption and entertainment.

Just outside Cypress, natural gas had been discovered, and

the fields that sprung up made rich men of many farmers and
landholders. It was in the hands of their wives and daughters
that Cypress culture rested, with women who had their names
written on the rolls of the Daughters of the Confederacy and
never let anyone forget it. There never was and never would be
anything for the ladies to do other than pour tea and eat lunch,
because the two towns together could support nothing more en-
tertaining than a roller rink, a bowling alley and a handful of
picture shows. And the ladies were a minority in a society whose
members' necks were as basically and determinedly red as the
clay in the hills just the other side of West Cypress. Therefore,
when the ladies grew so hungry for enlightenment and shopping
that they just couldn't stand it another minute, they had to drive
six hours south to New Orleans (where, if a lady was interested,
she could also indulge in some *serious* sinning).

On the other hand, when the ladies of West Cypress grew
restless with change burning holes in their pockets, they drove
across the bridge to Cypress, being of the opinion that the picture shows and the five and dimes on its main street were just
fine.

Why they were called the Twin Cities was a puzzlement to
those of the inhabitants who had ever given the question any
thought. Even their geography was different, Cypress's being
the richer. For the eastern bank of the Coupitaw, on which Cypress was perched, marked the very western boundary of the
Mississippi Delta, with all the rich loam and plantations and
wealth that that implied. On the west bank began the piney
land, the poorer farmland that might be prettier, with its rolling
hills, trees, and shade, but didn't hold a candle to the loamy
bottoms when it came to growing things.

The land around West Cypress did produce a plentitude of
trees, and as a result there grew up a paper mill, which, when
the wind was wrong, which was most of the time, caused West
Cypress to stink.

It was in West Cypress that Rosalie Norris, the woman whom
Jake Fine was coming to claim as his wife, resided—which was
appropriate, for Rosalie, like the town in which she lived, had
felt left out, put down and inferior all of her natural-born life.

She was standing now on the platform of the bus station in
Cypress, West Cypress being so much smaller and having so few

visitors that the bus didn't stop there. Rosalie nervously twisted the large luminescent brown beads of her necklace. A woman in a pink dress next to her, her cheeks flushed and her eyes bright, pushed a photograph of a uniformed young man in front of Rosalie.

"That's Fred. Isn't he handsome? I can't believe he's finally coming home on furlough." The woman stopped twitching for a moment and focused on Rosalie. "Do you have a picture of your husband?"

Rosalie smiled vaguely at her. Her husband? A photograph? No, Jake had sent her a picture of the baby Emma, but she'd never seen a photograph of the man she had agreed to marry. He hadn't sent one along with his letters, and she hadn't asked. She'd thought it enough to insist that he come to West Cypress rather than her moving to New York. She knew she couldn't— why, how could anyone—live *there*. She simply couldn't move, not a woman from a town whose inhabitants referred to anyone from more than fifty miles away as "from off." Jake had been amenable, saying that her prospects there, with her grocery store, sounded better than his, anyhow. So she hadn't pushed him for a picture.

She'd sent *him* one, though. She didn't want to be a complete pig in a poke to this man. She just didn't think she could stand it if he came all that way with Emma, took one look at her and then carried the baby away.

The tinted photo that she sent him had been taken in her best brown suit with the same brown beads that she was wearing this evening. The long narrow face that looked out of it was pleasant, with a prominent nose, hazel eyes and a pretty smile. She looked exactly her age, which was thirty-six. Her brown hair was dressed in a pompadour. She was tall, as all her family was, tall and lean, with long bones.

Rosalie Norris was never going to win any beauty contests, but then she wasn't trying to. She knew exactly who and what she was and what she could expect from life. She hoped that wanting Emma wasn't expecting too much.

"Do you think I've lost my mind?" she'd asked her sister Janey the week before.

"You don't have to marry him if you don't like him."

"Then I won't get the baby."

Janey nodded. "Well, that's true. I know that means a lot to you. There are always other babies, though, Ro. And you still could have one of your own."

Rosalie shook her head. There had been a baby, but Janey didn't know that. No one knew. That was a while ago—and had almost killed her. She'd paid the price, but then, as she'd always known, nothing in this world comes free.

The past few years had been a bit easier. Sometimes she allowed herself to lock the grocery store's front door at eight rather than staying on till ten. And on those nights when she went to bed early, she'd begun to dream, not the nightmares she'd had since *that* baby, but of *another* baby, another child. Of course, she would want one that was already here, one that she wouldn't be responsible for birthing but could raise as her own. Most people seemed to look at it the other way around, as if the birthing were the important part and the raising just incidental, but not Rosalie. She didn't give a hoot about the sex, and the birthing, or even the man. All *that* was incidental.

She shifted and fidgeted in the still-warm October air outside the bus terminal, pacing back and forth, looking at her watch. She had always been impatient, but if she'd waited this long, she guessed, biting her bottom lip and trying to keep her hands still, she could wait just a little bit longer.

She couldn't believe that it was only two months ago that she had received the first letter from the man named Jake Fine who was going to be on the bus, the man whose daughter was the blue-eyed blonde baby girl she had already fallen in love with.

In his letters he had laid it out plain and simple. He was looking for a mother for his daughter, for a good home, and that was enough for him. Well, that was enough for her too. She had learned to expect nothing of the world but grief, and any joy that came along was what in the southern part of the state the Cajuns called lagniappe—something extra and unexpected.

She opened her purse and looked again at the photograph of the smiling baby propped up against her daddy's wrist.

Wasn't she like a little doll?

Rosalie closed her eyes, and the lady beside her in the pink dress disappeared. The station disappeared. Inside her head a doll danced.

THE Christmas morning of Rosalie's eleventh year had begun at dawn like every other morning she had ever known.

"You girls get up in here," her mother, Virgie, stood at the bedroom door and called.

Rosalie rolled over into the still-sleeping body of her sister Lucille, who groaned and then, "Phewy," Lucille wrinkled her nose in disgust. Nancy, the third and youngest sister in the bed, had wet again, as she did almost every night.

Esther, Janey and Florence were still tangled together like puppies in the other cast-iron double bed in the square unpainted room.

"I'm not telling you girls again," Virgie said. "Get up now. There's chores to be done."

Rosalie fought her way out from between her sisters and slipped her white cotton shift and then her blue cotton dress over her head. The little pink sprigs that had blossomed over the fabric when she'd cut it out six months ago from a flour sack had faded through its many scrubbings in the big iron pot in the side yard. She pulled on a sweater that her older sister Esther had crocheted and then outgrown and passed down to her. She was still cold, as was the fireplace, last night's carefully banked fire having died hours ago. But she wouldn't be cold for long, once she took her place in the kitchen at the woodstove and began her morning chores.

"You better get those biscuits started now," Virgie said, pushing the flour sack toward her. "Your pa and the boys have already been up an hour. They're going to be back in here soon."

Rosalie nodded "Yes'm" and began cutting lard into the flour with two knives. She worked carefully and quickly as Virgie had taught her, handling the mixture as little as possible once she'd added the fresh milk from the pail that her father had already left on the back steps. It hadn't taken but one slap from the side of her mother's hand when she was careless and made tough biscuits to teach her the technique. Flour and lard, like everything else on the Norris farm, were too hard-earned to waste.

Rosalie tested the oven of the woodstove with her hand and slipped the first pan of biscuits inside. There would be three before she was finished. Her five brothers and her father would polish off the first two, dabbed with butter her mother had churned and sweet honey gathered from their hives. Afterward the menfolk would wipe their mouths on the backs of their hands, scrape their chairs back from the table and clomp back out the kitchen door to finish their morning work in the barn.

Only then would the girls clear away their debris from the big round table, scrape and wash the dishes in the pot of water that was always at the boil on the back of the black-and-silver stove, dry them and reset the table for their own breakfasts. Only then would Rosalie pull the third pan of biscuits from the oven, and the girls would settle down for a few minutes to eat while their mother, at her place closest to the door, drank a cup of boiled coffee while she nursed the baby.

"They've tracked in again," Virgie nodded at the bare wooden floor.

"Yes'm," said Janey and Florence. It was the two middle girls' job to scrub the floor clean with lye which bleached the pine pale as wild spring dogwood blossoms. What it did to their hands was another matter, but country girls couldn't worry about niceties like soft skin. They couldn't afford to.

Luxuries of even the most meager kind were unheard of in Virgie and William Norris's wide-hipped house set on top of a hill well back from the dirt road which led to the hamlet of Sweetwell four miles away. The acres surrounding the farm where William and his family planted cotton every spring were fertile, repaying with bountiful crops the backbreaking, finger-splitting labor of seeding, chopping, hoeing and picking—those years it didn't rain too much or too little and the boll weevil didn't come to dinner.

It was pretty country, northwestern Louisiana, green all the way to the nearby border where the piney lands of Texas began. A few miles south was the Cane River, with magnolia-lined plantation lands rolling back from its banks. The three-storied big white houses along the Cane, layered and decorated and sweet like wedding cakes, were so pretty they could break your heart.

But there was nothing but backs to be broken on the thousands of small farms like the Norris place, where the never-ending work spread itself out to fill all the days from sunup to sundown, and the more children there were to do the work, the more mouths there were to feed, and the more store-bought shoes to purchase, the more disappointments to worry about at Christmastime.

Virgie Norris plopped the baby, Will, down for a few moments and pushed her curling dark hair back from her damp forehead. Breakfast done, it was time to start dinner. The carcasses of three chickens lay before her on the countertop, chickens she'd raised from biddies, fed and, just this morning, before the girls got up, wrung the necks of. She'd had Esther scald, pluck and gut them outside the kitchen door. It was cold out, but the smell of the hot wet feathers had upset her stomach ever since Will was born.

She wondered if there was something wrong with her insides. What could she expect, twelve children in fourteen years. The childbearing hardly ever gave her innards time to take care of themselves.

She wished she could do more for her babies, all of them. She'd always wanted their lives to be better, but it looked like they were going to be just the same as hers, her parents' and their parents' before them. As long as any of her kin had ever been able to trace their family histories back, telling the long looping and relooping tales while they sat by the fire at night, stories full of great-grand-aunts and second cousins once removed, they had always worked the land, and they had always been poor.

Too poor, she imagined, to ever buy all their children what they'd like to, or even just something, for Christmas.

She glanced up from the chickens she was cutting into frying pieces, a special treat for Christmas dinner, three chickens for the twelve of them not counting the baby, and looked at the tree standing in the corner. The children had decorated it the night before with popcorn, bits of bright ribbon, and the few precious glass ornaments her mother had passed down to her. At the top was a tin star William had brought her from Shreveport so many years ago she could hardly remember, a present when they were courting.

Beneath the tree was one present for each child, wrapped in newspaper: a new pair of work boots, a sweater she'd knitted, a shift with tiny rosebuds she'd embroidered around the scooped neck, all necessities, with one exception. This was the year that Rosalie would get her doll.

The children knew better than to expect much, but each year there would be something special for one of them. At first the treats had been in descending order from the oldest, but then there had been the year that Virginia, her namesake, had taken ill and they'd known that she wasn't going to make it through the winter. So an older child had been skipped over and Virginia'd gotten the tin-backed mirror that she'd begged for. She'd lain in bed for many an hour, inspecting her pale face and watching herself braid her long red hair. Virgie had thought it a foolish gesture, but the children had all insisted that the mirror be buried with Virginia when she died.

After that, the order had gotten all cattywampus. The next year Lester had taken ill, and so he'd gotten his coveted basketball, but he'd made it through, praise the Lord, though sometimes Virgie regretted the present as the *slap slap slap* of it against the house threatened to drive her to distraction.

What with one illness and another, Rosalie had been passed over. Virgie knew that the child understood, but it didn't stop the tears of disappointment from welling in her eyes when the presents were all opened and once again hers was a pair of underdrawers or a new apron. Because Virgie knew that more than anything in the world Rosalie had always wanted a real doll.

She had seen the very doll of her dreams last fall in a store window in Natchitoches, the day William had loaded all the children into the wagon behind two mules for the trip for the Natchitoches Parish Fair. In the late afternoon, after a day filled with the wonders of the Snake Lady in her bespangled costume that made the boys gape and the girls avert their faces, caramel corn balls and meat pies bought with pennies saved all year, and the row after row of jars of prize golden peaches and bright red tomatoes, the hot dusty children had piled back into the wagon with Virgie and William to shop in Natchitoches for those store-bought items that couldn't be purchased in Sweetwell.

There, in the cool dark Kendall's Mercantile Store, while Virgie chose from the spools of thread and considered new needles for her treadle sewing machine, Rosalie saw the doll.

It was perched on the counter, out of her reach, but she wouldn't have touched it anyway. She wouldn't have dared.

The doll was like something out of a fairy tale, like Cinderella dressed for the ball. Its hair, real human hair, was like spun gold, parted down the middle and then twisted into a high knot atop her delicate head. A silver veil of the finest netting crowned the yellow curls. Her face was of porcelain, tinted blush pink at the cheeks and a rosier hue on her sweetly bowed lips. But the rest of the face was left its natural china white, and light seemed to shine through it, opalescent in the dim store. Her eyes were bright blue, with long fringed lashes that looked as if they had been dusted with gold. Beneath her slender neck began her dress of pale-blue taffeta, marked with what looked like rivulets of water. Virgie had once told her that the fabric was moiré, a kind of silk from France. Close upon her neck was a ruff of creamy lace. Below it marched a row of pearl buttons, tiny as seeds, down her slightly swelling bosom, ending at her wasplike waist. The sleeves of the dress belled out from the shoulder and then grew tight from the elbow down to her tiny wrists, where lacy trim matched that of the ruff. The skirt was full to the ankles, and just below the hem of it her delicate porcelain feet were enclosed in tiny black kid slippers. She was the most beautiful thing Rosalie had ever seen, beyond imagining.

Virgie had heard her daughter's sharp intake of breath and turned to see her staring, as round-eyed as the doll. Virgie's lips had tightened. Anger rose in her breast. She knew she ought to feel pity or sadness, but it was always anger that surged like bile when the children wanted something that they couldn't have. Their wanting and the naked hunger in their eyes made her ashamed to be a country hick standing in a city store with her passel of children strung out behind her like biddy chickens.

She reached down and jerked Rosalie closer to her.

"Don't you dare touch," she said.

"Ma, I was just looking at her." Rosalie's cheeks burned hot. She knew that everyone in the store must be staring.

"There's no point in wishing, girl. Your daddy works too hard for you to be having fancy ideas about things like that."

Rosalie ducked her head. She'd get a whipping, she knew, if her mother saw her quick tears; she'd get something to cry about, all right. She turned and walked slowly, but not smartlike to make her mother angrier, out of the cool darkness of the store and across the wooden sidewalk back to the wagon, which was tied up outside on the town square. She climbed back in and sat beside Esther.

"What's the matter, Ro? You look mad enough to spit."

"Nothing." Rosalie shook her head. Esther shrugged.

But something was wrong, Rosalie thought. Something was wrong when you couldn't even look at a doll and dream.

A few weeks later as Virgie and William whispered late into

the night in their bed, making Christmas plans, Virgie brought
the doll up to her husband.

"We skipped her, you know," she said to the long lanky man
who had lain beside her more than half of her thirty-eight years.
"If we don't get it for her this year, it'll probably be too late.
She'll come into her womanhood soon and be too old for dolls."

"Virg!" William shushed her. Though he had fathered all of
their twelve children right on this very mattress and had never
seemed shy about that, he was uncomfortable at any mention
of what he called "women's business."

"Well, I wish you'd think about it." Virgie snuggled closer
to him, but not too close. She didn't want to even think about
risking another baby so soon.

"It's a lot of money, Virg."

"I know." She rolled over and let it drop.

But a few Saturdays later, without saying a word more about
it, he'd ridden into Natchitoches and on his return pressed a
newspaper-wrapped bundle into Virgie's hand. She could tell
from the shape of it that it was the doll.

Now it lay among the clutter of the other packages under
the Christmas tree. Virgie couldn't wait for her family to finish
dinner so they could open their presents and she could see the
expression on Ro's face.

Now there it was. As the skinny little girl in her faded blue
flour-sack dress slowly unwound the string and then unwrapped
the paper, she raised her wide hazel eyes from the doll's long
blue watered silk, her mouth a perfect O.

She gazed first at Virgie, then at William, then back to the
doll again, shaking her head over and over.

"Momma, Pa," she cried, racing into their open arms and
crushing her thin chest against theirs, but carefully holding her
treasure to one side.

"It's all right, Ro," Virgie whispered into her ear. "Merry
Christmas."

The Norris boys expressed little interest in her special present,
disappearing into their room to try on new denim overalls, socks
and coats of sensible navy wool, but the girls all gathered round.

"Look," said little Nancy as Rosalie lowered the doll's head,
"her eyes close." They did indeed. Rosalie held her breath.
Were their brilliant blue lost somewhere in her head forever? But

no, when she lifted the doll perpendicular, there they were again.

The doll's jointed head moved, too. "Careful," Virgie cautioned. "Not too far." The arms, the legs moved, and the doll could even bend over at her tiny waist.

"Does she have drawers?" Janey whispered. Rosalie wiped her hand on her lap and carefully lifted the hem of the doll's dress to see lace-trimmed pantaloons.

Esther asked, "What are you going to call her?"

"Gloria," Rosalie answered without skipping a beat. She'd known the doll's name the first time she'd laid eyes on her in Kendall's Mercantile Store.

"Like morning glory, blue morning glory?" Lucille always seemed to know what was going on in Rosalie's head.

"Yes. And *Gloria in excelsis Deo*. From the hymn at church."

Virgie snorted, "Lord, Lord. Put her away now. Girls, come on. Let's get this table cleared."

For the rest of the day, Rosalie was on a cloud. She did her chores as always, taking her turn changing the baby and the other little ones, carrying water from the well, filling the big iron pot on the back of the stove, gathering eggs from under the hateful pecking hens, carrying in pails of foaming milk from the evening milking. But every chance she got, she slipped back into the girls' room and sneaked a look at Gloria, her blue eyes closed, asleep in a nest fashioned of an old baby quilt atop the chifforobe.

That night, after a supper of leftovers which had sat all afternoon on the table covered over with a clean tablecloth, she brought Gloria back into the kitchen to play with her while the family sat around the evening fire.

"Can I hold her?" Florence asked.

Rosalie hesitated, but Virgie caught her eye. Even if Gloria was hers, she had to share.

"Here." She handed the doll over. "But be careful."

Florence was careful, as were Esther, Janey, Lucille and even little Nancy. When Gloria had made the circle and was safely back in her arms, Rosalie sighed with relief.

Then, "What about me?" asked the gruff voice, still changing, of her older brother England. "Can I see the dolly, too?" He stepped forward, holding out his big rough hands.

Rosalie looked from his hands to Gloria to the eyes of her

mother. She found no help there. Nor in the half-closed eyes of her father, leaned back in his rocking chair enjoying his pipe, a pleasure reserved for special occasions.

"He won't hurt your dolly, Rosalie," Virgie said.

But England's sooty hands, never really clean in the cracks from his dirty work of smithing and shoeing, would snag and stain the fragile blue silk of Gloria's dress. But she'd just have to bear it.

"Well, isn't she a beauty. Look at that complexion. Bet she never hoed a row of cotton in her life." He teased and smiled into Rosalie's eyes. He held Gloria up and twirled her skirt, and, in the twirling, something caught, and she fell.

The porcelain smashed into a hundred little petal pink-and-white pieces, shining in the firelight.

Gloria's soft body was intact, but her head, her hands and her feet were broken, as was Rosalie's heart.

It didn't matter that England was sorry. It didn't matter when Virgie made her a rag doll to fill the blue silk dress. The beautiful Gloria was gone before Rosalie had had a chance to love her.

And Rosalie knew that that was the way of the world. It didn't do to want too much, to expect anything, she told herself when she'd finished with the mourning and the crying herself to sleep at night. Life was hard and painful, and she was poor, and that was the way it was always going to be. But life would be less bitter if she didn't expect it to be sweet.

THAT didn't mean that she had to spend the rest of her life on the farm, though. She was willing to work hard, to do anything, but Rosalie didn't want to spend all her days like her mother—washing, cleaning, cooking, tending after a whole mess of kids. The only way she could see to escape was to use her brains. Her teachers had always said she had plenty. There had to be a way they could earn her a living.

But when she finished the eleventh grade, where was she going to get the money to go on? It cost over four hundred dollars for the two years of normal school in Natchitoches.

Her brother England stepped forward. "I'll lend it to you." How would he scrape together the money from the few pennies he had earned on his small farm near home? But she was his favorite, and he'd always been a good boy.

The two years flew by. She was on her own, and though her job in the school kitchen was much like the chores she did on the farm, this was different, for there were her studies, the books, the lectures, the endless pages of empty blue lines to fill with notes that would enable her to stay away from the farm forever, maybe even to be a teacher.

And it was the twenties. Even in the rural backwater of Natchitoches there were short skirts, bobbed hair, jazzy music on the Victrola, new daring dances, and boys with slicked hair who came to call at the dormitories with silk bow ties beneath their sun-reddened Adam's apples.

Rosalie went out with a few of them but no one in particular. She didn't have time for all that foolishness. She had to get ahead in school if she was ever going to make anything of herself. She'd seen, boy, had she seen, in her mother's swelling belly every spring, what boys could do for you. That's all they were after, anyway, when you got right down to it. She was not interested. No, thank you.

For no matter how sweet the moonlight, the words, and the promises whispered out in a canoe late at night, they didn't mean a hoot when you had a passel of children underfoot and could see nothing looking you in the face for the next twenty years but the raising of them, with precious little help from that young man who sat next to you now trying to nuzzle closer to the buttons of your white organdy blouse. They could jazz her and razzmatazz her, but when it came to serious business Rosalie would make whatever she made of herself on her own.

So it was that two years later, with her normal-school diploma held proudly in her hand, she kissed her friends and family goodbye and set out alone to the eastern part of the state and nurse's training with the nuns at the hospital in Cypress. There were no teaching jobs to be had, so, as always, Rosalie would make do. It was her twentieth year, 1928.

It wasn't long, of course, before everyone began to realize that the crashing of the stock market that next year wasn't going to affect just the rich. The poor, like Rosalie, would become even poorer.

Soon there was no way to make ends meet. She couldn't find a job to pay for her training and there was no hope of help from home, for if they hadn't been able to raise their own food on the farm her family would have starved.

All of which was no more and no less than she expected. She hadn't really thought that she was going to get away with it, that even with education she could escape. Book learning wouldn't do it in these desperate times they had now started to call the Depression. Hard work, if she could find it, was what it was going to take simply to survive.

The next ten, eleven, twelve years ground by. Rosalie clerked in a grocery store six days a week, ten hours a day. She grabbed a bite when she could, often too tired when she got home to her rented room to make herself anything. After all those years over her mother's stove and in the normal-school kitchen, she'd lost her taste for cooking anyway. Food wasn't important; she'd rather sleep.

Her pleasures, an occasional movie, a visit to relatives, were measured out as carefully as spoonfuls of expensive store-bought sugar, pinched as tightly as the pennies she stored up, roll after roll. Rosalie was ever watchful for waste and ruin. There was always the danger that even the sugar could be spilled, the pennies slip into a crack or be snatched away.

She loved to count the rolls of pennies, watch them grow. When there were enough, she'd lease and maybe someday buy a little corner grocery store across the Coupitaw River in West Cypress. A wholesaler, Zeb Miller, had told her about it, and when the day came he stocked it for her on extended credit.

"You work too hard, Rosalie, not to have something of your own. My wife said, a woman like you, all alone in the world, we ought to help you all we can."

What he didn't say was that before too long he would present the bill—but she should have known.

He came making a sales call far too late one night just as she was closing, pressed himself against her as he pinned her behind the counter.

"Just a little sugar," he begged. Rosalie could feel the anger that was just on the other side of his plea. He wasn't going to like it when she said no.

"I did you a favor. Now can't you do me one?"

She loathed herself even as she gave away what she'd been keeping so long, her chastity now coin in a disgusting business transacted in her bedroom in the tiny four-room apartment behind the Norris Grocery and Dry Goods Store. Of course it didn't stop there. Zeb came to collect what he thought was his due once a week, just as regularly as if it were on his territory schedule. That's what she was, she thought, part of Zeb Miller's territory—until she became pregnant. Then he forfeited his leasehold, sent a junior man to take her orders for canned goods and housewares, orders she wrote in a trembling hand. For she was dizzy and sick to her stomach all the time, as much from shame as from the baby.

Finally she sneaked over to Aunt Georgia's house in the Quarters one night. The old colored woman was supposed to be able to cure what ailed you, no matter what, they said. Smelling of snuff, the tiny grizzled woman with a rag tied around her head had taken one look in Rosalie's eyes and muttered, "Unh uh. Cain't. Too far gone."

So Rosalie had gritted her teeth and lain through night after night of sweaty waking nightmares. In the midst of one halfway through her fourth month, she began to hemorrhage. At dawn, alone, she delivered herself of a tiny dead thing in her blood-soaked bed. She allowed herself a few tears and then closed her mind to the whole affair. It was over, buried. She couldn't afford the luxury of thinking about it, not with all the headaches and long hours attendant to running a business by herself, though the nightmares of the baby lingered.

And so it went, work and more work, and a few years later, just after that terrible Sunday and Mr. Roosevelt's somber words on the radio telling the country about a place called Pearl Harbor, she had stood behind the counter enough hours, weighed enough potatoes, measured enough fabric, pumped enough kerosene, ground enough meat that the deed to the Norris Grocery and Dry Goods was her very own.

It was after that that the night terrors lifted and the dreams began, the dreams of her rolling a baby carriage down the sidewalk, of people stopping her and saying, "How beautiful, what a beautiful child." There was no man in the dreams, or, if there was, he was a shadowy figure standing on the edges. He never had a face, not once.

But did she deserve a baby? Did she deserve that kind of happiness?

One Sunday she looked up from the sinkful of soapy dinner dishes she was helping Janey wash and asked, "What's the most important thing in your life?"

Though this was not their usual kind of conversation, Janey didn't hesitate a lick. "My kids," she said. "They're the only thing that makes it all worthwhile." There was a pause and they listened to Janey's husband, Cooter, snoring on the living-room sofa like a pig.

"Would you do it again?"

"With Cooter?" Janey laughed. "Next time I think I'd try to do better than that. But I wouldn't give anything for my kids."

"I've been dreaming about a baby girl."

Janey gave her a look out of the corner of her eye, for she knew more than Rosalie suspected. Then she put her arm around her sister and gave her a hug. "Dreams can come true, Ro."

ROSALIE didn't believe that for a minute. But Janey had put her up to answering that ad in the newspaper, and now a baby was on its way. Any minute now, Emma, with her china-blue eyes and rosebud mouth, would be hers.

Rosalie heard a heavy motor labor and shift gears. The headlights of a bus whipped the platform. She could recite the landmarks of its passage: New York, Washington, Richmond, Atlanta, across the widths of Alabama and Mississippi on Highway 80 and ninety miles into Louisiana, three days and nights of hard traveling, and here it was.

The bus door banged open, and off marched a fat old lady in a straw hat carrying a basket in her arms. Rosalie couldn't control her twisting hands. Then a tall gray-haired man, stooped, with a cane. Was that him? Was Jake that old? Rosalie lurched forward one step. But he had no baby.

A colored woman was next, trailing three cranky children crying over their interrupted sleep.

That meant he wasn't on the bus.

Rosalie's shoulders drooped, her pounding heart slowed almost to a halt. Negroes sat at the back of the bus, always got off last. This nigger woman was the signal. Rosalie shouldn't have gotten her hopes up. How could she have expected so much, especially from a stranger?

Rosalie turned and began to walk away, back to the turtlelike gray Chevy she'd parked under a streetlight.

"Rosalie . . . Miss N-N-Norris?"

She stopped and turned back, and there he was. He had to be Jake Fine, this slender big-nosed man in the dark-brown hat and tan suit. He had to be because in his arms, dressed in a long powder-blue coat edged at the neck and wrists with creamy lace, was her baby, her Emma.

4

1949

IT WAS ALREADY hot when Emma got up. The heat usually starts in West Cypress by mid-June, already blistering when you open your eyes unless you do it before dawn. Before air-conditioning, ladies rose with the earliest sounds of bluebirds in the hydrangea bushes, to have a first cup of coffee with their maids in the kitchen and then get them started on the serious business of washing, scrubbing, polishing and cooking before the sun rose high in the sky. Then the pace would begin to slow, and, like mechanical toys winding down, maids, mistresses, masters, children, dogs, cats and even the lowliest rattlesnake would creep through the middle part of the day, moving as if underwater, the elongated sounds of their conversation becoming even more monosyllabic and languorous. Naps were a necessity rather than a luxury for children to avoid afternoon fits of frazzle. Long cool baths, morning and evening, followed by blizzards of talcum powder helped stave off heat rash, heat stroke, and malodorous realities that Southern ladies didn't like to think about.

But the Louisiana summer sun is no respecter of class, burning down through airborne oceans of humidity to steam and stupefy the brain of the cotton chopper in the field and the clerk behind the counter in the airless store, as well as the lady reclining on her chaise behind drawn curtains, sipping iced tea from a sweating glass. The heat is something you simply have to live with, Rosalie would say. There's no use in trying to fight it, wasting electricity. It happens every year, just like death, disease and taxes. Wait till evening, and it will cool off.

The man on the radio was saying it was going to be near 100

degrees. Rosalie hurried Emma to put on her blue-and-white seersucker sunsuit and sit down to breakfast.

"It's too hot to stand here in this kitchen. I've got to get in the store and help your father. A delivery's coming this morning."

Already the backs of Emma's legs were sweaty, sticking to the green chair. She liked the little flowers' patterns on the chair's back and turned to trace them with her finger.

"Here, now, don't dawdle. Eat your breakfast."

Her mother plopped her plate in front of her, a fried egg, biscuits, and bacon. Before Emma could stop her, she poured a big puddle of Log Cabin syrup over it all.

"Momma!" Emma shoved her chair back. She *hated* sweet on the same plate, even in the same room, with her egg.

"I swear," her mother said, wiping her brown hair off her damp face with the back of her hand. "I don't know why a five-and-a-half-year-old child is so finicky. You should be grateful that you have food."

"But every morning I say—"

"No sass from you, young lady. Or you won't go swimming later."

Emma's bottom lip was still out, but she was thinking. Mrs. Cloutier next door had offered to drive Emma with her children to the pool across the river in Cypress late that afternoon. There she could play in the water—a welcome respite from lying out in the backyard under the fig tree panting for breath. She didn't want to miss her chance; Momma hardly ever let her go, because she said that was where kids caught polio.

Emma loved splashing in the baby pool, the one with a statue of a mermaid in the middle. It lay outside the bathhouse that led to the big pool, the one that Anne and Wayne, the older Cloutier kids, had to go through where they washed their feet in chlorine. Emma didn't know whether the chlorine was supposed to kill the polio or not. But she was glad little kids didn't have to do it. She and Mike Cloutier just pulled off their shorts and sandals and jumped right in in their underpants. Maybe kids too little to go into the big pool didn't get polio, so they didn't need the foot-washing. Just like Baptists in town didn't wash feet like the foot-washing Baptists out in the country did. That was the kind of church where her Uncle England preached— foot-washing Baptists. In Sunday School at West Cypress Baptist she'd heard something about Jesus washing the feet of the disciples. Probably they lived out in the country like Uncle England. Probably they got their feet dirtier there. Was that what caused polio? She'd have to ask Momma.

They'd been to Uncle England's church once last year, and she didn't remember any washing at all. She did remember that Uncle England let her stand up in front of the whole church and sing "Abide with Me" accompanied by Aunt Ida Lou on the piano. Everybody had hugged her neck and told her that she sang so sweet, sweeter than pecan divinity, one lady said. Even her daddy, who she knew really hated going to church, looked like he was crying and gave her a hug. And she remembered they had a big dinner on the grounds afterward, with mountains of the best fried chicken she'd ever tasted, golden brown and crusty, and fluffy biscuits that didn't come out of a cardboard-and-silver tube and potato salad with both sweet and dill pickles, and chocolate cake and lemon meringue pie. Her momma had fussed at her for making such a pig of herself and asked why she didn't eat that way at home, and Emma didn't want to tell her that this was a whole lot better than her cooking because she didn't want to hurt her feelings. But sometimes, when Momma just seemed to go out of her way to mess up her food, like this syrup on her egg, she thought she just might.

"Well, young lady, are you going to sit there and let it all get cold?"

Momma was in a bad mood again today. She looked tired already and like her stomach hurt. Emma knew better than to say her food couldn't get cold on a day this hot. She picked up a biscuit and a piece of bacon.

"That egg too. I want to see it down before you go anywhere."

"Yes, ma'am." Emma nodded and pushed the egg to the edge of her plate, as far away as she could get it from the puddle of syrup.

Then she heard her daddy calling through the screen door in the little hallway that separated their house from the grocery store.

Rosalie put down the dish she was washing and wiped her hands on her apron. She frowned.

"I've got to go see what your daddy wants. That egg had better be gone when I get back. Do you understand?"

"Yes, ma'am."

Emma watched her mother's back and waited until she could hear the slap of the screen door and then her voice asking Daddy what was it now. Quickly she chopped her egg into tiny pieces and scraped it in with the other trash in the garbage can under the sink. Her heart was pounding as she slipped back into her chair and reached for another biscuit. Momma would be really mad if she caught her. Momma never wasted anything, which probably meant that throwing away food was a sin they just hadn't got around to telling Emma about at the West Cypress Baptist.

She waited a long time, but Momma didn't come back. So she carefully lifted her plate, knife and fork up to the sink and gently let them go. Then she ran into her room and buckled on her red sandals. It was too hot to go barefooted today. The sidewalk would blister her feet.

In the store her mother's voice was loud. "I told you to tell the meat man that we didn't want that many this time." Emma paused in the doorway.

She loved the store. At night it was scary, but in the daytime it was her own special world.

She adored the neat rows of canned goods. Since Momma had taught her to read last year, she was allowed to stock the lower shelves, but she didn't really have to read to do that. The yellow label had a picture of spinach. Red was for tomatoes. The baby food was harder because all the jars looked alike. But even before she knew what the words meant, she could put all the same letters together. The Cs for chicken. The Ps for prunes. She still loved prune baby food. Her parents laughed about that. She didn't know why.

She took a few steps into the store and stood in front of the ice-cream freezer. It had six doors on top, and if you wanted chocolate you opened the chocolate door and reached down with a scoop into a deep can and took it—unless the ice cream was too hard. She could scoop it if she stood on a stool. And she knew how much it cost, too. Five cents for a double dip, but she didn't ring it up on the cash register when her friends came over. She loved the cash register especially; that was her favorite thing.

All the silver dollars that came across the counter were hers, kept in a little square cigar box on a shelf under the register. Every couple of months she carried the box downtown to the bank for them to put the money into their vault. The teller initialed the amount and the date with a fountain pen in tiny little numbers in her dark-blue savings book.

"It's important to learn to save," Momma always said. "There's nothing more important than saving."

Emma kept the little book in her bottom dresser drawer. There was her name, Emma Rochelle Fine, written in ink on the first page. Then all those little bitty lines with dates, and numbers, and initials. The total was the best part: ninety-six dollars. Her mother said it was the money she was going to use toward college.

She guessed college cost a lot. For as long as she could remember her mother had gone to college over in Cypress to finish her degree. Until one Sunday afternoon last spring when she and Daddy had sat on folding chairs in the sun and watched Momma dressed up in a long black robe like the church choir wore and a funny hat with a tassel. The diploma and the tassel were hanging on the wall in their bedroom now.

In the store Rosalie looked up from her conversation with Jake and saw Emma. Her face was red. Was she hot or angry? "Did you finish your breakfast?" she asked.

"Yes, ma'am."

"Good. Now put on your sun hat and you can go out and play before it gets too hot."

"And then swimming?"

"We'll see. If the Cloutiers go and Anne promises to watch you. Are you going over to their house now?"

"Yes, ma'am. Mike and I are going to play in the canal." And then she bit her tongue.

"Remember what I told you about that."

"Oh, Ro," her father grumbled from behind the meat counter. "They're just kids."

"Jake, I told you what I saw."

"And I'm telling you you're imagining things. Kids will play."

Emma flushed with the memory of what her momma had seen a couple of days before. She had been playing with the water hose out in the backyard they shared with the Cloutiers. She and Mike were in their underpants, Anne and Wayne in their bathing suits. They'd been spraying one another, screaming, jumping at the delicious shock when the cold water hit their hot skins. All of a sudden Mike stopped, pulled down his pants, and peed against the trunk of the catalpa tree.

Anne, his older sister, said, "Mike, don't!"

"Oh, leave him alone," Wayne laughed, showing his broad white teeth in what Emma thought was a movie-star face. She always felt excited around Wayne, the same way she did when she was close to her cousin J. D. who lived out in the country.

Emma turned from Wayne's laughter and stared at Mike with her mouth loosely parted. She'd sneaked looks when he was wet in his underwear, but she had never seen a boy naked except for little babies getting their diapers changed. Mike's pee made an arc like the water spurting out of the fish's mouth that the mermaid held in the baby pool.

Then Rosalie had turned the corner around the side of the yard, coming to get Emma for something.

"What on earth are you doing!" she'd yelled at Mike, then grabbed Emma by the hand and jerked her into the house. "What were you doing?" she demanded again inside the dark cool apartment as she shook her.

"Nothing."

Then Emma had stared at the brown and yellow squares of the linoleum on her bedroom floor. This had something to do with down there. She didn't know what exactly, but Momma always made her feel ashamed about down there. When she mentioned it, it made her feel queasy in her stomach, almost exactly like when Momma gave her an enema. Momma had said, "Mike is a nasty little boy," and she wouldn't let her play alone with him anymore.

Now Emma, who really wanted to go down to the canal to play with Mike, said, "Linda and Mo Moore are coming over, too, Momma. They said so."

Her mother looked at her sharply. "You just make sure that they do." She straightened the straps of the sunsuit covering Emma's tiny nipples. Her fingers were always rough, her touch a quick poke, leaving tingling red marks for a few minutes on Emma's pale chest. "You be good," she cautioned, and Emma skipped out the front door.

Rosalie watched her daughter's blonde pigtails disappear from view. She sighed and turned back to the invoices. School had been over for a week and a half, and she had looked forward to a summer of relative ease after her first year of teaching. She liked the work, but it was exhausting leaving before dawn to drive the twenty-five miles into the country to the three-room schoolhouse. Much of the trip was on gravel roads with wooden bridges that threatened to wash out in the winter rains. When she got there, she had to bring in wood and build a fire in the stove before her third and fourth graders arrived. She helped Jake in the store when she got home until it was almost suppertime. Then she would run back into the kitchen and throw something together. Saturdays were spent behind the store's counter, too. Only on Sundays could she relax, after Sunday School and the church service, with a nap in the afternoon.

She'd hoped to unwind this summer. But look at these invoices. They were a mess.

She stood with her hands on her hips, the yellow slips of paper in her right hand. The papers were covered with sums of money, most of which they hadn't paid.

"Jake." Her lips were tight, as was her voice. "Why haven't these been taken care of?"

"What?"

She knew that look he was giving her, as if she were speaking a foreign language. He was stalling for time.

"These bills. Some of them are past due. Which means we can't complain when we don't get deliveries on time. You'd think you could do something right."

Rosalie bit her lip then. She hadn't meant to go so far, so fast. But it was too late now. The words were out. Well, so what? She meant them. Almost everything Jake did (and she didn't think that was ever enough) had to be done over again. Well, she had to admit he was a good butcher, but he knew nothing about keeping books.

Behind the long refrigerated meat display case now, he slammed down the cleaver he held in his left hand. It made a dull thud on the end grains of the wooden butcher block.

"What the hell?" he sputtered.

"Don't you curse at me. Just tell me why you haven't taken care of these."

"Because I didn't want to, that's why!" Jake bit back. Then he tore off his bloodstained apron and stomped to the rear of the store, slamming the screened apartment door behind him.

Before the sound had even stopped, there was an echoing slap as a little colored boy walked in the front, letting the door close behind him.

Rosalie looked at him and wondered if he had heard Jake yelling. Jake embarrassing her in front of a nigger. It wouldn't be the first time. She wiped away quick tears with the back of her hand.

"What do you want?" she barked at the child.

The boy lowered his eyes, bit his lip nervously. "I . . . meat." He fidgeted as if he had to go to the bathroom.

"Jake!" Rosalie called to the back.

There was no answer. Of course not. Once he had had a fit like that and had raised his voice, there would be silence for a long time, for several days. She'd have to do it herself.

"You stand right there, boy," she said, pointing with her finger like she did talking to the children in her classroom. You had to watch niggers every minute or they'd steal.

Minutes later, she had the meat cut and wrapped and the charge written up in the book with "JOHNSON, H.," for his mother's name, Hattie Johnson, inscribed in pencil across the back.

She riffled through the two wooden cheese boxes full of charge books and wondered how much they were owed. If it weren't for the nigger trade they wouldn't have a cent. Even with most of those on credit paying up the first of the month, they didn't have much. But it was the niggers who kept what little bread they had on their table.

Rosalie hadn't wanted to locate so near the Quarters when she started her business, but that's where it was, the only store she could afford, and Zeb Miller had assured her the nigger trade wasn't bad.

"Just keep a loaded pistol under the counter," he'd said, "if it'll make you feel better. Probably never have to use it."

If she'd had any sense, she'd have used it on him, but nonetheless he had been right about the colored trade. Of course, they were slow payers, and you had to watch the little ones like a hawk so they didn't slip things out of the candy counter, but all in all she couldn't complain about the colored trade in her store.

Perched right there on the edge of the Quarters, separated from it only by a drainage ditch everybody called "the canal," her property had been so cheap that within a few years of paying

off the store she'd bought the lot next to it, too, the last lot right
on the white/black line. She'd built the little house the Cloutiers
rented from her. It had been a wise decision. The rent house
brought in forty dollars a month and every penny counted,
though she had to do all of the repairs herself. Jake hadn't
proved to be very handy.

Now Rosalie found herself staring into the eyes of the little
Negro child. She'd forgotten that he was there.

"What are you waiting for, boy?"

"My momma's meat, Miz Fine," he mumbled, lowering his
gaze to the floor.

Rosalie pushed the package toward him. That's what happened when Jake got her so riled up. She got all distracted. Her
nerves couldn't take it. She even found herself being short with
Emma, whom she loved more than life.

She'd said that to Emma once. "I love you more than my own
life, honey."

Emma had looked up from Rosalie's lap, where she was sitting with the book she wanted Rosalie to read to her.

"And how much is that, Momma?"

"Why, everyone loves his own life most of all, child."

But as she said the words, Rosalie had known they weren't
true. She didn't love her life at all. She never had, and she never
would. Since Emma had come into it, things had been better.
She'd been right about supposing that, in the first conversation
she'd had with her sister Janey about finding a child. But she
hadn't counted on the problems, the main one being Jake.

What she should have done, if she'd thought more about it,
was find a child who had no mother *or* father—an orphan was
what she should have sought. Then there wouldn't have been all
these complications—like sex. Though she'd made it clear to Jake
pretty early that *that* wasn't part of the deal. She never had been
interested and didn't plan on starting at this late date. No, sir,
thank you very much. Then there were Jake's grumpiness and
his moods, his temper and his foreign ways. New York Jew—he
might as well be from Mars for all he knew about how to get
along in the world.

And, too, she had to admit, the older Emma got, the child
herself was a bit more than she had bargained for. For Rosalie
had never really thought about a child having a mind of her

own, of her growing up, of her being anything but a beautiful blonde baby. Already, at five and a half, Emma asked hard questions. Why did her daddy talk differently? Well, if it was because he came from New York, why didn't Momma come from there, too? When did Daddy move to West Cypress? And why?

Rosalie was hard pressed for the answers, for she had convinced Jake that Emma would be better off if she didn't know the truth, if she thought she was Rosalie's own. It wouldn't be that difficult, she'd reasoned; with the exception of Janey, and the rest of her family whom she rarely saw, hardly anyone knew. She had very few friends in West Cypress, had never had the time for socializing.

Jake had fought her about it. "She ought to know about her real mother."

"*Real* mother," Rosalie had argued. "Then what does that make me, who's changed her diapers, raised her, given her a home?"

Jake had continued to grumble, but then things had slid along, and Emma had grown, and once the threads began to be spun, even if by omission, the lie became a fabric with a texture of its own.

But Emma's questions never stopped. It was astonishing, the things that grew in that child's mind and plopped out of her mouth. Why, just the other day, she'd come home from Sunday School—which Rosalie had thought would save her and make her like all the other children, even if (though she didn't know it) she had been born a Jew—talking about the song "Jesus Loves the Little Children."

"If Jesus loves them all, 'Brown and yellow, black and white, they are precious in his sight,' " she sang, "if He loves them all, why do we call the brown and black ones niggers? Why do they have to live in those ugly houses on the other side of the canal? Why can't I play with them?"

Rosalie didn't need those kinds of questions. They made her uncomfortable and gave her a headache. Southern children never asked them. She never had. Sometimes she wondered whether Emma's being born a Yankee had ruined her for life.

But she did love her. Oh, Lord, yes, how she loved the child. Though it was hard for her to reach out to her now that Emma was geting bigger. For Rosalie didn't really know about touching people, even Emma, once they got to the stage where they could hug and touch back. They scared her sometimes, Emma's grasping little hands. The child liked to touch, to pet things, to ask questions; she was constantly reaching out, as if she wanted to take the whole world into her hands and her eyes and her mouth. Rosalie had never seen a child so hungry, hungry for *everything,* in her whole life.

STILL shaking with anger at Rosalie's words, Jake sat at the kitchen table stirring canned milk into his coffee. He tasted it and made a face. The cloying taste was disgusting, but canned milk was a rule of the house. Rosalie thought cream a needless expense. He sighed and stirred some more.

In the past four, almost five years, there were many things Jake had come to dislike about his life in West Cypress, and when Rosalie nagged at him, like she had just done, all of his displeasure tumbled like a house of cards built on a poker table downtown at the Ritz.

For one thing, he hated the food Rosalie piled on his plate every day: squash, peas, beans, okra. And greens, all kinds of greens, turnip, mustard, collard, things he'd never heard of, cooked into a slimy mess with pork fat. His mother, Riva, would never have allowed such things in her back door.

The weather was sticky and hot like a damp blanket from May until October. Though summers in New York had been no picnic, there was the respite of the beach. You needed a boat to enjoy the Coupitaw. The Fines didn't have a boat.

God, it was so hot today. The little fan turning slowly in the store never hit him often enough for the sweat to dry. This afternoon he had to mow the yard, and his perspiration would pour until his clothes were soaked and he was faint.

Another thing, he would tell Ruth if she were here, he didn't understand about Southerners. They were supposed to be so polite, but they laughed at his accent, teased him about being a Yankee, while at the same time they pretended not to notice his stutter. But he knew they did—behind those nicey-nice smiles. They just waited to laugh about that until they got out the door.

He especially hated Sundays, putting on a tie and going with Rosalie to the West Cypress Baptist Church. All that malarkey about Jesus—what did he care? Didn't Rosalie understand that he was a Jew?

"It's a small town, Jake. People will talk about you if you

don't go to church, and they won't come in the store. Besides, think about Emma."

Riva would have had plenty to say about that too.

"If the Baptists are so good," he asked Rosalie, "how come Deacon Ledbetter is always trying to cheat you on the bills from his feed store?"

"Hush, Jake." It wasn't nice to talk about things like that.

Hooey. Hooey, that's what Christianity was. Rosalie said he had to go for Emma, so he went. But he hated it.

He hated it almost as much as working in the store every day, being left alone to talk to salesmen about things he didn't understand, to try to figure up bills and answer the phone and take deliveries and cut meat and deal with customers to whom he was supposed to be nice. He couldn't even make out what some of them were saying, they talked with so much mush in their mouths. And *they* couldn't understand *him!* Hooey!

"Be polite, Jake," Rosalie was always telling him, sometimes saying it in front of them, making him feel ashamed. He didn't understand their ways. They were all so slow, and talked so much, on and on about nothing. All that talking, that wasn't business. If they had to go to New York and order a sandwich in a deli, where you stood in line, said what you wanted, "Turkey on rye, Russian dressing, coffee regular," then paid for it and got out in a hurry, they would have all starved to death. How could he be polite to people who made him so impatient?

He was fidgety, too, with the rent houses, Ro'd just bought another one, she was always fixing up. He didn't know how to hammer nails, lay linoleum, hang wallpaper. Rosalie did. She liked it, let her do it. He didn't want any part of it. When he finished in the store, he wanted to relax, read a detective novel, look at the pictures of faraway places in *The National Geographic.* Rosalie told him he was lazy. He didn't know, maybe he was. But he knew for sure that he was all thumbs with a hammer, and hammering was the last thing on his mind.

He missed his family too, the big parties at Ruth's or Rhoda's, not that they'd always gotten along, but eventually everyone would kiss and make up. He missed the tables of good food and the rye whiskey and, later, poker with the boys. He missed Ruth's easy laugh, her teasing him, always making him smile. "Jakey, Jakey," she'd say, rubbing the top of his head, bald since he was twenty-two. Sometimes they'd all get dressed up sharp and go into the city, do the clubs, listen to the music and dance. Or there was Coney Island in the summer with the rides, the parachute jump, the boardwalk, the beach with all the family and their friends. There was no one who knew him like that here, who could tease him and make him laugh. There was no drinking, at least not family drinking, just a few to have a good time. No clubs, no dancing, no beach. They knew only a few people who came into the store. And then there was her family. Her sister Janey wasn't too bad, but like all of them she was a Baptist, living in mortal fear of having a good time. They'd rather argue and fight, like they did almost every time that he and Rosalie went to where her mother, Virgie, now lived, on a farm fifty miles away in Pearl Bank next door to her daughter Nancy. After a Sunday dinner of fried chicken they'd gather in the tiny living room and bring up grudges and pick at old scabs until they ran again, the blood mixed with the sisters' tears. Jake couldn't ever remember a Sunday afternoon that they'd left there without Rosalie snuffling into a handkerchief half the way back to West Cypress.

Jake stayed pretty close to home, except for the occasional evening he walked into town to play dominoes at the Ritz Bar. He would call Rosalie when he was through, and she and Emma would drive down in the gray Chevrolet and get him.

That was another thing, he'd never learned to drive. He hadn't had to in the East, and now it was too late. He'd tried, but Rosalie's poking at him to do this and do that while he was trying to watch the traffic made him too nervous. He'd given up. Not that there was much of anywhere to go. Nor much fun to be had. Not even *that* kind of fun.

Jake shut his eyes. He didn't think about that anymore, because if he did, it made him want to throw up.

The milk began to curdle in his stomach then, as he couldn't help remembering that night.

"No," Rosalie had said to him in those three days they'd courted after he and Emma had first arrived from New York.

That was fine. He hadn't wanted to rush her. After all, it *was* a marriage of convenience. She'd come to him in her own time. But the days and weeks and months had passed, and then one night he gathered all the courage that his need had constructed, like water building behind a dike, and reached out a hand.

She jerked away. "No!"

"But, Rosalie."

"No!"

"I'll be careful." He could be, if she were a virgin. Was Rosalie a virgin? He didn't know. And he'd bought condoms. They were underneath his handkerchiefs in his dresser drawer.

"No."

He couldn't talk to her about it. Whatever would he say?

So he let the time slip past. Rosalie treated Emma like her own. Why, it was practically as if she *were* her own, as if he'd come to believe the lie. He couldn't leave his baby, and he couldn't take her away, not now, not once Emma had a home.

The months turned into years. Emma was two, three, four. And then the night had come that he hated to think about, the night he'd tried once more. Only once more.

He'd been to the Ritz to play dominoes, and though he didn't drink at all anymore, that one night he did. Mr. Vance was celebrating his birthday, treating everyone to beers.

"Come on, Jake," they'd urged him.

"No." He shook his head.

"Come on, be a sport."

He always felt so separate. Why not? He reached for the beer. Why not have a sip or two and step inside?

He'd had three—or four, he'd lost track. It had been so long, the alcohol went straight to his head.

He decided to walk home that night; wobbling a little here, floating a little there, he convinced himself that this night would be different. Rosalie would be waiting for him wearing a flirtatious smile and little else.

She was asleep. He edged himself onto the bed and laid his hand over her breast.

"What are you doing?" Her voice was stiletto sharp. She sat straight up, instantly awake.

"Ro . . . I . . . th-th-th. . . ." He couldn't get it out.

"You thought what? You got yourself all drunked up," for she could smell the alcohol, "and came home with *that* on your mind?"

Jake jumped out of bed, that hand which had grazed her breast now holding his belly as if her words had stabbed him, which they had. He barreled out the door, barely making it to the backyard, where he doubled over. An almost-naked man in boxer shorts, he vomited into the grass. He heaved the beer and the shame over and over until there was nothing left. Then he sat in the wooden swing he'd hung for Emma from a green iron frame and pushed himself back and forth. The tears ran down his face, and he let them flow unobstructed from his chin. When he pushed off with his feet again, the tears flew in silver arcs into the night.

He thought of catching his tears in Rosalie's watering can and throwing them in her face. He thought of bundling up Emma in the night, going back north to his sister Ruth's house. But when he was standing on Ruth's doorstep, how would he explain? Then he thought of every hurtful thing that anyone had ever done to him. He cried and swung and cried some more. Finally exhausted, he curled into a ball in the swing and fell asleep.

He awoke at dawn. The Cloutiers' yellow tomcat had jumped up on the arm of the swing and was staring him in the face.

"Go way," he growled.

The cat licked its whiskers, then his toes. It tickled, but he couldn't laugh, for he remembered where he was and why. He was still alive, he found, even if he didn't want to be.

He tried to sit up. At first his limbs were so stiff and frozen, he couldn't. Slowly he warmed them, stretching like the cat. Then, not knowing what else to do, he got up and went inside and took a bath. He didn't speak to Rosalie for almost a month after that, but eventually his hurt and need, flowing along like the river of his days, smoothed out.

No, he didn't think about it much anymore. And, in a way maybe Rosalie was right. There could be that slip. There was always that chance, that a condom would break, and another child would be born. And look where that had ended, Helen lying dead on the floor.

But sex made Emma too, Jake, a voice whispered. Emma too. Yes, Emma, the only thing in the world that made him smile.

Darling Emma with her yellow curls, posing for the camera in her dancing costumes, holding out her little pink skirt and cocking one hip to the side. She was so pretty—and so smart. Already she talked a mile a minute. With that Southern accent, she reminded him of Helen, though he would never tell Rosalie that.

"She sounds just like you," he said instead.

He couldn't get over Emma. Not even in school yet and already she was talking about things sometimes he didn't understand. He was growing shy with her. Who was this child, chattering to herself in mirrors, talking with customers in the store, understanding what they wanted from him before he did?

Did that brightness come from Helen? But then, he had to admit Rosalie had done her part, was a good mother, so proud. She stayed up late into the night sewing for her, making little pleated dresses, silvery tutus for her dancing classes. "Dresses like I never had," Ro said. She read story after story to her, day after day, as soon as Emma was old enough to listen. At four she could read for herself. Now his Emma at five and a half read almost as well as he could. Yes, Rosalie had kept her half of the bargain, even though sometimes she was brusque with Emma. Well, that was her way. That was his way, too, now that he thought about it. Why did the two of them have such a hard time opening their mouths and arms and just letting soft words and caresses flow out? If only I could, he thought, if only I could relax my tongue, let the words flow like honey.

"Jake, are you coming back in the store?" Rosalie, hands on her hips, filled the doorway.

He hated it when she stood there talking to him as if he were a child. He didn't answer.

"Jake, I'm talking to you."

Well, of course she was.

"Are you going to answer me?"

Her voice had grown more shrill, and then its sound narrowed into a little sliver of pain that hurt Jake's heart. She didn't love him. She'd never held him. She never would. Oh, Helen, why did you leave me? What am I doing here?

"No! Goddammit! I'm not going to answer you!"

The words burst out of him. He wouldn't, either. He could be silent for days, for weeks, for months, when he wanted to. Rosalie might think herself a clever horse trader, but he'd teach her to be careful what she bargained for.

EMMA was relieved when the store door slammed behind her. She hated it when they yelled. Afterward everything would get really quiet and her daddy wouldn't talk for a long time. She couldn't decide which was worse, the yelling or the silence.

She knew everyone's house wasn't like that. Mike's mother hollered, but only when the kids were bad. She'd smack them on the legs with a belt and everybody would jump up and down like corn popping at the picture show. Then it would all be over and they'd go back outside. Emma spent as much time as she could at the Cloutiers'.

Mike had been waiting for her on his front steps, squinting into the glare, counting Chevys. Emma counted Fords. As of last week, she was ahead.

"She let you?" he asked, handing her a mayonnaise sandwich.

"I told her Linda and Mo are coming, too."

Mike made a face. Linda's little sister Mo was a pain in the behind.

Emma shrugged. "They may not, then we'll just pretend they did."

They crossed the yard then and walked carefully down the dirt path to the bottom of the canal, each holding a mayonnaise sandwich in one hand and pushing back the blackberry brambles with the other. The blackberries would soon be ripe. They were gigantic, big and sweet, delicious when they were picked in the sun and spurted hot purple juice like jelly into her mouth. But for now Mrs. Cloutier's sandwiches were enough, the mayo spread thick like frosting on one piece of white bread.

Mike's mother always had wonderful things to eat. She made banana pudding with vanilla wafers and meringue with little brown tears on the top. Once when Emma was over, they had fried frogs' legs that Mr. Cloutier had caught with his very own hands. *Gigged,* he said.

"Watch where you're going, you're gonna slip." Mike shoved the rest of his sandwich into his mouth and grabbed her arm as she started to go down. It had rained like crazy the day before, and there were still little patches of wet.

It seemed like it rained every other day in the summertime. One of Emma's favorite things was to lie out flat on her back in the yard and watch the clouds roll in. She could see them coming from way off in the distance, tall and puffy like scoops of soft ice cream piled one on top of the other until they must reach to heaven. Suddenly the air would change and the wind would come up and then in the distance she could hear the thunder and see the lightning flash. Sometimes if she was by herself she would just lie and smell the rain on the clover. The bees ran and hid from the wet. And even from the middle of the yard she could smell the odor of the hot sidewalks. She'd lie there until her momma yelled at her: "Get in this house before you get struck by lightning." Did anybody ever or was it just something grown-ups said?

Sometimes if she and the Cloutier kids were playing when the rain started, they screamed and ran with their mouths open, letting the rain fall right in.

The rain didn't always swell up gradually, though, giving them the choice of whether to keep playing or run inside.

Like right now. Just as she and Mike licked the last of their mayonnaise and started to argue about what game to play, Tarzan or cowboys, the heavens dumped. Following Mike's yellow head, his hair plastered in strings, she raced into the culvert that ran under the street and squatted down. The bank was only about a foot wide, edging the murky water that, if you fell into it, made you smell green and dead.

It was so dark under the culvert, Emma couldn't see a thing.

Mike inched his fingers carefully and then goosed Emma down the back of her neck.

"Spider!" she screamed.

Mike upped the ante. "Maybe it's a snake!"

Emma almost wet her pants. "Miiiiike," she wailed. And then she heard a giggle. "It's *not* funny!"

"I didn't say it was."

"You did, too! You laughed!"

"I didn't."

Emma was so wound up in the argument, she forgot the possibility of the spider—or the snake.

"If you didn't, Mr. Smarty Pants, who did?"

"I did," said a voice from across the canal.

"Yikes!" Both the children jumped up, crashed into one another, teetered on the edge of the water.

Then their eyes adjusted to the dark. There on the other side, not six feet away, squatted two little colored boys.

Of course she knew that Negroes lived right across the canal. The first house of the Quarters was just behind Skeleton Hill, which was what they called the empty lot with the rise in it bordering the ditch. They never played on the hill, because it was on colored property, but it figured large in their make-believe.

Many of their imaginary creatures lived there, including the Green Skeleton who haunted Emma's nightmares.

Every once in a while they would see a few coloreds playing on the Quarters side of the canal, but not very often. And when they did, they ignored one another just like when colored kids came into the store. Momma had told her she had to watch the pickaninnies, which she did, but she watched in silence. What would she say? Momma said you couldn't understand them because they barely spoke English, though a couple of times Emma had asked what they wanted and she had understood. Emma didn't know many of their names. Most of the time she looked right through them like everybody else did, like they were invisible.

But these kids sitting just across the canal under the culvert weren't invisible. Now she could see them just fine. She couldn't smell them. Momma said they smelled, but maybe that was because of the stinky canal.

For a few moments the four of them sat still as if they were playing statue, all squatting on their haunches.

Then Mike moved. "Hey," he said.

Emma turned her face to him, then realized he was speaking to the boys.

"Hey," the older of the two said back softly. The sound of his voice seemed to reverberate, wavy like the ribs in the steel culvert overhead.

"My name's Mike. This," he nudged her, "is Emma."

"Hey," the colored boys both said this time—and stared.

"What's yours?" Mike asked.

"Marcus," said the older. "This here's my little brother James." James nodded and ducked his head.

"Hey," Emma found her voice. Then, because she didn't know what else to say, she asked, "Where do you live?"

Marcus gestured wordlessly back over his shoulder toward the Quarters.

"We live over there," Emma volunteered, getting the hang of making this conversation. "Mike lives in the first house. And I live behind the store."

"We know," Marcus said.

Emma stared at him in the darkness. How did he know?

Then a shrill sound pierced the darkness. "Mikey? Emma!" It was Linda, calling them.

Mike stood up, stepped over Emma and out of the culvert. Then he poked his head back in.

"Come on, Em. The rain's over."

Emma stood and pulled the legs of her sunsuit down. On the other side of the canal Marcus and James stood, too.

"Come *on.*" Mike waved his hand at Emma. "You going to sit there in the dark all day?"

Well, no, she wasn't. But on the other hand, she wasn't quite ready to go, either. Emma didn't know what it was she wanted to do there, or to say, but she felt as if she'd left a gate hanging open somewhere.

"Okay, okay." She didn't have Mike to hold on to this time. He was already halfway back up the path. Emma picked her way carefully. Just as she got to the mouth of the culvert, she slipped.

A strong hand caught her arm and steadied her. She stayed. In the bright sunlight, for the rain had been a sudden shower and now had blown away, she looked down at his brown hand on her arm. It made her white skin look whiter.

"Thanks." She looked down at her sandals, suddenly shy again.

"You be careful, Miss Emma," the older one called Marcus said, and then they both turned, the younger brother a shadow to the older, and like dark butterflies they were gone.

Up at the top of the path Linda stood with her hands on her hips. Behind her was the fat little busybody, her redheaded sister Mo.

"*What* were you-all doing down there with those niggers is what I want to know." Mo was the most hateful six-year-old Emma had ever known. She didn't think Mo was going to live to be seven.

"None of your beeswax," Mike answered. He shot a look at Emma.

He was right, Emma thought. It was none of their business. But why did she feel so funny about it? Why did she feel like Mo would tell on them if she knew about their sitting in the culvert and talking to the colored boys? Had they done something wrong?

LATER that night, after a supper of macaroni and cheese, she and her daddy listened to *The Shadow* on the radio in the almost-dark living room while her mother did the dishes. It was so creepy, when the door on the radio opened, she could see it. *Cccrrrrreeeaaakkkkkkk.* It was shivery delicious.

"I don't know why you let her listen to that," Rosalie called from the kitchen. "You know she's going to have nightmares."

"Oh, Ro. What the hike?" His voice didn't sound happy, Emma thought, but at least they were still speaking.

She loved listening to the radio with her daddy. Sometimes they listened to the Dodgers games too. She adored the Brooklyn Dodgers because they were her daddy's favorite team.

"Rosalie, it doesn't hurt her to listen to the radio. She has bad dreams anyway. All kids have nightmares."

It was true. She did have nightmares. There were things lurking in the dark, waiting to get her.

After *The Shadow* she had her bath in the claw-footed tub and then Momma tucked her in.

"What do you want to hear tonight?"

" 'The Frog Prince.' "

It was one of her favorites from the red book of fairy tales that came with the encyclopedia. Momma acted out all the parts in different voices.

She loved it at the end when the frog turned into a prince.

"But it's not fair," she said at the earlier part where the frog insisted that he eat from the princess's plate and drink from her goblet and sleep in her bed.

"Just because he saved her golden ball from the well," Emma said. "He shouldn't expect all that. Why was he so greedy?"

Rosalie laughed. Now, *that* was a good question.

"Was he a Jew?"

Rosalie looked at her sharply. "What do you mean?"

"That's what they say at Sunday School. That Jews are greedy. What is a Jew, anyway?"

"Put your arms under the cover, and I'll pin you in."

"You didn't answer my question."

"Under!"

Emma gave up. When her momma and daddy didn't want to tell her things, it was always like this. She had another question, the one she was really leading up to. Mike had said that his mother said that her daddy was a Jew. Did that mean that she was one, too? Was it something you inherited? Or was it like

having polio, something you caught? If she was one, was that bad
or good?

"It's too hot to be pinned in," she whined.

"I'll leave the little fan on for a while, until you go to sleep.
You know if I don't pin you, you'll be afraid."

Momma was right. If even so much as her little toe was out,
the monster under the bed would snatch it.

Or the thing that could get out of her pine clothes closet when
the door was left open would grab her.

But the worst was the Green Skeleton who slept on Skeleton
Hill in the daytime. As soon as dark fell, it arose, its bones slimy
and green like the canal water, and dragged itself, creaking and
groaning, off the hill, through the canal, past the Cloutiers' and
up the sidewalk, leaving little globs of slime on her hopscotch
traced in chalk. Then it would wait for her just outside the
store's front door, where it crouched, sending messages to her stomach that there was something in the pitch-black store she just
couldn't live without: a Hershey with almonds from the candy
counter or a Coke from the big red box filled with blocks of ice.

"There's no one in there, Emma. If you want a Hershey bad
enough, go get it," Momma said.

But the pull light was over the counter, at the far end near the
plate-glass windows. Momma said those thumping sounds were
cans falling off the shelves, but Emma knew different. It was the
Green Skeleton, who'd already creeeeaaaked the front door open
and was waiting for her.

Even if she made it alive to the counter, then she had to stand
on the stool and feel around in the dark for the string. What was
there to keep him from grabbing her arm and, pop! chewing it
off? Once she had touched his finger; she knew it was his finger,
cold and icy. She screamed bloody murder, fell off the stool, and
cracked her head.

Momma said that was a lesson to her that little girls don't
need chocolate in the middle of the night. Emma thought they
did, especially if they didn't like the bony chicken spaghetti they
had for supper and were still hungry, so she hid Hersheys in the
dresser drawer with her savings book.

She still had to get up to reach them, worming her way out of
the tightly safety-pinned sheets and blankets. Something could
still get her, that something that had already sneaked into her

room and was waiting for her to get out of bed. But the chances of survival were better than in the store.

"Now go to sleep, Emma. I'll see you in the morning."

She hoped so. There was no telling what could happen between now and then.

Emma stared into the darkness. Even if the boogeyrun didn't get her tonight, in the morning Momma might ask her about the dollar. What was she going to say then? Maybe she'd wish that the boogeymen had killed her dead.

MOMMA had given her the dollar two weeks ago, a crisp new bill from the cash register.

"Now, be careful how you spend it. Don't go throwing good money away."

Emma turned and twisted as best she could beneath the tightly pinned sheet. A cold scary hand, even scarier than the Green Skeleton's, gripped her guts. It was possible that the Green Skeleton lived only in her imagination, but she knew that her mother's disapproval of her spendthrift ways was very real.

She tried to account for the money in her mind, but even using her fingers, the nickels kept rolling away.

Last Saturday she'd gone to the Strand with the Cloutiers to see a double feature of Lash LaRue, her favorite, and Tim McCoy, her second favorite, along with a Tarzan serial and three Bugs Bunny cartoons. That was twenty-five cents. A bag of popcorn was a nickel. That made thirty.

In the candy store next to the Strand she'd bought two Sugar Babies for a penny, five candy corns for two cents, five chocolate kisses for two more; that was a nickel. And a package of Necco wafers. Another nickel, a dime, that made forty.

Last week she and Mike bought chocolate éclairs at the bakery, though they were really pushing their luck in June. Everybody knew that the custard and whipped cream wouldn't hold up to the heat, and if you didn't eat them really fast, you could die of food poisoning, just like you'd get from eating tuna fish and drinking milk. The éclair was fifteen cents. Fifty-five.

At the swimming pool she'd had a chili dog, so good that it made her jaws go *squinch* at the first bite. Fifty-five plus fifteen made seventy.

She had a nickel left in her red coin purse. What had happened to the other quarter? Had she lost it? Maybe it was in the pocket of her shorts. She had to find it, but she knew she was going to be in trouble anyway. She couldn't tell her momma that she'd spent all that money on food.

"Emma, I swear. You'd think you didn't live in a grocery store. Just throwing good money away."

Emma couldn't explain to Momma how good the chili dog tasted, how the combination of chili, mustard and onions satisfied something deep inside her.

"When I was a little girl we were lucky to have cornbread and buttermilk for supper. We didn't need fancy things to make us happy."

Momma disapproved of fancy tastes, exotic chocolate and flaky pastry melting with snowy whipped cream, all thick and rich, luxurious on the tongue. She wouldn't even try them. She knew they wouldn't make her happy.

Momma was going to kill her, she knew. She was never going to get another dollar. She'd have to sneak coins out of the cash register or out of the bottom of her mother's purse if she ever again wanted a little glass dish of vanilla ice cream flooded with hot fudge sauce at Philips' Drugstore.

Maybe if she tried to do it all over tomorrow with a pencil and paper, she could account for the dollar in a different way. She closed her eyes and turned over, belly down. She'd try to go to sleep now.

She'd think about something good—like St. Jude's. She loved the Catholic church up the block. Sometimes she and Linda walked over there. It was one of her favorite places, though she never told Rosalie, who said the Catholics wanted to give the country to the Pope—whoever he was.

THE door of the church, next to the school, was always open. No one had ever stopped them from going inside. Even the nuns in black never said a word.

It was quiet and still in the empty church so different from the West Cypress Baptist. On the walls were things called stations of the cross, little statues of Jesus suffering. Emma had watched one day as a nun went around and stopped and prayed beneath each one of them. Down front there was a beautiful altar, silver and gold with a lace cloth and behind it a big statue of Jesus on a crucifix. Emma didn't like to look at that. She thought it was creepy, all that blood running down. The best parts of St. Jude were the candles and the smells.

In the back, just past the holy water which she always dabbled her fingers into, making them tingly the rest of the day, was a big stand full of candles, most of them burning. There was another one like it up near the altar.

Mike's big sister had told her that the candles were lighted by people for their dead relatives. The candles' burning saved them from hellfire for those same minutes. Then why didn't people burn candles for them all the time? And Baptists didn't even have any candles, so what kept them from burning in hell? Maybe they had to burn all the time. That's what the ladies in Baptist Training Union said on Sunday nights, that if the blood of redemption didn't save you, you'd burn in hellfire forever. She didn't know how blood could save you or where you got the blood, but the whole thing scared her. She'd come home one Sunday after Training Union screaming about brimstone and damnation, and her mother said maybe just Sunday School and church were enough. She thought so, too, though she didn't especially like them either. The only good part of Baptists was Vacation Bible school, where she got to cut out things from colored paper and play with white glue that smelled nasty but good and eat cookies with red and green sugar sprinkles and drink lemonade. They didn't talk about hellfire in Vacation Bible school.

St. Jude's didn't need white glue to smell good. There was something, especially right down near the altar, that made her nose twitch. Mike's sister had said it was called incense and that it came, like smoke, out of a silver ball the priest waved in mass. Emma couldn't picture it, but she loved the smell. It was sharp, like mustard, but there was something woodsy about it, too, like the sticky of pine trees.

That made her think of the woods behind Grandma Virgie's house where once she'd gone walking with her cousin J.D.

She snuggled, groggy, floating. It would be nice to have a big brother like J.D.—if he were as cute as J.D. Well, she couldn't have a big brother. What about a little brother or sister? How would that be? She thought about that, hugged her doll closer, and fell asleep.

"I DON'T know why you're always in such a bad mood. Why do you snap at me so?"

"I'm sorry. I don't mean to. But I told you before, I want to go, Rosalie."

"Then get on the bus and go."

"No, I want you and Emma to go, too, now, before she starts school."

"Why not next summer?"

"Why not this one?"

"You know why. It's too . . . dangerous."

"That's never going to change, Ro."

"Somebody will slip. She'll find out."

"You think Herb and Rhoda will tell her? Or Ruth? Or George? Or my father? What would they have to gain by that?"

"What about the children?"

"None of them know."

"How do you know what they might have overheard?"

"Ro, I don't think my relatives sit around and talk about us. Why should they? They haven't seen me in almost five years. For all I know, they think I'm dead."

"Don't be silly. Ruth writes."

"Yes. Ruth writes, and Rhoda writes, and they ask when we're coming to visit so they can meet you and see Emma. They want to see her, you know. And my dad's not getting any younger."

"You know I don't like to travel."

"I know you don't like to meet new people."

"Neither do you."

"They aren't new to me, Ro. They're my family."

"I'm just scared, that's all. What if she finds out?"

"If she finds out, she finds out. I always told you it was a mistake in the first place."

What was? wondered Emma, who had awakened from a nightmare of the Green Skeleton. What was the mistake? Who was? She was?

SHE had never seen anything like her Aunt Rhoda's house in Paterson, New Jersey. She'd never seen anyone like Aunt Rhoda either.

"Sit. Sit," Aunt Rhoda ordered, waving her bright fingertips at

them. Her fingernails were almost the exact same shiny red as
the dining-room table she was pushing them toward. The chairs
and the table legs were carved with dragons just like the ones
Emma had seen in pictures in her fairy-tale book. *Chinese,* her
mother had whispered. Emma didn't think Aunt Rhoda looked
Chinese. They had black hair, and Aunt Rhoda's was red, with
short little curls all over her head. *Dyed,* Momma had whispered
again.

"Eat. Don't be shy. Seltzer?" Aunt Rhoda held a silver can
with a black top in her hands. Seltzer? It sounded like something
you would take for a tummy ache. Aunt Rhoda pushed a button
in the black top, and fizzy water filled Emma's glass.

Now it was Sunday morning. They had all slept late, Emma in
an upstairs room with the cousin named Jeri who was asleep
when she got into bed with her and already up when she awoke.
When Emma went downstairs, they were all sitting around the
kitchen talking and drinking coffee.

Emma looked around the table at the adults and picked at the
hem of her nightgown. "Do I have to wear a dress to go to
church?"

Her Aunt Rhoda laughed and shook a finger at her father,
who got a funny expression on his face. "No, no church." That
was okay with her. But now she was starving to death, and she
didn't know what any of the things were on the white lacy tablecloth with the red surface underneath shining through its little
holes. And she was afraid to ask.

For one thing, her Aunt Rhoda seemed to think everything she
said was funny. "My little Southern shiksa niece," she kept saying, patting her on the head. Emma thought Aunt Rhoda was
pretty funny, too. She sure talked funny. So did Uncle Herb. And
now her cousin Jeri on her left. They all sounded a little bit
like her daddy. But they didn't stutter at all.

"Have some lox," Aunt Rhoda urged, pushing a platter in
front of her.

Was that orange stuff called locks? What was she talking
about? Emma was hungry; her stomach was growling and her
Aunt Rhoda was teasing her. She felt like she was going to cry.

"Show her," Aunt Rhoda said to Jeri, who took a hard brown
roll with a hole in the middle of it, spread it with what looked
like thick white butter and layered on the orange lox and raw

onion until she had a sandwich. Then Jeri handed her the lox
and bagel, as she called it. Emma glanced up at her Aunt Rhoda,
who was staring at her. "Eat," she ordered. Emma did. It was
delicious. Before they left the table, she had two of the salty
sandwiches. Her Aunt Rhoda laughed and called her Emmale
and sent her off to play with Jeri in the basement. Emma had
never seen a house with a basement.

In Louisiana the water is just beneath the ground, artesian
water that flows at the slightest provocation. And in the spring,
the rain and the melting snow from the North cascade down the
country, the water swamping up and flooding as it approaches its
muddy destination in the Gulf. Unless they're perched on some
elevation, smart people in West Cypress build their houses on
stilts or pilings so that water has a harder time rushing in and
carrying off their very beds while they're still asleep. In West
Cypress a basement would simply be a hole in the wetland, a
certain invitation to trouble that most folks would rather do
without.

So it was with amazement that Emma followed her cousin Jeri
down steps into a large square basement room with walls like
the knotty-pine clothes closet in her room at home. In the middle
stood a big table. Emma couldn't reach the top of it, but she
could see from where she stood that it was covered with green
cloth. Pool, Jeri said. It didn't look like any pool Emma had
ever seen.

A FEW days later Emma was standing in the center of a circle of
children in her Aunt Ruth's backyard in Connecticut. "Tell us
what you did in New York City," her cousin Ed demanded.

She told them about the Empire State Building, Nedick's
orange drink on every corner, Macy's escalators, Coney Island
and Nathan's—wonderful Nathan's hot dogs, better than at the
Cypress Natatorium.

Emma's eyes grew bluer and wider and her voice higher as she
told the children of her adventures, of all the things she had
now seen and had never even imagined. But she didn't tell them
the other things she felt. Even if she'd wanted to—and she didn't
because she knew that they weren't really listening to *what* she
said, but rather to the way she said it, giggling and poking fun
at her Southern accent—even if she'd chosen to tell them her

other feelings, she didn't have the words for those emotions bubbling up all at once, breaking through iridescent skins and releasing both remembrance and mystery, familiar yet strange. She couldn't describe how it felt, meeting these people for the first time ever who were the other half of her relatives. Could she tell her cousin Ed that his mother, her Aunt Ruth, with a voice that spoke sweet words, had a touch, a loving soft caress when their flesh met, that made her heart flutter and whisper *Yes, oh, yes!* She didn't feel this way about her momma's relatives at all (except J. D.), and she'd known them all her life.

Why, just the other night they had all been sitting out in the backyard, right about where she stood now, and Aunt Ruth was turning the lamb she was cooking on the grill. Emma had never tasted lamb before, nor the salad with something like rice, and tomatoes, and mint. It all smelled so delicious, Emma could hardly wait. And then she didn't have to, for Aunt Ruth had pulled off little pieces and given her tastes. And then Aunt Ruth had pulled her into her lap when she went and sat down by Uncle George. He had put his arm around Aunt Ruth's shoulder and pinched Emma's cheek. They were all tucked together in a kind of warm cocoon.

Later Ed had turned on the radio, and "Tuxedo Junction" filled the air. All of a sudden Uncle George had them both up on their feet. They were all holding hands, but close together, the three of them moving in a dance, swaying hips, shifting feet on the damp grass in the cool air while the others watched. Emma could smell the ocean over the lamb. The coast was only a few miles over that way. Then she watched Uncle George's hand slip out of Aunt Ruth's hand and onto her back, to her waist, and then it was cupping Aunt Ruth's rear end. Emma had never seen anything like it before. She looked up into Uncle George's face with astonishment, and he caught her look and winked.

GRANDFATHER Fine was the most elegant man she'd ever seen. Even on the hot summer's day when she met him, her grandfather was dressed in a three-piece blue-and-white seersucker suit. On his head he wore a straw skimmer with a black grosgrain band. Across his stomach was a gold chain that looped and then disappeared like a roller coaster.

He had caught Emma staring at it. "You want to see, *tuch-terle?*" he asked.

Emma nodded, suddenly shy, for he didn't smile much, this silver-haired old man.

He pulled out a gold watch. It was shaped like a small onion, and when he opened up the back two little girl figures held hands and danced across an enameled woods. Emma giggled with delight, and the old man crowed, "She's wonderful." Jake looked very proud, as if he were a little boy again and his father had patted him on the head.

"Beautiful," Isidore Fine continued. "And smart. Where'd you find this child, Jakey? The fairies bring her?"

Emma saw a cloud cross her father's face. But then her grandfather reached over and slapped her father across the back and Emma thought that then even the top of his bald head beamed.

They didn't stay long. Rosalie was very nervous meeting her father-in-law. She said she was getting a sick headache.

"You'll come back again," Isidore said. "Now that we all know each other, it shouldn't be so long."

Then he kissed Emma goodbye and slipped something into her hand. "You hold on to this tight for the rest of your life," he said to her. "This was my wife's."

Emma looked down to see a cameo on the front of a little gold box hanging from a golden chain.

"You can wear it when you grow up," he said. "Now, don't lose it or wind it too much."

And then he showed Emma the little knob on the back. When he wound it, out tinkled "The Blue Danube."

"You know how to dance?" he asked.

Emma nodded. "I take lessons. I do ballet."

Isidore bowed formally and took her hand, and to the music from the tiny box he and his granddaughter waltzed across the floor.

"Next time you come I'll teach you the foxtrot," he called after them as he waved goodbye at his apartment door.

EMMA loved many things about her Uncle George—his teasing, the way his arm around her made her feel, the long black Cadillac he drove, where all three kids and Aunt Ruth snuggled in the backseat. And she liked the smell of the cigar he smoked and the twinkle of gold in his front teeth.

One night he took them to a restaurant and sat them all down. With a big wave of his hand he said, "Order anything you want." Emma had never seen anyone like that. Her Uncle George must be rich as a king.

When she opened her mouth to say what she wanted her mother had frowned at her, but still, before her on a big round tray had appeared something hot and red and yellow and bubbling. She looked at Uncle George with a question on her face. He slapped himself on the forehead in disbelief.

"Jake, she doesn't know pizza? Where the hell do you live? Beyond the moon?"

"In Louisiana," Jake laughed, "the dark side of the moon." Rosalie frowned, but Emma's father had suddenly found his tongue. He told them about catfish and cornpone, a world where you couldn't buy pumpernickel bread. They all laughed, even Rosalie then, though Emma could see from the look on her face she didn't really understand.

Something in Emma's heart was battering blindly then, struggling like a butterfly to escape into the clear blue air where the possibilities existed for dancing and laughter and music and tall buildings and conversations long into the night, where people who were kin to one another gathered around breakfast tables and drank cup after cup of coffee and ate exotic foods and teased and shared secrets and told stories about the past.

THE last night in Connecticut before they had to pile back into the Chevy and begin the endless trip back home, Emma and Ed balanced each other slowly up and down on the teeter-totter in the backyard. It was twilight and the bushes thrummed with the voices of insects. A couple of stars shone, the bravest, brightest ones, but it would be a long time before the heavens filled. Darkness came very late to the Northern summer sky.

"That's the North Star," Ed said.

Emma looked and nodded. "We have that in Louisiana too."

Ed laughed. Their days together had been spent in comparing and contrasting, measuring the differences and similarities in their worlds. They had discovered that humor was one thing they shared that was not defined by geography.

"How do I know if you have stars? You don't have pizza."

"You don't have grits."

"Who would want 'em?"

"You don't have," Emma paused, searching for something, anything, that she had not seen in this place that seemed to encompass all the wonders of the world, "you don't have niggers."

"No," said Ed in a changed voice, "we don't."

"How come?"

"Because we have Negroes, stupid."

"That's what I just said. You're being dumb."

"No, *you're* being dumb. I didn't say 'niggers,' I said 'Negroes.' "

"They're the same thing. And I haven't seen any anywhere, except some in New York."

"Emma, do you know that 'nigger' is a bad word?"

She just stared at him, but something pinged deep inside and the blood of embarrassment began to rise.

"It's bad to use it to people's faces," she said. "You say 'colored.' But it's okay to use when no niggers are around. Everybody does."

"Not everybody here. It's not nice."

"Well, you're not so nice, either, Mr. Smarty Pants, charging all the kids in the neighborhood a penny to hear me talk."

"You just want your share, don't you?"

Emma was put out. She was losing an argument that she didn't even understand, and now she felt that Ed was making fun of her. "Right, you nigger," she yelled, and jumped off the teetertotter quickly, banging him hard on the ground.

Ed was three years older and many pounds heavier than Emma. Before she'd gone three steps he'd caught her by the arm, and now he was sitting on her stomach. He told her she could eat her words or eat the grass he held in his right hand.

"Nigger! Nigger! Nigger!" Emma was not going to give up.

She ate the grass.

Later, lying in a twin bed with her little cousin Sally, who was asleep, Emma whispered across to Ed, "Do your parents ever talk about me?"

"Sure, they talk about you all the time. They say you're a pain in the ass."

Emma giggled. "No, really."

"Yeah. They've said lots of times how they'd like to see you and Uncle Jakey. And your mom."

"Do they ever say I'm a mistake?"

"What do you mean, a mistake?"

Emma shrugged. "I don't know. Something I heard my parents say."

"You probably didn't understand."

"I don't understand lots they say. And they never answer my questions."

"All parents are like that. They make you feel weird. Like you're adopted. Or wish you were. They speak a foreign language when you're around. Sometimes mine really do—they think we don't understand any Yiddish."

"What?"

"Yiddish. Your dad must speak it, too."

"Why?"

"Because he grew up with my mom, silly. You know, Yiddish, Jews."

"Jews?" Emma whispered.

Ed was quiet for a minute.

"Emma, don't you know you're Jewish?"

"I am not!"

"You are! Your dad is. That makes you Jewish, too."

"No," Sally spoke up from between them, awake now, or maybe she'd never been asleep. "Not if your mom's not. Your mom isn't, is she?"

They whispered for a long time after that, their words tossing and turning, and finally fell asleep after exchanging promises of visits and letters. Emma dozed off with Ed and Sally's faces in her mind, then plummeted into a dream where the Green Skeleton waited.

But this time he was friendly. He came into the front of the store just as she entered through the door in the back looking for a Hershey bar, and before she could let out a good scream he bowed deeply at the waist just like her Grandfather Isidore and offered her his green glowing hand.

"May I have the pleasure of this dance?" he asked.

From somewhere came the strains of "The Blue Danube," and he slowly twirled her out the door of the store, across the squares of her hopscotch which she could see in the moonlight traced on the sidewalk, and down the bank of the canal. Blackberry brambles caught at the hem of her nightgown, but he gently untangled her and brushed them away.

"There's someone who would like to talk with you," the Green

Skeleton said, and then he swung her forward as if he were releasing her into the arms of another partner. And he was, for she flew into the embrace of Marcus, the tall shy colored boy who had caught her arm and kept her from slipping into the canal that day it rained—Marcus, who lived just beyond Skeleton Hill.

"So nice to see you this evening," Marcus said, speaking right up, as if he weren't shy at all, as if he weren't colored.

"Well, it's nice to be here," Emma replied, pretending there was nothing at all unusual about dancing on the surface of the canal's green water in the arms of a black boy. "How are you this evening?"

"Why, I'm just fine. I'm just pleased as punch to be here. But there's something I have to tell you." He dipped her and whirled her. The surface of the water was like glass, shiny but not wet.

"What's that, Marcus?" He's going to tell me that he's Jewish, she thought in her dream. She gave him her best smile.

But he didn't say that at all. He said, "I don't like it when you say 'nigger.' It hurts me." Whereupon his black skin became transparent and she could see, right through his white skeleton, his broken heart.

"I see what you mean."

"Good." He smiled a brilliant smile, his teeth white in his black face, silver in the moonlight. "I knew, Emma, that you would understand."

She nodded, and they smiled into each other's eyes, and the music swelled and then the surface of the water sparkled with stars which lifted like a flying carpet and they danced up up up into the sky, far far away from the canal and West Cypress.

5

West Cypress
1961

NEVER AGAIN, Emma had vowed to herself at fourteen. Never again would she travel with her momma and daddy across the Coupitaw Parish line.

Nor would she eat one more Vienna sausage in the backseat or sleep one more night in the car. Not one more time would she hang her head out the window like a collie dog, her heart lurching with hunger and sorrow, as Rosalie drove right on past hamburger stands, Holiday Inns and Howard Johnsons as if Emma had suggested they stop at the Taj Mahal.

So it was "No, thanks," she'd said at sixteen when Rosalie suggested New Mexico. "I'd just as soon stay home."

That was a lie, and both of them knew it. As long as she could remember, Emma had sat beside her daddy and looked at color pictures of faraway places he wanted to go to.

Emma wanted to go, too. But when she closed her eyes and watched herself waving goodbye, her parents were never in the picture. Sometimes there was a handsome man by her side. Or she was walking up a gangplank alone. A third version featured her jumping into a car with a sidekick like Dean Moriarty in a book she'd read, *On the Road*. Could girls do that? Just pick up and run away, driving to see what they could see? She didn't know, but she'd sure like to find out. She'd die if she had to spend the rest of her life in West Cypress.

Now Emma was seventeen, and on this bright November morning here they were, the three of them, in a car once again, a square white Studebaker heading west on Highway 80, breaking Emma's vow. But this time was different. Emma was driving. At

her right elbow Rosalie sniffled into a monogrammed handkerchief. In the backseat Jake and a rolling green thermos fought it
out for territory across an imaginary line.

It wasn't just Emma's driving that made this trip different.
For blazing the way ahead of them was the rear end of a long
black hearse. It in turn was trailing Emma's cousin J.D. sitting
tall behind the wheel of his state-trooper car. Jake could rest his
mind on the subject of navigation; Sergeant J. D. Tarley's head
was filled with maps.

Straggling behind them like so many biddy chickens in a gag-
gle of cars and pickup trucks were those of the Norris clan who
had attended one or the other, or in some cases both, of Virgie
Norris's funerals during the past two days. Now the cortege was
passing through the rolling piney hills that began at the Coupitaw, headed for Sweetwell and Virgie's funeral number three.

Some of the Norrises hadn't started out from West Cypress
that morning, but from fifty miles farther north in Pearl Bank.
That was where two days earlier they'd held Virgie's funeral
number one.

"Well, I hope Nancy's happy now that she's made us all late.
It's bad enough to keep all those folks in Sweetwell waiting three
days. They're probably standing on one foot and then the
other." Rosalie was twisting her handkerchief so hard that the
monogram had disappeared.

"Momma, I don't think Aunt Nancy kept them in Pearl Bank
on purpose. Aunt Flo said her kids overslept. Then the bacon
burned, and two collar buttons just disappeared off the face of
the earth."

Rosalie jerked her damp handkerchief to her face and dabbed
at a fresh flow. "You taking her side now," she cried. "I guess I
could have expected that."

"Ro." Jake tentatively placed a hand on his wife's shoulder,
but she pulled away smartly as if she'd been burned. "For the
lovamike," he exploded.

The blood rose in Jake's face. He shoved himself back into the
plastic seat. They were all crazy, he thought. Well, what did you
want from Baptists? Jews, sensible people like himself, buried
their dead, sat shiva and mourned for seven days, and it was
over. But not Southern Baptists and not Norrises and not in
West Cypress, Louisiana.

Now Rosalie was picking up an old thread of grief as if it were a stitch she'd been worrying and had for a moment dropped. "I knew it, I always knew it ever since we were kids."

"Now, Momma." There was a warning then in Emma's voice, but she kept her eyes on the road. She didn't need to look to see whether Rosalie was crying. The tears had been falling like spring rain determined to flood for four days now, ever since the word had first come that Grandma Virgie had passed on. She didn't need to listen either. She knew what was coming next.

"Momma always loved her the most because she was the baby."

"Now, you know that's not true," Emma said.

Rosalie ignored her and went on. It was her story. She'd tell it her way and as many times as she liked.

"Virgie loved you, Ro," Jake tried once more from the back seat, making a special effort, like putting on his dark suit. It occurred to Emma that sometimes her daddy didn't say this many words in a month.

"But not like she did Nancy," Rosalie insisted. "She was the favorite. She got sent to school."

"Because they had more money by the time she was grown. You've said that yourself," Emma countered, wondering why she tried.

Rosalie shook her head and, giving up on the handkerchief, fumbled for a tissue in her black plastic purse. "Nobody sent me to school. I had to work for everything in this world I ever got."

"Christ!" Emma exclaimed. The taillights of the hearse in front of them had popped on, signaling danger. Emma pumped the brake and shot a quick look behind.

They didn't call Highway 80 Old Bucket of Blood for nothing. It was a two-lane roller coaster built by that honorable thief and friend of the common man, Huey P. Long. Like Huey it specialized in making mountains out of molehills and throwing blind curves.

Emma checked her rearview mirror again. She could see the whole Norris clan rear-ending one another until they were all squashed together in a great ancestral jam.

"Be careful!" Rosalie said, pulling out of her grief to deal with the here and now. "You always drive too fast." She paused a moment. "And don't take the Lord's name in vain."

Emma glanced at the speedometer. She was doing thirty-five.

What can we talk about to change the subject, she wondered, before I have a screaming hissy fit?

Being a Southern girl, she put her mind on automatic pilot and the niceties fell out of her mouth. "It was a beautiful funeral, Momma. I know Grandma would have been proud."

"She did look pretty in her powder blue, didn't she? It went so nice with her silver hair."

"And that white casket," Emma added with a measure of pride. She had picked out the coffin, Rosalie being too nervous to choose, afraid they'd sell her something over the limits of the paid-up burial policy.

"I bet Nancy told everybody at the funeral in Pearl Bank that she made the arrangements."

"But, Momma, they know. They know you've been paying for that policy for years."

"I guess so. I just hope they appreciate all the trouble I went to." Rosalie snapped her purse shut in exclamation.

The car was silent for a few moments. Green pines, sweet gums, oaks floated by. A bunch of brown-and-white dairy cows clustered, staring over a fence into the highway as if they were counting trucks or had something on their minds.

Then Emma's thoughts leapfrogged over the top of the long hearse up ahead to the highway patrol car with its blue light flashing. She could imagine J.D. with his sunglasses on and his black nonregulation curls escaping from his wide-brimmed brown hat. J.D. looked more like Elvis Presley than any man she'd ever known. Her boyfriend, Bernie, had almost the same black hair, but not those eyes, not that mouth. That was what made her shiver when she thought about J.D., the curve, just like Elvis', of that wide mouth.

"Do you think she minded all this moving around?"

"Who?" Emma had to drag her mind back into the car.

"Momma," Rosalie answered.

"You mean leaving Sweetwell for Pearl Bank to live with Aunt Nancy and Big J.D.?"

Out of the corner of her eye, which she was trying to keep on the rear end of the hearse, Emma saw Rosalie shake her head.

"No, I don't mean that. I mean shipping her body from Nancy's to Cypress and the funeral parlor for the fixing, then back to Pearl Bank for that service Nancy insisted on."

"Those were her last friends there in Pearl Bank," Jake said, but Rosalie turned and shot him a look that made him hush.

"And then all the way back to Cypress for *my* funeral. Now over to Sweetwell, where I guess somebody's got to say a few more words before we put her in the ground beside Pa. Well," said Rosalie, dabbing at her eyes, "I hope Nancy's happy with all this running around."

"At least the weather's cool." Emma was just making conversation, trying to lead Rosalie in another direction. "At least it's not August." And then she fanned herself with one hand at the thought of three open-casket funerals in that heat when dogs lay motionless for days and tomatoes burst open by themselves sitting out in the sun.

But Rosalie would not be redirected from the worn path she was traveling on. "You know, I wouldn't have minded so much if Nancy had taken good care of her, seeing as how she was getting all of Momma's Social Security."

"For Pete's sakes," Jake said, still not having learned his lesson. "Nancy didn't starve her to death."

"You shut up, Jake. You don't know what you're talking about."

"Goddammit!" he began. Emma knew he was just warming up. This was like the old days, all those other trips in the car. But this time she was driving.

"If you-all are going to yell," she said, "I'm gonna pull this car off on the side of the road and stop."

Rosalie opened her mouth and then reconsidered.

Emma heard the echo of her own voice, sounding like *she* was the mother. But that's what had been happening for some time now, this sideways slipping of power, creeping from their hands to her own, as if they'd left it lying on the ground for her to pick up. At seventeen, she thought, I'm Big Momma of us all.

After the burst of yelling there was silence for the next thirty miles, except for Rosalie's hiccuping and a couple of times she blew her nose.

Nobody cares about my feelings, not even at my own mother's funeral, Rosalie thought.

In the backseat, Jake did the thing he did best, he sulked. He'd show Rosalie. He wouldn't say another word for the next seven days. He'd sit his own private shivah for Miss Virgie.

Miss Virgie'd been a nice old woman, he thought. And before she lost her mind she'd made a hell of a chocolate pie. It was too bad she'd never taught Rosalie how to cook. But nobody could teach Rosalie anything. No, Jake said to himself, as he'd said so many times the past seventeen years, Rosalie knew it all.

The silent thirty miles stretched slowly across the better part of an hour. Highway 80 was the main street of every little town. It poked along, widening and narrowing, giving the local folks a chance to stare. Old men, closer to their own last parade than they wished, looked somber and tipped sweat-stained felt hats.

In Grambling, a little colored boy had goggle-eyed the hearse and fumbled a sign at his chest, not exactly a cross. Voodoo, Emma thought. Then he'd mouthed the word, clear as day. *Cadillac.*

Emma smiled to herself. Did Grandma Virgie ever think she'd get to ride in a Cadillac?

Well, I'm going to, she thought. And not after I'm dead, either. When I'm *somebody,* I'm going to come back to West Cypress and show all those snotty girls in Delta Beta, all those girls with forty-two color-coordinated-to-their-sweaters-and-skirts net petticoats. I'll drive through the two blocks of downtown West Cypress, then over to Cypress, waving at them from a red Coupe de Ville. I'll wear my hair up in a twist and dress all in black.

But for now, for today, a ride in J.D.'s state-trooper car would do. She thought about his promise to take her out for a drive in Sweetwell later. A little shiver made her shoulders hunch. She bet J.D. knew all the back roads. He probably knew every piece of gravel in the whole northern half of the state—as well as she knew this road to Sweetwell where her grandma used to live.

Near Arcadia was a dirt road that trailed off at the edge of town. She craned her neck every time they drove past, looking for the splotches of red, though she knew they'd been washed away years ago from that place where the federal agents had riddled Bonnie and Clyde.

How exciting their lives must have been, saying the hell with it, grabbing up handfuls of their hearts' desire. Robbing banks, driving hell-bent for leather to make their getaways, holing up, making love.

Emma's outer eye checked the road ahead then. All was clear.

She could floorboard the Studebaker like Bonnie and pass J.D. in his trooper car, daring him to chase her to who knows where with blaring sirens, flashing blue lights. Her inner eye imagined what he would do with her once he caught her. She didn't have any bags of green, gold and silver booty to recover. What would Mr. Lawman take instead for his reward?

She shifted in her seat then.

"Are you tired?" Rosalie broke the silence. "I can drive for a while."

"Nope. I'm fine." Fine indeed. If Momma only knew what she was thinking, and about her *cousin,* she'd slap her face hard.

Did Rosalie ever even think about sex? Emma was sure they didn't do it. She had listened at her parents' bedroom door for years, rifled their medicine chest and dresser drawers. Not a shred of evidence.

All she'd ever found were old pictures that neither of them would ever talk about.

"Who is this," she'd ask, "and that?", pointing at a photograph of a woman with light-brown hair in a brown-and-white polka-dot dress. She had a pretty smile and looked, as the old joke went, a little bit pregnant.

There were so many things they wouldn't discuss, as if life were nothing more than gas bills, supper and the present. They'd *never* talk about the past.

And sex: Emma had never heard either one of them even *say* the word. But then she guessed Rosalie thought there was no need to voice the Southern Baptist assumption that a girl would remain intact until her wedding night. She wondered what Jews thought about that, for she had finally gotten her father to say that he was Jewish, but that admission was the end of *that*. She certainly wasn't going to be able to get him to talk about sex if she couldn't get him to talk about Jews. At least she had her boyfriend Bernie's father, Herman, to ask.

Suddenly the little Studebaker shuddered as an eighteen-wheeler roared past. Emma tried to catch a glimpse of the trucker. Now, *there* was a life of adventure she'd like to know more about.

Sometimes she wondered whether Bernie, who no more believed in Jesus or sin than she did, had been brainwashed by Rosalie. Had her mother's ideas concentrated themselves into little green rays, glowing in the dark like the Green Skeleton of

Emma's childhood nightmares, crawled into the car where she and Bernie sat behind windows fogged by their hot breath? That was ridiculous, she knew, but they'd had their hands in each other's pants for over a year now. Yet Bernie, only inches away from the prize, hesitated still.

Emma had thought about it a long time and had decided that their mutual virginity was a bore, one of those conventions that people in places like West Cypress insisted upon. She'd read books. She knew that people had been doing it out of wedlock for years in places like Paris, Rome, New York. Besides, so far, what she'd experienced with Bernie had been *fun*.

"Come on, Bern," she said to him, "take me."

"Not in the front seat of my car."

"Then let's get in the back."

"Very funny, Emma. I keep telling you, I want it to be special. That's why we have the Fund—to take us to New Orleans and the Hotel Monteleone."

"The Fund, Bern, is going to do me a lot of good as a petrified virgin in an old folks' home." Patience was not a trait that Emma had yet developed; in fact, she never would. "Who ever heard of a savings account dedicated to fucking?"

She knew Bernie didn't like it when she talked like that. The truth of it was, Emma thought, Bernie was just chicken. They'd practiced the preliminaries over and over like his basketball drills so that he had them down pat. But put him in the game for the big play, he choked.

Don't be ugly, Emma, she reminded herself. Isn't that what her daddy would say? Not about this, though. She glanced at him in the backseat, dozing. Don't be ugly, don't be mean. Don't be cruel. She could just hear Elvis singing that. She wished there were a radio in the car, but Rosalie didn't believe in such extravagance.

"You don't get in a car to have a good time," was how she put it. Oh, Momma, Emma thought, if you only knew.

Elvis knew—that you shouldn't be cruel to a heart that was true. Was Bernie's heart true? Of course. She had no reason to doubt him.

And yours, Miss Emma? Is your heart true blue? Is that why you want to take Bernie into your body, because your heart is so filled with love for him?

She didn't know. How did you know what love was? Emma
didn't feel like she'd had a lot of practice with it. She did know
she loved getting dressed up for the dances they went to. She
loved getting out of the house. She loved having someone to call
her own. And when Bernie went away that one summer, she
longed for him, and the longing was sweet. Was that what love
was?

But if she loved Bernie, if she really loved him, why did she
get bored with him sometimes? Why did she wonder how she
might feel about all the other boys she might meet, out there,
somewhere, who hadn't grown up in West Cypress? And most
of all, why did goose bumps pop up all over her flesh yesterday
when J.D. slipped a broad hand around her waist and whispered,
"Tomorrow, let me take you for a ride."

She thought a lot about J.D. and his curling lip, always had
since she was a little girl and caught him under a ladder in the
barn at Momma Virgie's, looking up the wide legs of her shorts.

And now he was leading this procession across the whole
northern half of the state with his blue light flashing in defiance
of his mother, Aunt Nancy, who, having had *her* funeral for
Miss Virgie in Pearl Bank, had stayed home.

Up ahead in his spick-and-span clean black-and-white car, J.D.
pushed his state-trooper hat back, easing it off the wide red
mark it left on his forehead. Because the mark reminded him
of the stigmata his father wore, the sun-reddened neck and arms
sticking out from his snow-white torso, the sign of a man who
worked out-of-doors, he'd leave the hat off for the rest of the
drive.

THE Sweetwell Baptist reminded Emma of her Uncle England's
church where she'd sung "Sweet Hour of Prayer" when she was
a little girl. It was small and plain and poor, the dark-brown
pews scarred with the boots of generations of little boys who'd
rather have been outside. The mint-green walls were peeling.

It was different from St. Jude's, where until yesterday she'd
attended the only funeral of her life when one of the Catholic
neighbor children had passed too close to a kerosene stove. She
loved St. Jude's stained glass, the gold, the lace of the altar
cloth, the sharp musty smell of incense that somehow made her
think of small furry animals burrowing in the ground. The

Southern Baptist Convention did not subscribe to such pomp or passion and wrinkled its collective nose at the actuality of frankincense and myrrh.

There was, however, *that once* that the Baptist Church had come alive for Emma—when Ricardo Martinez had come to preach a revival at West Cypress Baptist. Ricardo Martinez, dressed in pink and black. Ricardo Martinez with the shining dark eyes and the beautiful black hair.

Rosalie began snuffling loudly and Jake shifted in his creaking pew, bringing Emma back from that Baptist church to this one. In front of them, J.D. turned to see what was going on. Or that was what he made it look like—curiosity and concern. But Emma caught the glance he gave her, the glance from beneath long dark lashes that made her knees go soft and warm.

That's who J.D. looked like, she thought. Ricardo Martinez. And both of them looked like Elvis.

She knew Elvis was white trash from Tupelo across the Mississippi state line, but ever since she'd seen him on the TV she'd thought, If that's trash, I'll take a dump truck full.

Ricardo Martinez had made her feel that same way, that brown-skinned Mexican man of God who'd come to lead the West Cypress First Baptist revival meeting when she was twelve years old.

When he preached, pounding brown fists on the pulpit, his voice had raised her to the heights and then dropped her into chasms where the hellfire and brimstone glowed. Up and down, his baritone rhythms went, up and down. After the sermon he had sweated through his jacket and leaned heavily against the pulpit, spent. Then he issued the invitation, a personal invitation, to come to him and yield, and in so doing to give oneself to the Lord.

Emma had never believed a word she'd heard in all those years she'd been made to attend the First Baptist Church. She'd begged her daddy to take her across town where she'd heard there was a synagogue, where it would be different, wouldn't he please, but no, he shook his head, your momma says no one would like you then, I'm sorry, Emma, no.

And suddenly this same Emma had found herself standing up and marching right down that West Cypress First Baptist aisle just like she believed in the Lord and was willing to take him

as her personal savior, which she did not and had no intention
of doing. But when Ricardo begged her in that hoarse honeyed
voice to come to him, she hadn't seen that she had any choice.

A deacon had led her behind the pulpit and up a little stair
where she took off most of her clothes and put on a long white
gown. She stood with Ricardo in front of the whole congregation in the baptismal, which was like a big fish tank half filled
with cool water. The curtain was pulled back so everybody could
watch, and she wondered whether her robe had floated up. Were
her panties showing? With every eye in the whole congregation
watching and some mouths working, "Do Jesus, praise the Lord,"
Ricardo took her in his arms and said, "Just relax, this isn't going to hurt." She was dizzy with her faith in his words. He
pulled her close. She could smell his sweet breath. Then he
plunged her beneath the cool water. One hand was under her
back, the other over her nose. But she held her breath, which
she'd never learned to do in the Cypress Natatorium. She held
her breath and prayed that he would hold her in his arms forever.

But all too soon he lifted her, her hair streaming, and gave
her the kiss of Christian fellowship in the middle of her forehead. The spell was broken. He released her from his grasp and
from his thrall.

After that her friends had wanted to know what it felt like to
be truly saved, and Emma said it felt like being in love. They
could have thought she meant being in love with the Lord. The
Sunday School teachers talked a lot about that. But Emma's
friends knew her too well and gave her funny looks. Emma, the
word went, was a little weird. She knew she was. For one thing,
she asked herself a week later when she'd had time to dry off
and cool down, how many baptized half-Jews could there be
in this town?

Rosalie had been so proud of her. Jake had said nothing,
shrugged and frowned. This last year when she told Bernie the
story, he'd said, "You mean you did it because the preacher
turned you on?"

"Sure, Bern. Why else would I do it?"

Why else indeed? Just like now. Why else would she be
staring at the back of J.D.'s head as if she were going to burn
holes through it?

Finally the preacher finished what was the second tribute to her grandmother's life, a life long and good (and hard), that Emma had heard in as many days. The organist played "The Old Rugged Cross," one of Virgie's favorites, as the congregation filed by the open casket for one last look, thank God, the very last look at Virgie Norris's remains.

After the burial in the churchyard next to the grandfather Emma had never known, J.D. brushed past her and whispered, "Come with me in my car, now."

Emma nodded. It took her fewer than two minutes to get Rosalie and Jake tucked into the backseat of Aunt Florence's Oldsmobile.

"Aunt Flo's driven all the way here by herself. We ought to keep her company on the way to the dinner," she'd said, slamming the back door, glancing off the front, and then bouncing in a ricochet away.

"I'm gonna come along with J.D.," she called, just as the black-and-white car pulled up. J.D. threw the passenger door open, and one, two, even quicker than that, Emma slipped inside. They were Bonnie and Clyde, making their getaway. Rosalie gave her an openmouthed look that said an awful lot without any words, but Emma's practiced eyes went guileless and clear in return. Then J.D. stepped on it, and they were gone. Emma blew a kiss as they hit the boundary of the churchyard. As a little girl she'd sent away for one, and only one, picture of a movie star—because, like herself, she had blonde curls. Blow a kiss, she was sure that was what Betty Grable would do.

It was forty-five minutes since they'd watched that white casket lower, wobbly, into a fresh hole. J.D., who did indeed make it his professional business to know every back road in the northern half of the state, had them parked under a big cypress tree. On one side was a deep bayou and on the other a cotton field. Nothing except the two of them was moving, as far as Emma could see.

And moving they were. J.D., a grown man with none of Bernie's reticence, was unafraid of speed.

"J.D., I swear! Slow down!" Emma protested as he cut off the ignition and grinned, kissed her, tenderly at first, then with an insistent tongue. Next he grabbed the hem of her green-and-black watch plaid dress and pulled it straight over her head.

"Why?" he laughed, his big but clever fingers stripping off her white cotton underwear. "Is someone around here giving out speeding tickets?"

He did slow down for a minute, though, long enough to grab a blanket out of the trunk and spread it in the grass right beside the water.

Emma stopped in midflight and stared at yet darker smears on the blanket's midnight blue.

"What's the matter?" J.D. teased. "You afraid of a little nigger blood?"

Emma frowned and was opening her mouth to speak her mind when J.D. grabbed her so hard the little curls of hair on his chest left imprints on hers.

"Now, don't you start lecturing me about the niggers, Emma," he warned. "Fancy airs you put on for such a skinny gal." And then he tickled her in the ribs. "That's what comes of Aunt Rosalie marrying a Yankee. That's what my momma always says."

"Momma, momma, momma." Emma laughed and pushed J.D. (who let her) back on the blue blanket and sat on him as if she were strong enough to keep him down. "Momma, momma," she sang again.

The only idea they'd ever agreed on was that both their mothers were crazy, unless, of course, you counted as an agreement their as yet unspoken but mutual desire for each other's flesh.

"Don't worry about the blood," he whispered into her ear a little while later after he'd taken his tongue out of it. "It was just a joke. But I think it's time we added your cherry to it, if you haven't already given it to that boy Bernie."

Emma just smiled. That was for her to know and for him to find out.

Something rustled just then in the tall grass. Emma started and sat up.

"Never mind," J.D. said, and reached across her. His hard cock bobbled against her cheek as he stretched for his brown twill pants.

"There." He'd pulled his steely blue revolver out of its holster and set it on the edge of the blanket. He smiled an Elvis smile at her. "Let's just hope that we don't roll over on that thing and blow our peepees off."

Emma laughed, but inside she shivered. She was a little afraid of guns. But now that push had come to shove, she was afraid of J.D.'s cock too. To hide her nervousness, she reached for *her* favorite weapon, her tongue.

"Did Maylene tell you it was okay to be doing this with your cousin?"

While Emma was talking, J.D. pulled her down toward him and busied *his* tongue on her pink nipples.

He stopped long enough to grunt, "Forget Maylene."

"What's the matter, J.D., ain't your little preacher's daughter girlfriend giving you what you want?"

"Hush," he ordered, his voice thick with authority and lust. "Not so sure you are my cousin," he said and wished he hadn't, but then he *had* been provoked. He flipped the lightweight long-limbed Emma over on her back. He bet he knew something that would shut her up. With a swoop, J.D. buried his mouth between her legs, an act which Emma had never even *heard* of before.

"*What?*" she asked, but within moments there were other noises coming from her that you couldn't exactly call words.

"Are you ready?" she finally heard J.D. asking from somewhere that seemed very far away. He could have been standing over in the middle of the cotton field or neck deep in the black bayou sludge.

Little arrows of electricity were shooting back and forth between her bones. But *ready?* For exactly what?

She opened her eyes then, just in time to see J.D. start to roll what had to be a rubber onto himself. Though she tried to stop herself, she couldn't. Emma leaned her head back, and the sound of her laughter ran up the trunk of the cypress tree and bounced out over the deep dark water. Where it landed, a silver fish jumped.

"What's so funny, sister?" He was sitting on top of her now, having lost the impetus to do what he was about to do. "What's so fucking funny, baby girl?"

But he was laughing, too, and inching up toward her, laughing, laughing all the while.

"Here, darling," he said, having peeled the condom off his now soft self. Into her open mouth he inserted his cock.

Emma blinked her big blue eyes at him, once, twice.

"Suck, precious," he said. "Pretend it's a lollipop."

So for the second time that day, Emma experienced something completely brand-new. Her tongue explored the hardness wrapped in velvet. J.D. encouraged her with cooing. Emma congratulated herself on being such a quick learner.

"Now stay with me," J.D. said, probing inside her gently, then with more force and rhythm, with first one finger, then two. Emma relaxed. This was old familiar territory, one of Bernie's drills.

Then J.D.'s mouth lowered again and joined his fingers playing. Emma's mouth opened, too, and her ululation had no words. She was a holy roller seized with the spirit, speaking in tongues. J.D. needed no translation. He had heard women sprawled beneath him speak this language before.

He could read her, even if she didn't know what she was saying. *Ready, ready, ready when you are.* J.D. leaned back between her legs again, gently probing, pushing, this time with his cock.

"We're gonna take this slow and easy, baby. Breathe deep. Come on, now, don't hold your breath, breathe deep. Trust me. It's not going to hurt."

She did. She flinched, then fluttered with his coaxing, his gentle hands, his steady pressure, fluttered just like an unbroken filly, twisting, tossing her head, and before she knew it she was there, over the finish line, now that wasn't so bad, was it, he whispered, and they were riding together across meadows into a land Emma had never known.

And when it was over, because the excitement of his conquest made J.D. quick-like-a-bunny quick, they rested for just a moment, and then started, slowly more slowly this time, cantering, then galloping, before they raced home together once more.

"WHERE on earth have you two been?" Rosalie cried when, much too late for excuses, they joined the rest of the Norris clan gathered in Miz Robinson's backyard for a postfuneral feast. "We've been worried sick, looking all over the place for you."

"J.D. took me to get a fried pie," she answered. She knew she ought to be feeling guilt and shame, on so many levels she couldn't count them even if she uncrossed the fingers she held behind her back. But all she felt was trembling joy—well, and there was that one question.

"What do you mean we're not cousins?" she'd asked when it was all over and they'd regained their senses.

"Nothing. I just said that to make you feel better."

"What the hell do you mean—better?"

"Such a mouth on a young girl. It's unseemly."

"Better about what, J.D.?"

"About making love."

"I feel just fine about that. That's not what's bothering me."

"Aw, Emma. It was nothing. You know how my momma can be. Especially about your momma."

"What'd she say?"

"Well, hell, Emma, it didn't mean nothing. Once I heard her saying something to my daddy about a ready-made baby, but I think she was just fooling around."

No, she wasn't, thought Emma, who'd had more and more suspicions about what was what as the years passed, which made her feel crazy and wonder what other deep darks they weren't talking about.

"I know Momma was just teasing," J.D. said.

He knew that she wasn't. And he didn't tell Emma what Nancy had *really* said to Big J.D.: "If I was gonna go off and get myself a ready-made baby like Rosalie, 'course I wouldn't 'cause I can and *have* had my own, I wouldn't get me one that was a half a Jew."

"How do you know that she ain't a whole Jew?" Big J.D. had drawled, then spit from his tobacco.

"You know," Nancy had cried, "I never thought about that!"

"A FRIED pie!" Rosalie was saying. "With all this food here? Why on earth would you do something like that?"

"I guess Emma just had a taste for something different, Aunt Rosalie, ma'am," J.D. answered.

"I reckon." Goodness, that J.D. had turned into a handsome young man, Rosalie thought, with nice manners too. You'd never guess he was one of Nancy's boys, might even make something of himself. Rosalie shrugged her shoulders then, not quite satisfied with the answer to her question, but she knew she wasn't going to get much more. She went back to sharing remedies for constipation with Miz Robinson whom she hadn't seen in nearly twenty years.

Then Miz Robinson motioned for Rosalie to turn around. "Oh, I couldn't," Rosalie said to Flo, who was standing there with a big piece of lemon meringue.

"Honey, you need it to keep your strength up," said Miz Robinson.

"I guess you're right." Rosalie took the Blue Willow saucer. "Thank you, Flo. I don't mind if I do."

She glanced over at Emma, who was heaping a plate with fried chicken, potato salad and mustard greens.

Flo said, "That fried pie must not have been so filling after all."

"*Ordinary's* never been good enough for Emma," Rosalie said. "I guess she'll always have a taste for fancy things." Having polished off her pie, she licked her fork and put it down. "Sometimes I feel like I don't even know that girl, I swan."

6

TWO WEEKS LATER in that November of her seventeenth year, Emma was tromping in the woods with her boyfriend Bernie Graubart and his father, Herman. They were on the Graubarts' home place, two hundred acres of pine, oak and sweet gum that Bernie's mother, Mary Ann, had inherited from her father, Mr. Tim. It was good land for hunting and fishing.

Each of them was ruddy-faced in the crisp air of a cool Saturday afternoon, and each carried a rifle thrown over a shoulder. Ahead of them, her russet-and-black flags flying, raced Bernie's Gordon setter, Molly.

"Look at that dog snuffling all over the place as if she had good sense," Herman said. "She'd point an egg-salad sandwich as soon as a quail."

"And we're about as likely to shoot one, too," said Bernie.

"Are we out here to hunt or to run our mouths?" asked Emma. "If you-all don't shut up, there's not going to be a bird left in twelve parishes."

Herman grinned. There was almost nothing Emma ever said that Herman didn't want to hear.

The first time Bernie had brought this long, tall blonde home, Herman had fallen in love—and the feeling was mutual. Sometimes Bernie watched the two of them, Emma's bright head tilted toward his father's frizzle of gray, and wondered whether he wasn't getting in their way. Except, and now it was Bernie's turn to grin, as of two weeks ago he knew lots of things about Emma that his father didn't. For it was then that he'd become Emma's lover.

"Bernie, would you watch where you're going!" Emma snapped as he stepped on the heel of her old sneaker.

"Sorry." But then to prove he wasn't, really, he poked her in the fanny. She turned and waggled her tongue at him. In answer, his desire rose like sap inside his faded jeans. Things had been going like that since the day after Emma came back from her grandmother's funeral. She'd dragged him off to a girlfriend's family fish camp as if death and burial were the ultimate and irresistible aphrodisiac.

"I'm not waiting a second longer for the Fund to ransom my virginity," she'd said, running one hand up and down the front of his Levis as if she knew exactly what she was doing. "Forget the Hotel Monteleone. This'll have to do." Then she'd dangled the keys to the fish camp in front of him, and thirty miles, thirty minutes and four beers later they were standing on the steps of the empty cabin on Bayou Coupee and Emma was fumbling with the padlock.

"What's the hurry?" he asked.

"I've got to pee. Bad." Then the lock popped open and Emma raced past pine paneling, green plastic sofas and mounted fish trophies. Two minutes later she had taken care of her business. "Now," she said, "I'm going to take care of you."

And for the next two hours, she did. It crossed Bernie's mind that she went right ahead, on past that boundary they'd never crossed before, as if she were on familiar ground. But he knew she couldn't be. You could count on Emma to have done her research. She'd probably learned all this from books.

Because Bernie knew that, for all her mouth, Emma hadn't even had a date when he met her the year before, their last year at West Cypress High. But that didn't mean she was shy or ugly. What he didn't know was that until she spotted him on the basketball court she simply hadn't found anything closer to what she was looking for.

He had turned from his locker one day to discover the same tall blonde girl who screamed his name when he made a hook shot almost standing on his right foot. Bernie took a long look into her eyes, noted her profile, and wondered whether it was possible that in West Cypress there was another person who might actually be Jewish.

"What are you staring at?" she'd asked.

"Why are you following me?" he countered.

"Because I want your body," answered Emma, whose already-sharp tongue was impossible now that she'd read *Catcher in the Rye*. Underneath her bravado and her pink crew-neck sweater, however, her heart was pounding.

Bernie snorted, then leaned against his locker, stalling. Was this what Herman called seizing opportunity by the foreskin? Not that he imagined that this girl had one.

"You got it," he said. And that was pretty much that. They parked in the last row of the Star Drive-In the following Friday night and began on a course of serious exploration.

But Emma's lust for Bernie's body was nothing compared to what she felt for his father Herman.

She was following Herman now this bright cool fall afternoon as he blazed the way into the deep piney woods, his white baseball cap, as always, planted firmly. His bright-blue eyes, like Bernie's, like hers, sparkled behind PX-pink plastic glasses.

Herman Graubart, a Polish Jew, had been career U.S. Army, was now retired and had begun a whole new career as an auto mechanic. He had his own shop in West Cypress, worked when he chose and on what he chose, which did not include Volkswagens, Mercedeses or any other German vehicle.

"They are beautiful machines," he'd say, "but I did not escape the Nazis to repair their automobiles."

Bernie didn't know a trench from a hole in the ground. He didn't know how lucky he was to grow up in the United States, full of American vegetables from his father's garden, and now grown taller by almost a whole foot than any Graubart had ever grown before. He didn't know how important it was to learn everything you could, because, as Herman the career soldier who was a pacifist knew, it was knowledge, not force, that could free you.

Bernie would rather go out with his friends and drink beer and shoot baskets than read or listen to what Herman had to say. Well, let the boy enjoy himself. He was young. He needed to sow his wild oats.

Which, Herman thought, watching his son saunter through the woods, he'd finally begun to do. Look at that step, he thought, that grin, that swagger. The boy was finally getting laid. By Emma, lovely Emma, whom he and Bernie loved.

Suddenly, off to their right in the woods, Molly snuffled, yowled and took off, tail flying, through the brush.

"A coon!" Emma exclaimed.

"Probably an egg-salad sandwich," said Herman.

"If you have so little faith in Molly, why'd we bring her along?" she asked.

"To enjoy the exercise and the woods, just like us."

"You mean we didn't come out here to hunt?"

Bernie was stepping sideways, about to light out after the dog. And Emma was hoping he'd go, for there was something she wanted to talk to Herman about, if she didn't lose her nerve.

"Why should I hunt when I haven't lost anything?" Herman answered.

Bernie made a rolling motion beside his ear with one forefinger, indicating to Emma that his poor old father was nuts.

"Says who?" asked Herman.

"Says me," Bernie called. Following Molly's track, he was gone.

Herman leaned against the trunk of a sweet-gum tree, pulled a pint bottle of schnapps out of his old fatigue jacket. "Have a sip."

"You're a terrible influence," she teased, tilting her head and letting the clear liquid warm her mouth, her throat.

"Best you're ever going to have." He pushed his glasses back up on his nose. "Who else around here is going to teach you anything?"

"Don't my A's from State count?" Smart mouth, she thought, but if you're so clever, and she reflected on the thing that was on the tip of her tongue, why didn't you figure it out before? "Herman," she started, and then she stopped. Anyway, Herman was already continuing.

"Humph," he grunted, for Herman had no respect for the Louisiana state educational system. "Bunch of rednecks call themselves professors. You have to take that goddamned course, 'Americanism versus Communism,' don't you? Curriculum a cross between Oral Roberts and Orval Faubus. Come on." And then he stomped off on a trail that only he could see.

"Hey, what about Bernie?"

"Bernie knows his way home. He'll come when he's through running after that stupid dog."

That stupid dog, Emma thought, whom Herman cosseted and spoiled as much as he did her and Bernie.

"Where are we going?"

"Didn't I tell you I was going to show you something?"

Emma shook her head.

"Then you need to learn to listen."

"Watch it, old man," she teased, and goosed him from behind as earlier his son had goosed her.

"You should be ashamed of yourself!" But his eyes were twinkling. "Shhh. Now listen."

They moved softly, their footfalls little whispers through the brush, but clear as drumbeats to the creatures who made the woods their home. Birds called the news to their fellows farther on who had not yet cocked their feathered heads to the crackling twigs. "They're coming, they're coming," Emma imagined they said. "With guns, with loaded guns."

She and Herman would never shoot a bird. The quail hunt was a joke, an excuse to get out in the autumn air, walk, talk and, if they felt like it, blast some tin cans to kingdom come.

In between the bird calls there were long deep silences, more still even than those she and Herman often shared in the Graubarts' living room, their chairs pulled close, the smoke of their cigarettes spiraling up toward the pressed-tin ceiling after one of his lessons.

"You know nothing," he'd begin, and then he'd pull out his beloved *Encyclopaedia Britannica* which every three years he read straight through, then started over with Volume I. He told her Jewish history, customs, stories of growing up in the Warsaw ghetto, though he waved her off when she asked about religion, for Herman was not a religious man.

How strange, Emma often thought, that when she looked down onto the basketball court and zeroed in on tall, curly-haired Bernie Graubart, she'd found the only other half-Jew in all of West Cypress High, maybe in all of West Cypress—and with him had come Herman. What were the chances of her looking for a boyfriend and also finding a Jewish father, more of a father, in many ways, than Jake? Was it luck? Was it fate? Or was it genetic?

He taught her about the world too. "The French," he'd say. "No, before that, but we'll start with the French. This," he pointed to a map, "is Laos. This is Vietnam."

When Emma could absorb no more, they'd sip schnapps, and

Herman would put his favorite, "Scheherazade," on the record player.

Now they were in a part of the woods where Emma had never been before. Just ahead she spied a little clearing, to one side a small fire circle, charcoal within blackened stones. Beyond it stood a sloping one-room shack, its rotting wooden walls camouflaged beneath green moss and mold. It was like a fairy tale, something out of Grimm.

"Is this yours?" she whispered.

He nodded, reached into his pocket for a Camel and his nickel Zippo lighter. "I come here when I want to be alone."

"What do you do?"

"I read." He pushed on the door to the shack. Its rusting hinges groaned, then opened. Inside was a tiny room, a simple pine table, an old kitchen chair, a kerosene lamp, a faded rag rug. "I think." he rubbed his nose with the back of a wide hand. "Sometimes I write."

Herman waved her in. There wasn't room for two, so he stood in the open doorway.

"Sit," he said as if he were speaking to Molly. Emma did as she was told.

She ran her fingers across the top of the table, its unfinished pine worn smooth with use.

"What do you write?"

"Letters."

"To whom?"

"To Leo and Esther and Mo."

Emma watched dust motes floating in the golden sunlight. Herman's eyes were huge behind his thick glasses.

"Do they ever write back?"

"No." Herman laughed. "I'm not *that* crazy." He pulled off his baseball cap and scratched his head. "It just makes me feel closer. I miss them, you know."

Emma nodded. Herman's brothers and sister had died in a death camp twenty-odd years ago. Before he told her about it, she had never heard of the Holocaust. It wasn't something she'd ever been taught at West Cypress High.

He stood there for a moment, staring while faces long dead smiled their turns upon a stage only he could see. Then Emma sneezed. "Come on." He waved her outside again and brushed

aside some leaves. They sat perched above the shack's little yard
on a flat rock.

Emma felt that Herman wanted to change the subject now,
but she couldn't let go yet.

"Do you miss Jennie Lou too?"

He reached over and squeezed her hand. "You know I do."

"How can you miss someone who never was? I mean, even if
she was your daughter, she only lived four days, and that was
so long ago."

Herman nodded. "When Bernie was a year and a half old.
She'd be just about your age."

Emma nodded. She walked with him sometimes across the
railroad tracks, then down the road to the tiny churchyard
where his baby daughter was buried. His wife Mary Ann had
never gone, not once in all those years had she walked the path
to the graveyard door. "She can't," Herman said. But he could.
He placed flowers from their yard, sweet peas, roses, petunias, in
a china vase shaped like a baby lamb. And she knew that when
he looked at her across that little grave he saw in part the grown
Jennie Lou.

"What do you write to them about, to Leo, and Esther, and
Mo?"

"My cucumbers. How my scallions are doing."

Emma slapped at him. "Okay, forget it."

Then Herman shifted, sat cross-legged in his baggy khakis
facing her. His smile faded. "I write them about things I'm
worried about. Last week I wrote on the trouble that's coming
now for the Negroes."

They watched leaves fall for a few minutes. Then she spoke.
"I wonder sometimes what it would be like to go to school with
a Negro. To have one for a friend. What were they like in the
Army, Herman?"

"Like people. Good and bad. Nice and mean. Tall and short."

"Did you eat with them?"

"Emma," he laughed, "we ate, talked, played poker, slept,
crapped—we did everything together. It was the Army."

"It's just hard to imagine. I mean, when you think about it,
it's one thing, but in real life . . . it's another."

Herman picked up a stick and played with it.

"Well, you'll have your chance to see it all."

"You think things are going to change here? Will there be trouble?"

"No way around it." He leaned back and squinted. "Good people are going to die all over the South before this is over. But here? I don't think so. Probably not."

"Then what do you mean I'll see it all?"

Herman looked into her eyes as if in them he could read her future. She stood, waiting with her hands on her hips for his answer.

"Do you think you're always going to live in West Cypress, kiddo?"

"I hope not."

"So where are you going?"

Emma shrugged. "New Orleans, maybe. Atlanta. New York. San Francisco. Bernie and I talk about it sometimes, but we never decide."

"He wants to go where you go."

"Well . . . yes," she answered, not seeing, out of stubbornness, the point Herman was making.

For Herman knew that Emma thought she loved Bernie, and she did, in her own way. But he knew that even if she loved him with her whole heart, his son, his beloved son, was merely going to slow this girl down. It would be years before anyone could lasso Emma. And he felt sorry for any poor bastard who tried.

"Why stay so close to home? Why not Paris?"

"Well, hell, Herman, why not Katmandu?"

"Why not?"

Emma thought for a minute. This was her way into what she'd been thinking about for days. This was her opening.

"When you left Poland, wasn't it lonesome to leave behind everybody you ever knew?"

"Sure, but sometimes you don't have a choice."

"If I go away, I'll miss you."

"Me too, sweetheart."

Emma stood up, stretched, swung her arms in a big circle.

"What's on your mind?" Herman asked.

"You know what you were talking about earlier, about missing people who are dead, who you never knew really, like Jennie Lou?"

"Yep."

"I miss people I don't know, too," she said.

Herman looked up at her, waiting.

"I miss all the relatives on my daddy's side I never met. And the others I know but never see." *You're getting warm, Emma, but you're not there yet. Do it.*

"Well, everybody does that," Herman said. "Families don't live together like they used to. Back in the old country they were all around you forever. Their noses in your business till you were sick of them, *feh!*"

This is it, she thought. *Don't back away. Don't laugh at Herman's joke. Say it now.*

"I miss my mother, Herman."

Herman laughed, "What do you mean, you miss your mother? She probably misses you, too. You're always here or off with Bernie. As much as I love you, you know you ought to go home every once in a while, Emmale."

"I mean my real mother."

"Mein teiere Emmale, what the hell are you talking about?"

She opened her mouth and the words tumbled out. "My cousin, I mean I guess he's my step-cousin, J.D., told me something a couple of weeks ago that I've always known—or anyway suspected." She took a deep breath. "Rosalie's not my mother, Herman."

Herman stared at her. "You've had too much schnapps."

"No, really. I've been looking for proof for years, when they were out, and finally, in a little suitcase at the back of the hall closet, I found it."

"What?"

"My birth certificate."

Herman's eyes grew wide. "All kids think they're adopted . . . but you're not joking, are you?"

"No." And then Emma's heart thundered in her chest as she said the words aloud for the very first time. "Her name is Helen, Herman. It says my real mother's name is Helen Kaplan."

Herman picked up another stick and drew a circle in the soft blanket of leaves. What the hell was he going to say to her now? "Have you talked with them about it?"

"No." Emma's voice faltered. She was close to tears. "I don't know *what* to do."

Herman reached over and gathered her into a hug. The tears began in earnest then, rolling down her cheeks, her nose running, but she struggled through. "You know, I overheard little things they'd say now and then when I was growing up, and I'd ask them questions. They'd pretend they didn't hear me. Or change the subject. They'd never talk about the past, not like you do, it was like there was something awful there, something dirty."

"Emma." He hugged her closer, as if he could squeeze away her pain.

"So I'd try to trick them. I used to do things like, in the middle of supper, I'd say, 'Daddy, could you pass the peas, please, and how did you and Momma meet?' " She smiled at the memory, laughed a little. "Like if I did it fast enough, they wouldn't notice and would answer before they thought. And then once, I called Daddy from school, when we had to fill out some form with our mother's maiden name. As if asking on the phone would make a difference."

"What did he say?"

"He said 'Norris.' "

Herman struggled for an explanation, but he didn't understand these people. Why would they do this? But Emma was looking for an answer. "They have a reason for this, Emma. I'm sure they thought they were doing the right thing."

"Do *you* think that was the right thing? To lie to me all these years? To hide that from me like it was something awful? What could be so awful, Herman?"

He shrugged. "You never know what people think. People have pain, Emma, that you don't know about."

"What about *my* pain, Herman? All that whispering and lying? It made me crazy—to wonder who I really was . . . am. It's weird to know you can't trust your parents . . . *if* they're your parents!"

"You're not crazy, sweetie. You're one of the sanest people I know. Now, what are we going to do about this?"

"I don't know. I want to talk to them."

"And you should. But you must be very careful, Emma. Very careful. They had good reasons for what they did. They're not bad people. Have you talked with Bernie about this?"

"Not yet, I—"

"Don't, not yet."

"Talk with me about what?" Bernie struggled into the clearing then, having heard his name as he came through the bushes.

"About what to get you for Christmas." Emma quickly wiped

her nose and gave Herman a look. He was right. She wasn't
ready yet. And then, as always, her tongue covered up her feelings. "A jock strap or a nose guard? Which should I get him,
Herman? Which do you think, Herman? Which is bigger?"

Herman laughed at his son's blushing. Then, behind him,
Molly rushed up, her speckled tongue lolling. She ran over to
Emma and snuffled in her crotch.

"Get away, you pervert!" Emma managed a laugh.

"Well?" asked Herman.

"It was a chipmunk," Bernie snorted. "She led me over half
the parish and treed a chipmunk."

"Ha!" Herman crowed. "I told you that dog was stupid." He
stood then, brushed off the seat of his pants. "Let's head back.
Your mother will have supper waiting."

But as they headed out together, Bernie's arm around Emma's
shoulder, Herman and Molly trailing behind, Emma turned
and saw Herman slip Molly a meal bone. He looked up at her,
winked, and waggled a warning finger.

Okay, Herman, she thought, I'll talk to you about it again.
I won't go home screaming. I've held it in all this time. I'll hold
it a little longer.

Supper was early in the Graubart house, even earlier as the
days grew shorter. At the back door Emma could already smell
Mary Ann's pan-fried steaks. On the table were three kinds of
vegetables and a bowl of Herman's cucumbers, sour cream and
onions.

"You going to stay?" Mary Ann called from the kitchen. "You
know you're welcome."

Mary Ann Graubart wasn't the warmest of women. In some
ways she reminded Emma of Rosalie, afraid of things Emma
couldn't see. But she was nice because of Bernie, so Emma was
nice to her in return.

"Thanks," she said.

Herman warned, "Call your mother."

Emma shot him a look.

"Hello?" Rosalie answered on the fourth ring, her voice filled
with alarm. She was always sure that a nighttime call meant
Emma was dead on the road.

"I'm not going to be home for supper."

"We're having chicken spaghetti."

"Thanks, no. Bernie and I have some studying to do."

"Drive—"

"I'll drive carefully. And I won't be too late."

Rosalie sighed and returned to the stove. She knew that neither of the things Emma had just told her was true.

She'd be late, as always, and drive like a house afire to make up for it. As Rosalie poked at the chicken, steam fogged her glasses, hiding her hurt feelings. Jake, reading the paper at the table, slowly devouring every word, didn't notice. Only when Rosalie placed his full plate before him did he look up.

He blinked then as if he had come inside after sitting out in the dark.

"Emma?"

"At the Graubarts'."

Jake frowned, lifted the food to his mouth and chewed, but it was tasteless. He never saw Emma anymore. And when she was home, she was behind her closed door, studying. Not that he minded that. But he was afraid that soon he was going to lose her forever. She'd get married and move away. Or she'd go off to graduate school. He knew that if she left West Cypress, she'd never come back. *He* wouldn't. Maybe she'd go to California; he'd visit her—oh, to stand on the edge of the Pacific again and look at all that blue.

"I said are you finished?" Rosalie was leaning over him, waiting to take his plate. He looked up at the kitchen clock. He couldn't have been daydreaming more than ten or twelve minutes. Their meals never lasted longer than that.

Ahead of them stretched the long hours of darkness.

"Do you want some more coffee?" Rosalie asked.

"No, thanks."

Jake moved to an easy chair and picked up a Carter Brown mystery he didn't think he'd read before. Neither he nor Rosalie would say another word until ten o'clock when Emma came racing in the side door.

Rosalie pulled a bright lamp up to the kitchen table, wiped off the plastic tablecloth, and laid out her sketch pad and her pencils. Propped beside the gooseneck lamp was the first photograph she had ever seen of Emma as a baby, the one Jake had sent her from New York.

The house was filled with Rosalie's watercolors and pencil

sketches. Hers was a small talent, she knew, but when the ladies in her Bible group visited and fussed over her work, she was always pleased.

Sometimes she prettied up other pictures, adding snow to branches, smoke to chimneys. Recently she'd done a watercolor of her old home place that she liked a lot. But her best were her pencil sketches, renderings from photos of her mother, Emma and Jake. Emma was the hardest. She couldn't get her eyes right or her mouth. Something always eluded her.

But this photograph of Emma when she was a baby with a big toothless grin, this was her favorite. She did it over and over again. She held the photo up now at arm's length. What a sweet little thing Emma had been—so helpless. All she could do at that age was creep and crow and gurgle. She'd held on to Rosalie's arm, her hair, her skirttails so tightly, as if Rosalie were the only person in the world. Those had been the best days of Rosalie's life, before Emma got big enough to let go.

Rosalie glanced over at Jake, still reading. She sighed. This was all he ever did, it seemed, and all he wanted to do when he came home from his job butchering at the supermarket. It was better, in a way, though, since their store had closed. At least he got out of the house a little.

Jake sat turning the pages of a *National Geographic*. He stopped at a story on East Africa. In one of the pictures beautiful bare-breasted black women were pulling little pieces of meat out of a pot. He thought for a minute about the meat he smelled cooking when he walked home from the Ritz Bar through the Quarters, about the low laughter he heard from their porches, the soft voices every once in a while that called, "Hello, Mr. Jake." And then, as if Rosalie could see that thought and would ask him what on earth he was doing walking those dirt streets of the colored ghetto, he pulled his mind back to the magazine and turned the page. The next story was about Singapore. People were eating there too, nibbling things off little sticks.

Then he closed his eyes and could see himself handing a hot dog to Helen. She loved to eat outdoors. One afternoon he'd taken her to Coney Island, and she'd eaten three Nathan's franks without stopping and laughed and laughed when he warned that she might get sick.

Helen would have loved Singapore. In his mind he took her hand, and they turned the corner, right there off the page, around that corner where the photograph couldn't see. They ran down the sidewalk together, but not too far. He slowed her then, and they stopped. She tipped back the brown straw hat she was wearing, grinned, and then she gave him a kiss.

Rosalie paused at the door and looked at Jake leaned back in his chair, his eyes closed. Why, she wondered, was he smiling?

7

San Francisco
1962

JESSE TREE had spent the whole morning on the Union Station platform waiting for a train. The day was a brilliant blue, the blue of Van Gogh's Provence.

Clifton, his art teacher from his childhood days in Watts, was on that train, coming to teach drawing at the university in Berkeley.

"Hell," Clifton had said to him on the phone. "I reckon if a young twerp like you can find fame and fortune in Baghdad-by-the-Bay, why not me too?"

Things *had* gone well for Jesse Tree, once he had left behind charcoal, acrylic, oils, and had found himself to be a sculptor in wood.

He'd taken the advice of Clifton, who'd warned him that the life of an artist was a tough row to hoe. " 'Less you like starving, boy, you better find some way to make your art pay. Fine art's fine, but so's eatin'."

And Jesse had. He'd studied sculpture at the San Francisco Art Institute, but he'd learned woodworking, carpentry, furniture making too. He supported himeslf building cabinets, at first journeyman work, but now he was on his own, carving woodwork for Pacific Heights mansions in cherry, oak, price be damned, ebony wood. He'd begun to make tables and desks on commission for these castle dwellers, and those were indeed works of art, a fact which Jesse had just begun to recognize.

Maybe he wasn't waiting until he could do his art. Maybe he was doing it now at twenty-four.

In the library he found the work of 1920s furniture designer

Jacques-Émile Ruhlmann, discovered that in eighteenth-century France there was no more exalted title than Cabinetmaker to the King. With that inspiration, he stretched, he dared, he soared. He inlaid hundreds of ebony valentines in a hall stand of purple heartwood. He experimented with silver and gold leaf. "Craft furniture," they called it in his first group exhibition. Now a small gallery out on Sacramento Street had called, to talk about a one-man show.

He'd telephoned Clifton with the news. "Hot damn!" Clifton had exclaimed. "But tell me, boy, have they seen *you?*"

"I sent them an eight-by-ten of Tab Hunter."

Clifton laughed, but saw in his mind's eye a young man who almost glowed in the dark. He was a black prince, handsome, big-shouldered, strong-limbed, intelligent—best of breed, one would have called him had he been a horse. Clifton, who loved men but didn't lust after them, could nonetheless smell Jesse's sexuality as if it were sprayed around him like a fine perfume. He reeked of sex; it wafted in and out of his pores. But Clifton knew that that kind of attractiveness didn't exactly make white people comfortable—including gallery owners.

"Just keep your pecker in your pants," he'd said to Jesse. "You ain't no white starlet, gone fuck your way to the top."

Clifton had been telling him the same thing since he was just a boy.

In the distance a whistle blew and behind the whistle there was a chugging, and a whooshing, and then the crackle of an announcement overhead which Jesse couldn't understand, for a tiny old Chinese man was asking him a question. The man held a squawking parrot in a great gilt-and-enameled cage. From behind the cake peeked a little girl, a granddaughter doll with long black hair. She stood on her tiptoes and whispered into Jesse's lowered ear, "The time, please, sir, the time?" Jesse smiled, remembering his sisters Clarissa and Allison at that age.

Before he could check his watch and answer, he felt a sudden clap on his back. "You leave that little girl alone!"

Jesse whirled and fell into Clifton's embrace.

"You son-of-a-bitch," Clifton shouted, "why didn't you tell me it takes three days to get from LA?"

"If you'd paid full fare and ridden up front, you'd have been here yesterday."

"You little bastard," Clifton laughed at the young man who towered over him now by half a foot. "Never gave me any respect. Nothing ever changes."

Jesse stood back and looked his friend in the face. No, some things never did. He didn't realize how much he'd missed Clifton until he saw his face, his stiff-legged gait.

"Say, there room for one more nigger painter in Frisco?" Clifton laughed, his big voice carrying out across the tracks. Several heads turned and stared, but Jesse didn't care. Hell, he and Clifton were going to turn more heads than that.

Jesse struggled to take Clifton's battered suitcase from him at the same time the older man slapped him on the back.

"Goddamn, it's good to see you, boy." Clifton rubbed his hands together. "So where do we start?"

"Let's drop your bag off at my place. You can stay with me till we find you something in Berkeley. Or if you want to stay over here where it's happening, we'll see if we can talk my landlady Maria into giving you a room. She owns space all over the city." Then Jesse winked.

"Maria, huh? You telling me something?"

Jesse shook his head in a gesture of innocence. "Pretty woman, but not for me . . . maybe for you. She's just thrown out that fat wop she was married to. Maybe she's got a taste for something older and darker."

"Then lead on, my man, lead on."

Much later they stood side by side in a smoky jazz club on Upper Grant drinking shooters. The bassist was playing his lick, the too-low-to-even-imagine notes that sounded like a joke, like watching a fat man waltz.

"My Uncle Slideman played here a few weeks ago," said Jesse. "You see him?"

"Yeah, he's really bad, man, the cat can blow."

A blonde cocktail waitress in a short black skirt elbowed her way into the bar.

"Anything I can do for you?" she murmured into Jesse's ear.

"No—no, thanks, I'm just fine."

She turned and walked away, then Clifton poked him. "She wanted more than your drink order. Boy, like I always told you, you don't watch out, you going be the spit and image of your daddy."

"Clifton, you're always blowing that same note, singing that same tune."

"Well, it's true. Between your looks and the way your daddy raised you, there's a severe danger you just gone fuck all your talent away. Be nothing more than an old cunthound."

"My daddy raised me! Hell, Clifton, you know better than that!"

"Yeah, well, and you know what I'm talking about too."

Jesse did. He paused a long moment. The saxophonist played a spiraling riff as if he were a bird looking for a place to light.

IN Los Angeles, where he'd grown up except for summers with his mother, Blanche, Jesse had no parents other than his paternal grandparents Lucretia and Josephus Tree. He'd felt like a father himself to his sisters Clarissa and Allison, trying to stop them from following in Blanche's wild path, bouncing pebbles to her rolling stone. Only from time to time did his father Jessup, put in an occasional appearance.

"Hello, boy," he would say, that handsome man of whom Jesse was indeed the echo. He was slow and somber when he came to Lucretia's house, knocking at the front door like an acquaintance making an obligatory social call. Gravely, he always offered Jesse his hand but nothing more except that once, on the fifteenth anniversary of his only son's birth.

"Come with me," he'd said, and Jesse's head reeled, for never in his entire life had he walked out a door with his father.

"You ever had a woman, Jesse?" The big boat of a dark-blue Oldsmobile was sailing through the back streets of the neighborhood, making waves at crowded corners where men hanging out tipped their hats—for Jessup was a respected man of property. More than likely he rented them the hovels they called home.

"No, sir." Jesse wasn't sure whether that was the right answer or not, but he didn't think diddling with Sharleen next door would count.

"Well, it's time, son," he'd said. "And it's a father's duty to break you in."

Jesse didn't dare ask why Jessup suddenly had been reminded of his paternal duty after a space of fifteen years, though the question of why his father, or his mother for that matter, didn't love him and his sisters was something he often wondered about.

They drove a couple more blocks and stopped. Jesse stared at a little house with a crooked front door and falling-down steps.

"She's behind," Jessup said. Jesse didn't know that his father was talking about the young woman who lived inside and her relationship to her rent. Her baby and her little boy, both high yellow like she was, almost as fair as Jesse's mother Blanche, were tossed in corners of the soiled sofa in the living room, down for their naps.

The woman nodded at Jesse, smiled at his dad.

"He do look like you. Like father, like son, they say. That true?" Then she winked. "I hope."

"Depends on what kind of teacher you are, Lorinda," Jessup said. "Like I told you, we'll subtract it at the usual rate."

Again, Jesse didn't know what his father meant. But he did understand when Lorinda took him into the tiny bedroom that was almost filled by her double bed. There she stripped to a bright-red nylon slip that was plastered onto her like a silken flag. Then she took Jesse's hands and placed them on her breasts. He had been this far with Sharleen. The rest of it, with Lorinda's gentle direction, pretty much took care of itself.

Later, driving back home in the Oldsmobile, Jessup had delivered the longest speech Jesse had ever heard from him, the words floating out from around his cigar.

"Remember this, son. A man has only so many fucks in him. You don't want to waste them, but then, too, you don't want to die with some of them still left in your account. That's what women are for, son, to help you balance your books." He paused and took a hard look at the end of his cigar. "Remember, now, they'll try to short-change you. They have deals they're working on their own, and the biggest one of all, the one that cancels all their markers, is holding on permanent to a cock like yours. Whereas you're just trying to dip in and out of their honey pots, stealing all the sweet you want, without getting caught. All the flavors are different, son. Try as many as you can. But remember that you always the one in control. You always the one on top. Don't ever let an uppity woman think because she got a piece of your thing she can get the best of you. You hear what I'm saying, boy?"

Jesse did, and he followed his father's advice.

When Jesse was seventeen, Clifton had peered at him across the top of his half-glasses.

"Where you get all these naked women, son?"

For Jesse kept him supplied with figure models who tossed off their clothes with happy nonchalance, modeling gratis as if they were guests of honor at a party in Clifton's studio.

"I've just been doing what my daddy told me," Jesse answered. Then he explained what that was.

"Sometimes women come up and ask *me*, women I don't even know."

"What do they say?"

Jesse laughed. "Last week one yelled at me across the street, 'Say, give me a piece of that, I could love you forever, honey bun.' "

"You believe them?"

Jesse shrugged.

"You want to believe them?"

"Hell, no. All I want to do is get laid. Don't you?"

"Listen to me, boy. You too young to know it yet, but when you take off your pants, you exposing more than your fine black ass."

"Like what?"

"Ought to be at least a piece of your heart."

"Old man, you don't know what you talking about," the young man had flung back as he bounced out of the studio.

But he knew that Clifton was onto something. For all those times that he'd dipped his wick, that he'd buried himself between some willing young girl's legs, he kept coming up feeling empty. Even now at twenty-four, with everything in his life going so well he was constantly holding his breath, afraid he'd wake up, he had to admit that he was lonely—even with all the sweet ass he could handle, with him always in the driver's seat, always calling the shots.

"How's your family doing, anyway?" Clifton asked. The bird-like saxophonist's melody found the home it was looking for.

Jesse shrugged, signaled for another round. "Oh, you know how it is. My momma's up in Sacramento living with I don't even know who. She hasn't come to see me in two or three years. And I get tired going up there watching her act like she was still sixteen years old, always looking for the man who's going

be the answer to her prayers, always ready for another party,"
he gestured with his glass, "another shot of hooch."

"You sounding like your Grandma Lucretia now for sure."
Clifton smiled. "Sounding mighty Old Testament for a man
who's never settled down."

Jesse ignored him. "Then I see the girls. Allison's already got
three kids, Clarissa's got a second one on the way. Hell, Blanche's
gonna be a grandma five times over, and she's not even forty."

"They ever come down to see your work? Come to that group
show?"

"Hell, Clifton, they don't know what any of that means."

They drank silently for a few minutes. The bassist was again
working his big fiddle, a giant trying to sing a lullaby.

"Ran into your daddy a couple weeks ago. He looked tired."

"He still buying up all the property in sight?"

"Asked him, but he didn't say. Did say if I saw you to say
hello."

"Ain't that something?" Jesse laughed. "Think the man didn't
know white boys had invented the telephone."

"Maybe that's why he don't want to use it."

They both laughed again, and the air lightened in the room.

"Hell, I don't know why I got in this mood." Jesse held up his
glass and took a long look at it. "Must be this demon rum. We're
supposed to be celebrating, not crying in our beers, celebrating
the arrival of Professor Jones. That is why you came up here to
the North, sir, to profess?"

"No, cocksucker, I came up here 'cause I can't get laid in LA."

"All the women find out you were queer and tell you to go
fuck yourself?"

"Did, be the best piece of ass I ever had."

Jesse slapped Clifton on the back. "Are you sure you got a job
up here? Sure they ain't got the wrong Jones?"

"Hell, I don't know. Maybe I am the wrong one. Then I'll
just go on welfare, suck for a while on Uncle Sam's tit. Hell,
that cheap bastard ain't ever paid me all he owes me for giving
him my second-best leg in the war." He knocked on his artificial
limb. It made a hollow sound.

"How come it was second-best?"

"Hell, boy, ain't I ever told you? I used to be part white. That
was it, that leg."

8

West Cypress 1964

IT WAS ONLY nine o'clock, the sun not all the way up the summer sky, and already Rosalie had to stop every five minutes to wipe the sweat off. She leaned on her hoe and squinted out across her garden. Sixteen rows were up, marching from the back fence halfway up the yard, stopping at the edge of the sunken bathtub where she'd tucked some cucumbers, and the bathtub's border was tiny strawberries planted all around. Her fruit trees were doing well; the pear and the peach were both loaded. The plums would fill several cupboard shelves with rubylike Mason jars of jam.

Now that it was June and the real heat had begun, she was going to have to get up earlier for the garden. She'd been at it three hours, snipping and picking peas and keeping after the weeds.

First thing this morning her hoe had unearthed a nest of baby rattlers right over there at the edge of the garden in that bunch of shrubs. They'd scattered every which way, then each had stopped and struck, their tails clattering as if that was going to frighten her off. She'd chopped them in half neatly, every one.

Momma Snake hadn't been home. Probably she'd gone for a drink of water over to the deep bushy-banked ditch that Rosalie kept after the city to cut. But the city didn't care if she was going to have to be on the lookout for a momma rattler. She'd called the mayor about the ditch, but with no results. Well, the city had bigger fish to fry. The whole town was in an uproar about next fall's school integration. And if her choice was between that and snakes, she'd take the snakes.

She'd handed in her resignation at the end of the year. Three years shy of twenty, but it couldn't be helped. She'd had enough misery in the classroom, putting up with those nasty junior-high-school children. She didn't need to add the niggers. The whole situation was just going from bad to worse. She didn't care if she didn't get her full retirement. For the first time in her life she'd said, What difference would a few dollars more make? She couldn't imagine what it would be like, looking out at a classroom and seeing those nappy heads. It was going to be a mess. She'd said that, and others in the teachers' lounge had nodded, especially those heads that were gray like hers. Who she really felt sorry for were the younger teachers who still had years to go.

Well, that wasn't her problem now. Rosalie wiped a drop of sweat from off the end of her nose and got back to work, reminding herself to keep an eye out for Momma Snake.

But maybe the snake didn't even care. That thought occurred to her. Maybe she'd slide up to that nest and, finding it empty, just go on about her business. As if it didn't matter. Her children, out of sight, were out of mind, forgotten.

Rosalie wished that she could do that. Since Emma left last fall, this had been the worst year of her life. And most of it was Emma's doing.

Rosalie winced as she thought about Mary Ann Graubart's phone call yesterday, one more thing to worry about. That too was Emma's fault. In fact, Rosalie had hardly slept all night. If it wouldn't be too much trouble, Miz Graubart had said, she'd like to drop by. Rosalie had talked to Bernie's mother only once before in her whole life, not counting saying hello at Emma's graduation, and that time liked to have killed her. What misery was the woman carrying to her doorstep now?

Rosalie pulled the long green hose across the yard. The grass, mowed only last week, was already getting too high. She'd have to speak to Jake about cutting it today. He'd remind her once again how much less yard there'd been to take care of at the old place before they moved. You'd think that he'd be grateful for a new brick house, but all Jake could do was complain about the yard.

She knew he was going to be little help with Mary Ann Graubart today. Last time when the woman came to call, tripping in as if she were bringing them a sweet pineapple upside-

down cake, Jake had sat there for the longest time without saying a word.

Rosalie could see that day. She'd seen it over and over again
for months now, every time she tried to fall asleep. The pain of
it throbbed worse than even her rheumatism.

"I GUESS you know that Bernie and Emma haven't been getting
along so well," the short round woman had begun, rolling little
crumbs of cake around on the plastic lace tablecloth, never
looking up.

Yes. Rosalie knew. Well, she suspected. It wasn't as if Emma
ever told her much. She'd become quiet as a clam around her
when she and Bernie had started getting serious, almost three
years ago. Rosalie overheard her laughing and carrying on with
her friends, though she never brought them home. With other
people Emma was a completely different person.

But Bernie, yes, she wondered about what would happen when
Emma went away to Atlanta to graduate school, though Emma
had let on that when she finished they were going to get married.
Bernie had stayed behind to graduate. A year older than Emma,
but she'd passed him right on by.

Emma had always been in a hurry, ever since she was a little
girl. With her late birthday, she'd begun first grade when she
was still five. Then at the end of the eleventh grade, right after
she met Bernie, Emma had come home and announced that she
was graduating after summer school.

No one had ever heard of such. But Emma was bound and
determined to go right ahead, as if senior parties and proms
meant nothing, just leapfrogging right over into college and her
freshman year when she was still only sixteen. At first Rosalie
had thought that Bernie was the cause of it, that Emma hadn't
wanted him to leave her behind at West Cypress High. But then
when she put up a stink to go away to college, as if Cypress State
just across the river weren't good enough, as if they were made
of money, Rosalie realized that it wasn't just Bernie Graubart
that she had on her mind. Emma was in a hurry to get on to
something else.

Why, you'd think that the child would be grateful, but then
gratitude didn't run in the Fines.

Going right on to college, just like that, like it was the most natural thing in the world. Rosalie could tell her a thing or two about it, how hard *she'd* worked in the kitchen to go to normal school for those two years. How many nights she'd sat up late studying after working all day, struggling to finish her degree so many years later.

But Emma didn't want to hear about it. "Oh, Momma," she'd say, "it's not like that today." It most certainly was. It was the same money, except it cost a lot more. Well, maybe not so much, since the tuition at State was free and Emma had a scholarship to pay for her books. But if she'd gone away? Lord only knew how much that would have been.

She'd explained all this to Emma, who had just stared at her with that expressionless face she put on when she didn't like what she was hearing. Where had the smile gone, Rosalie wondered, that used to light up her face when she was a little girl? Then Emma had said, "All right, then I'll just have to do it my way."

Which meant that she'd zipped through Cypress State too as if it were a kindergarten, racing toward graduation in three years.

"*This* time I'm going to do it right," she'd announced at the beginning of her last year. Eighteen then, she was only nineteen when she finished, and already she knew her mind as if she had a picture of what she wanted her life to be hidden in her room.

"I'm going *away* to graduate school, Momma," she said while licking stamps for applications—to Georgia, Virginia, Pennsylvania, New York.

Atlanta was where she'd won the biggest fellowship, and though her face had broken into a grin as she waved the offer like a flag of victory, Rosalie knew that Emma was really disappointed. Atlanta was the closest of all to home.

What *was* it Emma was looking for? What was she running away from?

Was it Bernie? That shouldn't be so hard. Emma's tongue had never been shy when she had something on her mind. No, it was something more than that. It felt like there was something about home that she just despised. The older she'd grown, the colder she'd gotten. It made Rosalie shiver when she thought about it.

Why, only this past Thanksgiving, when they'd gone to Atlanta to visit, Emma had said to her, how could she, "If you don't like Daddy, cut him loose. I'm probably not coming home again. Don't stay with him for me. I'm gone."

"Why, whatever are you talking about?"

"For years you've complained about him. You were just telling me how lazy he is. About how you can't stand the yelling when he's mad. What I'm saying is you don't have to put up with anything for me any longer. Do what you want."

Rosalie had left the room then, walked down the hall of Emma's dorm blindly bumping into walls. But then she had to come back because she was afraid if she went any farther she'd get lost.

How could Emma say those things to her? What was she so angry about? She'd gotten more and more like Jake, quiet on the outside, but furious inside. It had gotten worse and then never any better—when was that?—sometime around Rosalie's momma Virgie's funeral.

I didn't know it was going to be this way, she thought. Is it all over so soon? Did I get so little for my bargain with Jake? Of course, Emma didn't know about the bargain, but still, Rosalie had always thought, even if unspoken, her investment would bring her interest in return. Wouldn't you think so?

Well, she couldn't say that to Emma. But they didn't say much of anything for the remainder of that Thanksgiving in Atlanta, because, within minutes after that hurtful conversation about Jake (Rosalie hadn't even dried her tears) the announcement came over the radio—John Fitzgerald Kennedy was dead.

The whole Thanksgiving visit had gone that way, just one awful thing after another.

It had started with Bernie, who was going to Atlanta to see Emma, too, not wanting to share the trip. She couldn't imagine why he'd want to drive all that way by himself, waste all that gas. But then, he'd never had much to do with them, just poking his head in and saying hello to be polite.

Once in Atlanta, Rosalie knew there was something up between him and Emma, even aside from the assassination which put everybody in a terrible mood. They were all crammed together, watching Jackie grabbling over the back of that limousine in that blood-smeared pink suit. But there was a tightness in Emma's mouth that didn't have anything to do with the President, and no matter how he tried, Bernie couldn't seem to get his face straight, either.

When Emma stood that last rainy morning on her dorm steps, waving them all goodbye, Rosalie had seen the tension in her face loosening. It was only a couple of weeks later, in that space between Thanksgiving and Christmas, that Miz Graubart had first come to visit.

Rosalie had served pound cake and coffee to her and made polite conversation. Jake sat, and, as usual, after hello he didn't say a word.

"I guess you know that Bernie and Emma haven't been getting along," Mary Ann began.

Rosalie nodded. Yes, she'd suspected as much.

And then as if that nod had turned a switch, the woman spit out, "She's sending him to Vietnam. She lied to him, broke his heart, and now he's being drafted!"

Rosalie didn't know what to say. Mary Ann raced on. "He dropped out of ROTC two years ago. His father and I didn't want him to. It was his insurance. As an officer, he could go to Europe, Taiwan, somewhere other than the war. But no. Emma didn't want him to. She wanted him to take his chances so they could get married. But now she's changed her mind. Bernie says now that she's gotten away, she doesn't think he and West Cypress are good enough for her." Her voice cracked. "He'll never come back. I know it."

"You don't know that."

"I don't know what?" The look she threw at Rosalie was sharp as a razor. "I don't know that he won't come back in a box with a flag for a blanket? Or with one leg? Or blind? I'll tell you who doesn't know. *You're* the one who doesn't know a damned thing!"

Rosalie's heart, which had been picking up speed, began to race now as if it could run away from these words which she knew she didn't want to hear.

"You don't know how she got him, do you? Your precious daughter, Emma?"

"What are you talking about?" Jake's voice was froggy, like a seldom-opened door. Both the women turned and stared at him. They had forgotten he was in the room.

"What do you mean?" he repeated.

Mary Ann's face was scarlet now. Her mouth worked. Even in anger, the words didn't come easy to her. "I mean she . . . she . . . *slept* with him."

Rosalie turned away, a hand to the side of her face as if she'd been slapped.

"How do you know?" Jake asked flatly.

"I know." Mary Ann set her mouth in a prim straight line of defense.

"Well, *I* want to know!"

Watch out, Mary Ann Graubart, Rosalie thought. Watch out when Jake is riled.

"I read her letters," Mary Ann spat. "Dirty letters. Trash. And if you paid attention, you'd know. She's your daughter, isn't she?"

"And *your* son!" Jake was shouting now. "Isn't he your son? Who's ruined her?"

Rosalie stood up and ran out of the room. She'd heard enough. Then there was the back door slamming, a car door, and Mary Ann Graubart was gone.

It had taken her days to get over that. Well, really, she never would. But she'd decided to let it go for a little while, at least not to mention it to Emma until Christmas, until she came home.

ROSALIE sighed at that memory and took one last swipe at the weeds around her pole beans—too hard, too close. The tall wooden stake fell down, the green-bean tendrils grasping at the earth as if in seconds they would take a new hold there, sink roots, then fight their way back up.

I'm like those pole beans, Rosalie thought. Cut me down. Throw me in the dirt. I keep on struggling. Jake and his daughter aren't made of the same stuff. They think life is easier, sweeter than that. They think you can have anything you want if you want it bad enough. They don't seem to know that life is going to cheat you at every turn. Emma's young. She has an excuse, though God knows I've tried to teach her differently. But Jake, Jake's lived through the hard times, the hungry years, just like me. You'd think he'd know.

It was just like she'd explained to him in that first letter she'd written him. *The world is a terrible place. Cold and hard and cruel. No place to bring an innocent child into. But if you al-*

ready have one, if you have a baby who needs a mother as much
as I want a little girl, then that's what I'm looking for.

You'd think Jake had never understood a word she'd ever
said. You'd think that life was just one long dime store novel.
He sat there, at the kitchen table, on the sofa, and watched life
flicker by like images in a book, dipping into a paper bag now
and then for a bite of chocolate. Jake liked things sweet.

And comfortable. Rosalie's eye fell now on the green metal
yard chair he'd moved to the edge of the garden the last time
he mowed the yard.

"You can sit here and watch your garden grow," he'd said.

What on earth was the man thinking about? Gardens weren't
for watching. You had to work at them, bend your back, break
your fingernails in the dirt. Hard work and survival, that's what
gardens were all about.

Rosalie had finished with the pole. *There, now.* She patted
down the dirt with her foot. It was straight again, firmly rooted
in the ground, green and tall, almost as high as her head. A
Christmas tree in June, her beans.

Then the Christmas just past tugged at her thoughts again. She
saw the silver tinsel tree she'd bought on sale at the last minute
at the five-and-dime.

"But it doesn't smell like a tree," Emma had said, walking in
the night before Christmas Eve, the all-day drive thrumming
around her as if the miles and towns across Georgia, Alabama,
Mississippi were slipping beneath her yet.

"I don't know how you do it," Rosalie had said, remembering
that awful trip they'd made in the other direction at Thanksgiving, only a month before.

"You know I love to drive," Emma answered.

But not now you don't, not now that the journey is over,
Rosalie thought, looking at Emma's face which snapped shut as
soon as she stepped in the door. You don't love it now that the
adventure is over. Because this trip was in the wrong direction.
You're happy when leaving, not coming home.

Two minutes in the door, and she was complaining about the
tree. She always crabbed about Christmas, as if Rosalie never got
it quite right.

Well, Rosalie had a few things she wanted to complain about,
too. But she'd waited this long; she could wait a bit more.

She followed Emma into her bedroom, stood and watched her unpack. Emma was holding a cream-colored lacy undergarment that Rosalie had never seen before. It was like a teddy, the kind of one-piece vest and step-ins Rosalie had worn as a young girl.

"What's that?" she asked, reaching out for it.

Emma pulled away and quickly tucked the garment into a drawer.

She'd always acted like that about her underthings. As if Rosalie hadn't changed her diapers as a baby. As if she hadn't bought her her first brassiere.

Of course, she'd carried on as if the falsies Rosalie had pinned inside were meant to hurt her rather than to make up for her still-flat chest. Emma had tucked the bra into the bottom of a drawer just like she was hiding this lacy thing now. What else was she hiding with it, Rosalie wondered, what else that Mary Ann Graubart had warned about?

"Well," said Emma then, closing the dresser and the closet doors, "I'd better make a few phone calls."

Not five minutes in the house, Rosalie thought, and already she's trying to get away. Rosalie followed her up the long dark hall.

She reached for a saucepan in the kitchen, filled it with exactly three cups of water and put it on to boil. She could use a cup of tea. Emma was on the phone now, leaning against the refrigerator door.

And as she rang up first one friend and then another whom she hadn't seen since September, the bright excitement colored her voice. Rosalie thought she could almost see her words glowing against the dimness of the single kitchen light. She and Jake sat at the kitchen table, pretending they were doing something else but listening to every word.

"Tomorrow," Emma was saying. "Tomorrow about one, and then we'll go to Delia's and open all our presents there." She laughed then, a high-trilled laugh as if she knew a secret. Her cheeks were bright red. The phone connected her with an energy that electrified her in this quiet room where the only other sound was that of the gas flame.

Emma had complained that she was cold, so Rosalie had turned on the oven for a moment. She listened to the sound of the gas, the sound of money burning.

"I can't wait to eat some of Snooks's chili," Emma was saying. There was a pause. "*Of course* Bernie will be there." Then she lowered her voice to a whisper. "I've got to talk to him again. He's taking this something awful."

Such assurance, little miss, that you can toss him out and then come back and see him again? What is it that makes you think you have that power? Is it the thing that Bernie's mother whispered, her words hissing like this gas?

Rosalie watched Emma filling in the spaces in a little book that said "Hallmark" on the cover. She leaned it against the refrigerator and wrote in names and times.

"Come and sit," Jake said when Emma finally got off the phone. "Have a cup of tea."

Emma smiled then. She smiled at her daddy and sat right down. Like him, she stirred milk and a couple of teaspoons of sugar into her cup.

"So how's school?" he asked.

"Fine." She smiled again and took a sip. "But it's harder than I thought. I am really having to work."

"I'm sure it couldn't be that bad. Not for a smart girl like you." Rosalie placed a loaf of fruitcake on the table as she said the words. It, like the silver tree, had been on sale at the dime store.

"No, thanks,'" Emma gestured and then pushed back a forelock of her blonde hair. It was getting longer, gave her a different look. "Everybody in the program's smart. But they all went to better schools."

Rosalie stiffened, her lips tight. "I'm sure you got a perfectly good education at Cypress State. After all, you won all those honors."

Emma spread her hands on the tablecloth and looked up at Rosalie. "You don't understand. Some schools *are* better than others."

"I'm sure I don't know. It seems to me that all you have to do is apply yourself."

Emma's hand trembled as she lifted her cup of tea. She always sees things her way, Emma thought. It's as if she looks at the world through the wrong end of a telescope, so that everything is smaller, not larger.

But already, just four months away from home, Emma knew

that the world was so much bigger than West Cypress—just as
Herman had always promised.

She'd have to go see him while she was home. She'd have to
explain how she felt about Bernie. Would he understand that it
was all tied together, getting away, looking forward, looking
backward?

Atlanta was huge—it seemed to go on forever. And everything
was different. She wasn't getting A's on her papers in graduate
school. But on the other hand, she was swamped with calls for
dates. She'd hung out in Manuel's Tavern, with paintings of
naked women on the walls. She'd eaten Chinese food. She'd met
a poet in one of her classes who had long hair, smoked marijuana and lived with a bunch of other strange-looking people
in a house they called "the commune." She'd seen a Fellini movie
and another by Bergman, *The Seventh Seal,* she hadn't understood a word of. What did all this have to do with Bernie?
Maybe the point was that it had *nothing* to do with him. She
felt like she'd been given one tiny bite of strawberry shortcake.
She wanted more.

She knew that she was breaking Bernie's heart, and she was
sorry. She truly was. But she simply didn't have any choice. She
couldn't keep pretending that she was going to marry him in
June when every single fiber in her body said, "No, you're not."
It was as clear as if she had a radio signal in her head that broad-
cast the words: *You've only begun. Keep going.*

"Well," Emma said brightly, "I've made lots of friends. And
Atlanta's *so* beautiful. It's too bad when you were there we
didn't have time to drive around and see the gorgeous old
homes."

"Rich people." Rosalie said the words as if she were spitting
something nasty out of her mouth.

"I beg your pardon?" Inside, Emma started to shiver. This
house made her feel cold and deprived. The windows were bat-
tened down, the rooms clammy with the stench of arrested time.

"Rich people," Rosalie repeated. "Not for the likes of us."

"Well, it doesn't hurt to look."

"Just as long as you keep in mind who you are and where
you're from."

Emma stood then, pushing back her chair. She had to get out
for a minute. "Excuse me," she mumbled, "bathroom."

She stood at the sink and scooped cold water on her face. She stared at her dripping image in the mirror and whispered, "Calm down. You're letting her get to you already."

And then she asked herself, Why are you here, Emma? You finally got away. Why didn't you stay gone?

She hadn't come back for Christmas, when Jake would sleep late and leave his presents untouched under the tree for days.

"He hates it," she'd told Rosalie for years. "Jews don't do Christmas."

Rosalie sniffed, "He just does it to be mean."

It certainly wasn't for the Christmas meal, a fatty hen masquerading as a turkey, devoured in silence, as all their family meals were, in ten minutes.

It wasn't because she missed Rosalie, her *stepmother*, to whom she'd never said that word.

No, she'd never confronted her daddy and Rosalie with their secret. It was as if the knowing of it was enough. And once she knew, she'd rolled it up and swallowed it and kept it deep inside in a little room, shut off. It was as if their secret had become *her* secret. She knew, but she wasn't going to tell them.

And through those two years that she'd nurtured the secret inside her, her affection for Jake and disaffection for Rosalie had grown. He lied, too, she told herself when she thought about it. And he was the same distant, difficult, silent, mercurial Jake. But he's your *daddy*. He's your *blood*. And he married Rosalie, she'd begun to figure out, for *your* sake.

Back in the kitchen, Rosalie blew on her tea and said, "She's just wasting her time at school. Wasting her time and our money."

Jake shook his head. He didn't agree with that.

"I knew that's what would happen the minute she got away. She's gone over there to play. And Lord only knows what else."

"Ro . . ." he began to answer that playing wasn't such an awful thing, but Emma walked back in and he stopped.

Emma's voice was light again, though tight. If she was here to talk to Bernie again, and to Herman, and to say hello to Jake, she'd grit her teeth and make the best of it with Rosalie. You can do it, Emma, she cheered herself on, you've had lots of practice.

"I've been tutoring too, in Atlanta." She picked up her tea. "Helping kids who are behind in school."

"Where do you find the time to do all this?" Rosalie shot Jake a look: See, it was just as I thought.

"It's only a couple of hours a week. Some of us take a bus to their neighborhood from the campus."

"Children don't try very hard these days. Most of them need a paddle, not a tutor." Rosalie stood from the table then and rinsed their cups in the plastic basin of saved tepid water that stood in the sink.

"These kids need special help."

Emma knew she was heading down a path toward trouble. But hadn't she known, since she started this conversation, that the punch line was something that Rosalie wasn't going to like? Big surprise. There was no completely neutral territory. Every conversation they'd ever had was laced with mines.

"Why do they need help?" Rosalie turned from the dishes.

"They're colored. You know how it is. They haven't had a lot."

"Niggers! You're teaching niggers?"

"You know I hate that word!"

Rosalie felt a sick headache coming on. She wouldn't sleep all night.

"Here I am giving up my teaching job that I've worked so hard at all these years, and you're over there in Atlanta going out of your way to help the niggers. Emma, I swear, I don't know what's come over you!"

"Things are not the same everywhere as they are in West Cypress."

"They have schools, don't they?"

"Separate schools. And everybody knows they aren't as good."

"I don't know why not. It's their own who are teaching them. If they want them to be smarter, they ought to do a better job."

"You just don't understand."

"I understand plenty. I understand that you've been gone four months and already you've turned into an integrationist—and I don't know what else!" Rosalie could feel the tears rising. She knew that any minute she was going to start to cry.

"This isn't new. It's not as if you haven't heard me say these same things since I was old enough to figure them out."

"It's all those books you read. And that Herman Graubart. You think I don't know, all those ideas he put into your head?"

"He's never told me anything but the truth." And you? What have you told me? The words hung unspoken.

Rosalie knew that this wasn't the time, but she couldn't stop herself. "I guess he told you that it was all right to . . . to . . . sleep with his son, too?"

There. There it was. All the cards lay face up on the table. Now let's see how you play this hand, Miss Emma.

Emma looked as if she'd been slapped—which was what she ought to be, Rosalie thought, slapped until she had good sense.

"No," Emma answered slowly then, staring Rosalie straight in the eye. *You want it? You're going to get it.*

She has no shame. The thought took Rosalie's breath away.

"He never told me sex was right. He never told me it was wrong either. We talked about it, though; we didn't hide it in some closet like a dirty secret."

Rosalie held a hand over her heart. "I don't want to hear it."

"I don't want to hear it, either. I walk into this house five minutes, and you're at me—picking at my underwear, for Christ's sake."

"Emma!" Rosalie was white around the mouth.

"Emma what? There's lots worse things than taking the Lord's name in vain, Mother."

"Yes, and I guess you're proud you've done some of them."

Emma placed both hands flat down on the kitchen table. "What exactly is it that's gnawing at you? What is it that you want? You want to talk to me about my underwear, about my ideas on race, religion, sex, education? Do you want to sit down and have the very first intelligent conversation we've ever had, or do you want to just stand there and pick at old scabs?"

Rosalie's hands fluttered. "You've gone crazy! Off to school for four months and you've thrown Bernie over and you're too good for us! But you always thought that . . . that you were too good for your father and mother."

Three beats passed. Then Emma opened her mouth and said it: "You're not my mother."

Rosalie reeled back against the counter.

Then everything moved in slow motion, and it was like she was watching Rosalie from a far distance, as if she were standing on a faraway hill. This must be what it feels like to be in shock, Emma thought. I didn't really mean to say that. I've walked around with it all these years, not knowing, then knowing, but not knowing how to say it, to ask it, once I knew it.

Yet *there,* as if the thought had birthed itself, it just plopped out.

"Emma." Jake was standing now, moving toward her, his arms outstretched.

"No! Don't touch me!"

Tears banked on Jake's cheeks, then fell. He looked from Rosalie to Emma, then back again. "I told you it would never work, Ro. I told you that from the start."

"My fault! That's right, make it all *my* fault," Rosalie screamed. "As if I haven't suffered enough."

Emma wheeled on her, furious. "Exactly what is it that you've suffered, Mother? Why is that you always think that you have such a monopoly on pain? Why do you think that your life is so much more terrible than anyone else's? What about my mother's life?" And then her voice climbed and broke. "Who the hell *is* Helen Kaplan anyway? Or *was* she?" Then, strangling through tears, she sounded like a little girl. She turned to Jake. "Where is my mother, Daddy?"

Rosalie wheeled and fumbled through the double hallway curtains that she'd nailed in place to keep in the precious heat. She ran blindly from the room.

Later, lying on her bed, Rosalie could hear Jake and Emma murmuring in the kitchen. Their voices rose and fell, but she couldn't make out the words.

THERE wasn't that much to tell, though Jake tried to answer Emma's questions: No, he and Helen hadn't known each other very long. They met in New York. He didn't know exactly why she was there. No, he knew nothing of her past. A little town in Georgia or Alabama—he wasn't quite sure where she was from. He didn't know her relatives, didn't know whether there were any. What she was like? Why, she was very nice. She was a very nice woman.

He didn't have the language to describe how he'd felt about Helen. He couldn't tell Emma that he thought about her every day, that her softness and her warmth still filled his daydreams and nights. To explain, he'd have to talk about himself, and he didn't know how to do that.

He didn't stutter when he talked about Helen, Emma thought. Though he fumbled when he tried to explain why they'd kept the secret so long.

"Rosalie loves you, Emma. She thought if she raised you as her own, it would be better."

Emma shook her head. She still didn't understand. She doubted that she ever would.

Yet she did feel easier toward her daddy, though not toward Rosalie. Rosalie—that's what she'd decided to call her from now on.

Herman had warned her not to do this in anger. But that was what Rosalie always made her feel, anger, as if she were personally responsible for all of Rosalie's hurt. Hell, she didn't even know what the woman was hurting *about.* But whatever it was, she wasn't going to feel ever again that it was her fault. Nope, not now that her daddy had told her all the secrets.

And he had—well, almost.

Rosalie didn't sleep a wink that night, except sometime in the early morning, she must have dozed off for just a second. And in that second Emma had dressed and was gone.

A few days later a long letter with an Atlanta postmark arrived. It read: "Dear Daddy and Rosalie, Why didn't you tell me? Explain to me what the secrecy was about." Then she went on to talk about the coloreds and school and how she'd said goodbye to Bernie and how she felt like she had to be free to grow.

Rosalie didn't know what she was talking about. Jake guessed.

In her reply Rosalie didn't address Emma's first question. Instead, she wrote how Emma was way over her head, how she was going to have to pay for her sins, how she'd ruined herself with Bernie, and now what did she think she was going to do? Rosalie didn't think she was pretty enough to make up for it; Bernie had probably been her only chance. And now that she'd turned away from him, she'd better be prepared to get by on her brains. She had plenty of those, if she'd only use them. If she'd only wake up and smell the coffee and see the error of her ways. Maybe Bernie would even forgive her, take her back. She could return to West Cypress, settle down with him, and teach school.

Emma ripped the letter to pieces. Then she'd leaned over the wastebasket and shouted into it, "Don't you tell me what to do.

You don't know me. You don't know me at all!" She stared at the black metal basket for a few minutes, then picked the shreds of the letter out of it, tore them even smaller, and burned them in an ashtray, cremated them a few at a time. She poured the ashes into a plastic bag from the Kroger's, walked over to the lake by the university president's house, and tossed the ashes of the letter across the water until they were all gone.

That had been January. Now it was June. In that time, Rosalie and Jake had heard from Emma exactly five times. She wrote a one-page letter the first of each month as if she were paying a bill. The words filled the page, but they didn't say very much.

She was fine. School was fine. The weather was fine. She wouldn't be home for vacation; she was working a part-time job for a caterer, had discovered she had a knack for cooking, was going to summer school.

She never mentioned Bernie. Rosalie wondered whether she knew that, just as his mother had predicted, the Army had called his name. He'd been in Vietnam since March, since right after his birthday.

Now Rosalie stood in her garden and stretched. Her back hurt from the leaning over. Her squash was looking good. So were her tomatoes. Maybe she'd make a sack of vegetables to give to Mary Ann Graubart when she came to call.

Why *was* that woman coming here again today, a little over six months after her first visit? Was she coming to tell her that Bernie was dead, that, just as she'd predicted, Emma had laid waste to more than his heart?

"Rosalie!" That was Jake now calling from the back door. He was standing with the sliding screen door pushed aside, still wiping sleep out of his eyes in the bright morning sun.

"I've put the coffee up. Come and get some."

He was pouring hot water into the plastic cups, the instant coffee foaming as she came inside. She was blinded for a moment. After the sun's glare, it seemed so dark. She'd pulled the screen door to with a bang, hoping he'd notice and remember that he should close it, too.

There was another sound then, the slamming of a car door. Rosalie peeked out. There was Bernie's old two-tone green Ford in the driveway. She was here, Mary Ann Graubart.

Now she was rapping on the screen door.

Rosalie, still wiping the sweat off, welcomed her in.

"No," Mary Ann refused coffee. She wouldn't even take a chair. She stood there, once again in their kitchen, her feet planted firmly, her jaw set like a bulldog's. It was like a rerun, like watching the same television program over again.

"Herman's ill," she said, "probably dying. So they're sending Bernie home. With Herman gone, I'll get to keep Bernie, because he's an only son. It's a trade-off. I don't get to keep both."

Having said her lines, she was back out the door now, standing in the carport which was only a tad cooler than being out in the blazing sun. The heat made her look wavy, her image disappearing in the carport's dark. Rosalie blinked. Looking at Mary Ann made her eyes hurt, which in turn gave her a stomachache.

I'm going to be sick, she thought, as a yellow taste filled her mouth.

"You be sure and tell Emma that."

Rosalie couldn't see Mary Ann anymore. It was like listening to a ghost.

"Tell her she's helped kill Herman, and Bernie doesn't want her anymore."

"You get out of here!" Suddenly Jake was yelling. "Emma never killed anyone in her life."

His head was out the screen door now. "She never killed anyone. Do you hear me? It's not her fault."

He yelled those words, *It's not her fault, fault, fault,* over and over. They echoed out into the hot June morning, as if the words could save Herman, as if they could bring back the long-dead Helen, the image of whose body lying in a long-ago bedroom, quiet except for the wails of the infant Emma, never disappeared. His words rumbled through the air long after Mary Ann Graubart, that hit-and-run artist, was gone.

9

Los Gatos, California
1970

JESSE AND CLIFTON sat at the long bar of the Claremont House in the little town of Los Gatos, seventy miles south of San Francisco, having a late-afternoon drink.

"Another?" Jesse caught Clifton's eye in the mirror.

Clifton stared back at the younger man's reflected face. Jesse was looking better and better every day.

"Sure. I told Maria I'd be a while."

"How's she doing?"

"Fine. Fine." Clifton leaned back on his bar stool. "I'll tell you, coming up here and marrying your landlady is the best thing I've ever done."

Jesse slapped him on the back and laughed. "Things going pretty good for you, old man?"

"Hell, Jesse, I hear you're not doing too badly yourself. Not from what you just showed me over at Montalvo. How's it feel, son, to be having a retrospective of your work at thirty-two? What did that reviewer in *Art News* call you, 'The Redwood Tree of Craftsmen'? Not bad at all for a little colored boy from Watts."

And Clifton was right, for both Jesse's skill and his fame had grown. Two of his pieces were in New York's Museum of Modern Art. He had spun his furniture back to his sculptural roots, crafting trompe l'oeil pieces, wardrobes hung with clothes so realistic that it took a close look to discover that they too were carved of wood. Both the Metropolitan and the Boston Museum of Fine Arts were asking for works from this newly opened Montalvo show.

"Yep, I sent Lucretia a clipping. She called and said, 'Boy, you're stepping in high cotton.' "

"What's next?"

"Think I'm going to take a break for a while."

"A break! You made it to the big time and you're laying off? No time to stop."

"I've been working like a madman since I was a boy, Clifton. Think I want to take some time to do something for myself."

"Humph. Don't sound like the Jesse Tree I know. You got something in mind?"

"I just closed the deal on an old inn up Highway 17 from my house. Think I'm going fix it up."

Clifton shook his head. "Houses eat you alive, boy, you know that even with your little place. An inn, you say? How big is that?"

"Oh, about fifty thousand square feet."

"Sheeeit! You mean you're going to hire some men to do the work."

"Nope. Think I want to do it all myself."

"Have you lost your mind?"

"Maybe. I just feel like I want to get out of the rat race for a while. Still make art, but coast. Maybe it's the scale of this that appeals to me." Jesse spread his arms. "Miles and miles of woodwork."

"Yeah, well, by the time you finish it, *Art News* is going to have forgotten your name. I think you're making a mistake."

They drank in silence for a while, each man pondering his and the other's words.

"You know what's wrong with you, Jesse?"

"I didn't know anything was, but what?"

"You need to settle down."

Jesse threw up both his hands. "Jumping Jesus H. Christ! You are infuckingcredible. You sound just like my grandma."

"Lucretia always was a smart old broad."

"You call her that to her face."

"Nah. I may be bad, but I ain't stupid. Anyway, what I said is true."

"I've settled down before. It didn't take."

"Marrying a woman for three months because she tricks you into thinking she's knocked up ain't my definition of settling down."

Jesse smiled. "Well, it counts. It makes me divorced."

"We're not talking about what the State of California calls it. We're talking about your stopping all this tomcatting around. You're getting too old for it."

"Mr. Marmaduke here don't think he's too old." Jesse was looking down past the front of the starched white shirt to the pressed jeans which had always been his uniform.

"I ain't talking about your dick, no matter what you call him. You too old to be thinking with you dick anyways."

"You know when you get mad you talk like a street nigger?"

"Next thing I know you gone tell me when I get mad I'm cute. Is that what you tell the women right before you break their hearts?"

"I don't break their hearts. I just don't make any promises I can't keep."

"And why's that? Why can't you just find some nice woman and settle down?"

"I think this is where I came in. We gonna sit here all night and argue?"

Clifton muttered under his breath.

"You say something, old man?"

"I said, 'Shut the fuck up and drink.' "

Jesse laughed. "You always were the sorest loser on earth."

Clifton pulled on his beer for a while before he started in again.

"Jesse, I want to talk about this. Serious."

"Well, I don't."

"Being married don't mean that you're tied down. If you got the right woman it *adds* something to your life, not subtracts from it. But the way you do it, how could you ever tell? Never been without a woman since you were fifteen, but none of them worth the time of day. They're like this inn you're talking about, reclamation projects."

"What do you mean?"

"Did it ever dawn on you that the women you spend your time with are not exactly what you'd call the cream of the crop?"

"Watch it, old man. I let it go once. Don't push me now."

"I mean it. Maybe if you thought about upping the quality of the company you keep, you'd find someone who was more your style. Somebody you'd want to come home to."

"You saying I go with trash?"

"Nawh. I'm not saying that. But I do think you're afraid to get tangled up with a woman who can give you a run for your money."

"And why do you think that is?"

Clifton leaned back on his bar stool and gave Jesse a long look. "You really want to know?"

"Yes, Professor Freud. They been letting you teach art up at the university on the hill so long, you think you know it all. Lay it on me."

"I think you're afraid if you let a real woman, a smart woman, get close to you, she'll run off. So it's just easier to hang with the good-time girls and never have to know."

AT a table just across the room, Emma Fine tasted a bowl of cioppino and her face lit up.

Not bad, she said to herself. Not bad at all. The fish soup could use just a touch less tomato and a hint more oregano, but it was good. Now, if aioli were served alongside the sourdough—but that would be asking too much. If you want that kind of cooking, Miss Fine, you ought to go down the street to your apartment and make it yourself.

But she didn't have time for that. That's why she was here grabbing a bite, because she didn't have time for anything these days.

How could she have gotten herself into this? What had made her think she could juggle two full-time jobs?

She looked at the list of things she had to do today.

She'd already driven the fifteen miles into Santa Clara and taught her two writing classes at the junior college. Her satchel was stuffed with compositions to be graded.

She had to pick up the wheel of Brie.

The bakery was going to close before she got there if she didn't hurry up.

She needed to call the butcher and remind him to butterfly the lamb.

Why did she think she could cater a sit-down wedding dinner for thirty-five in the middle of the week?

Don't you ever stop? her friends at school asked.

Nope, never.

But now she did. Just now, as she looked up from her list.

She ran her gaze down the bar, and then it stopped dead.

That, thought Emma, that is the goddamned handsomest man I've ever seen in my entire life.

She shook her head, took another look.

Well, but he *is* black, Emma.

Jesus Christ, I'm not blind. I can see that. My God, I bet he tastes like homemade chocolate ice cream.

Was the man next to him, the man he seemed to be arguing with, no, now they were laughing, was that his father? No, the older man was much too dark. But maybe the handsome man's mother was white.

Oh, Emma, you're such an expert, aren't you? Why, in your whole lifetime you've dated one black man. How many blacks do you even know, except at school?

This isn't a sociology lesson. This is sex.

Well, in that case, let's get down to it. Do you think he's so handsome *because* he's black? Because he's forbidden?

Forbidden by whom? This is 1970. This is California. This isn't West Cypress, for Christ's sake.

Come on, Emma. Don't you think he's kind of scary? So big and dark? Doesn't he conjure up your every little-white-girl fantasy?

Oh, no. I bet he's intelligent, even brilliant. I bet he's a nuclear physicist over at Lockheed.

You do not. You think he looks like something you'd like to wallow in for a few days even if he couldn't say an intelligible word. And you think he probably has a lovely cock.

At that Emma burst out laughing, sitting there alone holding a soup spoon.

A few minutes later, having paid her check, she was racing back up the steps of the restaurant. As if she weren't already late enough she'd left her satchel of papers under the table.

Inside, Jesse and Clifton were walking toward the door.

"Think about what I said."

"I will, old man, but lighten up. You're double-dogging me."

With that, Jesse shoved the front door. On the other side, Emma dropped her keys, leaned over to pick them up.

"Jesus, are you okay? Are you hurt?" The pretty blonde was crumpled over with a hand to her forehead. "Here, let me help you up."

"No, really, I'm fine."

Jesse didn't think so. He gripped her with an arm around the waist and lifted her to her feet.

"Do you want to lie down?"

"No." But inside she was reeling. It was true you saw stars.

"Let's take her inside and set her down." Clifton suggested. "And we'll call a doctor."

"No, no . . . I mean . . . yes, I'll lie down . . . but no doctor."

She was even prettier up close, soft, and this moment, in his arms, limp, loose as a goose. He had heard her Southern accent. Weren't all Southern women helpless?

Clifton caught his eye, and was that?—yes, it was, a wink. Jesse looked down at this woman. Holding her didn't seem like such a bad idea.

Then Clifton opened the door wide, and Jesse swooped Emma up in his arms.

"No, I can—"

"Shhhh." He carried her up up up the foyer steps.

My God, he was strong. What a lovely voice he had. She felt giddy. Miss Scarlett, she thought, you've just had a bit of brain damage, you silly.

JESSE ordered another drink. Across from him Emma shook her head. They were still in the bar of the Claremont House. She was playing with the straw in her ginger ale.

He didn't want to move. He was afraid even to excuse himself to the men's room, for fear he might break the spell. He wanted to keep her talking, so he crossed his legs, held his water and his breath.

Her blue eyes, bright and clear as Crater Lake, were truly, as the people who said those things said, mirrors of her soul. She had nowhere to hide behind those eyes. As she talked, weaving stories the likes of which he'd never heard, through them flickered as clearly as subtitles on a screen joy, hope, fear, disappointment, pain. Behind those beautiful blue windows lived a woman who could never pull her shades, tell a lie, and get away with it.

He watched her slender hands flutter. She could tell stories for the deaf. Every once in a while her fingers crept up and brushed her long pale hair. She flung it back behind her ears, grabbed it with one hand and twisted it atop her head, then let it fall like water down into a golden pool on her shoulders again.

He didn't think she knew she did that—any more than she knew how lovely she was.

"You're a very pretty woman," he said.

She brushed the compliment off as if it were lint. But he saw, for just a moment, inside those eyes, Emma smile, blush and hold her breath. Me, pretty? Yes, you, his eyes smiled back, but the moment was gone, had passed, as Emma's words raced on, the honeyed sounds filling the bar's smoky air with the smell of magnolias and hot summer evenings until she hit the word "New York." Only New Yorkers said it like that.

"How long did you live there?"

"Two, three years." She waved a hand as if a year, more or less, made no difference.

Jesse had visited New York, of course, its museums, galleries. He had always found it exciting. But he could never imagine leaving California for all that frozen unyielding and judgmental concrete.

But look at this golden girl before him, sipping ginger ale through a straw. She'd lived in New York as if it were nothing and had survived to tell the tale.

"And why did you move to New York from . . . Atlanta?"

"Correct, Atlanta." She nodded and he felt her approval for his having listened well.

He was already memorizing her words so that he could take them home with him, run his tongue over their sounds late at night.

"It's a long story." She hesitated.

"Go on."

"Well. Atlanta seemed so big when I first got there, after I left West Cypress."

She said her hometown's name as if she were saying "Ibiza" or "Saint Moritz." *West Cypress*. The initiated would know that hamlet. It was an in joke, between Emma and herself.

"And then all of a sudden, after three years, it started to feel like a small town."

"How can you keep 'em down in Atlanta after they've seen New York?"

"That *was* part of it. But then, too, I needed to get the hell out of Dodge."

"Do I smell a rat in this scenario? Or just a broken heart?"

"A little of both, I guess. The second year I was in Atlanta, I was teaching composition at this downtown college, and one of my students, she was about a year younger than I, said, 'My brother Will's coming back to town, and when he does, you've got to meet him.' Sure, sure, I said, and then one day I was waltzing down the hall toward my office, and leaning against the door was the—" Emma stopped herself then, as she rarely did, for usually she just blundered on, never letting tact get in the way of a good line.

"Yessss?" Jesse asked with a grin, as if he could read her mind. Though come to think of it, he wasn't so sure he wanted to hear the rest of this story.

"Was the handsomest man I've ever seen," was how she usually finished that line. But sitting there, looking at Jesse, she'd have to say handsomest white man.

And, lordy, Will had been that. Tall and lanky and blond, his hair almost white, with deep-green eyes. It had been Katie-bar-the-door-love-at-first-sight throughout one of those springs in Atlanta, well, Emma thought every spring was like that there, with the lilacs, azaleas, wisteria and dogwood blooming all at one time until the air was so heavy with their perfume that the whole city smelled like sex. Springtime in Atlanta made Emma crazier than thunderstorms in West Cypress ever had. And watching Will enter a room was ten times more exciting than lightning flashing. She was positively disoriented with love, perfume and lust. Between the spring and Will, all she did was sit on her back steps with him and kiss, spoon, then together they'd lie naked in her bed under the moonlight. Every once in a while she'd get a fit on her, jump into her little beat-up convertible and drive hell for leather until she got to the Chattahoochee River. She almost drove off into it several times after Will announced one morning that he thought he'd be moving on.

"I guess I deserved the broken heart," she said now to Jesse. "Reckon in the balance of things it was my just desserts for Bernie."

Jesse remembered Bernie. She'd mentioned him about twelve stories back.

"But I tell you what. I like to have died." When Emma reminisced about old times her accent always got cornpone Southern.

"Cut you up bad?"

"Something terrible. It drove me nuts, see, that I never could convince Will that I truly loved him. He said he always felt that I was holding something back. That I really had something else in mind, was on some other track."

"Was that true?"

"No. It wasn't." She looked Jesse squarely in his big brown eyes and wondered, Why the hell am I telling this man this? Which didn't stop her from going on. "Will was the love of my life. But I know what he was talking about—well, I sort of know."

What Emma knew, even at twenty-one, was that she had the ability to confound the bejesus out of men. But she never quite got the mechanics of their quandary. She'd tell them exactly what was on her mind, good or bad, Emma was frank, up front, forthright, way beyond a fault. And that either unnerved them completely, so that they turned and ran immediately for the shelter of some softer, gentler, easier woman's skirts, or, like Will, himself no uncomplicated man, they thought the honesty was itself a cover.

"It's a weapon, Emma," he'd said, frowning at her. "It's all about control. It's a way of keeping it all in your hands, calling the shots, and in the end nobody really gets close to you."

Well, Jesse thought, I know what *that's* all about. But he couldn't imagine that he'd ever admit it, not the way Emma did—or was that not exactly what she was talking about?

"I really wanted to let Will in," she said to Jesse.

"So why didn't you?"

Emma shrugged. Her smile was wry. "I guess I didn't know how."

"And since then?"

"Since then I've rarely met anyone that I didn't, in the middle of the first date, think I'd rather be home washing my hair."

Didn't she know, Jesse wondered, that she should never *ever* say things like that to a man, who would ask himself, as he did, whether she wished she were home washing her hair right now?

"So you left Atlanta because of Will?"

"Well, I was still mourning for him a year later, couldn't figure out what the hell I wanted to do, so I spent a lot of time feeding the ducks in Piedmont Park, pining and thinking."

"Thinking about what?"

"Where I wanted to be. I just felt so restless. By then Will had married somebody else and I'd sat behind them once at the movies. When she stood up and I saw she was pregnant, I was sick. I said to myself, Girl, this is over, done, you've got to figure out your next step. What do you want? Who the hell are you? I decided that if I went somewhere else, somewhere big like New York, one day I would turn a corner, run into someone on the street, and it would be me."

She still carried a calling card that read: "Emma Fine, Traveling." It was a Holly Golightly conceit, but it had fit then, and did yet, for Emma was still traveling and still looking.

"So Atlanta wasn't the place to find yourself?"

"Nope, never bumped into her like I bumped into you." They both smiled, and Emma touched the lump on her forehead that was turning purplish black.

Jesse waited. He had already learned, in the past almost three hours, that she would come full circle if he'd just wait. Was this Southern, he wondered, her way of talking that flung bits of a story way out like a wide net and then took its own sweet time in pulling them back? Or was it Emma?

"But before I pulled up stakes, and I don't think this was very logical, nor was it very kind, I back-pedaled a little before moving on down the road that third spring. I went to see Bernie."

"Can we blame it on the azaleas? Were they blooming that spring, too?"

"They were," she laughed. "We could say I was blossom crazed."

"And what happened? Bernie shot you? Told you to jump off the Chattahoochee Bridge? Was married?"

Emma ignored him, refusing to ruin a perfectly good story by rushing the punch line. She took her own sweet time telling him how she'd visited Bernie in Miami, how he'd told her that he had a fiancee, thank you, and didn't need her stepping on his heart and mashing it flat again, how he thought she ought to be talking with Herman anyway, not him.

"I think you got the wrong Graubart here, sweetie," was how he put it. "It's my old man, not me, who answered your questions when you were confused. You ought to go see him anyway."

For Herman was still alive; he hadn't died as Mary Ann had predicted, but he wasn't well.

"So you went to see Herman?" Jesse asked.

"No, I didn't. And that's something I'll always regret. I didn't feel like going to West Cypress. So I went back to feeding those goddamned ducks in Piedmont Park. They were beginning to look like blimps. And only a week later the call came from Bern. It was forever too late to ask Herman's advice about anything, because he was dead."

Emma stared off into space for a while, picturing Herman in his white baseball cap.

"And then?" Jessie's voice was soft.

"When he died? I went crazy. Got in my car and ran away up to north Georgia. Ever been there?"

Jesse shook his head.

"Beautiful country. Foothills of the Smokies, blue-hazed. Not, of course, that beauty made much difference in the state of mind I was in. *Berserk.* I bought half a case of bourbon and a sackful of Hersheys, crackers and tuna fish. I checked into a motel in a town called Helen, stayed there for a week, drinking, listening to the radio, mourning Herman who was like my dad, I mean, not like *my* dad, because Herman talked to me and my daddy hardly does, but you know what I mean. Anyway, outside the sign flashed off and on: OTEL, OTEL, OTEL. Herman would have loved it, the way I sat shivah for him. But then he always thought everything I did was wonderful. Except instead of bourbon, he'd have preferred schnapps."

Emma paused a moment, and Jesse thought for just an instant that he could look straight through those blue eyes, out the back of her head, and see mist-covered hills and that motel sign.

"Helen was my mother's name. That's why I stopped there, I think. Well, I know it was."

Jesse paged back to something she'd said about an hour ago. "I thought your mother's name was Rosalie."

"My *step*mother. My *real* mother was Helen. And she was from right near Helen, Georgia. From Tallulah Falls, just south of Rabun Gap. But I never went there."

"Your real mother—"

Emma shook her head. "We don't have time for that now." But then added, as if Jesse would know what she was talking about, "I finally wrote for her death certificate."

"Whose?"

"My mother Helen's. My father still won't talk about her much, I guess really he doesn't remember. But *I* would," she added fiercely. "Don't you think if you really love somebody you remember *everything*, the rest of your life?"

Jesse didn't have time to nod or shake his head as she raced on.

"But anyway, just that spring I had sent off to Baltimore, and the certificate says she was born in Tallulah Falls on Independence Day in 1906."

Did she always talk like this? He knew she couldn't be drunk. One cognac and three ginger ales couldn't do the trick.

"After that," she said, making another leap, "after I got over Herman, I packed up and went to New York."

"And you found yourself, the person you were looking to bump into in New York?"

Well, no, not quite. For a while she had loved the city, loved Europe the two summers she'd been, had felt that she'd walked before, perhaps in a past life, the streets of London and lanes of southern France, and that she was only rediscovering the pâté, the bread, the wine. The food itself reawakened in her a hunger for something she couldn't quite put her tongue or finger on. That's when she'd begun taking cooking seriously, attended night classes at a Manhattan culinary school—though she wasn't sure to what purpose. She'd visited northern California and felt an attraction so strong she's moved out there. She loved California, but still she was restless. To this day, nothing, no one, neither career nor lover, had ever filled her up. Though, as if cooking were the literal answer to her hunger, she was most content in her kitchen, playing with food.

Which reminded her, she had completely blown it. She was never going to get this meal together. Thirty-five people at a wedding day after tomorrow were going to starve.

She said as much to Jesse, who replied, "Hell, let 'em eat cake."

But she was gathering her things about her now. She picked up her satchel full of papers off the floor where hours ago she'd left it.

"No. It's late." She looked at her watch. "I've really got to go." She stood.

"Your head?"

"It's fine."

"It's not *that* late," he said. And then panic rose in Jesse's breast. He was afraid if he didn't move quickly this woman was going to walk forever out that door, for his smack to her head had only slowed her down. And for the first and only time in his life, he didn't think he could stand that.

WITHIN five minutes of watching Jesse carry Emma inside, Clifton had said, "Got to shove off, old man."

Then, leaving Los Gatos behind, he had headed north, the long way up the windswept coast. He could still see the look that passed between Emma and Jesse as he settled her on a sofa, a look bright as neon. He could project it out onto the highway now as if it were burned on his retina, a scarlet road sign pointing toward home. Standing in the chill at a pay phone overlooking the Pacific, he crossed his fingers as the silver coins he dropped sounded—bong, bong.

Maria said, "I'll wait an hour. Then I'll put your coffee on."

Clifton grinned. There's nothing finer in this world, he thought, stepping back into his battered Karmann-Ghia. He tuned in KJAZ on the radio. Ray Charles and Betty Carter were singing together, "Baby, it's cold outside." There's nothing finer in the whole wide world, he thought, watching the red sun drop off toward China, than heading home to your baby's arms.

"HERE, let me walk you to your car." They stepped outside. Each took a deep breath.

"God, it smells good out here."

Jesse agreed. "After all that smoke."

And then an awkwardness fell upon them along with the twilight. It was different outside with no drinks to hold, no straws to twiddle, no props.

Emma ran her eyes up Jesse's jeaned legs, up the starched white shirt, out across the broad shoulders that made him look even bigger than he was.

I like this man, she thought.

Come, now, Emma. *Like* is not what you feel when you spot someone across a room. And all this time you've been running your mouth, *like* is not what you've been thinking about.

SHE's wearing no rings, no jewelry except a cameo locket on a golden chain. Has she ever? Despite what she says about being bored by men, how tightly has she been wrapped with another?

Can I count her ribs through her slenderness with my tongue?
If I do, what kinds of sounds will she make? When she's played
in the proper key, does she hum with a Southern accent? Is she
too much of a lady, or does she scream when she comes?

Up close, what does he smell like? Did all black men have that
musky scent that rubs off, like David, her only black lover?
Sometimes, after she'd left David in his closetlike apartment on
New York's Upper West Side, she'd sniff the oil his skin left on
her hands, her arms. She's sit on the subway breathing in his
aroma and get turned on all over again. There was a lot about
David to get turned on to. Not that they'd had much to say to
each other; in fact, as with many other men, she'd wanted to put
her hand over his mouth. Hush, she'd wanted to whisper, don't
ruin it by saying something stupid. Just make me happy for a
bit with all those clever tricks you know so well.

But she wanted to hear this Jesse Tree's tales.

Like the one he'd told her about spending childhood summers
in Sacramento in a stepfather's whorehouse. About sketching a
whore named Loubella with gigantic breasts. She could listen
to him all night, it was foreign, fascinating stuff, if she could
only get past the thrumming in her thighs that was reverberating
in her head.

She looked down at his wide beautiful hands. She'd seen his
work once in a show and many times pictured in magazines.
What other clever things could those hands do?

I'd like to tell her how much I want to reach out and cup her
butt. I'd like to sketch it, too, sculpt it in rosewood. Sculpt it
with my warm self.

I don't want to go home alone to my big bed. Tonight I want
to be held and loved.

And then I'll add his name to the list in the little notebook
in my bottom dresser drawer, the list of men I have known—in
the biblical sense.

Though she could no longer put faces to some of the names,
there were several who had established respectable tenure. But
then the time would always come when she would push them
away, usually because she was bored, but sometimes because she

felt she was suffocating, for they wanted to confine her within some small vision that felt to her like the city limits of West Cypress. Only once or twice since Will had she met someone she'd thought was the one, and then, ah, then something in her had set up a panic, a scenario of betrayal and abandonment. *Then* her touch had become as mucilaginous as wasp's saliva, and, of course, the men had run. She'd never know whether she would have tired of them or not.

She could see his name now in her back-slanted script, perhaps the most famous of them all, except for that gray-haired novelist in New York. She could see the words in the purple ink she saved for the little notebook: *Jesse Tree.*

He touched her elbow and she jumped.

"I said, 'Why don't you come with me for a ride up the mountain?' There's something I'd like you to see."

I bet I've seen it before, thought Emma.

Which just goes to show you how wrong she could be.

LIKE Louisiana's Highway 80 of Emma's childhood, California 17 had a well-earned reputation for murder and mayhem as it snaked its way from Los Gatos up and over the summit of the Santa Cruz Mountains.

Jesse was an expert driver, but still Emma flinched at every curve. She looked out into the rapidly darkening twilight. In a moment it would be pitch-dark. "You live along here?"

"Off there." Jesse pointed to a marker on their right that read CANYON ROAD. "Been up that way?"

"Probably. I've done lots of exploring, driving around. I love these mountains. I wouldn't mind living up here or over there in Santa Cruz by the ocean, but I think the drive would make me crazy. They say it's getting worse all the time."

"It's not so bad from here. It's worth it to get away from everything."

"I know. But I guess Los Gatos is far enough away for me."

"Nice place to visit. But I wouldn't want to live there."

Emma laughed. "I can just see you in New York."

"Never. I like being a hermit up here in my little house on my little hill."

"You've always lived alone?"

"For the most part."

So what did that mean?

They whipped around one curve, then another, on up the mountains. There wasn't much traffic. Now the road was *really* dark. And then a finger of fear tapped Emma lightly on the shoulder. Where was she going with this stranger, even if he had a name that was known, up this highway that led to little roads, that led to paths, that led to lonely woods, that led to who knew where?

His old Morgan's tires whooshed on the snakelike pavement. He could secretly be a murderer or one of those men you read about in the paper who spirits a person away, locks her in a little room and holds her captive from the world for months or years or eternity. And what more perfect hideaway than these mountains. Who would know?

The mountains did have a reputation. They had been home to bandits and robbers in the Old West. Now there were rumors of armed helicopters landing at Scott's Valley smuggling in bales of pungent Mexican grass, tales of hitchhiking coeds from UC Santa Cruz found headless in shallow graves. People hid out here in remote cabins, safe at the ends of deeply rutted roads, odd, strange folk who didn't fit in below in the valley.

They were slowing. Jesse turned at a sign that said SUMMIT ROAD.

"It's only a little way now."

"What are we going to see?" She hoped her voice sounded calm.

She *could* open the door and jump. But jump to where in this lonely darkness? From this skillet into what fire?

Suddenly Jesse threw an arm across her, swerved, and slammed on the brakes.

She screamed. Her heart leaped out into the road, where it joined a bounding fawn, his white undertail flashing now as he melted back into the darkness.

For a minute the car was still. There was no sound. Neither of them was breathing.

Then Jesse put a hand on her shoulder. "I'm sorry, I didn't mean to scare you or to hurt you—again."

She relaxed back into the leather seat.

"Lots of animals up here," he said then, pulling the car back onto the road. "Possum, racoons, rabbits, some say cougars, but I think that's a myth."

"Do you hunt?"

"Nope. Don't believe in it."

Good, she thought.

The headlights swept a half-hidden sign then, and they turned off to the right.

"What did the sign say?"

" 'Skytop.' "

"What's that?"

"Hold on a couple seconds and I'll show you."

They drove only a few more yards now, off onto a rutted drive. The low little car bounced along, moving at a crawl that seemed to be as much vertical as lateral, and then its headlights swept onto a large log structure. Jesse stopped the car and turned off the ignition. He reached under the seat and pulled out a large flashlight with which he pointed.

"My baby," he said.

JESSE leaned over and gave her a hand up onto the wide-planked porch.

"Be careful. Nothing here's as substantial as it seems."

That was for sure. Emma skirted a large gap in the flooring that suddenly appeared, a rabbit hole that led to God knows where. And then a flash of déjà vu hit her—Herman opening the door to his secret forest house.

"Just hold my hand. I've been here a million times before."

The pine-finished front room was ballroom-sized, two stories high. A stone fireplace big enough for a couple of steers dominated the back wall. Along another ran a gallery at second-story height. A series of evenly spaced doors opened off the gallery.

"Bedrooms," Jesse said.

"What *was* this?"

"A lodge, a hotel of sorts. It's been abandoned now for a long time. But once this was *the* spot in the mountains. People used to drive down all the way from San Francisco, over from Santa Cruz, to dance and drink and gamble till the small hours, and then they'd stay in a room upstairs for the night."

"You're kidding."

"I've never been more serious in my life."

"How come I never heard of this place?"

Jesse shrugged. "Why would you? All that's been over now for almost forty years."

"A saloon?" Emma imagined spangled dancing girls, swinging doors, silver revolvers flashing from holsters laced against hard cowboy thighs.

"'Speakeasy' would be a better word. Come the end of Prohibition and the beginning of the Depression, it fell on hard times. But it sure saw its share of good ones."

Emma crossed over and ran her fingers along the dust-shrouded rosewood bar. The mirror behind it was splotched and blackened in spots but still intact.

"How do you know all this?"

"Bart, my neighbor, brought me up here. His family's lived in the mountains for three generations."

"Who owns it now?"

"I do. I just bought it—am about to start fixing it up. When it's finished, I'll run it again as an inn.

"Like the Awahnee in Yosemite?"

"Sure. Smaller, of course, more intimate. But . . ." He paused and Emma knew that he was seeing his dream in his head. "It would be more than that, too."

And then Emma's own fantasy raised its hand. "Would it have a restaurant?"

"Sure, and a gallery." He swept one arm wide, along with the flashlight, and Emma saw the acres of space.

"For your work."

He shrugged. "And others'."

"An art gallery in the woods." Emma walked right into Jesse's dream. "With all this height, the work could be hung one above another like in Gertrude Stein's living room. Huge paintings that can't be hung anyplace else. For openings, there'll be chamber music, giant potted palms. It'll be like the Plaza. A Sunday afternoon saloon salon."

Jesse laughed. "And after they're drunk on culture and champagne, they can spend the night. Here." He took her hand. "There's another wing. I'll show you."

He pulled her with him in a rush to show it all, through a cavernous kitchen, a pantry, a storeroom, down a hall and up a flight of half-broken stairs. There were ten more rooms opening off a narrow hall. Some still had beds that now looked like nests.

"Do you think people sneak in to sleep here sometimes?" Emma whispered in the dark.

"Probably not now. But who's to know?"

Emma's imagination took another leap. She shivered. It *could* harbor criminals, robbers, bandits. It could.

"Follow me," Jesse was saying now, leading the way back down the stairs. "I'll go ahead and catch you if you fall."

He took her hand again. *Oh!* She'd been so swept away by Jesse's dream that she'd forgotten for a time about the actual physical man. But now the electricity that had for hours in the Claremont House kept her sitting on the edge of her chair traveled up through her fingers, down her arm, warmed her breast.

She clutched his hand tighter.

He turned, and the glow of the flashlight illuminated her face.

"Are you okay?" he asked.

She looked into his eyes and then she had to look away. For she was drawn into them, into him, like a moth. And he knew that in an instant. She could see recognition of his power in the corners of his eyes, his mouth. He knew that he could pull her back the other way, lead her into one of those little rooms, and have his way, her way, their way.

"Sure," she said, "just a little out of breath."

Their steps were loud as they made their way back down the stairway.

Then they were again in the living room, Jesse's flashlight once more lighting the hearth, the fireplace.

But there, just there, leaning against that wall, what was that?

Emma took his wrist and redirected the light.

"Look!"

Jesse said nothing, but held the torch steady.

Emma moved forward from his side. "It's a painting."

"Yes."

"God, it's so beautiful. *She's* so beautiful."

The strong golden light fell upon a woman's face that stared right back into her own. The seashell skin was like porcelain, all of the naked flesh from her forehead right down to her feet. There was a hint of Botticelli about her, the translucent drape, the long swinging rope of silver hair.

"She's breathtaking."

"Umm," Jesse murmured.

"Is that your work?"

He nodded yes. "I used to work in oils when I was young."

"But why did you hang it here? Someone will steal it."

He laughed a little. "It's not hung. It's painted on the wall."

Emma turned and looked at him. His eyes were still on the woman.

"Then you can't ever take her away."

"I don't want to."

Emma looked around the dilapidated room. "Lot of work here."

But she really had no idea. Her imagination ran ahead, skipping right over the renovation to the finished product. She had moved right into Jesse's fantasy, merging it with her own most recent dream of opening a restaurant. She saw herself in a white apron, stirring huge stock pots, cooking astonishing meals, just one menu each night, what she had was what you ate, like a favorite place in Provence. Wouldn't it be the most fun in the world, to own a place like this where you could feed people, tuck them in at night, see them like family in the morning? A place where they'd feel at home?

"I didn't think I had the eyes right till now."

Emma started at the sound of Jesse's voice. In her mind she'd been out gathering lettuce from the kitchen garden she'd planted outside the door.

"What?"

"The eyes. I didn't think I had them right till now."

Emma followed his gaze back to the portrait. She found herself staring straight into lake-blue eyes. It was like looking into a mirror.

Jesse switched off the flash. In the moonlight the painting shimmered.

He moved one step closer and placed his hands on her shoulders.

Then the fantasy in which she'd been playacting dropped away. This was the here and now. She reached up and with one forefinger touched his bottom lip.

"You have the most beautiful mouth." She'd been wanting to say that for hours. They both leaned just a fraction closer and their mouths joined in a kiss.

His arms held her closer and tighter until she felt that she had stepped through the wall of his chest and was now inside.

"Jewish eyes," he murmured. "That's what I was thinking about when I was doing the painting."

"Southern Baptist–Jewish eyes."

"You'll have to tell me about that." And then he ran the edge of his tongue down the side of her neck. Her flesh tingled as if his tongue were electric.

"Another time," she said.

"Sure. We've got plenty."

But not right then they didn't, for their mouths had so much to do without talking.

From behind the remnants of a sofa Jesse produced a drop cloth and laid it on the floor. He lit a kerosene lantern, turning that corner of the room sepia.

He stared straight into her eyes as his fingers unfastened the buttons of her blouse. She didn't look away this time, but held his gaze fast.

Later, she didn't remember what he did with her lace-trimmed camisole and panties, but they disappeared as if he had sucked them off and chewed them up before he began to nibble on her flesh.

"Ears," he whispered. "You have the most wonderful ears. You saved them for me under all that golden hair."

He explored every crevice with his tongue, his teeth, his lips, until she moaned with the thrust of his tongue as if he had penetrated her and pinned her to the floor. Her ear was burning, hot, open, and she heard herself screaming into the big reverberating room, *"Jesse, fuck me, fuck me,"* when he wasn't even close.

"Oh, no," he whispered. "My dear, we've only begun."

For Jesse was good, very good. He flipped her over on her stomach, one hand pinned beneath her. The other he bent against her back.

He held her in poses. In her mind, which always saw pictures when the sex was good, they were still lifes, spare in composition, illustrated haiku.

> *The swan tucked her long neck into the dark water*
> *Pierced by his gilt stake.*

But he didn't enter her. He took her with his mouth again, his tongue tracing the curves of her behind.

His control was complete. She couldn't move a hand. She couldn't caress him in return but could only receive what he chose to give.

Her whole body was alive, hungry, parched for his lips as he concentrated on only one place at a time, giving it his total attention while the rest of her quivered, waiting in line.

"I want you everywhere," she moaned. "Touch me all over."

Jesse stopped for a moment, lifted his head from her as if he were a drinking animal who had heard a rustle in the forest.

And in that moment he loosened his hold and Emma turned beneath him. She was desperate for his touch, his weight, everywhere upon her.

He withheld himself for just an eternity more, lingering above her, only an inch of air separating them as he leaned upon his elbows staring down into her face.

"Please," she pushed the word between clenched teeth.

"Please what?"

You could butter your bread with his words, she thought, and eat it for your lunch.

"Please touch me, please fuck me, please be with me."

"Where?" he whispered.

She pushed her breast up into him.

"There," she answered.

"Where?"

Her pelvis grazed his.

"Where?"

Her mouth sucked his into hers, her teeth devouring his lips.

"I want you," she said.

"Swear?"

"I swear."

"Swear?"

"I swear."

"There now, then," he cried, and he pushed himself into her with no further preamble, but then none was needed, as she had never been more ready in her life. He lifted her knees upon his shoulders, and her screams bounced off the walls where just minutes, or was that hours ago now, they had talked about pictures being hung. They rode together for what seemed like days, but then Emma would never know, for she was completely adrift in time and space. They rode through foreign landscapes, along paths, beside silver streams, and then finally Emma could see a clearing at the top. Together they were approaching a high mountain plain.

Beneath him Emma hummed. Butterflies swarmed around her breast, around her knees, and then they dove right through her center and fluttered, fluttered now in waves, fluttered out her mouth, her ears, her nose, her eyes, out the top of her head, and on, free now, out the windows.

SOME time later as they lay stretched out upon the blanket with the lamplight shining on their damp bodies, Emma murmured, "I have to go and buy a wheel of Brie."

Jesse's laugh rumbled up to the high ceiling, where Emma, with her eyes closed, could still see one butterfly stuck. "I don't think so. Not tonight."

"Jesus. I've really screwed up. What am I going to do?"

And then Jesse opened his mouth and out flew the words before he had time to think.

"You're going to come and live with me."

"Yeah, yeah, yeah, but what am I going to do about the cheese? What am I going to do about that wedding party night after tomorrow?"

"What the hell do you mean, 'Yeah, yeah, yeah'?" Jesse was leaning now on one elbow, staring down into her face.

"I mean, yes, I accept, and thank you very much. But that still doesn't get me a wheel of Brie."

" 'Thank me very much.' *Fuck* me very much."

"Oh, Jesse, don't be so melodramatic. Didn't you know this was going to happen from the moment you hit me in the head with that door?"

He paused. Well, yes. He'd hoped so.

"So? So what's the big deal? Why the big surprise if you could see it coming a mile off?" Then she burst into laughter and gathered him into an embrace.

But she was bluffing, Miss Emma Fine was, trembling with terror and bluffing all the way. For she knew no more about living with love (nor did he) than she knew about renovating houses, much less an undertaking as large as Jesse and Skytop Lodge. And she didn't know that when she held her nose, for she'd never learned to hold her breath, and jumped off the diving board into the depths of Jesse Tree, she was way, way, way over her head.

THAT first year went like quicksilver. Emma didn't have time to think.

Jesse had bought an old Ford pickup truck. They named it Elvira.

"You choose," Jesse said, standing before her with a fan of color samples.

She didn't hesitate a moment. They painted Elvira the rosy pink that had become Emma's trademark. Then they loaded her up with Emma's things. It took two trips just for her kitchen stuff.

"We should have used movers."

"Yeah. But they wouldn't let us sing."

They sang up and down the mountain. He took the low parts, she the high, and then they reversed. Jesse's falsetto was something to behold.

> *Row, row, row your boat, gently down the stream.*
> *Merrily, merrily, merrily, merrily, life is but a dream.*

And it was. Emma couldn't believe her good fortune, when she had moments to catch her breath. What had she been so afraid of all these years? She had never been so happy or so busy in her life.

There was much to do. For starters, though Jesse had had a world-class woodworking studio built in the side yard, his decorating efforts on the house hadn't gone beyond knocking out most of the interior walls and painting it all white.

"It looks like a hospital in here."

He held out the color samples again.

The stairs to the two little rooms above shone with a lacquered blue. The front door was bright yellow.

"Friendly, don't you think?" Emma stood back and inspected their handiwork.

"Yes. But who are we being friendly with?"

For no one ever came up the winding little road looking for them—their rare invitation was to Maria and Clifton. The truth be known, they didn't need anybody else. They were a world within themselves, round, fat as a tick, complete.

They didn't own a television.

They lay in bed propped on a sea of pillows and stared at each other's toes.

"Yours are beautiful. Just like your hands. Mine are weird."

"You can say that again."

"Mine are weird."

Then he took a footful of her toes in his mouth.

"If I suck on this little middle one, do you think it will grow?"

"Nope, my father's never did. It's part of my inheritance."

"Do all Jews have a short middle toe?"

"Do all blacks have little bitty dicks?"

"Yep. All of us. Now why don't you suck on this one and see if it'll grow bigger than your toe?"

"Lawdy, Mistah Jesse, leave me be, I don't know nothing 'bout sucking dicks."

EMMA asked, "What do you think about puce for the bathroom?"

"I think your cousin Wanda June's tastes has rubbed off on you."

Wanda June Cooter was one of Jesse's favorites. She was Emma's stepaunt Janey's only girl.

"Tell me another Cooter bedtime story," Jesse begged of Emma sitting beside him in one of his old T-shirts.

"I don't think it's nice you making fun of my relatives, Jesse."

"They're no more your kin than I am, honey bun."

So once again Emma would tell about how when they were children Wanda June got to pick all the colors of the Cooter house. The living room was bright orange. The dining room chocolate brown.

"You'd drop something in there off the table, you might as well have thrown it down the outhouse for all you could see. Smelled like that, too, sort of. Their house was way out in the country, out past Bernie's, and always smelled like cold dishwater, sorghum syrup and beans."

Wanda June's room was deepest orchid. The boys' rooms were red, navy and snow-pea green.

Jesse picked it up. "And in her purse, just in case, she carried . . . you tell it."

"Why, you know it all by heart."

"Nope." He stuck his tongue out. Now they were sitting out in the carport they'd screened in and planted like a florist's shop with begonias, fuchsias and ferns.

"She carried a bottle of Mercurochrome and the number of the FBI."

Jesse slapped his leg. "Now do Lollie, do Lollie," he begged.

So once again she told him about Wanda June's brother Lollie Cooter who invented his own religion which had all the trappings of Christianity except Jesus. "I told him he didn't know it but he'd become a Jew." He quit his job as a washing-machine repairman and devoted full time to proselytizing. He built a billboard in front of the house he and his mother, Janey, lived in when they moved to town. "Look Here, Sinners," it began.

"Do you think I'm getting fat?" Emma asked.

"Well, you might be. If you're leading up to being pregnant, go pin it on one of the dudes you screw when I'm up in the studio." It was one of their running jokes. For Jesse had had himself fixed after the woman named Patience whom he married for three months had tricked him with her false pregnancy. And Emma wouldn't have looked at another man if she'd had the energy. Which she didn't. Jesse used it all up.

"Is there a square inch of this house on which we haven't banged yet?" she asked.

Jesse pulled on his mustache. "How about the doormat?"

"Pull the sucker in here. Can't hurt its feelings, leaving it out."

"Is it May yet?"

Emma checked her watch. Actually, she'd completely lost track of the seasons. Sometimes she was so consumed with Jesse, his taste, his smell, his voice, his touch, that she didn't even know what day it was. Her students at the junior college thought she was on drugs.

"I think it's May fifteenth," she said.

"By God, we've missed the beginning of outdoor fucking season by over two weeks. I want your sweet ass on this doormat at good dark."

To answer Emma's question, they should have been getting fat, for her genius in the kitchen had gone berserk. She cooked in at least eight languages now. Her catering was getting to be a problem. She had to expand or quit.

"Why don't we just move down into Los Gatos to the Safeway?" Jesse asked. "It'll save us carting all those groceries up the hill."

Emma just smiled and kept on cooking, twirling her wooden spoons and her French knives as if she were a magician dressed in kitchen whites.

Besides, she liked taking Jesse to the grocery store with her. She liked handing him a list and his own cart and then trailing behind as if she were a stranger, watching the looks women gave him. Some of them crashed their buggies into his on purpose, some because they had seen him only at the last minute and had been stunned like a deer in the light. They winked. They dimpled. They twitched their behinds. Driving back up the mountain, Emma could hardly keep her hands off him. Sometimes she didn't.

"Emma, Emma, stop," he said to the top of her head buried in his lap. "Stop. I can't drive while you do that."

"Then pull over."

SKYTOP was the only blemish on the peach of their contentment. It just wasn't going as planned.

"How long's the new subflooring on the porch going to take if I come help you pound nails?"

"A weekend."

Three weekends later Emma was still pulling splinters from her ruined manicure, and it wasn't finished yet.

"Do you think this is going to take longer than you planned?"

Jesse frowned and grew silent and Emma bit her tongue.

WHEN they met, Jesse was a scotch drinker, but after two or three she didn't like him much.

"You ought not to do this to yourself—and to us."

"You got a better suggestion?"

"I'd rather dance."

"Apples and oranges," he said.

Emma did some research.

"You want the Giggles, the Zombie, the I Need a Cookie, or the Motha, Just Let Me Lie Down?" Emma had the marijuana separated, nicknamed and labeled in cannisters on a kitchen shelf. She bought it from their next-door neighbor, an entrepreneur of wholesale smoke.

"Just roll one of each and we'll decide when we get to the Catalyst."

On the way to Santa Cruz, they never smoked until they were

over the mountains with the ocean in sight. Otherwise, like so
many others, they'd have been roadkill, victims of the unfor-
giving Highway 17.

The Catalyst met all of Emma's requirements: it was old and
funky, a bar, a dance hall, a good café, a coffeehouse, all in one.

Somewhere between the car door and the Catalyst's palm trees,
Emma lit up.

"I can hear the colors of the music," she said as they passed
through the swinging doors. She took Jesse's hand.

"Let's dance to the purple, Jess."

"Just a minute, hon."

Jesse didn't really like to dance, but she was twirling already,
out on the floor with the couples, the trios, the children, the
dogs. It was that kind of place. One old man swayed every night
before a speaker that was twice as tall as he.

"Never," said Emma, looking a gigantic whole-grain tostada in
the face while a Stones tune shook the table, "never eat anything
bigger than your head."

"If one could find your head." Jesse smiled, for he knew it
could be anywhere. He loved to watch Emma when she was
stoned. God, how the woman flew. Loosey-goosey. She giggled.
She shook her booty to the music. And more than once she'd
taken his hand and led him out to the street, where she'd pulled
him into the nearest darkened doorway and lifted her skirt above
her hips.

"Do me, Jess," she whispered. 'I can't wait till we get home."

Oh, yes, Jesse loved Emma and the naughty woman she became when she was stoned.

Now, if things would only go right with Skytop. He couldn't
get a handle on it. He couldn't figure out what was wrong. He
couldn't get the flow going. He kept bumping into corners, running into blind alleys. He'd start in one room, and then another
would seem to be calling to him.

Emma stood with a hand on one hip, the tip of her tongue
poised to point to the heart of the matter.

"You're all over the lot here, Jess. Why don't you just pick a
room and finish it, as if it were a piece of furniture, then move
on to the next?"

"Why don't you just shut up? Go home and tend to your cooking, woman."

He was sorry afterward when he saw her tears. But he couldn't help himself. Skytop, which was supposed to have been such fun, his retreat from hard-driving obsession, was driving him nuts. And he didn't know why. Sometimes he wondered whether the place was haunted, but if so, with whose demons?

"You want to send them eight-by-ten color glossies?"

"Of the two of us or of me, the darky lover, alone? Do you think Rosalie and Jake would like that?"

"Seriously, what do you want to do?"

"Emma, I've told you before, I don't see that we have to do anything. It's not as if you've ever made them privy to the details of your life."

For Jesse knew that since that long-ago first-time-home-from-Atlanta Christmas, Emma had written a letter to her parents every two weeks that was less revealing than her shopping list. And even though she visited dutifully once a year, for all they shared she might as well not have bothered. It was all one-way travel. After the JFK assassination weekend, they had never visited her.

"I'm willing to tell them all about us, Jess, though you know they'll never begin to understand. Jake won't mind so much deep down, but he's been corroded by all that cracker shit."

"Emma, let's just skip it. It means nothing to me. I don't need another set of relatives, God knows. Look at my own."

Emma tried to, but they were as much fictional characters to her as Rosalie and Jake were to Jesse. For though Jesse had mentioned Emma to his mother and his sisters, they had never met.

"Don't worry about it, Em. I don't."

"We'll just be orphans together, then," she said.

At that, Jesse pulled her into his lap.

"I'll be your momma and your daddy and your sisters and your brothers. Your grandma and your grandpa and all the family you never had."

And for a while he was, that first year. He made Emma feel at home. She had found a safe harbor which would give her passage to the adventures of the sea while at the same time protecting her from its raging terrors. That first year, Emma felt she was his beloved. Why, there was no way she could drown.

10

California
1971

CALIFORNIA IS a roller coaster. Pay your money, step right up, and it takes you for a ride. A thrill a minute, this state of the United States that is also a state of mind.

It was in a roller coaster mood that Jesse and Emma set out one morning in their second spring together to a serendipitous Sierra destination, perhaps Lake Tahoe.

They started from a giddy peak, perched on their little mountaintop. Then down they rolled, pointing Jesse's Morgan into the Santa Clara Valley, Valley of the Heart's Delight, where the springtime orchards bloomed. Up again, up, up eastward over a transmission-eating incline before dropping over the other side into the Sacramento Valley that stretched brown and flat as the Holy Land. They followed the Sacramento River as they turned north toward the capital city of the same name. The delta land was damp and swampy like Louisiana bayou land. Rice grew in diked bogs along with crawfish, called crayfish here. But, when boiled, served with a pungent sauce in the beached paddleboat of a restaurant where Emma and Jesse had stopped for lunch, no matter what the pronunciation, the small crustaceans tasted the same.

"God, I'm stuffed." Emma patted her stomach and pushed back from the Formica tabletop.

Through plate glass windows the sun shimmied like a Bourbon Street fan dancer on the levee-hemmed water. Emma felt lazy with food, sunshine and beer, floating in a delicious afternoon dizziness called "the fantards" back home.

"Why don't we find someplace cozy and take a long nap?" She reached under the table and squeezed Jesse's blue-jeaned knee.

In answer he grinned, then fingered a corner of his mustache, twirled it like the villain in a melodrama who was certain that, if not now, surely in a minute he'd have the upper hand.

"We've got a long way to go before nightfall if we're going to make the Sierra," he said, playing hard to get.

But he motioned to the waiter all the same, the waiter who had eyed them throughout lunch, this Southern-voiced long drink of water and her lunch partner, dark as himself, whose bigger-than-life voice betrayed no origins at all.

"Check, please," Jesse said.

Emma stretched and yawned. "I don't know if we ought to try to drive it all in one day. Maybe we ought to take it slow."

Jesse reached for his wallet then, dropped money on the table, headed toward the door. "Come on. Let's go."

Emma followed, but with a bit of hesitation.

"Are we driving on, or what?"

"Aren't you the one who likes surprises? Or do I have you mixed up with someone else?"

This particular surprise had been nibbling for months at the edges of Jesse's mind. He still wasn't sure—but then he hadn't yet given it words. Until the words, well, an unborn surprise could be anything. A surprise was a surprise, right?

The waiter watched as the blonde hesitated. Then her face jumped the fence of indecision and beamed into that of the big black man who held her hand, pulling her arm into full extension as if he held short reins.

"Sure I do, Jesse, but nothing you do surprises me now."

"Oh, yeah? Already you got me figured out?" He shook his bull-like head. "Come on, then. In that case, I'm gonna show you something you've never seen."

"Ha! I've heard that before!"

"Ha yourself." And then with one arm he reeled her in, held her close.

The waiter watched as this uppity woman who had more than one trick up her sleeve snaked a long silent hand over to a table that hadn't been cleared, dipped her slender fingers into a water pitcher, then dropped a handful of ice down the jeans of her escort, who yowled and smacked her upside the head with a softly pulled punch. Then they laughed their way out the door, this electric couple.

The waiter listened for their car door's slam and clucked to himself like a chicken under his breath. Who were *they?* he wondered. Must be *some* story behind what they were all about.

THEY spent the night in a motel near Roseville in the Gold Country, snuggled together like spoons in a family silver chest. They slept late, the curtains drawn against the light.

Emma awoke to Jesse's kisses on her forehead. He'd been awake for a while, thinking.

"Rise and shine, sleepyhead. Let's hit the road. Got miles to go before you get your surprise."

She rolled to him then, sleep-warm, pressing her full length against his. He ran a hand along the curve of her behind. His behind. Emma was his. And in that moment he made up his mind—even before she whispered, "I love you, Jesse."

He answered, "I love you too, baby. And you're going to love this surprise."

SHE did love the little town of Lodestar, perched up on the side of a hill out of which had once poured gold by the ton, making this one of the richest boom towns in the West.

All that was left now were a couple of gilded mansions, a single street lined with saloons for the tourists, three motels, one hotel and a million-dollar sky-blue view out every window.

The wide-open rip-roaring good times that the nuggets bought —traveling magic shows, dancing girls, Chinese cooks and hot and cold running whores—had petered out into a clot of mobile homes with a sign flashing "Playland" at their gate. Pull the glad wagons into a circle. For this was Miles County, Nevada, whose major source of income, now that the ore had played out, was legalized prostitution. Second in dollar volume was the marriage business, which some wags said was more or less the same thing. No waiting. No blood tests. Just twenty-five dollars to a justice of the peace and you were man and wife, joined with no more effort than stopping for cheeseburgers at the drive-in.

Emma and Jesse were sitting at the bar of a saloon called the Silver Dollar. Old coins, embedded in the wood like stars, probably would have twinkled had any light ever penetrated the bar's permanent gloom.

"Think we ought to do one like this at Skytop?" Jesse asked.

Emma ran a hand down the smooth surface. "Might not be a bad idea." Might not be a bad idea to get a move on with the big stuff, like the staircase, before we start on the details. But she didn't say that. Give your tongue a holiday, too, she thought.

"Why don't you finish up that drink and let's go on a little tour. See what else we can find." Jesse threw a proprietary arm around her, led her toward the rear of the saloon.

They passed the ubiquitous slot machines that had appeared in every gas station, fast-food shop and grocery store since they'd crossed the Nevada line. Emma fished in her pocket for nickels. You could get an awful lot of excitement for a dollar's worth of nickels. But Jesse was moving too fast for cheap thrills.

In the far corner was a small, dusty latticework grotto trimmed with plastic flowers, lace curtains tacked over old wallpaper, photographs of couples smiling down from all angles.

"It's the chapel," Jesse ventured.

"You mean people get married right here in this saloon?"

He laughed at her indignation. "That's the same tone you use when you say 'canned beans.' "

"And why not?" slurred a voice from behind them, heavy with bourbon.

A short balding man in a black suit almost as shiny as his pate smiled before them. He held out a hand. "Silas Marner Jones." Then, "What's so funny, little lady?"

"Nothing." She wiped the grin off her face.

"My name? Well," he said, "better that my mother had moved on from books of the Bible to the library shelf. I have a sister named First and Second Thessalonians. There were fourteen of us altogether, and I could have done a hell of a lot worse. But," he raised a hand as if he had just reached out and grabbed hold of the slippery but holy part of himself, "though my name isn't from the Good Book, I am a man of the cloth."

Emma and Jesse traded a look.

"Ordained not only by the state of Nevada, but by the Holy Empirical and Evangelical Church of the Moving Spirit, to join those who have been living in love but yet in sin in the name of all that's holy, as one."

"I beg your pardon," Emma said.

"I'm a justice of the peace," Silas said then straightforwardly, realizing through the fog of that morning's booze that if he didn't just spit it out he might lose a possible twenty-five dollars. "You two here to get hitched?"

"I don't think so," Emma said. "Thanks anyway." And turned to go.

"Wait a minute," said Jesse. "Why not?"

"Why not?" Emma's voice rose and rose again as the room seemed to grow brighter before her, all its edges shining. "Why not?"

Jesse grinned at her. Was he joking?

"Yeah. Why not?"

"Is this a proposal?"

Silas Marner Jones shifted his weight from his right foot to his left. Each was shod in a black-and-white high-topped tennis shoe that had seen better days. If the blonde said yes, he could drive into Carson City to the Army-Navy surplus and see about getting a new pair. Recently, the marriage business had been dragging.

Jesse's grin grew wider. Hell, yes, it was a proposal. *This* was the surprise. Initially when he'd dangled a secret delight, he'd meant their destination, the town Lodestar which he'd visited once when he was young. But then there was the idea that for months he'd been noodling around.

He hadn't been able to focus on it wholly, to set aside each part of it and look at it with a cold and logical mind. But last night, just before he tipped over into unconsciousness, in that dreamy land of phantasmagoria, that vestibule to the territory of deep sleep, he had seen an image of Emma as if she were on the other end of some magical teeter-totter, rising like a fairy princess. Behind her was a blurred parade of all the other women he'd ever known, including his quick-grab-her-while-you-can fire-fly of a mother—with whom he'd never been at home. Then that parade had receded and there was Emma, golden, his, just his, alone.

"Sounds like a proposal to me," Silas said. And then, as the big black man frowned at him, he realized that he'd overstepped the line. Don't sell so hard, Jones, he said to himself. Let the suckers do the work. He listened to his own advice and took three steps back.

"It is a proposal," Jesse said. "What do you think?" Emma heard how light his voice was, so that if she said no she wouldn't think it mattered, wouldn't think him hurt.

What did she think? She thought this wasn't the proposal of the movies, a man kneeling, staring adoringly into her eyes, his very heartbeat dependent on her answer.

"I married him because he asked me to do it in a saloon," she'd later say glibly to others—or when she needed an answer to the question for herself. But she might have said other things.

Because he was one of the handsomest men I'd ever seen.

Because after a year he still made me laugh.

Because we'd shared a dream called Skytop.

Because I liked to hear him sing.

Because he hadn't bored me yet, and nothing about him reminded me of West Cypress.

"Are you serious?"

"Serious as death."

Emma smiled.

"Is that a yes?" Jesse asked and traced the curve of her mouth with a finger.

"Yes!" She was jumping up and down now, her feet dancing.

"Yes!" Jesse shouted. They joined hands and swung each other around and around like children in a schoolyard. Silas Marner Jones moved farther aside, not wanting to do anything to queer the deal.

But he needn't have worried. They were swept away with themselves. All he had to do was lead them. And, this being Nevada, where marriage was big business, the state officials in their infinite wisdom had made the process so simple that a drunken dull-normal teenager could follow it, and many did.

Within fifteen minutes, having handed over the requisite amount of cash and signed in the proper spaces, Emma, in purple corduroy jeans and her buckskin jacket, and Jesse, as always in his carefully pressed Levis, white shirt and Emma's Christmas gift, a black leather jacket, joined hands and themselves in holy matrimony.

Miss Cat Miles, a round-faced matron who just happened to have the same surname as the county, and Jimmy Lavell, a tall loquacious drunk with a crew cut and a permanent twinkle, were two regulars who earned much of their bar change by signing their John Henrys at the appropriate moment. They did that very thing for Jesse and Emma, and then settled back at the bar with fresh boilermakers.

The ceremony took ten minutes, stretched out because Silas

Marner Jones did a bit of quoting from both William Shake-
speare and e e cummings, running the two together in a most
peculiar combination.

But it would do. And Emma had a cigar band from behind
the bar on her finger—Jesse having rejected Silas's offer of a bar-
gain-priced gold ring—to prove it.

They stepped out onto the wooden sidewalk and exchanged a
movie clinch so steamy that, had there been horses in the street,
it would have scared them.

Then Emma looked Jesse square in the face. "What's next?"
she asked.

"Next!" her brand-new husband roared. "Getting married
wasn't the cherry on the top?"

"I don't know." Emma winked at him. "Was it?"

Jesse took four more steps backward from his bride of five
minutes and gave her a long hard look.

Then he reached a decision. "Wait right there," he said, reaching into his pocket. He disappeared back through the swinging
doors of the Silver Dollar.

Emma waited five minutes, then sat down, dangling her feet
off the edge of the high wooden sidewalk. She held her left hand
out and inspected the cigar band, excited, and wondering at what
she'd done.

"You got it," Jesse said then, sneaking up behind her.

"Got what?"

"Your cherry on the top. Come."

He shoved a bottle of champagne and two glasses into her
hands as he jumped into the Morgan without opening his door.

Showy, Jess. Very flashy. What are you doing for an encore?

What he did: the little plane was waiting for them on the
edge of town, and the grinning pilot flew them in blue spirals,
rolls and somersaults above the craggy tippytops of the Sierras
before, a hundred miles farther south, he finally put them down.

"Jesse, Jesse," she laughed, breathless, "I'm going to throw up."

"Oh no you're not," he said. "Not for this kind of money."

A jeep straggling tin cans and pink and silver streamers was
waiting to drive them through the Yosemite Valley, where the
sun was glinting off the face of Half Dome. A smiling porter was
at their service at the Awahnee's door.

"No luggage," Jesse said as he tipped the porter anyway. "And
I can carry the bride."

At that he swooped Emma out of the jeep and, shades of their first meeting, carried her up the wide steps of the old stone-and-redwood lodge, Skytop on a grand scale, through the endless lobby where sedate blue-haired couples gaped at them from tapestried high-backed chairs, past the desk where he called, "Tree," and the clerks answered, "Congratulations sir, ma'am," and up, up, up the wooden stairs to a set of double doors.

"Jesse, how did you pull this off? It takes months just to get an ordinary room."

He plopped her down across the wide bed, having kicked shut the door of the bridal suite behind him. "Don't ask," he said.

"But—"

Then his mouth lowered to hers, and that was the last question Emma asked for a long while.

11

West Cypress
August 1972

THE SUMMER-EVENING streets were still and empty. The frame houses in this older part of town were beginning to show their age, but then, Jake thought, what wasn't?

New houses were going up out past the Northside, out in what used to be the country, columned mini-Taras with wide yards full of St. Augustine sod. But here, close to the river, close to town, such as it was, steps sagged, chimneys tilted. The freeway was coming right through the middle of it for those who were in a rush to get from where they'd been to where they were going. The folks who lived in its path had to be in a hurry, too, to relocate. Their houses stood empty now, abandoned. Once people were gone, Jake thought, how quickly their houses gave up, dropping shutters and screens and sashes as easily as a fresh widow strewing hairpins, girdles, all pretense of caring.

Jake wiped his brow. The night was hot and close, nothing stirring except air conditioners, window fans. He thought of Emma. She had always hated this August heat.

"Rich people go away in August," she'd announced once at the table when she was quite young. She'd read that in a book. And then she'd gone away for far longer than a month to Atlanta, New York, California. There were two whole summers full of postcards from Europe once. For a long time, the bad time, she hadn't written much. But then those postcards. He had them all in a scrapbook. His Emma, flying to all the places he had only dreamed of, had never been to, writing back about museums and wines and foods he'd never heard of as if she had been traveling forever.

And here he was, still here, walking these same streets, in this same hick town where nothing was ever going to move or change, except to grow older, or hotter, or colder.

Something had been different this evening, however, something that upset Jake enough to have him talking to himself now as he walked the two miles home from the Ritz.

"Cheating," he said aloud to himself. "Said I was cheating. I never cheated anybody in my whole life."

He crossed the intersection of North Fourth and Bienville without looking—which was no real danger. It was almost eleven o'clock. Most everyone in West Cypress had been sleeping for hours.

Jake muttered to himself, "Maybe Rosalie's right. Maybe people are jealous of you when you're good. And I *am* good at dominoes. But that's no reason for Mr. Vance to get huffy. I've been beating him for years."

Jake pulled a handkerchief out of his pocket and wiped his brow again and the top of his bald head. Walking through the August night air was like walking on the bottom of a tub of hot water.

"Maybe the heat's getting to him. Goddamned heat. Getting to me. Accusing me of cheating."

What he didn't remember was that he'd been sitting through the game with the double five in his lap. It was when he played it that Joe Vance had snapped. He'd warned Jake five or six times in the past few months that he had to stop that. Jake remembered neither the cheating nor the warning. To his mind, none of it had ever happened.

Now Jake cut back over to River Road, which wound by the side of the Coupitaw, a seawall and then a levee separating the two all along the way.

It wasn't the most direct route, this toing and froing, but though his memory of the immediate past was fading, he remembered what Emma had said to him the last time she was home. "Daddy, you miss the fun of it, always doing it the same way. I know Momma tells you there's a *right* way, the *only* way. But that's crazy. You've got to learn to meander."

There was some truth in that. Rosalie had patterns and rules for everything, from washing dishes to mowing the lawn. He hadn't given in to them at first, he'd been angry all the time, but in the long run it was easier. But Emma hadn't. She always amazed him, Emma. How had she grown up to be so smart? And not just about books.

Emma. He smiled into the summer night, and his leapfrog memory, which was much more comfortable with decades than with yesterday, took a big jump.

Why, it seemed like only yesterday that he was standing in the kitchen of the old apartment, the one behind the store, trying to place an order to a wholesaler on the phone.

That black instrument was like a king snake. It didn't matter how many times Rosalie told him that the telephone was harmless, that he ought to be able to face it unafraid. He picked it up and it turned on him. His tongue cleaved to the roof of his mouth with terror.

"And a sack of p-p-p . . ."

He couldn't get it out. His stutter kept the word inside as tightly as if it had turned the lock and thrown away the key. His face was red. He could just imagine the face of the woman on the other end, not even having to hide her grin, waving other people in her office over to listen to the popcorn sounds on the telephone.

The more he struggled, the more he resented Rosalie's insisting he do this. "You could at least place the orders, Jake. Do I have to do everything?"

He started over. "A sack of p-p-p."

Three-year-old Emma had been sitting in a chair at the kitchen table, playing with a bowl of cold oatmeal she'd refused to eat. 'Potatoes!" she yelled suddenly in her high fluty voice. "Potatoes! Potatoes! Potatoes!"

"Potatoes!" Jake had echoed her into the phone, as if *p*s weren't an obstacle as tall as Mount Everest.

And when he'd hung up, she'd stood up on her chair and held her arms out to him, crowing at their triumph. He'd picked her up and hugged her to him.

He'd never had a problem with *that* word again. And "potatoes" had forever after been their running joke.

Ah, Emma. He missed her so. Why did she have to go?

Well. He knew the answer to that. She'd have suffocated in West Cypress. But he doubted that she had ever looked back; she had inherited his roving eye.

Not for love, no, he didn't mean that. And he didn't know anything about Emma's boyfriends since Bernie. It would have embarrassed him to ask. It seemed like prying. And Emma didn't volunteer.

No, he'd meant his yen for places. *New York.* He could close his eyes, and the towers of Manhattan glowed before him in the night sky. *California.* Beautiful warm California. San Diego. Ah, those sweet brief Navy days; he could never forget that bay. All that blue. Even the Dodgers were in California now. They had known a good thing when they saw it.

Though—he laughed a little to himself—Emma never saw it their way. She had never forgiven the Dodgers for deserting Brooklyn, moving to LA. Like her daddy, she'd been a diehard Brooklyn Dodgers fan.

All those summer afternoons they'd listened together, the announcer's voice flying high as a home run when Campanella hit one over the fence. There was no other sound in the world like that of a baseball game. "A high fly ball," and he and Emma would groan together on afternoons as hot as this very one had been. Emma would dance in front of the radio, cheering her Dodgers on with the pennant they'd brought back from Coney Island when she was almost six years old.

Yet when the Dodgers moved, she'd turned her back on them, switched off the radio or put her fingers over her ears. As far as she was concerned, they were dead.

"Just like Baby Snooks," she'd said.

Her beloved Baby Snooks. She'd been about five then. He'd told her that the newspaper said Fanny Brice was gone.

That was okay, Emma said, but Baby Snooks would still be on the radio.

"Fanny Brice *is* Baby Snooks," he'd explained.

"No." She understood about actors and characters, but she refused to accept this particular truth.

She sat by the radio that night, waiting for her show. Her face was expectant, about to burst into a gleam of "I told you so." She *knew* that Baby Snooks couldn't die. Baby Snooks was her favorite, better than chocolate ice cream.

When the hour arrived, there was no explanation, just a new program of recorded music played in Baby Snooks's place as smoothly as waters closing over a spot.

Emma had raced sobbing out of the room, had been incon-
solable for days. And then suddenly it was over. She turned a
cold face toward his and said, "Baby Snooks is dead."

"The Dodgers are dead," she'd said with that same face, but
no tears.

It had scared him a little, the way she could close down her
heart. She could just turn it off.

In high school. "She lied about me," she said about Linda,
her until-then best girlfriend. And never mentioned her name
again.

Jake didn't know how it had gone for her much after that.
Except for whatever it was she had decided about Bernie, once it
was done, it was over.

Well, that was how life was, wasn't it? Things were done. They
were over. That was that.

Just then Jake came to the place by the river where he and
Mr. Beasley used to go fishing. Suddenly, without having thought
about it, he found himself standing on top of the levee, which
was covered with long grass.

The moon was bright enough for him to see the outlines of
the trees below, where the bank sloped into the water. There
was the little dock down there where Mr. Beasley, a neighbor
and an acquaintance of his and Rosalie's from church, had fished
before he got impatient behind a truck on Highway 80 and
turned himself to mush.

Jake always wondered about that. He remembered the man
talking about the hardware business he'd retired from and about
how after that the days had seemed so long. He said that each
one stretched on and on for years, that he felt like he was just
marking time, waiting to die. Jake wondered whether he'd just
gotten tired of waiting.

He looked down at the black water, far down beyond the trees.

If Jake could have forced his tongue to talk to Mr. Beasley,
to say what was on his mind, he'd have said this: If you let them,
the days flow. They flow one into the other, on and on, just like
the Coupitaw. Sure, there are snags. Like Rosalie fussing at him,
wanting something, but you can stop that with silence. If you're
quiet, eventually, they all go away and leave you alone and the
days continue flowing. When you get really good at it, you can
go off into little turns in your mind, like Emma's meanders. You

can go and spend the day somewhere. You can sit on the front stoop in Baltimore and listen to the kids playing stickball up the block.

He took a last look down at the black and moon-spangled water, raised one hand and waved to the memory of Mr. Beasley, scrambled back down the levee and across River Road, and then, instead of following it two more blocks toward home, he looked back over his shoulder and made a sudden left turn.

It was time for another meander, though he didn't know whether he could call this deviation from the straight and narrow path back home to Rosalie a meander, since he'd been doing it for over twenty years.

It was more like an ox-bow lake, a pool of still water that had once been a curve in the river until the current got tired of going around the long way and cut on through the shorter distance and left the lake behind.

That's what Hattie was to him. A pool of still water that the rush of other people's lives had left behind. And when he bathed in her waters, sometimes literally, because she liked to get into her tub with him and take turns scrubbing backs, he felt like there was nowhere in the world he'd rather be. But as the years had passed, that wasn't quite as easy as it once had been.

"We gone have to stop eating or get a bigger tub," she'd laughed just last week.

But then, after they'd had their bath and were done with their loving, she'd put a whole sweet-potato pie topped with whipped cream on the table in front of them anyway. And they dug right in. Finished the whole thing, along with cups of light coffee sweetened with a big tablespoonful of sugar.

Hattie was the most wonderful cook.

Thinking about her made his mouth water.

Well. One more block and he'd be there.

The blocks weren't quite as regular here in the Quarters as they were in the rest of town. The streets still weren't paved, and when it rained they were a mess.

Years ago, when he first started with Hattie, she'd told him he was going to have to be careful of his shoes. If he went home full of mud, Rosalie would know he'd been walking the Quarters and want to know why on earth he'd come that way.

So he changed into his galoshes whenever the weather was bad.

He left them in a bread sack under a bush of pampas grass—
pompous grass, Emma called it as a little girl—right at the
Quarters' edge. The pampas would cut you to ribbons if you
weren't careful. No one would go bothering with his shoes in
there.

Of course, everyone in the Quarters knew that that was where
Mr. Jake left his shoes, and that he came back and got them
when he and Hattie were through—but Jake didn't know that.

Tonight he didn't have to worry about mud. It had been dry
for almost three weeks. The clouds had been rolling in every
afternoon and hovering heavy like a tease, but nothing happened. It was getting to be a drought.

He was still thinking about the weather when he reached
Hattie's house. It looked like all the other houses in the Quarters,
wood frame, four-roomed, a little front porch and a tinier one
behind. No sooner had he set foot on Hattie's front step than
she opened the screen door.

"Hi, sugar," she said in her deep voice. It was like cane syrup
pouring out into the dark.

She always did that. He didn't know how she knew, because
he never knew himself which night he was going to make the
turn and head toward her arms.

"Come on in." She opened the door wider.

He ducked his head, still a little shy the first few minutes after
all these years.

Then she put her round brown arms about him and he felt the
familiar pillows of her breasts. How he loved to rest his head
there after their lovemaking and take a little nap.

"Honey, I am so happy tonight. I be's beside myself with joy."

"Why?" Jake asked from his usual place where he had settled
himself in her tiny front room, an antimacassared easy chair.

" 'Cause I heard from Viola."

That was her youngest child, her only girl.

"And she and Brownell be coming to visit from Seattle. And
they bringing me my grands."

Jake nodded, smiled. "That's good," he said.

But it always took him aback, even though he could count as
well as anyone, to think that Hattie was a grandmother. Though
he certainly could be a grandfather, too, if Emma had ever married and settled down. After all, he was almost sixty-six years old.

"And look, I got letters today from both Marcus and James. And pictures too. Almost more in one day than I can stand." She waved the colored photographs of her two sons in his face.

He took her wrist gently and pulled Hattie to his lap. He snuggled her and rocked her like a child.

"Get away with you," she laughed. "We be too old for this."

"Since when? We're not too old for the other."

"Hush," she said and patted him on the cheek. "Leastways *I* be too fat."

But she couldn't hide her dimples from Jake. Here she was a woman of fifty-five, and still this man made her feel that way. She had had years of praying about it on Sundays, but then, since her husband had left her so long ago, she thought the Lord understood. Viola hadn't even been born, was still in her belly, when in the middle of the night her man, overcome by the thought of yet another mouth to feed, had pulled on his clothes, eased out of bed and slipped away out the door. She'd heard him, but what difference would it have made if she'd hollered out his name? Words were no cement when it came to men.

So she'd done what any other colored woman in her situation would do. She left her own with her mother and went to take care of a white woman's children, washed their diapers, ironed their ruffles, kissed their bumps and bruises, all the time pretending that she was home with Marcus, James and Viola her baby girl.

At the end of the week, she had almost made enough money to feed them. Almost, but not quite. So she was very careful how she spent her money at the corner grocery store.

The first time she noticed that Mr. Fine hadn't written up everything in the charge book with her name on it, she hadn't said a thing about it, except to give her thanks to the Lord.

"It's not the same as stealing, Jesus," she'd said. "Not the same if the man just made a mistake."

But it happened again. And yet another time. Then there was the once she'd found, in the bottom of the bag Marcus had brought home, two candy bars.

"You stole!" She stood waving the chocolate right in Marcus's face.

"No, ma'am," he said, his face serious as death.

Marcus was her oldest, the one she'd sent away first, as soon as he was big enough, off to her brother in San Jose. He was there still, south of San Francisco, an engineer with Lockheed. He made more money now than she'd ever thought possible for a black man on this earth, and sent her a check every month. After she bought herself a refrigerator, and then a window-unit air-conditioner, she had put the rest of it in the bank. When she was gone, he'd have it for his children's or their children's college. He fussed at her, but there was nothing else in the world that her heart could want.

But that day he'd looked at her with those serious eyes and said, "No, ma'am. I never stole nothing in my whole life."

"You sure you didn't take them when no one was looking? Was that little girl Emma behind the register, and you just slipped your hand by her into the candy counter?"

"No, ma'am. Mr. Fine was what rung me up."

He didn't tell his momma that she was warm. She almost had the story right. Emma *had* been standing right beside her daddy, and it was her hand, with a little silver-and-pearl ring on one finger, that sneaked into the counter and lifted the two Hersheys just as pretty as you please.

Then she'd climbed up on the stool beside her father, who was busy writing in the book, and dropped them into the bag, only then catching Marcus's eye with a little smile.

She'd whispered the words, no, not whispered, because there was no sound, just mouthed them so clearly that he could have read them even if he'd been deaf. *Thank you.*

Thank you, he guessed, for having caught her a few days before, caught her and kept her from slipping on the muddy path and falling into the canal.

But she couldn't say it out loud. He understood. Even though they hadn't been playing together, had just happened to be there at the same time, him and James, and Emma and that little white boy Mike.

Emma couldn't say it out loud, and it was too complicated for Marcus to explain to his momma now. His hand on Emma's arm, her hand dropping chocolate into his sack, puzzled him, made him feel funny inside, good and bad at the same time. But he didn't begin to have the words to explain it, not even to himself.

So he just said the words again, "Mr. Fine rung me up."

After that, Jake's little gifts to Hattie continued, an extra pound of hamburger meat, a loaf of bread, a couple yards of blue cotton fabric. Emma and Viola had matching dresses in that pattern that their mothers on either side of the canal had run up.

Jake told himself that he was just being kind, but it was more than that. For there was something about Hattie, even though she was colored, that reminded him of Helen—a roundness, a softness, her smile. These things touched a place in him that he thought had died in a row house on Independence Street in Baltimore.

Soon he'd begun to lie in bed beside the snoring Rosalie buttoned up to her chin, thinking lusty thoughts of Hattie. He looked at the space, wide and sharp as a bundling board, between him and his wife and watched the sheet rise between his legs and make a little tent. He would wait all day to see if Hattie would come into the store, but she sent Marcus most days and sometimes James.

Nights, he found himself walking home from the bar out of his way through the Quarters. It took him months of circling through the unpaved dusty streets to get up the courage to approach Hattie's house.

The colored people had watched him, the old men and women sitting on their front porches dipping snuff. No white people ever walked here except sometimes Cowboy Lou, but, they said deep in their throats, he be'd crazy.

They watched Jake and slipped one another looks out of the corners of their eyes.

"Reckon he be working up his courage."

"Reckon that ain't all he be working up soon."

For white men had *been* in the Quarters before, sliding by in their big long cars, furtive like cockroaches looking for a hiding place in the light. They stopped for just a second while the woman whom they were buying ran to an unlatched car door. Then *zoom* they were gone.

But not Mr. Jake, walking Mr. Jake. 'Course he was different. Couldn't talk straight, what with that stuttering, and even when he got it out he had that New Yorky way of talking. Folks said he was a Jew. Most of the Quarters wasn't sure what that meant, but there were those that knew said it was better than being a cracker. Said they'd heard tell the Jews up North were good folk.

Treated a Negro like he was a man. So they watched Mr. Jake to see how he was going to play his hand.

He didn't have to play anything, as it turned out.

When he finally got up the nerve and turned down Hattie's block as if it were nothing, he had pulled almost even with the corner of her house when she spotted him from behind her screen door.

"Jake," she called, in that warm low voice. Not Mr. Fine, Mr. Jake. No, none of that. "Jake, come on in," she said.

He stepped up on her front porch. She opened the door, and he entered as if paying social calls were something he did every day.

"I want to thank you for all your kindness," she said, then turned her face up to his and kissed him, right in the mouth.

He'd been so shocked, even though this was the stuff his dreams were made of, that he'd fallen back and hit his head against the wall.

"Ha!" she laughed in a laugh that made him wonder whether he'd ever heard anyone laugh before. "Ain't that what you come for?"

"I . . . I . . ." he sputtered. But he didn't even know what he was trying to say.

"That and a piece of my famous chocolate cake?" She pointed at the oilcloth-covered table, on which sat a prime example of that very thing, taller than Miss Virgie's had ever been.

It had just gone on from there—for all these years—as if their love affair, because that's what it was, were the most natural thing. It developed a life of its own. Somehow she always seemed to know when he was coming, would have herself and the sweets he loved ready as if he'd called ahead. In the old days, when the children still lived at home, they'd be safely tucked in or off at her mother's or a neighbor's house.

Jake and Hattie had never gone anywhere, not that they could have, even if Jake had been a single man. It would have been hard to hold hands in the picture show with Jake downstairs and Hattie upstairs in the colored balcony. The *White Only* signs that marked even the drinking fountains drew lines in the public world of West Cypress. They never saw each other outside the walls of Hattie's house. Jake continued to slip her his little gifts. After the store closed for good, she said for him not to worry. She didn't need them anyway. But Jake continued to bring her small things—cologne, embroidered handkerchiefs, a Whitman's Sampler of chocolates with a little map on the inside of the box. She liked the jellies and the creams. He liked the caramels and the nuts.

"Honey, we be's a perfect match," she'd tease. But she was right.

Tonight he'd brought her a pair of pink nylon panties.

"Lord have mercy, Jake," she laughed. "What if you die of a heart attack walking here and they find these in your pocket? What's anybody going to think?"

He laughed, too. Emma would have had a quick answer for her. Emma was good at that. But he wasn't. He didn't have the words. He had only his feelings that lived inside.

She knew that. She patted his bald head and smoothed the few strands that wanted to pretend that they belonged on top.

But later, when he left, she lifted the panties from the arm of the easy chair where he'd left them and shook her head. They were panties for a young girl, not for the likes of an old woman like herself whose rear end was spreading into a barrel butt.

Jake knew what her fanny looked like. What could he have been thinking about?

But more and more she'd asked herself that question. He was getting unmindless, as folks said, distracted. He forgot things. And a couple of times recently she'd noticed that he kept peeking at her windows like someone was out there and he wanted her to draw the shades.

Not that she ever flaunted herself for the neighbors. They knew what was what, but there were limits to how far she wanted their noses to grow. So she'd always been careful. She'd always been discreet.

But this was something else. Jake was getting to be afraid of something. For him there *was* something out there in the darkness. He wouldn't talk about it when she asked him, but, she shook her head, that was Jake.

12

Los Gatos, California
July 4, 1973

"I WISH YOU HAD come up to Berkeley and let *me* do this," said Maria. She was sitting in Emma's kitchen, watching her chop onions into the coleslaw. "Much as I love your cooking, it's my turn, you know."

"I don't keep track of turns, do you? I love having you-all, and Jesse wanted Clifton to come down and see the windows at Skytop. I do wish you'd stay over; it'll be dangerous driving home tonight with all the drunks on the road. You know we have plenty of room."

Maria shook her head and smiled thank you, no. After his years long ago in the Army, Clifton was never comfortable sleeping anywhere but in his own bed.

Emma dumped the onions into a big blue-and-white ceramic bowl and started chopping pickles and peppers.

Maria watched her. "When is Jesse ever going to finish this kitchen?"

"I don't even want to talk about it."

"But wasn't that the first thing he was going to do when you moved in, two—"

"Three and a half years ago. Yes, it was. But you know he puts every living breathing minute into Skytop."

The kitchen wasn't awful, it was just inconvenient. The freezer was out on the back porch, and the stove was awkwardly placed. She and Jesse had talked about a six-burner professional range and new shelves. But he'd never gotten around to them.

All the beautiful cabinets Jesse used to build. "The shoemaker's children," she said.

"So how's the Winchester House of the Mountains coming?" The now-dead Sarah Winchester, heir to the rifle fortune, had spent decades and millions building a house in San Jose with secret passageways and numberless rooms.

Emma rolled her eyes, "Please, don't get me started. The hours I spend traipsing back and forth to the hardware store, lumber store, plumbing, paint, tile, socket, plug, wrench, hammer, screw store." She paused, knife in hand. "You know, Rosalie owned some rental properties, and when it came to fixing them up my daddy used to bitch. I always thought he was just lazy, but I'm beginning to see his point. If you don't love the process, it is *the* world's biggest drag."

"But it will all be worth it someday, don't you think? When Skytop's finished?"

Emma poured them each a glass of iced tea and joined Maria at the dining table.

"I never thought I'd hear myself say this, but no, I don't. Besides, we'll never live that long. Jesse gets off on tangents, like those stained-glass windows in the great hall—they belong in a church! Four of them, each six feet wide and twelve feet tall. Do you know how long that's going to take? And he didn't even *do* stained glass before. He's up there teaching himself to be a Renaissance man. Meanwhile, the porch is still falling down, the kitchen is a shambles, the bathrooms—just the everyday carpentry work always takes three times as long and costs twice as much as he plans. It's like owning a boat—a hole in the water you pour money into. Sometimes I think about going up to Skytop and burning it to the ground."

"You can't convince him to stop, to sell it and get out? Go back to his art?"

"I've begged him, but he's lost all perspective. It started as a little break, remember, a diversion? Right after that Montalvo retrospective. But for Jesse it was a dream too, and I guess I bought into it. We were going to create this hotel with a gallery and a restaurant. Jesse would do such a wonderful renovation, it would be a showplace—with the Tree touch. I think he had visions of Frank Lloyd Wright. I would be the chef. Then, after it opened, a manager would take over, and Jesse would go back to his art. I'm afraid by that time they'll have forgotten who he was."

"No. Jesse was on top."

"What if he's had his time in the sun?"

Maria stirred her tea. "Fame's not *that* fickle."

"He gets calls. His agent in New York thinks he's gone nuts."

"Is that what *you* think?"

"Sometimes, I swear to God, I believe he thinks if he tries hard enough, if he does every little thing about Skytop perfectly, he can go back and do his childhood over, his parents won't divorce, he and his mother will be just like *that*." Emma held two fingers twisted together close.

"Does he talk about that?"

"He talks *around* it, sometimes."

Up at Skytop, Jesse and Clifton were leaning over a worktable stretched across two sawhorses.

"I never did glass," Clifton said. He picked up the soldering torch. "Show me how this goes."

Jesse smiled. "Going to let *me* teach *you* something, old man?"

" 'Bout time, don't you think?"

Jesse joined the pieces of carefully fitted glass, explained that this was the easy part. It was cutting the glass that was difficult. He had a pile of bright shards of discarded pieces and Band-Aids on his fingers to testify to that fact.

"It's different from wood. Every color is a completely different experience. You never know how it's going to act until you start working with it. And in the same sheet, the minerals can run different, making strong, resistant spots that you don't know about until you start to make that cut." He held a piece of amethyst glass up to the light, and it cast a pool of violet across his shirt.

"Ain't it that way with most everything?" Clifton asked.

Jesse turned and looked at him. "I guess so." Then he dropped the amethyst and picked up a piece of emerald which was to become part of a lily, turned it in his hands, inspecting it as if it contained a key to the universe. "Say, what do you mean by that?"

"Nothing. Just that most things aren't what they seem, I mean you don't know much about them till you handle them a while, get down in the dirt."

"That's for sure," Jesse nodded.

Clifton approached the stairs that led to the gallery level, where Jesse had carved a magnificent newel post. The stairs themselves were still broken.

"Fine-looking piece of work," Clifton said, running his hand over the flowering cherrywood forms that swirled around a woman naked to the waist.

Jesse turned away and walked the full length of the great hall, thinking of the little brunette who had modeled for it. She hadn't been able to keep her hands off him—or vice versa. He stared for a long moment at the painting of the woman with Emma's eyes he had done on the wall, what now seemed like eons ago. Ah, Emma. He hadn't meant to be unfaithful to her—but then that was *her* fault.

Clifton came up behind him, put a hand on his shoulder. "When you getting back to it? Ain't you fooled around here long enough?"

"What are you talking about? I haven't been fooling around." Jesse's tone was suddenly sharp.

"Don't shit a shitter."

"Exactly what are we talking about?"

"I don't know. You tell me—pussy or art?"

Jesse stared at him for a moment.

"Don't stand there looking like a chicken deciding whether or not to cross the road. You think I don't know you better than that? I'd hoped Emma would settle you down. I hear things, too, you know. I know you been philandering. Sounds to me like the symptom of a man who's lost track of his priorities, all tangled up in this place that don't mean a goddamned thing."

"Careful, old man."

"Careful, shit. Careful is what I was being when I stepped on the mine." Clifton tapped loudly on his false leg. "I'd been going on, taking care of business, never would have happened."

"Nothing to do with me," Jesse grumbled.

"We're not talking about careful, son. What we're talking about is that it's time you got back to paying attention to your marriage *and* your work."

"Emma been talking to you?"

"Emma don't have to talk to me. She probably don't even know. To me looks like she's still in love with you. Don't quite have that down-in-the-mouth disappointed look—yet. But close, close. You keep messing around, boy, she soon will."

They had stepped out on the front porch now, looking out across fir and redwoods. The Pacific was in the distance.

"I know you're right—about Emma," Jesse said. But what he

didn't say was how more and more, as Skytop grew, he felt Emma slipping from his grasp. Was there some correlation? Or was it just the passing of time?

At first she'd been right there. She was spirited, of course, that's one of the things he'd loved about her. But then she drifted. When he'd take her arm to lead her through a door, something just as simple as that, she'd shrug him off.

"Is this some kind of fucking symbolic act?" he had asked. "You don't want me to open doors for you? Go on ahead. Help yourself."

"Don't be silly, Jesse," she had said. But she went right on doing what she wanted to do. And they just didn't feel as close.

She *was* busy, he'd grant her that. Out in the world with her teaching, her students, catering clients were calling all the time for her. She was booked for special dinner parties, at seventy-five dollars a head, past the first of the year. And he was proud of that. But it felt like she was spreading herself awfully thin, like there wasn't enough of her left.

"That's because you've locked yourself up in Skytop," she said. "You really need to get out. You never see a soul anymore. All that isolation will make you nuts."

"I've always spent time alone. Artists *do!*"

Emma had given him a look. "I'm not your evening entertainment, Jesse, after your day up the hill."

Why couldn't she understand how important the lodge had become to him? It represented—well, he found it hard to talk about. A *big* canvas. A monumental work. When he was dead and gone people would come to see the Jesse Tree House. It would be the noblest thing he'd ever done. Couldn't Emma see that? Couldn't Clifton? Couldn't they sense the enormity of his vision?

"Come on," Clifton was saying. "We better get back and give those pretty ladies a hand."

A while later, out in the screened-in lanai, Jesse tipped open the lid to the heavy rectangular smoker. "Never made a better investment in my life than this baby crematorium," he said.

Everyone laughed, though all of them had heard the joke before.

"That's what it looks like, doesn't it?" Jesse said.

"Indeed it does, my man," Clifton answered.

"Can I freshen your drink?" Jesse asked. "Anyone?" They all shook their heads. "No takers, huh? Well, the Fourth is young, and I say you're all a bunch of pikers. I think we have an obligation to drink to our country's birthday and keep these home fires burning till—well, at least until Rupert comes."

"Did he call?" Maria asked.

PATRIOTISM is a funny excuse for drinking, Emma thought. Especially for a man who referred to "your President" and "your Governor" as if Nixon and Reagan were *her* responsibility and he weren't a citizen of the country or the state.

But then, in a way, he wasn't, for Jesse had always seemed to occupy his own particular territory. She wondered sometimes what its geography looked like, for the longer she lived with Jesse, the less the felt she knew him.

There were those things that hadn't changed. He was still a most handsome man. In fact, his looks seemed to improve with age—his carriage, his imposing presence, this larger-than-life black prince. When he entered a room, conversation stopped. And he had a wonderful way with words. The two of them were so clever, they thought, that once sitting at the table after dinner they'd made a tape of their conversation. It was still here somewhere, in the bottom of a bureau drawer. And there was drama about the man: his beautiful bass-baritone that even when he talked with her quietly in a restaurant caused heads to turn. In the realm of the practical, he could do those things she hated to do: fixing locks, plugged sinks, creaky doors. (How, she asked herself often, could a woman who wasn't interested in hanging a picture let herself be talked into Skytop? What *could* she have been thinking about?)

And, of course, he enjoyed a certain fame, or he had when they'd met. Everyone in Bay Area art circles, and beyond, even in New York, knew Jesse's name. That, perhaps, had changed. As had their bank account. More and more of the reserve that Jesse had saved when he was at his peak was pouring into Skytop. He needed to get back to work.

Not just for the money. He needed a wider audience. He hardly saw anyone outside of Clifton—and his old friend Rupert from time to time. So it fell to Emma to provide the applause.

It was tough being an audience of one, especially when she

was tired of the same old show. The burden was far too great; he wanted her to see, *come up and see,* every little bit of work. She had begun to feel like a mother watching her child in the swimming pool: *Look, Ma, look.*

Besides, if she was the only audience, she had to be perfect, didn't she? And Jesse's rules of perfection were unwritten. Yet if she loved him, she would know them or intuitively figure them out.

Just as she ought to know how he'd like her to iron his white shirts, cook his eggs. She ought to know what size washers, screws, nails he'd like her to pick up at the hardware store on her way home.

She needed to be finely tuned to hear the vibrations of the mines that lay in the fields of the territory that was Jesse's private world.

For when she misstepped, made the wrong move, said the wrong words, the explosions were fast and furious. They burst out of Jesse like cherry bombs. Then the silence would fall.

The ensuing quiet covered the house and the yard like a thick blanket of fog. It was familiar; it reminded her of Jake, whose angry outbursts had punctuated his long silences throughout her childhood. Once, when he had already been angry at Rosalie, he'd flown at Emma in a rage because she hadn't swept under her bed. The price for those dust bunnies was a stillness that lasted two months.

Jesse's silences weren't as long. But they were long enough, so that by the time he decided to speak again Emma had developed a rainbow of bruises from beating her head against his implacable will, and they hurt. She wanted them kissed and made well before she kissed and made up again. Jesse, on the other hand, wanted to be rewarded for returning from his muffled kingdom back into her less-than-perfect world. So he'd pull the drawbridge back up before she even crossed it, and she would fall back into the moat to swim alone.

After a while, she'd gotten used to it, to being alone again. For hadn't she been like that for most of her life? Hadn't she protected herself from all those names in her little notebook, the names she'd inscribed in purple ink, of men she'd given her body to but from whom she'd oh so carefully hidden herself? And maybe she'd been right to do so. Maybe the mistake had been in giving in to Jesse, who had seemed so different from all the others, who had charged in and swept her up before she had time to think.

Not that he was like those men. He didn't bore her. Well, mostly not, though she was getting awfully tired of talk of Skytop. How different from the reality had been her fantasy of what their life together would be. For when they met, he had been at the apex of his career. She had imagined openings, shows, a circle of his scintillating friends. Little did she think that he'd become the hermit of Skytop.

Nor did he suffocate her, as so many of those old beaux had done, with their tiny vision of the world, as tiny as West Cypress. No, of course not.

But he was choking her—with his need. Sometimes it reminded her of Rosalie, who had wanted her, needed her in some way that Emma couldn't understand, expecting her to fill a void that she didn't want to be, *couldn't* be, responsible for.

Jesse had said to her recently that she'd been hiding from him, that he didn't feel like he could reach out and touch her.

"I'm not hiding," she had answered. "I'm right here."

Yet when he reached for her, she pulled away. "Honey, I'm not . . ."

"You were tired last night."

"But I wasn't the night before."

And then his beautiful voice had grown so cold that she imagined it a wedge of steel.

"I never knew another woman who didn't want to make love."

"Every night?"

"Every night I wanted to."

"That's not normal, not year after year."

"How do you know? Did you read that in a magazine?"

Yes, she probably had, in an article or a book. There were statistics on things like this. Besides, she knew what she felt and didn't feel; and she *didn't* feel passion every night.

"I never have time to build any need. You never give me any breathing room."

"I'll give you breathing room." Then he'd jumped out of bed and pulled his jeans on.

"Where are you going?"

"What do you care?"

"I care a lot."

"Why? You don't love me." His eyes brimmed with tears.

"I do love you." Then her tears too began. "I love you very much."

"Why do you find me so loathsome?"

She shook her head. "I don't."

He reached out again and touched her breast. And despite herself, she flinched.

"There!" he shouted.

"Does it always *have* to be sex?" she yelled back.

What had ever happened to kissing, necking, making out? She remembered never being hotter in her life than sitting in the front seat of Bernie Graubart's old green Ford touching and exchanging spit.

She'd told Jesse that once.

"That's what you want? Some adolescent groping in the dark?"

"Yes," she cried, "sometimes. And sometimes couldn't we just be? Just sit? Just talk?"

"And snuggle?" he asked sarcastically.

For that seemed to be what Emma enjoyed most about their time in bed together.

"Snuggle me," she said almost every morning. "Hold me for a few minutes."

That was what was important, more important than anything else, though she could never convince Jesse of it, those few minutes, only seconds out of unconsciousness, of feeling loved, safe.

His morning erection always got in the way of that.

"EMMA!"

"What? Sorry." Then she pulled herself back into the lanai, back into the Fourth of July barbecue.

"Did Rupert call? Say when he was coming?" Maria was still asking the same question.

"Where the hell is that white skunk, anyway?" Rupert was a very very light-skinned black man. His father, when he left his mother, had moved to another state and passed for white.

"He's always late," said Emma, answering Clifton. *"Did* he call, Jesse?"

But Jesse's attention was on the radio. "Why is it you can't find the classical station when you want it?"

Why is it when we have people over, you drink instead of

smoking dope? Emma asked herself. And how long was it going to be before he crossed the line from mellow to mean?

"Man may not be dark, but he sure does operate on colored people's time," Clifton said, talking about Rupert.

"He's bringing Lowie?" Maria asked.

"No, I don't think so." Jesse was back with them again.

Emma gave him a questioning look. "Why not?" She had liked Lowie, a woman as funny as she'd ever hoped to meet, Rupert's second cousin as well as his wife.

"How you think we always kept this blood so white?" Rupert had laughed at Emma's surprise when she'd first learned that fact.

Lowie did look like Rupert, with blue-green eyes and fair skin, though hers was dotted with a million round freckles that looked like M&Ms across her broad nose. Her hair was crinkly orange, and she wore it in a big natural halo. Besides Lowie's sense of humor, Emma had been looking forward to her playing the piano. When Lowie came to visit, they'd gather around the square rosewood grand piano. Emma had found it in an antique store and couldn't live without it, both because she thought it would be perfect up at Skytop and, as Jesse said, because it made her think she was living on a plantation in the South.

"Was no plantation behind that corner grocery store," she reminded him.

"Yeah, but we all have dreams, darling, we all have dreams," he teased.

"Where *is* Lowie?" she repeated in the here and now.

Jesse shrugged. "I'm not his keeper, Emma, just his friend. Rupert called yesterday while you were out and he said he might be bringing someone else."

"*Someone else?*" But before Emma had a chance to ask him whether he meant what she thought, she heard the blast of Rupert's horn, and there was his Oldsmobile eating up the hill's last turn. Dust flew and gravel popped and Rupert shouted his big hello. Nothing about the man was ever quiet.

Through the screen of the lanai, Emma could see the figure of a short woman, a smudge of long black hair, but she couldn't make out the details until they'd climbed the flagstone path.

The Oriental woman Rupert had thrown his arm around in a proprietary fashion was definitely not Lowie.

"Howdy." Rupert smiled with a grin so bright it dazzled. He

grabbed Jesse in a bear hug, and Jesse grabbed him back. Then
Rupert began an elaborate routine of hand-slapping and wrist-
popping that made everyone laugh.

"This man might as well be speaking Swahili, the way he
shakes hands," Jesse said.

"*Arigato,*" Rupert answered with a clownish bow.

The Japanese woman who was standing there still unintro-
duced smiled ever so slightly.

"That's 'Thank you' in Japanese," Rupert said, then pressed
the woman to him. The top of her head came about halfway up
his chest.

My God, doesn't she speak English? Emma wondered. Has Rupert brought his honey into my house to spend the Fourth of
July and I can't even be rude to her because she won't understand?

For Emma *was* offended at the idea of Rupert's flaunting his
unfaithfulness. It seemed like awfully bad manners, not to mention poor taste. She knew that Jesse would tease her about her
proper Southern upbringing when she complained about it later.
The gall of Rupert! And this woman, what nerve! But wait,
Emma, she caught herself. Maybe she doesn't know he's married.
What could she know, if she didn't even speak English?

"I'm Caroline," the woman said as if on cue. "Caroline Kitana."
She had a lovely low and musical voice. "Rupert's told me that
you're very good friends of his," a beat passed, "and his wife."

Well, that certainly answered those two questions, didn't it?

CAROLINE might be lots of things, Emma thought as the afternoon wore on, but she was not stupid. If *arigato* was Japanese
for "thank you," Emma wondered what the word was for "vamp."
For she knew Southern belles, and she knew Jewish princesses,
but Caroline was a new variety of that seemingly helpless female
who laughed at the men's jokes and smiled sweetly at the women,
with clever eyes that looked right through them. But behind all
the lightness and birdlike flutter, behind the geisha fan, was a
mind that knew—and almost always got—exactly what it wanted.

Emma wondered what she wanted from Rupert.

"Caroline is a physical therapist," he'd answered for her when
someone asked her what she did. Then he'd winked. "Gives a
great rubdown. You wouldn't think a girl this little could."

Caroline smiled up at him as if he'd just paid her a great com-

pliment. Lowie would have slapped him upside his head and
said, "Man, what the fuck are you talking about?"

Emma wanted to know more. "Where do you work?"

"At the VA hospital in Palo Alto. Most of my patients are
boys from Vietnam." Caroline shook her head. "Very sad."

"Well, they must perk right up when they see you coming,
huh, sugar?" Rupert grinned.

Emma wondered about that. How did men perceive Caroline?
Emma couldn't decide whether she was pretty or not. Her round
flat face was pleasant, her mouth wide, her nose a nubbin. Her
hair fascinated Emma; long, silky and inky blue-black, it curled
in ringlets at her shoulders.

"Oh, it's a perm," Caroline said and dimpled, and then, in
that moment, she was as lovely as a peach.

But seconds later, when Jesse said something clever about Governor Reagan and Caroline laughed, her teeth grew big as a
bunny's, and her skin, the exact shade of an old ivory bracelet
Emma wore, pulled back until Emma thought she could see her
skull.

But the transmogrification wasn't only when she smiled or
laughed. There was something chameleonlike here at work. On,
off. Pretty, ugly. Helpless, strong. Was this geisha-princess routine the Japanese version of that dual role Emma knew so well
from home, the Southern lady who hid her iron fist in a velvet
glove?

Now she and Caroline stood together in the living room. The
others were gorged, resting around the dining table. Emma was
playing hostess.

"I love your house," said Caroline.

"Thanks, but it's got a long way to go."

"Well, I think it's lovely. And look at that gorgeous coffee
table!" It was one of Jesse's pieces, an ebony slab resting on a
pile of golden balls. "Rupert told me that you are both so clever
with your hands. You *are* a wonderful cook. And of course I
know Jesse's work. I've always wanted to meet him."

Really, Emma thought. Rupert not enough of a conquest for
you?

"Oh, what a pretty piano! Do you play?"

"Not really. I took seven years of lessons as a girl, but 'Chop-
sticks' is about all I can manage. Do you?"

"A little," Caroline said and tucked her chin modestly.

"Please. Help yourself."

"You're sure you don't mind?"

"No, not at all. Lowie plays it all the time."

She bit her lip. She hadn't meant to say Lowie's name, as if
speaking it in front of Rupert's girlfriend besmirched it somehow. If she just kept Lowie out of this afternoon, she wouldn't
have to think about her own culpability in not showing the
woman the door.

She could imagine doing that, pointing in outrage. "Out, out,
you shameless hussy! You son-of-a-bitch!"

If Jesse had showed up at Lowie's house with a piece of fluff
in tow, she'd have expected Lowie to do the same.

"Man, what the hell are you thinking about?" She could just
hear Lowie. "Have you lost your ever-loving mind? Get that
tramp out of here. Git, you no good dog!"

Caroline smiled. "Yes, I know. Rupert told me Lowie plays."
She paused. "You don't like me, do you?"

Well, she had brass. Emma would give her that. "No, I don't."

"I'm not going to take Rupert away from Lowie. You needn't
worry about that." Cool, that's what Caroline was, very cool.

Then she settled herself on the piano stool which Jesse had
made of exotic bubinga wood with little gargoyles reaching up
for the player's derrière. The best of Jesse's work was full of
jokes like that.

Caroline began with a Chopin study. It was all flash, a bravura
performance for a woman who played "a little"—or a lot. The
others bounced into the living room to witness the musical fire-
works.

"Isn't she wonderful?" Rupert asked.

Caroline thanked him prettily and smiled beyond him to
Jesse, where her glance stayed, Emma thought, just a moment too
long.

It turned out that Caroline, like Lowie, could improvise
(Where *did* Rupert find these piano-playing women?), and they
spent an hour gathered round her. Jesse, playing host, kept their
glasses brimming, though Emma had long ago switched back to
iced tea—as had both Clifton and Maria, with an eye toward
the drive back home.

"Do 'Go Down, Moses,'" Rupert urged. "You must hear Jesse
sing."

"I don't know it," Caroline answered. "But I'll try."

What a little trouper, Emma thought.

Caroline revolved on the stool and looked at Jesse from beneath her lashes. "Start and I'll catch up."

Jesse winked at Emma. He was having a good time, as was everybody else. "For my lady," he said and bowed formally toward her. Well, wasn't that sweet? But she kept an eye on Caroline, who, unless Emma was mistaken, was flirting with her husband, and the other on the drink he had forgotten now, placed on a corner of the polished rosewood. It would leave a ring, Jesse of all people should know that, but she bit her tongue.

They began. The song, though an old chestnut, was one of his best. It gave him a chance to show off his vibrato, his deepest, most dramatic notes.

Caroline clapped her little hands when they were finished. "That was wonderful." Jesse smiled back at her.

"You make anyone sound good."

"Rupert," Caroline turned to her escort now, "you're so lucky to have such wonderful and talented friends."

I may, thought Emma, have to excuse myself to puke.

She glanced across the room to Maria, who returned a look of cool assessment and an imperceptible nod.

"Well, we hate to break up the party." Maria rose, smoothing her skirt. "But Clifton and I have to hit the road."

Clifton, who appeared to have been dozing on the sofa like an old bear, but never missed a trick, shook himself and stretched.

"What say, Rupert?" He slapped the man on the shoulder. "You headed back to Oakland? Want to drive on up to Berkeley with us? It's not too late to hear some music."

"You dragging my party away, old man?" Jesse asked. There was a storm flag ruffling ever so slightly in his voice.

"No, 'course not. It was just a thought. Why don't you and Emma come, too? You can stay over at *our* house."

"What do you think, sugar?" Rupert asked Caroline.

"We can go if you want to, but I'd just as soon stay here. If that's okay with you, of course?" She directed the question to Emma, who wanted nothing more than to usher them all out and shut the door—and then tuck into bed. She was even in the mood for a little loving. Caroline make you appreciate what you've got? she twitted herself. Well, maybe, maybe not.

"Why don't you *all* stay?" she heard herself, the perfect Southern hostess, saying. "The evening's young."

"Thanks, bro," Rupert said and returned Clifton's slap on the back. "But I think we'll hang here and help Jesse finish up this bottle of scotch."

"There's plenty more where that came from," Jesse said.

"Well, it was just a thought. Some other time." Clifton had his hand on the door.

Declining Maria's final offer to help with a wry smile that wasn't just about the dishes, Emma said, "You clean at your house, next time." Then Clifton and Maria kissed their thanks and farewells and were gone.

BECAUSE Caroline couldn't talk and act at the same time, and the scotch she'd been sipping all afternoon had loosened her tongue, she stood holding a dish in one hand, telling Emma about her two children, the husband who had left her, her apartment in Palo Alto, her job. The dish never moved.

Suddenly she remembered her manners. "Rupert said you teach?"

"Yes, in Santa Clara at—"

But before Emma could continue, Caroline burbled, "*I've* always wanted to teach. I was thinking about going back to school to study art. I love to draw. And I love kids."

"You should have talked to Clifton about that. You know, he runs a workshop for art teachers at Berkeley in summer school."

"Oh, really?"

He talked about it for half an hour. Where was *your* mind all afternoon?

"Does Jesse teach, too?"

"He did for a while, a few private lessons. But Clifton's your man."

"I should talk with Jesse about it."

Was the woman stupid, or just drunk? Emma took the dish out of Caroline's hands, dumped the remaining coleslaw into a plastic refrigerator container and said, "That's enough. Let's get out of this kitchen." Before I scream, she thought.

Things weren't much better in the living room, for Rupert and Jesse were well into their cups.

"Coffee, anyone?" she asked.

The answer was no.

"Come on over here, Emma." Jesse patted the dark blue leather sofa beside him. "Come and have a little drink."

"I think I'll stick with my iced tea."

"You're such a prissy schoolmarm," Rupert teased. "Come on, loosen up, live a little."

Emma smiled stiffly. How many times did she have to refuse?

"Rupert's right. Caroline's going to have one, aren't you?" Jesse stood and took Caroline's glass out of her hand. "See?"

See what? That Caroline is a good sport who doesn't know when she's had enough?

But there was no point in resisting. "A light bourbon and water," she said. Jesse made her one, dark and stout. It didn't matter. She'd just hold it for the rest of the night, however long that eternity promised to be.

When he was sober Rupert was funny. When he was drunk, he wasn't. He was well into a routine that went "And I says, 'Bro, you full of shit.' "

"Say what?" Jesse answered, and they laughed, slapped hands as if they lived in the street. Jesse's grandmother Lucretia, who had taught him to speak, if not the King's English then a close approximation thereof, would have washed his mouth out with soap.

"And so I axed him, 'Is that why yo eyes be's so brown?' "

This was going to go on all night, and she couldn't go home, because this *was* home. Emma closed her eyes and imagined excusing herself with a headache, slipping into the bedroom. She'd sneak her flashlight on under the covers so that they couldn't see the light, and settle into her new book, *Fear of Flying*.

"Excuse me," Caroline said suddenly. She staggered slightly as she stood. "Bathroom."

"Are you okay?" asked Emma.

"Sure," Caroline answered, but she tripped as she left the room.

Rupert looked up, and then the men went on. And on. Emma disappeared into the kitchen for a while, put the dishes away now that they'd drained. She drummed her fingers on the counter. She dawdled as long as she could.

"Can I get anybody anything?" She poked her head back in.

No one answered. That meant no.

"Where's Caroline?" It must have been fifteen minutes she'd been gone.

"In the bathroom, I guess," Rupert said.

"Do you think we ought to check on her?"

"Don't be such a mother hen."

Fuck you, Jesse. She smiled and retreated back into the kitchen. What the hell was she doing here—hiding? Yes, hiding with nothing to read. She should cache books all over the house the way the squirrels did nuts. She could never tell when she might get caught in a boredom emergency, and though clean under-wear was one thing, how much worse to be without a book. But her purse book was in the bedroom. Her car book was in her car. Her truck book in the truck. Then she spied some old *Gourmet* magazines she'd meant to file.

In minutes she was arm in arm with Elizabeth David on a journey through the countryside of southern France. They were hot on the trail of the perfect chanterelle when she heard the sound of breaking glass. She dropped the magazine and hurried into the living room.

"What was that?"

"What was what?" Jesse looked up.

"Didn't you drop something?"

He grinned. "What are you smoking in the kitchen?"

She took a quick look at the ebony coffee table. Nothing broken there.

"Where's Caroline?"

The two men exchanged blank looks.

"Still in the bathroom, I guess," Rupert ventured.

"Jesus Christ, she's been in there for half an hour. You ought to go and see about her."

Rupert didn't move.

"Hell, I'll do it myself." Emma strode across the room, knocked and, when there was no answer, threw open the bathroom door.

Caroline was passed out on the toilet, her skirt up above her knees. Her head had crashed backward into the mirrored shelves behind. Shards of silvery glass glinted on the floor.

"You guys better get in here," Emma yelled. Caroline didn't move.

"WELL, they say God protects drunks and fools."

Emma closed the door behind Rupert, who had come back in

to say one last loud farewell, having thrown Caroline over his shoulder and carried her out to his car. *She* was fine. Only one shelf was broken. Rupert had insisted that he drive her home now rather than spend the night, and Emma put up no argument.

"Lord, am I glad *that's* over," she said as the door closed.

"You're awfully tough on people. You should learn to relax and have a good time."

"I did have a good time, up to a certain point."

"And then?"

Emma wanted to say, "And then I'd rather be reading a good book, or washing my hair, or doing almost anything," but she knew better. Jesse had been drinking far too long for her to tell him that most late nights with his friend Rupert bored her to death.

Instead, out fell the words she'd been thinking all night.

"That woman has the hots for your body."

"Who?"

"Caroline. Who do you think—Maria?"

Jesse looked at her with narrowed eyes, measuring whether she was putting him on or not.

"You're kidding."

"I am not. Are you blind?"

"Well, I didn't notice."

How could he not see Caroline's fluttering approach? She'd watched other women do it, too, and it had ceased to amuse or flatter her as it once had when they sidled across a room, chest first.

Well, never mind, she'd let it drop. "Why don't you go on to bed," she said. "I'll clean up the glass so we don't step on it if we get up to pee." She patted him on the shoulder. "I'll be there in a minute."

Emma dawdled in the bathroom, took her time with the dustpan and broom. The sexy thoughts she'd had earlier had long since evaporated. She was exhausted and had the first cranky twinges of a headache. She swallowed two aspirin. Then she wet a paper towel and carefully mopped the tiles for invisible slivers.

Suddenly the thought struck her: For whom was this broken mirror going to be bad luck? For Caroline or for her?

Jesse was snoring when she joined him. The bedside lamp was still lit. She picked up *Fear of Flying* and found her place. Soon she was reading about the zipless fuck, the one-time encounter with a stranger, no ties, no recriminations, no goodbyes. Just guiltless pleasure in the dark with a blind, deaf and dumb cock. Sounded like old familiar territory to her.

"Happy Fourth of July," she whispered to Jesse and turned the page to the next adventure with a dampened fingertip.

13

IT SEEMED TO EMMA that for the rest of that summer the phone never stopped ringing.

Jesse never answered it if Emma was home, and she began jumping at the sound the way Rosalie always did—as if the phone couldn't possibly bring good news. That summer Rosalie would have been right. It didn't.

Caroline's voice was high and fluty with a thrill of laughter running through it, though she seemed a little surprised that Emma had answered.

"*Emma!*" she said, and then once again, "*Emma!* I want to apologize for my behavior on the Fourth. And I want to replace your mirror."

"Oh, don't be silly." Emma waved a hand in dismissal of the idea, and the pie crust she was holding almost bit the dust. She rested it atop a pile of papers on the bookshelf.

"Well, I felt like such a fool. I really can't drink, you know."

Which is why you shouldn't, thought Emma, biting her tongue and thinking, I've been doing a lot of that lately.

"Anyway, I'd like to speak to Jesse about the mirror."

Jesse? Was he in charge of the mirrors in the bathroom?

"Sure, I'll have him call you when he comes in. He's up at the lodge, at Skytop."

"Thanks." Caroline left her number. "Thanks so much. And again, I'm really sorry."

For what, Emma wondered, exactly what?

"Ummm," Jesse murmured that evening over dinner when Emma told him Caroline had called.

"I wonder why she wants to talk with you?"

"Beats the hell out of me." He shrugged.

.A couple of nights later, just before they got into bed, he said, "Caroline wants to have us by for coffee and to give us the piece of glass."

"What?"

"She took the measurements for the mirror so she could have a piece cut."

"Why the hell didn't she just drop five bucks in the mail if she felt so goddamned guilty about it? We go to the hardware store almost every day of our lives. Didn't you tell her that?"

"I didn't want to make her feel worse than she already did."

"So it's going to make her feel better for us to schlep all the way the hell to Palo Alto to get her stupid piece of glass?"

"What are you so angry about? You don't have to go, you know. I can do it."

"I bet you can," Emma muttered, not quite managing this time to keep her tongue in tow.

"What?"

"I said I'd love to go." Emma pulled a T-shirt over her head, slipped into bed and turned out her light.

CAROLINE'S apartment was exactly what Emma had expected. Everything was very neat, in straight lines, her furniture a mix of black lacquer and light bleached oak. She did indeed paint—large floral watercolors. They weren't bad, Emma thought. They weren't good. Her children were five and seven, a girl and a boy, well-behaved and beautiful like little windup toys.

But Caroline wasn't beautiful today. She wasn't even pretty. The mercurial quality Emma had spotted on the Fourth had landed wrong side up. Caroline looked as though she'd been run over by a truck. Her hair was drab and lifeless, her face was pale, except beneath her eyes where there were liver-colored spots. She wore a limp pink Indian cotton dress. Pink was not her color.

She smiled as she presented them with the piece of mirror which she had prettily gift-wrapped. But she couldn't seem to think of anything to say. She managed her hostess duties, pouring tea for them into tiny cups. And she'd made little almond cakes. But nothing came together. Time hung there—a suspended afternoon.

Little fits and starts of chatter fizzled, then died out. From the children's room came the drone of a television, a sound Emma detested, but welcomed now, as it filled the vacuum in the living room. Jesse, never good at small talk, sat staring at Caroline with a puzzled expression. Did your bubble of fantasy pop, my dear? his wife wondered to herself. Finally she took pity on all of them and opened her mouth.

"Didn't you want to talk to Jesse about art?"

"Oh, yes." Caroline brightened a little. And Jesse picked up the ball. He gave her a mini-lecture, telling her all he knew about art programs, advising that she call San Jose State, maybe talk with Clifton. He was as helpful as he could be.

Emma sat back and watched. There was something very strange about this woman. Very strange indeed.

"What do you think *that* was all about?" she asked as they headed afterward into Menlo Park for cheeseburgers at the Oasis, where once, like thousands of other couples, they'd carved their names in a wooden picnic table.

"Maybe she's depressed about Rupert."

"What about Rupert?"

"He dropped her. He's moved on."

Emma remembered Caroline's saying she wouldn't take Rupert from Lowie. Who had dropped whom?

"Moved on? Does Rupert screw around a lot? Does Lowie know?"

"I doubt it. Which question am I answering? Who knows?"

"Jesse, I haven't talked with you about this because . . ." She paused. "But I feel insulted that Rupert thinks he can bring his girlfriends over to my house."

"*Your* house?"

"Okay, *our* house. But Lowie is our friend. I like her. How am I supposed to act the next time she comes over with Rupert when I know he's screwing another woman?"

"How do you know he was screwing her?"

"Come on, Jesse. Please."

"It's none of our business." And as if that would end the conversation, Jesse gulped the rest of his beer and slapped his mug down.

"Rupert makes it our business when he drags his stuff into our house."

"*Stuff?* Where do you learn words like that?"

"His piece. His honey. His cunt. What do you want me to call her?"

"*Whoa.* A little while ago you were being nice to her and now you're coming down on her like she's a whore."

"Well?"

"She's not a whore, Emma. She's a perfectly nice woman with two kids who's probably lonely."

"Well, let her be lonely somewhere else."

"Jesus Christ. You don't have to make such a big production of it. Forget it, okay? It's over."

BUT it wasn't. Because a week later Caroline called again. This time Emma was even less friendly on the phone. But it didn't seem to matter. Caroline got straight to the point.

"Hello, may I speak to Jesse?"

Hello? What am I, some sort of answering service? Emma wondered.

"Yes?" Jesse said. This time he was home.

Emma sat and listened to his side of the conversation, imagining the other half, hearing Caroline's breathy little voice that sounded as if she'd only just escaped from a boogeyman that very minute.

"Well, I guess I could. Where are the catalogues from?

"No, some programs are better than others. It *is* something you want to take a close look at.

"I don't know. I'll have to check my schedule. I have your number. I'll give you a call."

"She wants help picking out a school," he said, looking Emma straight in the eye. Too straight, she thought. Guileless people don't look at you like that.

"So I gathered. Does she think you're her guidance counselor?"

"Emma, you don't have to be so ungenerous. Just because you got all the breaks."

"Breaks? Breaks? Tell me about all my breaks."

"It's hard when you're alone with two little kids."

"*I* didn't tell her to have them."

"What are you being so hysterical about?"

Emma thought about that for a minute. Was she overreacting? Was she imagining things? She turned back to the jeans she'd been ironing for Jesse before she answered the phone, fingered a thin place. She should put a patch there. How many times had she washed and ironed this same pair of jeans?

She ran her finger down the zipper. She still loved the preliminaries, watching Jesse unbuckling his belt, unzipping his fly. And then something disconnected. When he reached for her, it was as if she were watching a porno flick and suddenly the bulb blew out. The film kept going, but she couldn't see the picture.

Maybe she ought to face it. Maybe she didn't really want him anymore. But if she didn't, what did she want? Did she want to be alone again, free to flit from man to man like a hummingbird?

She flipped his jeans over. On the back pocket was a heart she had embroidered their first year together in red satin stitches. In yellow she'd done the words "Jesse + Emma." Fancywork was the only kind of sewing Rosalie had ever been able to teach her when she was a girl. Nothing practical, like dressmaking, Rosalie had sighed.

"Jesse," she began, not knowing what her next words would be.

"Yes?"

She looked into his face, now soft and open. His irritation was gone. She put the iron down, reached across the ironing board and ran one finger across his cheek. He looked so sad, poor little boy.

Want me, Emma, he was thinking. Want me the way I want you. Let me get inside you—the only way I know to touch you anymore. Hold me in your arms and save me from myself, from women like Caroline who whisper sweet words to me on the phone.

Emma smiled. "What are you doing this morning?"

"What I always do. Going up to Skytop."

"What are you doing right this minute?"

"Nothing. Talking to you. What do you mean?"

She switched the iron to off: "Come with me," she said and took his hand. "I want to show you something."

In the next room she pushed him slowly back on the bed.

"No, sit up," she said. She hadn't meant for him to recline completely. She plumped two pillows behind his shoulders, leaned over and kissed him, softly, with just a slip of her tongue between his lips. He reached for her. "No," she said. "Don't move. Let me do this."

She turned and opened her chest of drawers and took out something, using her body as a shield so he couldn't see, then left the room.

She was only a few minutes in the bath, slipping quickly in and out of her clothes. Returning through the living room, she dropped a record on the stereo, rummaged through the little brass box on the coffee table until she found a joint. She lighted it, took a deep drag and, as she glided back into the bedroom, handed it to him.

He laughed in mock protest. "Emma, we can't smoke dope before noon."

"It's our house, and we're consenting adults," she said. "We can do anything we're big enough to."

Jesse took a hit, held in the smoke, and grinned as he heard the first strains of Jim Morrison from the living room. Emma had placed the stylus on the cut "Back Door Man," the sexiest song she knew. She'd seen The Doors once in New York, Morrison in his black leather pants. She closed her eyes now, standing at the edge of the bed, swaying in time to the music, thinking of Morrison, listening to him sing about unnatural acts.

She slowly began to unbutton her blouse.

"Here, let me help you with that."

"No." She gently brushed his hand away. "I can do it by myself." Still her eyes were closed. "Watch," she whispered.

As he saw the first lacy edge of black, Jesse made a sound deep in his throat. For Emma had donned the underwear he'd bought her once on a trip to San Francisco. They'd been standing in a sexual novelty store on Broadway, laughing together, fingering the goods.

"You'd look great in this." He'd held up the tiny strips of black lace.

"Don't be silly."

"No, you would."

Emma had recoiled a little at the thought. She didn't need props. But what the hell?

He'd been at the counter paying for the lingerie when a drunk Greek sailor approached him. The sailor looked back over at Emma, who was flipping through a magazine, and asked in broken English, "How much?"

"I don't work here."

"No, the girl, how much?"

Emma looked up. Then it dawned on both her and Jesse simultaneously. A black man and a white woman in a porno shop—the man thought Jesse was her pimp.

"A thousand dollars," Jesse answered, and over the man's head he winked at her.

"No!"

"Yes!"

"She must be something pretty good."

Jesse grinned now, remembering that night and the words he'd said. He repeated them now: "She's the best."

Emma slowly dropped her blouse to the floor. The wisps of black lace barely covered her small breasts.

"More, more." Jesse clapped his hands.

Emma played with the zipper of her jeans, released it slowly, wiggled out of her pants. Morrison was still singing in his bad-boy voice. Behind her closed eyes she watched him drop his black leather trousers on a stage.

Now she leaned across Jesse, slowly trailed the length of her blonde hair across his face.

"Your turn," she said, pulling him up till they stood together against the edge of the bed. She loved that feeling, of being almost nude against a body fully clothed. She felt him hard behind his zipper, through his jeans.

The rest was slow and gentle, Emma whispering, "No, baby, let me, here, let me show you, come to Momma, there," lifting her head for a moment, "now, doesn't that feel good?"

For the first time in a long while, Jesse let her lead the dance, followed her shifting rhythms.

Behind her closed eyes, Jim Morrison pulled her onto the stage and the crowd screamed. Emma screamed, too.

"I think you woke up the dog," Jesse laughed.

Emma dragged most of herself back into the room.

"What do you mean?" she asked. Her voice was still far far away.

"He's scratching at the front door."

Emma giggled. "Do you think I woke up the whole canyon?"

"Most of them aren't still in bed at this hour on a Monday morning." His voice too was languid with lust and the laziness of marijuana.

The sound at the door continued.

"Jesse, I don't think that's Elmer. I think someone's knocking."

"Hell, let 'em, they'll go away."

"Is anybody home? I need some help," a man's voice called.

"Stay there," Emma said. "I'll get it." She grabbed her terry-cloth robe.

When she opened the door and saw the man standing there, tall, with wavy white-blond hair almost to his shoulders, she started. For at first glance she thought it was her long ago Atlanta lover Will. His eyes were the same sea-foam green. This man's eyes crinkled at the corners as he looked down into hers.

"I'm awfully sorry to trouble you," he said, shifting from one blue-jeaned leg to the other. "I'm your new neighbor up at the top of the hill."

He wasn't Will. Of course he wasn't. The voice was different. Get ahold of yourself, girl. "The Bradley place?" she said.

"Yes," he said and smiled, showing a gap between his two front teeth. "I'm sorry as hell, but I seem to have run my van off in the ditch in front of your place. I'm stuck."

Emma pulled her robe tighter around her. "No problem. Let me get my husband. *Jesse,*" she called.

Fifteen minutes later Jesse was back in bed. Emma, naked again under the covers, handed him a cup of just-brewed coffee.

"You got him out of the ditch?"

"Yeah. We lifted the sucker out."

"You lifted his van?"

"Sure, have you forgotten that when he's stoned your old man has superhuman strength? Here. Let me show you." Jesse jumped out of bed and pulled Emma to her feet. He tossed her above his head and twirled her around.

"Jesse," she screamed, "put me down. I'm going to throw up."

"Don't do it," he warned.

"Then you stop!" she shrieked.

"What'll you give me to stop?"

"Haven't I already given you enough? What do you want?"

"I want you to—"

But Emma never knew what Jesse was going to say, because the phone rang.

"Saved by the bell," he said instead.

Jesse brought her her terry-cloth robe as the conversation went on. She nodded in thanks. She was freezing, naked, her feet bare on the cold dining room floor. The inside of their house never warmed beneath the redwood shade, not even in early August. He listened to her side of the conversation.

"What do you want me to do?

"Well, what did the doctor say?

"You didn't take him yet?

"Then how do you know?

"Rosalie, this isn't a time to be so cheap. There must be a psychiatrist over in Cypress.

"Oh, I forgot.

"I guess you're right.

"Okay, okay. Try to calm down. I *know* it's hard. Just keep him as quiet as you can until I get there.

"I don't know. I'll have to call the airlines. *Today* if I can. I'll be there soon."

She hung up and turned to Jesse, "My daddy's gone crazy," she said. "I've got to fly home."

14

West Cypress

EMMA hadn't been able to get on a plane that day and had hardly slept at all that evening. What *was* wrong with her daddy? she worried. She'd been trying to read to take her mind off the question, but her book rested face down in her lap.

She checked her left hand one last time. Yes, she'd remembered to take off her wide gold wedding ring as she did every time she went south. She'd left it atop her chest of drawers at home. She rubbed at her finger. The fat woman in the seat beside her gave her a look and Emma tried to be still. At least she wasn't tan, otherwise she'd have had to wear a cigar band on her hand and have told Rosalie it was the latest thing in California. The naked spot felt numb. Well, thank goodness she'd paid attention to one thing Rosalie had drummed into her, to protect her fair skin. It had never crossed Rosalie's mind to warn her against *marrying* a dark complexion.

"To your left is the city of Shreveport," said the pilot in that comforting good-old-boy voice that Emma thought they must be taught in flying school. "We'll be landing in Cypress in fifteen minutes. Take your seats, please, and fasten your seat belts."

Fifteen minutes from Shreveport to Cypress. She thought of all the times she'd driven the distance on old Highway 80, three and a half hours of two-lane winding road.

She looked out the window at the gentle pine-covered hills. Somewhere down there was where she and her step-cousin J.D. had rolled together on a dark-blue blanket in a cotton field by the edge of a bayou.

Good Lord, that seemed like a long time ago. How many years

was it? She subtracted. Thirteen—an unlucky number. Well, Lady Luck surely hadn't sat on J.D.'s shoulder. Emma still couldn't get over it, though it must have been five, six years ago when Rosalie had written her about his accident and sent the newspaper clipping.

J.D. had become the sheriff of West Pettibone Parish. She could just see him, growing fat and sassy with power. "Hey, Bubba, you want to run over to the 7-Eleven and get me an RC Cola?" He *looked* fat in the picture in the paper, no longer the sleek long-limbed boy she remembered.

He'd learned to fly. His mother, Aunt Nancy, must have been so proud of him. He was on his way to Arkansas to pick up a prisoner who'd broken out of the West Pettibone jail. J.D. must have been hot for that one; the nerve of that peckerwood, making him look like a fool. Sheriff J. D. Tarley had been flying his little plane over a silver Arkansas lake, just as pretty a fishing hole as you ever hoped to see, when suddenly something went wrong. There was a quick boom, then a flash of crimson, and *splat*. The lake put the fire out. Once the water settled, little blue and silver fishes swam up to stare goggled-eyed at the man inside, his inky ringlets floating gently, gently.

Rosalie had written that she and Jake had climbed into the car and driven up to Pearl Bank for the funeral. They hadn't been there since before Rosalie and Nancy's mother, Miss Virgie, had died. Rosalie hadn't seen her sister Nancy since then, either, not since all that hullabaloo over the double, no, triple funeral. Well, she hadn't seen her to speak, anyway.

"There was that once," Rosalie had told her on the phone when Emma called to talk after the news of J.D.'s death. "I was standing there in the Dollar Store with my hand on a pair of pale-green polyester pants, thinking how high they were. I could make them for half the price. I was just about to head back to the piece goods to see what remnants they had on sale, when I looked up, and there she was—Nancy, just as big as life and twice as mean. Mean as ever! Do you think she spoke to me? Well, stop wondering, she didn't. She looked me straight in the eye, and I looked her back, and then she let go of the other leg of the pants I was holding and turned on her heel and stomped off. Disappeared in between the pots and pans and the hair dryers."

But nonetheless Rosalie had felt that she ought to go up to

Pearl Bank to pay her respects. After all, J.D. was her nephew
and an important man too.

So she did. She and Jake had driven straight to the church
where J.D.'s widow Maylene's father was preaching the funeral.
Afterward, Rosalie had gone up to Nancy.

"I hugged her neck," she told Emma. "Then we got in the car
and drove back home."

"You didn't say anything?"

"Well, yes." Rosalie paused a moment thinking till she remembered that the long distance was burning up money. "Yes, I
said, 'I'm sorry. About J.D., I mean.' Because I didn't want her
to think I was sorry about anything else, that I was apologizing."

God, Emma thought, nothing ever changed in West Cypress.
Well, she was almost there now. Below was the winding brown
snake of the Coupitaw lined with thick green trees. Home.

What *was* wrong with her daddy? Emma wondered for the
four hundredth time since the call last night. It was hard to
know what anything meant when Rosalie told it. Once she had
diagnosed Jake's appendicitis as indigestion. He'd almost died
before they got help. But usually her diagnoses went the other
way, on the side of overstatement. And her idea of treatment!
Rosalie was of the go-ahead-and-get-it-over-with school.

Like when Emma was twelve and it looked as though she was
going to spend the entire summer in a dentist's chair, Rosalie
had said, "I don't know why you don't go ahead and get them
all pulled out. Get yourself some dentures like mine. With teeth
it's just going to be bridges, crowns, one thing after another.
Might as well go ahead and get it over with."

Emma had burst into tears. She could just see herself in the
eighth grade with false teeth. "Isn't life just one thing after another, Momma?" she'd wailed. "I'd might as well go ahead and
shoot myself in the head and get life over with, too."

Rosalie had backed off and admitted that Emma had a point
there, and she had begrudgingly paid the dentist. "But it'll all
have to be done over again," she'd said. "Just you wait and see.
They don't know what they're doing, any of them. They're just
after your money."

That was the same thing she'd said about veterinarians too
when Emma's one and only dog, Skipper, had had terrible
eczema. Rosalie had said it was no use fooling with it, she'd
seen it before, and had had him put to sleep.

Emma wondered whether Rosalie was thinking Jake's case was hopeless and was contemplating putting him to sleep, too.

He must be pretty bad off if Rosalie didn't think she could fix what ailed him with a little Mercurochrome, vinegar and hot saltwater. She always said most doctors didn't know any more than she did anyway. She remembered more than a body would think from her year of nurse's training. And most of what ailed folks just called for a little common sense. No use traipsing off to a doctor's office to sit and wait to hand him your hard-earned money. You could sit at home and wait in your own living room. Most things got well by themselves anyway, or you died, without your spending a cent.

Rosalie, crazy as a bessybug, Emma thought, but you couldn't say she was boring. For, as the years passed, Emma had developed a bit of a sense of humor about her stepmother. Not, however, that she'd embraced her to her bosom. But every summer she flew to West Cypress to spend a week, to say hello, because that was what she felt she ought to do. Like Jesse, she still wished that her folks were like everybody else's—which to her mind meant Robert Young and Jane Wyatt on "Father Knows Best." But they weren't. So she tried to be grown-up and make the most of it. Or at least, that's how her visits always started out.

"Honey?" The fat woman in the blue hat sitting next to Emma suddenly patted her on the arm.

"Yes, ma'am?" God, Emma thought as she heard herself, just let me fly over the South, haven't even touched ground yet, and I get mush-mouthed and full of Southern manners. At least that kept the locals from staring at her, though this old gal was doing a pretty good job of it.

"You just hold on to my hand when we land, and I'll pray for both of us. Everything's gonna be all right, I promise."

"Are you scared, ma'am? There's really nothing to be frightened of. The percentages are much higher that you'll die in a car wreck," Emma answered.

"Why, no!" The woman drew herself up, her chest heaving like a sack of flour that had been dropped. "I'm not scared. But aren't you?"

"Whatever gave you that idea?"

"That book." The woman pointed at the paperback on Emma's lap. She'd been trying to finish it since the Fourth of July, but what with one thing and another, she hadn't been able to. Across a picture of a woman's torso with her dress half unzipped marched the title in bold black letters: *Fear of Flying*.

Emma laughed. "This is a novel," she said. "It's about . . ." She hesitated, realizing she couldn't very well explain the protagonist Amanda Wing's sexual exploits and the zipless fuck. "It's not really about being afraid of flying."

"Well, I wondered." The woman sniffed. "With that cover." And she turned away and closed her eyes as the plane came in for a landing. She prayed, but only for herself.

I'm home, Emma thought. Help me, Lord, Jehovah, can anybody hear me? I'm home.

ROSALIE was waiting for her at the airport, had been there half an hour early as she always was, pacing and craning her neck to look up through the plate glass window at the sky.

She hoped she could get Emma to stay the rest of the summer. That would be a nice visit. And God knows she could use the help.

But she knew Emma probably wouldn't. She was always fidgety, nervous as a witch. Always kept at least a thousand miles between herself and West Cypress, and then when she did come home she wasn't in the house five minutes before she was on the phone, laughing and talking, calling up friends and making arrangements to run off here and there. Just like when she was a teenager, in and out.

Well, this time would have to be different.

"Flight 106 from Dallas will be landing in just a few minutes," said a voice from somewhere out of the ceiling.

Rosalie turned from the plate glass window to the seat where she'd left Jake. Behind thick glasses his blue eyes were swimming.

"That's Emma's plane," Rosalie said.

"No, not Dallas. She lives in California." There he was, being crabby again.

Why did Jake always have to cross her? Most of the time he didn't know what he was talking about—not that this craziness had made *that* any different; he never had.

"She changed planes in Dallas, Jake." She used the same tone of voice she'd used with those generations of junior-high-school children who always thought they knew everything. "Miz Fine, pay a fine," they'd sung behind her back, down the hall.

"Oh," Jake said and then shook his head. He looked down at the floor sadly. There'd been the time he would have gone on with it, yelled at her right out here in public. But recently most of the spunk had gone out of him.

Rosalie felt sorry for him now. God knows he hadn't been an easy man to live with all these years, what with his moods, his bursts of temper, long silences—and his laziness. And all that talk of faraway places, as if they were made of money, as if West Cypress weren't good enough for him. That's where Emma had gotten her restless ways. Atlanta, New York, California. Lord only knew where she'd light next. Though you could be sure it wasn't going to be here. Rosalie was surprised Emma'd even agreed to come this time, since she'd already done her annual week in June. That was probably how she thought about it, "doing a week," as if she were serving time. But she'd come for Jake. She'd always loved her daddy. Rosalie scrabbled in her black plastic purse for a tissue and wiped her eyes. That was her lot, wasn't it, to never be appreciated.

Well, it was high time Emma came and helped out. She needed her now. Jake was about to drive her round the bend.

She'd known for a long time something was coming on. For ages he'd been pulling all the curtains at night, peeking around them into the backyard like there was something out there.

Rosalie herself had been a little nervous, what with their living so close to the Quarters and the niggers having gotten so uppity since integration. You just couldn't tell what might happen. Of course, nothing ever had. But you couldn't be too careful. It was after all of that started, mixing in the schools, that she had begun locking the door for the first time in her life. Because give them an inch, you just never knew what would be next.

But this business with Jake. This was something else.

"Is she here, is she here?" he was saying.

Rosalie knew he couldn't see that far, but he must have felt her, for Rosalie had gotten distracted and the plane *was* here, the last passengers looking a bit stunned as they picked their way down the steps of the little plane onto the blazing-hot runway. Where was Emma? Rosalie was always afraid that one time she'd come down those steps and she wouldn't even recognize her.

"Hi," the tall blond woman suddenly beside her said. Yes, that was Emma. She'd know her anywhere.

"No, I don't really want anything. I ate on the plane."

"But I saved dinner for you."

Emma looked at all the pans sitting on the stove. "Save it for supper, okay?"

"I've got okra mixed with squash. Some rice with tomatoes. And those nice pears I put up. Did you want some chicken? I can thaw some out."

I have a Southern stepmother who can't cook and a black husband who doesn't like to dance. Isn't it funny how the stereo-types somehow don't work out? What if they switched roles? Jesse *could* cook if he wanted to; he just never did. And could Rosalie dance? Had she ever? Emma had no idea. She watched her hovering near the stove as if she were just dying to fire up some-thing. Rosalie looked great for her age. She wore a new silvery wig from Woolworth's, and her figure was still as trim as it had been when she was a girl. Only her wrinkles gave her away.

"No, I'm fine. Maybe just a glass of iced tea." Emma fanned herself. "It's awful in here. How hot do you think it is?"

"Maybe ninety-six, ninety-eight. It's always hot in August. You'd think you'd be used to it."

"But remember I haven't lived here for over ten years. And where I am, near the coast, it never gets hot like this. The sum-mers are cool."

"I know you tell me that, but I never can believe it. I just can't imagine." Rosalie placed a glass of tea in front of Emma, who took a big gulp.

And then before Emma could stop herself—and she'd meant to watch her tongue, this time especially—she said, "What *is* this?"

Rosalie averted her eyes like a child caught doing something wrong. "It's tea. Instant iced tea."

"And what else?"

"Cherry Kool-Aid. Your father and I like it mixed. And it's cheaper that way."

Cheaper than what? Emma wondered. She put the glass down on the table and tried to rearrange her face. "It's good. Just a little different." And unimportant, she reminded herself. But it did matter, it all did, all the little things. They added up, one by one, and twisted in her gut. Grab it now, grab the edges of the mask of your polite face. Open your mouth, it's not so hard, and say the proper, the kind thing. "Rosalie, I know this has been hard for you. Come sit down and tell me all about Daddy."

Jake didn't look or act a bit differently, as far as she could see. Perhaps a little more hesitant, a little more slow. Had Rosalie made it all up?

"Just a minute." Rosalie slipped out of the kitchen, through the plastic curtain that separated it from the hall. She was back now. "I wanted to see if he was napping. Though I don't think he can hear, anyway. He's getting so deaf."

They both were. Each complained to Emma when the other was out of the room. And when they were together, it was like the Abbott and Costello routine, "Who's on first?"

Emma fanned herself with a church program she found resting on the table. It was so hot she felt nauseous and slightly faint. "Can we turn on the air-conditioner?"

Rosalie frowned at the wall unit. "I don't think it works very well."

"When's the last time you used it?"

"Oh, when your Uncle George came to visit."

"Ma, that was three years ago."

"Well, you know *I* don't need it. I've lived here all my life. And it didn't work right then. I was so embarrassed. There was a wasps' nest up in it, and the fan couldn't turn. They stayed at a motel. Wasting all that money when your bedroom was perfectly good—and empty." Rosalie was rising now. "I'll go get that little fan out of your room."

Emma tried to stop her. "Couldn't we turn on the attic fan and cool off the whole house?"

Rosalie pretended that she didn't hear. Emma was always like that, no sooner in the door than she wanted the lights on, the air conditioner on, or in wintertime the heat. She wanted special, expensive things to eat. Or she was talking on the phone, so after she left Rosalie would have gone over her limit for her reduced rate. Well, it was only a nickel or dime each call, but it mounted up. It was a good thing Emma had never had to live through the Depression. She never would have made it. She was so spoiled, so used to having every little thing. Rosalie didn't like to think about what was going to happen to Emma in her old age. She bet she wasn't laying away a dime. What was she going to do then? Rosalie thought of the money in her own savings account. All those nickels and dimes multiplying into dollars. This was what they were for—it was here now, her and Jake's old age. Though now that they were old, she didn't want to let any of it go. But she could see it dribbling away with Jake's illness. Oh! She *was* going to leave it all to Emma, who, God knows, was going to need it. She'd probably go through it all in one year. Her whole lifetime of scrimping and saving—Emma would blow it all on who knows what? Last time she was here, she'd been talking about investing in real estate. California real estate! Why, Rosalie told her, she'd put money into a couple of lots in West Cypress and they'd never done a thing.

And Emma was talking more and more about leaving teaching. You're just going to have to do better than that, Rosalie told her. Why, she'd have to be crazy, leaving a good job with a pension! Then Emma had gone on about how she wished she'd had some guidance when she was a girl—that all she'd ever been told she could be was a teacher, a nurse or a librarian. As if there were anything wrong with that! Good steady jobs that a person ought to be proud of. Rosalie had said to her, maybe she ought to come back to West Cypress and teach. It wouldn't cost nearly as much to live, and she could put more by for her old age. Or if it was the students who were bothering her, and Rosalie could understand *that,* then why didn't she just come on home and get a job clerking in a store? But she could tell by the expression on Emma's face she thought she was too good for *that*. Emma had always had fancy tastes—like air-conditioning. As if there weren't more to life than being *comfortable*.

Just then she got the fan situated so that it oscillated back and forth across Emma's face. There, that ought to cool her off.

Then she began: "He was out in the backyard with money balled up in his fist."

"Doing what?"

"Well, that's what I asked him the first time. I said, 'Jake, what on earth are you doing out there in the middle of the night?' I hadn't heard him get up."

"Did he have a flashlight?"

"No. He was stumbling around in the dark. He could have fallen in a hole and broken a leg. And *then* what would we have done with him?"

You could have shot him like a horse, Emma thought. And then in her mind she slapped her mouth for being so smart.

"He didn't want to tell me at first, but when I got him in the house he said, 'I was looking for the people who kidnapped the baby. They won't give the baby back if I don't give them the money.' 'What baby? What money?' I asked. And then I saw that fist and I said, 'What do you have there, Jake?' Well, finally he showed me. It was three hundred dollars! He was walking around with three hundred dollars wadded up!"

"Where did he get it?" Did he steal it out of the bottom of your purse, Emma wondered, a little at a time like I did when I was a kid, copping nickels for chocolate éclairs and hot dogs?

"He saved it from his Social Security."

"It must have taken him a while."

"Yes, but he said the voices had been asking him for it for a long time. And he could hear the baby crying—out in the yard. He knew he had to do something about it."

Then Rosalie broke down.

Emma reached across the table and patted her hand.

"It's been so awful," Rosalie sobbed. "Being with him here alone. He won't stop talking about them—the voices. He hears them all the time. And he wants me to hear them, too. He says, 'Listen, Ro, listen, there, there, can't you hear them?' And I don't hear a thing. They're not real!"

"I know."

"Then one night he got up, I usually stay awake as long as I can because there's no telling what he's going to do, but I guess I'd just drifted off, and I woke up, and he was standing there in the bedroom with a gun."

"A gun!"

"You know, that old pistol that I keep in the bottom dresser drawer. It hasn't been shot in probably forty years. I kept it in the store in case somebody broke in. Remember that time I told you, when that drunk nigger tried to hold me up?"

Emma nodded. She did remember the story, though it had happened before she was born.

"Anyway, your daddy was holding the pistol. It was empty, I discovered later, but it scared me to death. So I got up easy, and I said, real soft so as not to scare him, 'Jake, what are you doing?'

" 'They're going to kill the baby,' he said. 'I promised Helen nothing bad would ever happen to the baby. So now I'm going to have to kill them.' "

Helen, oh, the mysterious Helen. Emma had continued to ask

her father questions about her every time she saw him, but the
bare skeleton of his story never put on flesh. And now, whatever
it was that had happened with her mother, whoever she was, it
was all coming back to haunt Jake in his old age. Those terrors
he had been carrying around, hidden like the wad of money in
his hand, were out now, ordering him to stand alone and face
them in the dark.

"What did you do?"

"I just talked to him. And then I got closer, and I talked him
into giving me the gun. 'There's no one there, Jake,' I said.
Finally I think he believed me, and he started to cry. He was
afraid, he said. He was afraid of the voices, and he was afraid
for the baby, and he was afraid of being alone. But he's not
alone. I'm here."

"Yes, you are," Emma said, and she reached over and gave
Rosalie an awkward hug. For they never touched each other except upon first greeting and final leave-taking. "And I'm here,
too. We'll work this out. We'll find out what's wrong."

"The doctors won't know anything."

"Well, let's don't say that until we try."

"I don't know who you think you're going to call. There's no
psychiatrist here. I told you on the phone, that Stewart man got
run out of town because he was . . . funny . . . what do they
call it now?"

"Gay."

"I guess so. Well, anyway, he's gone, and there's no one else.
At least not that I know of. And anyway, how can we afford it?"

"Medicare, Momma. And I can help you some."

"They won't pay all of it."

"Let's worry about that later. Right now, I want to put in a
call to Marshall."

"But he's a medical doctor. He won't know how to do anything about your daddy losing his mind."

Emma always had a drink with Marshall Stokes, Bernie's best
friend in high school, and now Cypress's most successful intern-
ist, when she came home. Marshall had the best bedside manner
she'd ever known, even when he was handing her a gin and tonic
by his and his wife Sally's pool.

"Maybe Daddy's problem is physical. Let's have Marshall look
at him first."

Rosalie didn't resist, though Emma knew this was hard for her. She'd asked for help, but when she stepped off the very narrow path to which she held her life, dragons lurked.

Emma returned from the phone. "He'll see us first thing in the morning."

Rosalie looked up at her and nodded. Then she reached into the bundle of things she'd been worried about and said, "A colored woman came here."

"What do you mean, a colored woman?"

"Hattie. She used to trade in the store when you were a little girl. She had three children, a boy about your age. She came a couple of weeks ago and knocked on the back door."

"What did she want?"

"She said your daddy had taken to walking home through the Quarters at night, on his way home from the bar, and the colored people over there were worried about him, because he seemed lost."

"Well, that was nice of her."

"Yes," Rosalie answered. "It was. It was right after that that I woke up and found him with the gun."

"How do you feel, Daddy?" Emma asked him later that evening. The two of them were sitting on the screened-in back porch. He'd slept all afternoon. Rosalie had run out to the store.

"Okay," he said. He looked at her with his blue eyes, owlish behind big lenses. Then he looked down at the floor. "You didn't have to come," he said in a voice that was apologetic. "I'm all right."

"I think you are, too. But we need to make sure of that."

"I wish they didn't, didn't talk to me about the baby," he said. "But-but-but . . ." Then he looked at her very strangely. He wasn't just stuttering. He was struggling with something he didn't understand.

"There is no baby, Daddy," she said. "I'm here. The baby's grown."

"I know." He smiled then, as if that was the answer to everything. "You're all grown up. B-b-but . . ." and then she could see him going away again, to somewhere terrible in his head, "I promised Helen, it didn't matter, it never mattered, I would never give the baby up."

"You didn't, Daddy. You didn't give the baby away. You kept her."

"I was scared. The baby was so little, and she was hungry, and Helen was lying there . . ." His voice choked. "I was all alone. I was so afraid, being all alone."

"It's okay. You did the right thing," she said and went to sit beside him on the chaise. She took his hand, which had become as soft and white as her own, no longer the strong hand wielding a meat cleaver when she was a child. The sound of a night baseball game wafted across the backyard from a neighbor's television.

"Do you remember all those games we used to listen to on the radio when I was a little girl?"

"The Dodgers. The Brooklyn Dodgers. They were something." Then he laughed the way he always did when he paid a compliment, as if in the giving of it he was receiving praise too and was a little embarrassed.

"Yes. They really were."

"I don't listen to them anymore."

"They moved to LA, Daddy."

"I *know* that. They moved a long time ago. I'm not crazy, Emma."

She looked at him in the half-light of dusk and smiled gently. "No, of course you're not."

Then he faded out again, like the voice of the announcer saying, "A high pop fly to . . ." Someone changed the channel and she couldn't hear the game anymore. "I promised I wouldn't tell you, but sometimes I think I ought to."

"You already told me about Rosalie and my real momma," she said. "A long time ago."

Jake shook a warning finger at her. "No, no. You don't know . . ." he trailed off. Then he leaned over and whispered, "The baby shouldn't be out there in the dark alone."

LATER Emma listened to both Jake and Rosalie snoring in the next room. They had always slept just beyond the door, across the hall.

Her room, the guest room, though she'd never lived in this house to which they'd moved shortly after she left for Atlanta, was a recreation of the one she'd left behind the grocery store.

She lay in a curlicued metal bed, a replica of a brass one she'd seen in a magazine as a teenager and thought romantic. Piled on it were the long dolls in satin dresses that Jake had won for her, pitching baseballs at targets at the parish fair. On the night table lay books she'd never gotten around to reading: *The Red and the Black, Swann's Way, The Joys of Yiddish.* That last one she kept meaning to take home with her, wherever home had been over the many trips and many years, but it never found its way into her suitcase.

She wondered whether she left it here to remind Jake that he was a Jew—just as she was. After she found out about Helen, which made her, by anyone's rules, Jewish, she'd gone for a while in Atlanta for religious instruction. When she told the rabbi about her upbringing, he'd seemed much more interested in talking about that than in teaching.

"It's like a mystery story," he'd said. "Where was your mother from? What was she doing in New York? Why don't you track down her family?"

"I wanted to know about her, but I wanted my father to tell me," is how she put it later to her Jewish roommate in New York, "just like I wanted him to tell me about what it means to be a Jew."

Her roommate undertook the latter task, picking up where Herman had left off, took her home for the High Holy Days, for Passover, gave her a basic New York Yiddish vocabulary, so she knew a shmuck from a shmatte and wouldn't embarrass herself. "You can't go around with a name like Fine and not know the difference between a fool and a tacky dress. Though with your accent nobody's going to believe you're Jewish, anyway, even if your name was Esther Goldblatt."

And after a while Emma realized that her cultural heritage was what she was interested in anyway. But she was going to be no more religious as a Jew than she'd been as a Baptist.

Jesse had never quite understood it. "Why do you want to identify with a group that's been so persecuted, if you don't have to?"

"Would you pretend that you weren't black if people couldn't see your skin? Jake and Rosalie pretended for so long that I was something else, the label is important."

Jesse shook his head.

When she tried to talk with Jake on visits home, he'd smile, as if it really pleased him that she thought of herself as Jewish, but he always said, "Not too loud. It'll upset Rosalie."

So Emma left behind *The Joys of Yiddish*. She wondered whether Jake had ever read it. But he probably never came into this room. (He did, though. He had done it for years. When he was lonesome for Emma, he sat on the edge of her bed and patted the pretty dolls he'd won for her.)

Rosalie was in and out of the room all the time. She filled the closet with the overflow of her scores of polyester pantsuits. When she found the fabric on sale, she couldn't resist. The quilt on Emma's bed was made of little scraps of all those garments, patched together with her sewing machine's zigzag stitch.

Around the walls marched Rosalie's drawings of Emma. Some of them were hung side by side with the original photo. Was that so that the viewer could see how close she'd come to capturing the image? Emma wondered. Or was it some kind of voodoo—casting a spell that would bring her back home again?

Did Rosalie think about things like that?

They had never talked about their feelings for each other since that awful Christmas when Emma had snapped out her suspicions about Rosalie being her stepmother. That had been nearly ten years ago, that first trip back from Atlanta. Since then, on her annual duty calls they politely walked around each other. They smiled and exchanged pleasantries, that was all.

Yet she was my mother, Emma thought. She raised me since I was ten months old. But I live in California and she might as well live on Mars.

It was so strange: for all the trouble Rosalie had gone to to have a daughter, Emma couldn't remember Rosalie's ever having said the words *I love you*. Neither to Jake nor to her. She said them to her little dog Bootsie, but never to people.

Instead she talked about being hurt, cheated, slighted, about things being overpriced. Was love too expensive for her, too? Was the chance of being short-changed just too great—so that she'd decided simply not to deal in that commodity, even though the husband and child she'd cut a bargain for in a moment of emotional profligacy were already in place?

Had the deal been sealed before she realized, too late, that she just couldn't play? For if she truly considered the world too ter-

rible and hurtful a place to bring her own child into, why did
she think things would be any different for a stepchild?

Suddenly the air in the room felt even more close. Emma sat
up again and pulled her T-shirt off. It was too hot to sleep in
anything. Except for the little oscillating fan, nothing moved.
The room smelled musty.

"Rosalie, you really ought to get someone in to clean once in a
while and to help you with the yard," she'd said early this afternoon.

"I can keep my house myself. It's perfectly clean." Rosalie had
the same disdain for housekeeping that she had for cooking. She
slapped a dust mop around every once in a while. "And no one
else knows what I want done in the yard."

"They could at least mow the lawn. How much could it cost?"

"Too much." And that was the end of that, like a door slamming shut.

It was Rosalie's life, Emma reminded herself. If she wanted to
be out there in the broiling sun pushing a lawn mower, it was
her choice.

Emma stretched out, trying to find a cool place in the sheets.
They felt like polyester, too. Perhaps Rosalie had been running
up bedclothes from sheet-sized remnants.

She would be scandalized if she could see Emma lying naked
in her bed. But, God, it was *so* hot.

Emma wiped a trickle of sweat from between her breasts. And
for the first time since she'd left him standing in the airport that
morning, she thought of Jesse.

They'd done the right thing, choosing to never involve him in
any of this. What would be the point? He didn't want to be part
of West Cypress and her family any more than they would have
wanted him to be.

She closed her eyes and saw his handsome face. She rubbed the
fingers of her right hand across her naked wedding-ring finger. It
still felt a little numb.

What was going to happen to them? she wondered. Was their
story going to have a happy ending? Were they going to grow
close again? (They were nice, weren't they, those moments they'd
spent together in bed before the phone call from Rosalie. She
couldn't remember when she'd last felt so close to him. She'd
whispered, "I love you." He'd whispered the words back.) Was it

going to get better when she went home—life with Jesse, her secret husband?

Or worse? Would she one day tell Rosalie and Jake, "I have a good-news/bad-news joke. The good news first—I'm divorced."

God, she was never going to get to sleep with those kinds of thoughts. She should read a little while. She reached for the lamp, fumbled, and then there was a crash as all the carnival dolls fell onto the floor. One of them suffered a shattered skull beneath its blond wig, and its blue eyes rolled under the bed. What could they see under there? Were there monsters? Was the Green Skeleton waiting?

"Emma? What was that?" Rosalie, alarmed, was standing in the doorway.

"Go back to bed. Everything's all right. Go back to sleep, Rosalie."

And for the thousandth time in her life, Emma thought, who's the momma here? In all the secrecy and hush-hush, did we swap places?

A WEEK of tests passed. Then a week and a half.

"You've had a little stroke," Marshall said to Jake. "Probably several tiny ones."

Jake's eyes looked frightened behind his glasses. He turned to Rosalie, who was twisting the strap of her plastic purse.

"What does that mean, Marshall?" Emma asked.

"You're going to be okay, Mr. Fine. It's going to take a little while to see the effects of the medication we're putting you on. You'll have to take it every day."

Jake nodded obediently like a child.

"The voices?" Rosalie asked.

"They'll disappear."

Jake looked from Rosalie to Emma, then down at the plushy brown carpeted floor of the doctor's office, as if the hallucinations were something of which he was ashamed.

What did I say, Jake wondered, when I was out of my mind? Did I tell them everything? I must not have. Everyone is being so nice.

"They're not your fault, Mr. Fine. I know the images are very real to you, but they're only triggered by the lack of oxygen to the brain. It's funny how the brain responds when it doesn't get enough air to breathe. We're going to give you some tranquilizers to make you rest easier until they subside. So you'll be sleeping a lot at first. But we're going to keep close tabs on you."

"He doesn't need to go to the hospital?" Rosalie asked.

"Oh, no. I'm sure he'll be safe in your hands. You'll see that he takes his medication. Home is where he needs to be."

"I NEED to go home, too," Emma said later that afternoon. They were sitting on the back porch drinking iced tea. Now that the crisis was over, she couldn't sit still. When they walked back into the house after stopping by the pharmacy for Jake's medication, the old claustrophobia had grabbed her by the throat. She could stand it as long as she had to. Now she didn't have to anymore.

Rosalie looked up from the peas she was shelling. Each one pinged into an enamel pan. She'd picked them at dawn that morning before the blistering heat rose. Her garden was in full harvest, popping out vegetables almost faster than she could gather them. "You're not going to go so soon."

"I have to. I really need to get home."

"But you don't have to be back at school till after Labor Day."

Emma looked down at her hands. The vacant spot on her left hand no longer looked naked. She had ceased to miss the heavy gold band's weight. But Jesse was waiting for her, and her house, her work, and Skytop. There was so much straightening out to do.

Suddenly she'd missed Jesse with a palpable ache. It was good to have gone away—now she had a fresh perspective. She needed to get back. They could make a new start and make things work. She knew they could.

She looked over at her father, who had just taken his pills. He had a pleased expression on his face, like a little boy who had been very bad but now was being good.

She needed to be good, too, she thought. She needed to try harder with Jesse. She could be more loving if she tried, more patient. She didn't want to strike out on her own again. They'd have a long talk when she got back.

"I'm going to call Susan and tell her when to pick me up at the airport," she said, using the name of her imaginary roommate.

"Okay," Rosalie answered, deciding to be brave. It didn't

make any difference what she said, for Emma had always done exactly what she wanted to. "That's awfully nice of her."

"Yes, it is." Emma smiled. "Susan's always gone out of her way."

JAKE insisted on making the drive to the airport, though Rosalie thought he ought to stay home and rest. "Let him go," Emma said. Later, when Jake was out of hearing, she whispered, "I don't think he ought to be home alone." There was that, but she knew he felt it was his duty to wave her off.

The airport was crowded. Businessmen clutched briefcases, sample cases, under the arms of their pale-blue and -tan rumpled ice-cream suits. Running in and out of the crowd were a passel of black children all dressed up in their Sunday best. The little girls' patent-leather shoes squeaked on the shiny floor.

"Would you look at that?" Rosalie whispered behind her hand.

"What?" asked Emma.

"All those Nigras flying—with money from their welfare checks."

Emma didn't answer. But in her mind's eye she saw winged blacks filling the skies like crows—or black angels.

She focused on the group of black people clustered by the gate. There must have been twenty of them, laughing and talking, all standing close together as if they didn't want to say good-bye. Then one of the women, a round short woman in late middle age, nodded at her. Emma smiled tentatively and nodded back.

She turned Rosalie's shoulder in the direction of the woman. "Do you know her?"

"Who?"

Emma didn't want to point.

Suddenly Jake beside them said, "I do."

"Why, so do I," said Rosalie. "That's Hattie, the woman I told you came to the house. Jake, you remember Hattie, don't you?"

"Yes, I said I do." He smiled at Hattie across the room.

Rosalie was distracted by the announcement of incoming planes. But Emma caught the sweet look that passed between the black woman named Hattie and her father. It made her catch her breath. She took Jake's hand in hers.

Hattie was coming toward them, now she was only about three

SARAH SHANKMAN 241

feet away. "These here's my grands. My daughter Viola's kids." Then she turned and caught a tall black man by the shoulder. "This is my oldest, Marcus. He's on his way back to San Jose, California." San Jose was just north of Los Gatos, where Emma lived.

Marcus, a handsome man in a yellow polo shirt and tan khaki slacks, reached over and extended his hand to Emma, who shook it. Behind her she could feel Rosalie's discomfort. Men and women didn't shake hands in West Cypress, and certainly not black and white. But this was almost California. Once she stepped foot on the plane, West Cypress would be gone.

"I remember you," Marcus smiled. "You were the little girl with the chocolate."

"Yes." Emma laughed and she could see her own hand, small again, slipping two Hershey bars into Marcus's grocery sack. Then her memory flipped back a couple more days. It was his hand now reaching out to stop her from slipping down the muddy canal bank. A few months later, he was waltzing with her in a dream. She'd never forgotten that dream, the Green Skeleton, the boogeyman of her childhood, releasing her into this man's arms. Except then he had been a little boy.

"So you got away, too," Marcus said as they settled into their seats on the plane.

"Yep, I made it out alive. And never looked back."

"You were home visiting?"

Emma told Marcus about her daddy.

"I'm sorry to hear that. The doctor said he's going to be okay?"

"Yes, he'll be his old self again soon, I'm afraid." They both laughed. "A gin and tonic," she said then to the waiting stewardess.

"Make it two."

Marcus insisted that the drinks be his treat.

"I owe you at least one for those candy bars." He winked. "To West Cypress," he toasted her. Their plastic glasses bumped silently.

"To getting out and coming back and getting out again."

JESSE greeted her at the airport with a big hug.

"Did you miss me?" she whispered into his ear.

"You bet," he said. "I almost starved to death."

"Is that the only reason?" She poked him in the ribs.

"Nooo. That's not all I missed. But you'll have to wait till we get home for that."

She smiled, but inside she stiffened a little. Relax, relax, she reminded herself. Everything's going to be different.

"You've eaten?" he asked as they were about to pass Los Gatos on the highway. "Last chance. You want a hot dog or something?"

"No. I ate on the plane."

"You smell like you did a little drinking too."

"More than a little. I think I'm still a little drunk."

Jesse raised an eyebrow. "Can't let you go anywhere. Well, I've got some leftovers in the refrigerator. If you're hungry later we can fix you up with something."

"You cooked?"

"Of course I cooked."

Oh, it was good to see the canyon again. She loved this little mountain road, the wooden bridges, the death-defying curves up the final hill.

"And the windows are almost finished? Great!"

"Yep. It's been going well—beginning to see daylight. I've even been sleeping up there." He paused. "I had a phone installed."

"Where?"

"At Skytop."

"Really? Why?"

"I just told you. I've been up there so much, and I've been thinking about what you said about being isolated."

"But you never even answer the phone." Emma didn't know why she was being so contrary, but something was niggling at her.

"Don't you get tired of driving up when you need me?"

"I've been doing it for almost four years."

"Well, now you don't have to anymore."

The bottled salad dressing was the first thing she saw when she opened the refrigerator door.

"Jesse," she called, "who's been here?"

"What do you mean?" He was in the bedroom.

"There's Roquefort dressing in our fridge." Jesse hated Roquefort cheese.

There was just a pause, a two-beat hesitation. She felt him taking a deep breath.

But his voice was ever so natural as he answered, "I had some friends over."

"Friends?"

"Rupert. You know."

No, she didn't know at all. Rupert had been here twenty, thirty times before. He'd never asked for Roquefort.

And then she did know, had already known in her heart, in a place where a door had begun to open with a warning creak and she'd kept kicking it shut. Caroline and Jesse must have had quite a love feast in her absence.

"Are you getting something to eat or are you coming to bed?" Jesse asked.

She couldn't go into their bedroom yet. "I need to call Rosalie and let her know I got back okay," she said.

Emma looked around her kitchen, where nothing was different—the same old cabinets, the same testy electric range—but suddenly everything had changed.

15

MONTHS ROLLED BY. Summer slid into fall, the rains began, and Emma closed her eyes to Jesse's affair with Caroline. If she didn't admit that she knew, she wouldn't have to deal with it. And since she wasn't sure she *really* wanted him, but wasn't willing to let go, either, since she couldn't decide whether or not to get off the pot, she pretended to be deaf, dumb and blind, and she coasted.

There were some rewards. In the place of the intimacy of their early days there was a sort of calm. Jesse seemed kinder, more solicitous, less fractious. Well, he was getting what he wanted, she guessed—whatever that was.

Sometimes she stood off and looked at her teaching, her cooking, her long tight body, and she thought, Let Jesse go, why not? You'll be exactly where you were before him, just a little further along. And wouldn't it be delicious, to take a good deep breath without feeling that he was worrying at you about that thing he had so long referred to as your secret part?

As in: "There's a secret part of you, Emma, that's self-possessed and far away. You don't really need anyone. You think you do, for a while, but you don't. It's like you popped out whole, Aphrodite from Zeus's forehead, but you did it all by yourself."

"You make me sound like some kind of machine, an automaton. I'm not like that."

But she was, Jesse thought, sort of. For what she did, without knowing it, was use people up.

He'd watched the phenomenon again and again. At first, if someone appealed to her, Emma would turn to him with her unique warming focus—like a magnifying glass in the sun—asking questions, paying a kind of attention that was as flattering as it was unusual. It was as if the object of her attention were a new dish Emma wanted to taste. But once she'd rolled it around in her mouth, chewed on it until she had discerned the ingredients, well, then her curiosity was slaked, and she was ready to move on. However, the someone would by that time consider himself or herself (gender was not an issue here) a friend, certainly more than an acquaintance.

"That's what you did with Bernie," he'd told her.

"How do you know?"

"Because I listen when you've talked about the men in your past."

"You asked me!"

"That's not the point. The point is that you tossed them all away—like used tissues."

"Not all. There were survivors, a few who lived to tell the tale." She thought of long-ago Will. But then, too, hadn't he suspected something like what Jesse was saying, something that scared him so that he moved on? Then she mugged a mouth like the devouring shark her husband accused her of being. "You're full of shit, Jesse."

But perhaps there was a bit of truth in his words—an idea that, when she thought about it, made her more than a little uncomfortable.

IT was early December, and getting out of the canyon on weekends was impossible, the roads clogged with flatlanders driving to the mountains to cut their own Christmas trees.

"You better start early if you're going to get across the highway," Emma said.

"That's what I'm doing." Jesse was pulling on a flannel shirt, a jacket. "I just need to run up to Skytop first. I left some measurements."

"Where did you say you were going to be all day?" She asked it lightly, as if she were inquiring about the weather.

"Place in Oakland I want to check out, has Victorian salvage." Just as lightly he asked, "Sure you don't want to go?"

How polite we are, she thought, in our conspiracy not to stumble over the body of Caroline which might as well be lying on the rug here between us.

"No, thanks. I don't think so." There was a time, oh, there *was* a time, when she would have pulled on a jacket and jumped into the truck, happy as Elmer to be taking a ride. "Today I'm going to run down to Boccia's. Tony's talking about doing a cookbook and wants me to help him test some recipes."

"Great," Jesse said. She knew he wasn't listening to her. His mind was already on his first destination, Caroline's apartment in Palo Alto.

"Have a good time." She waved him out the door. "I hope you find what you're looking for."

He turned on the heel of his boot and gave her a look.

Emma smiled brightly and blew him a kiss.

SHE hated being late. Jesse was just out the door and once again the washing machine had exploded. The chipmunks thought it was a larder, had filled it with nuts. Now water had backed up and blown out the hoses.

Where was Jesse when she needed him? By now, screwing his little sweet patootie.

But on the other hand, if she lived alone, there'd *never* be anyone to help.

And then on the third hand, she said to herself, stripping off her pants, soaked from the washing machine, and struggling into another pair, why don't you just shut the hell up?

She grabbed her bag loaded with cookbooks and raced out the door.

At the end of the canyon road she could see the line of traffic to the highway ahead. From the valley side were station wagons full of children with expectant faces. Big green firs on wheels rolled down from the hilltop. Damn! She was never going to get out.

Finally someone waved her and the van behind her into line. She should have called Tony Boccia: "Christmas trees are clogging the road, and my washing machine was full of nuts." She looked at her watch. She'd never make it.

Then she glanced into her rearview mirror. The man in the van behind her waved. Who the hell was that?

She crept forward a foot.

Bump. Bump. Her tires made a funny sound. Probably a broken Christmas-tree branch.

The van behind her tooted. She glared into the rearview mirror. "I'm doing the best I can, you bastard."

He honked again. *Okay. Okay.* She rolled forward another foot. *Bump. Bump.*

Then a tall man with long white-blond hair was leaning down looking into her face. Her heart leaped. Will! No, no, she'd made this same mistake before. But where, when?

"You know you've got a flat?" By God, listen to that. He was Southern! When he smiled, a gap showed between his two front teeth. "And now I get to return the favor," he said. "Three, four months ago your husband pulled me out of the ditch."

That was it! He was the man at the door that day she and Jesse had made love stoned, the day Rosalie had called her about Daddy.

She looked at her tire. He was right, left rear, flat as a fritter. Now lots of horns were honking.

"Goddamned flatlanders," she said. "Why can't they buy their Christmas trees in stores like other people?"

"Minor Daniels," the man laughed and extended his hand. His sea-foam eyes crinkled at the corners.

"Where are you from?"

"Up at the top of the hill. I bought the old Bradley place."

"Before that?"

But his answer as to his origins got pushed aside by a man yelling, "Get that thing out of the road."

"Some Christmas spirit!" Emma volleyed back.

"Here," Minor said, still grinning, "let me push you off."

He did. Now their vehicles stood side by side at the level pull-off by the highway pay phone. He opened his hand for her car keys. "Shall I?"

"Be my guest." His head disappeared inside her trunk. "I appreciate your help, but I hope this doesn't take very long."

"What?"

She raised her voice. "I said, 'I hate to sound ungrateful, but I'm in a hurry.'"

"Well," his head reappeared, "I could change your tire a hell of lot quicker if you had a spare."

"Shit! I forgot!" She slapped herself in the forehead as she remembered the tire she'd left at the station in Los Gatos the week before. She looked at her watch. "I'm never going to make my appointment."

Minor reached into his jean pocket and handed her a dime.

"What's this for?"

"Call," he said, pointing at the phone.

"Now." Minor wiped his hands on a red bandana. He'd insisted on checking her oil while the station attendant changed her tire. "How about a cup of hot chocolate?"

That wasn't a bad idea. "Sure, come on up to the house, and I'll make us some."

"Let's go to my place instead."

Emma paused. She couldn't go to his house with this man whom she hardly knew, even if he looked like Will, even if he was a neighbor.

He saw the look on her face, and his gap-toothed grin reappeared. "I meant over the hill to my restaurant in Santa Cruz. You have the time?"

"*You* own a restaurant?" With his long hair and round gold-rimmed glasses, he didn't look like any restaurateur she'd ever seen.

"Yeah." He laughed. "Half of La Rosita, at the marina. I keep my hand in a few other things too."

"Like what?"

"Ah—Southern women. You-all never give up, do you? Get in the van and while we drive over the mountain I'll tell you my whole life story."

Emma thought about it. The road beside them was still filled with Christmas trees, happy families, smiling kids. She'd rescheduled her meeting with Tony. Her husband was off with his lover. The morning mist had cleared. It was going to be an absolutely gorgeous day.

She locked her car and turned to Minor. "Why the hell not?"

"WHERE are you from?"

"South Georgia," he said. "Little town you never heard of."

"I used to live in Georgia."

"I thought you might've."

"So try me."

"Dexter," he said.

"Nope." She shook her head, then pointed at herself. "West Cypress, Louisiana." She paused. "How'd you get to be called Minor?"

"My daddy's Major. Really Beaufort Marion Daniels the Fifth.

I'm the sixth. My son's the seventh. We call him Seven. All the men in my family have nicknames."

Through the van's windows an apple orchard paraded in uneven rows down the side of a hill.

"Like Big Beaufort."

"Little Beaufort, Major, Minor, you got it." He lit a cigarette, pausing two beats. "Your folks still living in West Cypress?"

Emma nodded.

"How they cotton to Jesse?"

"They don't know about him."

Minor laughed. "You never told them he's black?"

"I never told them I'm married."

"Whowhee! That's some brass. They'd have a fit, right?"

"A screaming hissy."

"What other skeletons you hiding, woman?"

She just smiled. That's for me to know, Bubba, and you to find out.

THEY sat at the bar of the Rosita sipping spiked Mexican hot chocolate. Minor had made the drinks himself.

"What else do you do?"

"Fried chicken," he said. "Best pecan pies and fried chicken in the whole world."

"*I* make the best fried chicken."

"Challenge you to a cook-off sometime."

She shook his hand. "Deal. And other than chicken?"

Minor pushed back on his bar stool, tilting himself almost supine with his long legs. "I can see you've heard the gossip. I'm going to have to come clean."

"Well, I heard something. But I can't remember what."

"Well, Lord have mercy, woman, that's no good. That's like not remembering the punch line to a joke."

"Are you going to tell me or not?" Emma made a ferocious face.

He laughed. "Where do you want me to start?"

"At the beginning."

As she said it, Emma realized that she *was* curious about this very attractive man who reminded her so much of Will. She liked it that he kept smiling at her with his crinkly eyes as if she pleased him all the way down to the tips of his cowboy boots.

"Half my youth was misspent hanging out at the Dexter truck

stop listening to tales of open roads and memorizing country-
and-western tunes. When I got out of reform school"—and now
she knew he was lying; for reform read military, no, prep school—
"I pulled myself together and went to Emory—"

"*I* went to Emory."

"Couldn't have. I wouldn't have missed you."

Emma sniffed. "I didn't date undergraduates."

"How the hell old are you anyway?"

"Thirty."

"I'm thirty-two." Minor figured for a minute. "In a hurry to
get out of West Cypress?" He lit another cigarette and then
grabbed her arm. "Isn't this too pretty a day to be inside? Drink
that thing down and let's go for a sail on my boat." He pointed
down to the marina. "That one there." It was a beauty.

Moments later he gave her a hand aboard.

"It's a shame to give a boat this beautiful such a silly name,"
she said, reading the word *Grits* painted on the side.

"Ain't it?"

"AND then I did my hitch of alternative service 'cause I didn't
want to go kill Vietnamese who'd never said a bad word about
my momma."

"Where?"

"Hospital in Atlanta—mostly peeled potatoes for two years."

"Made you want to go into the restaurant business?"

"Naw. Made me want to kill."

They both laughed.

"After that did lots of stuff. Played guitar fair-to-middling well.
Traveled in a band for a while, Looney Toona. Got married.
Had a baby boy. Went on tour. My wife got bored. We got di-
vorced. Ended up here in California."

"You married now?" Emma held her breath.

"Yep, she's an actress—down in LA."

"Your son's with her? He lives down there?" (*You're* married,
too. Remember? What you getting so huffy about?)

"He is now. Seven bounces back and forth, be here for the
summer."

(She too?) "Why don't you all live together?"

"Sometimes we do. But I don't like it down there—where her
work is. Too easy for me to get in trouble. I find enough here to
amuse myself."

(I bet you do.) "Ought to be easy for a man who can fry chicken."

"And sail. Which I'm doing a pisspoor job of." The mainsail was flapping. "Get ready to come about."

Emma ducked under the sail as Minor maneuvered it to the other side of the boat.

"And then?" she asked when they got back on course.

"Then? After Looney Toona, you mean? Then I got involved in selling dope."

Emma tried to keep her face straight. Minor laughed.

"Not hard stuff. Just marijuana in wholesale lots. I'd go down to Mexico and arrange for shipments in through Scotts Valley airport."

"I always thought those Scotts Valley stories were just that—stories."

"Well, the Feds believed them. That's where we got caught. Yep." He played with a rope. "Served my time in Lompoc, two years."

(He'd been in *jail!*)

"Yep." He smiled, reading her mind. "Sitting right before you is a genuine jailbird. Peeled a hell of a lot more potatoes. But all the while my money was doing pretty well in the stock market. Kept in touch with my broker by mail."

"The money you made dealing grass?"

"Yep. They can put you away, but if they can't find the bread they can't make you give it back. So when I got out, I put some of it in the restaurant, some in that health food store down on the plaza. And I putter a little in mountain real estate."

"Good Lord."

"Shocking, huh? But I'm reformed. Now I do good works."

"Like what?"

"I fund part of the day-care center in town and volunteer one day a week. I like little kids."

Emma shook her head. A Grade-A Southern talespinner and bullshitter. She'd met his kind before—well, similar, but hardly ever as cute.

THE late-afternoon sun felt wonderful on her face. The hell with her complexion. Emma lay on her back on the deck as they slowly headed back toward the marina. Her eyes closed.

"This has been a wonderful day," she said.

"We'll have to do it again sometime."

She'd love to, but she couldn't.

"We can invite Jesse to come along next time," Minor said.

Emma sat up and stared Minor straight in the face. He winked.

"DID you find anything at the salvage place?"

Jesse had awakened her getting into bed. She squinted at the clock. Eleven. The sea air must have knocked her out. She'd already been asleep for a couple of hours.

"Some old school lamps with long brass rods and white globes. Now go back to sleep."

She did and dreamed of Minor giving her a hand off the *Grits* onto a bamboo dock in the South Seas. Out of the midst of a welcoming party marched the king. He was wearing a grass skirt, a big grin, and looked exactly like Marcus from West Cypress— now San Jose. Jesse was not in the dream.

But it was Jesse she snuggled up against when in the dream she and Minor began making love. Minor whispered, "Hey, darling," into her ear while rubbing a hand across her behind. "Great fanny."

"Ummmm," Emma murmured.

"Well." Jesse awoke, hard against her. "What a pleasant surprise."

"MEETING Rupert for lunch tomorrow," Jesse said the next Saturday. "Want to join us?"

"Nope. I'm going to stay home and work on some of Tony's recipes."

Neither of them ever mentioned Caroline. The affair was now five months old.

Emma had barely closed the door behind him when the phone rang.

"What do you think about this rain?" Minor asked.

"Who is this?"

"Don't play coy with me, woman. You've been hearing my sweet Southern voice in your dreams."

(How did you know?) No, she didn't say that. Instead she said, "You shouldn't be flirting so shamelessly with a married woman."

"A pretty woman whose husband shouldn't leave her alone so much."

"How do you know I'm alone?"

"Because I have a telescope aimed right at your front door."

"You're kidding."

"Would I kid about a thing like that?"

"Prove it."

"Put down the phone for a minute and walk out the front."

Emma never knew what got into her. She slipped out of her robe, opened her front door, and stepped naked onto the flagstones.

"Whoowhee!" he yelled when she picked the phone back up. "I *knew* you were beautiful. Hold it right there, lady. I'll be down in a flash." He hung up.

"No."

Minor slipped his hands under her robe. Now he opened it.

"Come to Daddy," he breathed. "What sweet little breasts."

She shook her head again; her heat was rising fast.

He ran his fingers up and down her body, avoiding the obvious places.

"No," she repeated.

His head rose. "Why not? Jesse won't be back until tonight."

"How do you know that?"

He never stopped touching her, here, there, but not there, ever so gently. She was fighting to keep her hands off his zipper.

"Take me to bed," he said. He gave her his hand. "Take me because you want me."

He leaned over and licked her eyes, her nose. She began to tremble. She had to distract herself or she was lost.

"How do you know how long Jesse will be away? He just went to the store."

"No he didn't. I know where he went, and so do you."

"How do you know?"

"I've followed him."

Emma pulled back from Minor then and stared into his eyes.

"I was curious because I've wanted you from the first time I saw you, when you came to the door in this robe"—he looked to where he'd thrown it on the floor—"with the smell of sex all over you." Emma leaned against his chest and closed her eyes. "That was August tenth—four months and ten days ago. It's five days till Christmas, Emma. I'm a mighty patient man, but I'm ready for my Christmas present." He tickled her ear with his tongue. "Won't you be my Christmas present?"

Jesse was with Caroline this very minute, she rationalized. Doing this very thing. She ran her hand under Minor's flannel shirt. His nipples hardened.

"Howdy, lady," he whispered and kissed her gently. Then, in a while, not so gently.

She took the hand he'd offered her and led him into the bedroom. The room was cold, but neither of them felt the chill.

"Come to me, Emma." He smiled, leaning back as she fell upon him. "Come on home."

WINTER rolled into spring. Along the highways the ice plant and acacia and mustard bloomed. Then in May the rains stopped. By the last week of June the hills were golden, edging toward brown, and dry. The threat of fire in the mountains was constant.

Emma and Minor saw each other almost every week, though never in the canyon again, always aboard his boat. While they bobbed happily in the ocean, Minor strummed his guitar and sang, "Lay, Lady, Lay." They smoked grass and made love.

The drill went like this: the minute Jesse left for Caroline's, one of them called the other. "All clear. Let's go."

Then came the day when Jesse forgot something and doubled back up the canyon road just as they were heading out. They met on the second wooden bridge, a sandwich with Emma in the middle.

Jesse got out of his truck.

"Where you headed?" he asked Emma. "I thought you were staying in." Then he looked behind her at Minor, who waved.

Emma mumbled, "I need some things at the store. Got to get ready for the Fourth."

"Hi, stranger," Jesse called. "Haven't seen you since you fell in our ditch. Been almost a year, hasn't it?"

"I've been real busy," Minor answered with his easy drawl. "You know how it is when you're having a good time." Then he reached out his van window and shook Jesse's hand. They talked for a few minutes about the canyon waterlines, the potholes in the road that needed fixing.

"Well, we haven't been very neighborly ourselves," Jesse was saying. He turned back to Emma, who was leaning out the window of her car. "We ought to have Minor for dinner. How about next week?"

"Sure," said Emma, swallowing hard. "Great."

"Monday?"

Emma and Minor traded glances and answered in chorus. "Monday's fine."

"Okay." Jesse smiled at both of them and headed back to his truck. "Let me pull off here and let you both by." He waved as the two vehicles passed.

Emma trembled all the way down to the bottom of the road. At the foot of it, she signaled a left turn to Minor, down toward Los Gatos.

Jesse had found them out, she knew it. He was going to catch them and kill her.

Minor nodded and turned right, in the other direction, headed over the hill alone to Santa Cruz. When Emma pulled off the highway into Los Gatos, she looked into her rearview mirror Jesse waved and smiled and kept going.

"EMMA sure is a fine cook," Minor said, helping himself to seconds of fried chicken and potato salad. "I thought I made some good chicken myself, but I take off my hat to you." He tipped an imaginary one to Emma, then turned back to her husband. "You're a lucky man, Jesse Tree."

"Yes, I am." Jesse smiled as he answered, slowly and deliberately, as if he meant what he was saying, but something else too.

Emma's hands were clenched in her lap. She didn't dare smoke, because she couldn't hold a cigarette still.

I don't know this man, she kept reminding herself. I don't know a thing about him. She'd been chanting that thought like a rosary for the past two days.

"What part of the South are you from?" Jesse asked Minor as they pushed back from the table and retired to the living room.

"Georgia."

"Emma lived in Georgia, too."

"Really? Where?" He turned to Emma, his eyes big and green.

"Atlanta." Don't ask me where I went to school, Minor, she willed him. I can't waltz through this charade. Keep it simple, please.

"You ever been to the South, Jesse?" Minor veered off as if he could read her mind.

"Nope. Never really wanted to."

"Well, there's some beautiful country. Great fishing and hunting. Funny people, wonderful sense of humor."

Jesse concentrated on pouring glasses of cognac. "I guess I'd have a hard time finding much amusing."

Minor pushed his imaginary hat back on the top of his head. "Well, I grant you there's lots of assholes in the South. But you can't lump them all together. Some of us are worse than others." His big grin kept grinning.

Jesse had on what Emma called his bull look. Made him look twice as big and four times as scary. "It's hard to know, isn't it? I guess to me all Southerners look alike."

Emma wanted to scream, Okay, you caught us. We're fucking our brains out. So there! Now what are you going to do about it? She opened her mouth.

But before she could say anything, Minor, like a Southern gentleman avoiding an unpleasantry, changed the subject.

"You do that mighty handsome portrait over the fireplace?"

Jesse nodded. "A long time ago."

"Beautiful woman."

"My mother."

"She looks a little like my wife, Kit."

Emma sat up. Well, that was news to her.

"Your wife's black?" Jesse asked, then his eyes narrowed, as if he was taking some new measure of this man sitting in his living room.

"No, but she's part Spanish. Her skin has that same golden tint."

Emma never asked questions about Kit, and Minor never mentioned her, except to say he was flying to LA or she was coming home.

Emma felt a little twitch of jealousy then, but that was silly—wasn't it?

She and Minor had talked about it. Minor wasn't interested in leaving his wife, and Emma didn't know what the hell she was doing, she'd said, except enjoying him, enjoying sex again, as if Jesse's need for her had made that part of her numb and Minor had warmed it up again. They were good friends—and lovers.

"Tell me, Emma," Minor was saying now, drawing her back into the conversation. "I understand you teach at a junior college."

She couldn't seem to find her voice just then. She nodded.

"Great vacations, huh?" he filled in the space for her.

Come on, Emma, you can do it. Talk. "Yes," she agreed. "Especially this year." Then, as if Minor didn't know, she explained about her cooking, that after summer school she was taking the whole next school year off to apprentice in kitchens in Italy and France, that she hoped never to teach again.

"Maybe I'll join her for a couple of months after Christmas," Jesse said. "It's been far too long since we've been in Europe."

Emma stared at him, her mouth open. They'd *never* been to Europe—together. They'd never even been to New York. She hadn't been able to get him off this goddamned hill, away from Skytop. What was this, a pissing contest?

"Emma's been so busy with her friend Tony Boccia, we never go anywhere."

Her mouth, like a fish's, was flopping open and shut. She felt like she was going to have a stroke. *She'd* been busy! *She* never wanted to go anywhere? She wanted to scream: What the fuck are you talking about?

Instead she smiled at Minor and said, "Jesse's jealous of Tony because we've been testing recipes and I haven't been cooking at home much." She turned to Jesse. "But you know he's gay, sugar."

"Couldn't prove it by me." He turned to Minor. "I've never laid eyes on him. Could be Tarzan for all I know."

"You're going to be very embarrassed when you meet him, Jesse. I've been trying for ages to get you to come down and join us for lunch."

"Let's have him up here," Jesse said, waving his cognac glass and spilling a little. Uh-oh, Emma thought. "Let's see this *Tony*." She blinked. Was he really jealous of her friend? Was she missing something?

"You ought to have a wife who spends all her time in LA kissing other men for a living," said Minor. *"That'd* give you something to think about." Then he explained about Kit's acting.

"Doesn't bother you?" Jesse swung his big head in Minor's direction.

"No more than it would bother Emma, I guess, for you to use life models."

"I used to use nudes years ago, when I sketched and painted some," Jesse said. "But not anymore."

"What about that newel post?" Emma asked. "Didn't you use a girl for that?"

He had indeed—used one. He'd forgotten.

"What was her name?" Emma was staring at him. Had she suspected something then? That was over a year ago.

"I can't remember." And he couldn't.

Minor laughed. "See, that proves my point. Nudity in the name of art, doesn't mean a thing, does it?"

And then Minor went on to admire Jesse's furniture in the living room. They started talking about wood, which it seemed Minor knew quite a bit about, having enjoyed woodworking as a boy. The next thing Emma knew, Jesse was inviting Minor to visit him up at Skytop soon. Great, she thought. Then we can invite him and Kit over the next time she's home, and we can all become great friends. Maybe *she* and Jesse could have an affair. Maybe we could *all* get into bed together. Maybe I'll fall in love with *her*.

"Nice fellow," Jesse said when Minor was gone. "We should have gotten to know him sooner."

"Yes," Emma said.

"Didn't you like him?"

"Sure. Why?"

"You don't sound very enthusiastic. I think he'd be someone you'd be most curious about. Want to collect—as one of your specimens."

Determined not to rise to the bait, she changed the subject. "That's one dinner party down this week, another to go. You sure you want to do this on the Fourth?"

"Yes." He seemed willing to move on to another subject, too, now that he'd fired his shot. "We'll barbecue like we've always done."

THE day, no different from any other July day in California, was sunny and bright. Three couples gathered again—Maria and Clifton, she and Jesse, Rupert and, this year, Lowie.

"I can't believe I missed last Fourth. No summer colds for me, ever again." The three women were in the kitchen while their husbands were out in the lanai, stirring the coals.

"Can you just wish them away like that?" Emma asked.

"A woman can do anything she puts her mind to," Lowie answered.

Maria and Emma exchanged looks. What did Lowie know about the last get-together when Caroline had been on Rupert's arm?

"Ain't that the truth?" Maria said with a smile.

Lowie laughed. "You've been so long with Clifton, you're starting to talk black."

"Well, *Emma* always does." Maria defended herself. "I don't hear you teasing her."

"Nope. Emma talks Southern."

"Sounds like the same thing to me."

"Well, you may have a point there." Then Lowie handed a bowl of her Waldorf salad to Emma to put into the refrigerator. "You know what, Emma, I think the only person here who doesn't talk black is Jesse. He's always sounded like a white man to me."

"I know. He does, except when he's playing. My stepmother, Rosalie, thinks he's white when she's talked to him on the phone."

Lowie laughed. Her orange halo of hair wobbled. "You still playing that charade?"

"Sure am. It's not hard, Lowie. My parents never visit."

"But they call?"

"Mostly we write. But Rosalie calls every once in a while, and a couple of times when I wasn't home she's gotten Jesse. She's never asked who he was."

"Maybe she's smarter than you think she is. You can never tell with these old gals. Maybe she'd just rather not know."

"How's your dad?" Maria asked.

"He's doing fine. My friend who's Daddy's doctor was right. The medication fixed him right up. Rosalie's been letting him out of the house again at night to play dominoes for almost six months. He walks home just like he used to."

"I expect the exercise is good for him," Lowie said.

"Yes, it's good for him to get out," Emma agreed. Then, as she said the words, she remembered again, as she had many times, Hattie smiling at her father in the airport. She'd gnawed on that smile a lot in the past year. No, it had to be her imagination. Her father was an old man. And Hattie was a colored woman. In West Cypress?

After dinner, Maria and Clifton left early for the drive back up to Berkeley. And true to form, as usual, Rupert wanted to stay for a while. Everything changes, Emma thought—Caroline and Jesse, Minor and me, Rupert and Lowie—and yet nothing. And, as always, I want everybody to go home.

"Come on." Lowie took Emma by the arm. "Let's leave the men to their drinks. I need to take a walk."

Emma held back. She'd seen Lowie only once during the past year, and that had been at a party where they'd never been alone. What if Lowie had found out about Caroline and Rupert?

"It's too dark," she said.

"Don't be such a sissy. Come on."

"Go ahead," Jesse said. "Just holler really loud and we'll come to the rescue if the boogeyman gets after you."

Emma capitulated.

"Let's go this way," Lowie said, heading up the hill. Emma *never* walked in that direction, up the road which dead-ended at Minor's house. She couldn't think of a good excuse not to. Then Elmer wagged his way out from under their house, carrying a rock.

"You want to go, boy? Give it here."

Elmer dropped it. Emma threw it up the one-lane road, and Elmer scampered on ahead, wriggling.

"Takes so little to make that dog happy," she said.

Lowie took slower steps now, scuffing up dirt. "Takes a lot more for people, doesn't it?"

Uh-oh. Emma's stomach lurched. Here it comes. She's going to ask me about Caroline. She willed her not to. God, I don't want to be the one to break her heart.

"Are *you* happy, Emma?"

Emma relaxed. She hadn't realized she'd been holding her breath. She could answer this. One word. Easy. "Sure," she said.

Lowie kicked at a rock, then took a deep breath and looked Emma straight in the eye. "There's something I think someone ought to tell you."

Emma froze. Elmer was waiting patiently for her to throw his rock again. Finally he barked.

Oh, shit, she thought. This isn't what I suspected it was at all. She's not *asking* me about Caroline. She's going to *tell* me—about her and Jesse.

"I don't think I want to know."

"But you ought to." Lowie's voice was eager, almost as if she were delivering good news.

Don't tell me, please don't. If you tell me, I have to *do* something about it. I have to figure out what I want.

Then Lowie let her have it, all in a rush. "Jesse's making a fool of you with a woman named Caroline. Everybody knows it."

There. There it was. She'd pretended ignorance for a whole goddamned year, and now Lowie had laid it out for her to see as clearly as if she'd written the words here in the dust.

She was cold, clammy. Something acrid burned her nose. She felt as though she was going to throw up.

"I know Caroline," Emma finally answered in a thin tight voice.

"Yes, she was here, last Fourth of July, wasn't she? I'd forgotten that."

"Forgotten it?" Emma turned to her. "How could you forget it if you knew she was with Rupert?"

"Oh, Rupert," Lowie said with disdain as if she were naming a little-loved pet. "He's always played around. I don't let it bother me anymore."

"Then why are you telling me about Jesse?" Emma's voice rose. "Isn't it the same thing?"

Lowie shrugged and looked away, up the road. Then Emma understood. Lowie wasn't telling her this because she wanted to save her or her marriage. And it wasn't that she didn't care about Rupert. She cared, all right. She wanted Emma to care, too. She wanted Emma to feel exactly what she felt. She wanted to spread the hurt around.

"They meet at our house sometimes," Lowie said in a conspiratorial tone, as if she were gossiping about someone else's life.

Emma tried not to rise to the bait but failed. "In Oakland? All the way up there? They involve you and Rupert—after he and Caroline . . ." She let it trail off.

No, Lowie wasn't going to have any answers. That wasn't in the bag of tricks she'd brought with her to unload on Emma's doorstep. She'd already done what she came to do.

"It's been going on for a long time," Lowie said. "I'm surprised you haven't figured it out."

They were at the last big loop in the road now. Above them

gleamed Minor's living-room windows which looked across the canyon and down toward the Trees'. Inside there somewhere was Minor's telescope. Was he looking at them now? Could he see how masklike, how closed, her face had become?

Emma felt exactly the way she did in an emergency, cold and calm.

Lowie wanted an answer, and until she had it she was like Elmer worrying a bone. "Didn't you even suspect?"

Emma turned and stared at her. She felt she hardly even knew this woman, an acquaintance, not a friend, who was serving up the cold remains of her marriage to her on a platter and asking, "How do you like it? Does it taste good?"

"No," she answered, "I never knew a thing." Then she turned her back, her hands clenched so tightly her nails cut her palms. Had she been fooling *herself* all this time, thinking that she really didn't care? Then why did she feel so awful inside? She understood now why kings once killed the bearers of bad news, and it wouldn't take much more for her to push Lowie off this mountain. Then the messenger reached out to her with a small neat hand, which Emma shrugged off, saying, "I'm going back home now."

"Well, you needn't be so . . . I mean, it's not *my* fault." Lowie's big eyes were full of tears.

For whose hurt is she crying, Emma wondered, mine or hers?

"No," Emma said. Her voice seemed to her to have the most peculiar ring, like high heels clicking on marble, cold gray marble tombstones laid side by side. "No, it's not your fault at all."

Lowie and Rupert left shortly after the women returned, Lowie insisting that she had a bad headache. "I need to go home and lie down in my own bed, Rupert," she said.

Yes indeedy, Emma thought, the one you've made. And I, in mine, in just a few moments—if I can get you out the door. But Lowie had signaled Rupert, and in no time at all they were gone.

Emma stood staring at the closed door. Is this a scene that's going to play over and over forever on the night of July Fourth, she wondered, my ushering people out of my house who've stayed too long, who have left me with ashes in my mouth and a sink full of dirty dishes? Though this year there were no shards of slivered glass to clean up.

But maybe if I'd looked into those pieces of mirror more closely last year, if I'd looked at my face in those fragments that Caroline left behind and asked, *What do you want, Emma?* I wouldn't be asking myself that now. When you cleaned up that broken mirror so quickly you didn't save anybody from bad luck.

"What are you doing?" Jesse asked. He was settling into the sofa with a drink. "They sure ran off in a hurry. Did you and Lowie have some kind of argument?"

"Jesse," she said, crossing the room toward him. She felt so very odd. She wasn't thinking about what she was doing, just standing off watching herself do it.

He heard something in her voice, looked up like Elmer with his ears perked, his expression watchful, sniffing the wind.

"I know about Caroline."

His gaze didn't waver. She'd give him that.

"How long have you known?"

"Lowie just told me."

"*Lowie.*" He spit the word out like a bitter seed. "That cunt."

"It's not—" She began, but he cut her off.

"It's none of her goddamned business. She's always sticking her nose in where she doesn't belong."

The room was so dark and quiet around them, Emma felt that she was floating, as if the two of them—she in a high-backed chair he had bought at an auction, and Jesse on the leather sofa—were suspended. She blinked and the edges of the sofa seemed to be rimmed in light. The whole world had come down to this. There was nothing outside this room, nothing anywhere. Was this what it felt like when two people faced each other with drawn guns, life narrowed down to just one pinpoint of space and time? But that was life or death. This was *love,* or it used to be. She wasn't sure what any of it was about anymore, or what she was doing here, but whatever it was, she had to play it out.

"You didn't know before?" Jesse asked.

She had rehearsed this scene so many times in her head, the moment of confrontation when she would play the wronged wife. She'd run her lines, his. But that question had never been in the script.

She hesitated. This was crucial. He was very crafty, Jesse Tree, turning this into a game. What was he holding in his hand? What should she show him in return? There was real danger

when the stakes were this high and you had to make up the
rules as you went along.

"No."

"No what, Emma?" His full attention was upon her. He leaned
forward, studying her face.

"I didn't know!" But her voice was rising. He'd win if she got
rattled.

"Come on, Emma. You're a very smart woman. You knew all
the time."

"I didn't."

"Don't play stupid with me."

And she rose to the bait, the challenge to her intelligence, as
he knew she would. "Yes, goddamn you, I've known from the
beginning!"

"So why didn't you say something?"

Why, he was pushing the move back to her, putting her on the
defensive. Wait a minute. *She* wasn't the one in the wrong here.

"What could I have said? If I'd asked you to stop seeing her,
would you have stopped?"

Instead of answering, Jesse rose and left the room. Then from
the kitchen she could hear the tinkle of ice falling into his glass.

"You want anything?" he called, his voice light now, as if this
were any other time. He was stalling.

Did she want anything? As in: *I'm going to the bank, can I
bring you anything? Sure, how about a million dollars?* But what
did she want? Even now, as she stood upon the precipice, knowing that any step could be the one that tumbled them over into
the abyss, she didn't know the answer to the question.

"Emma?"

"Some cognac, please."

For a woman who had almost always known her mind—who
could run her finger down a row of dresses, through a catalogue,
yes, no, yes, no, ticking them off—here, in the big time, she was
adrift.

More than once she'd flipped a coin and said to herself. "Go,
stay," to see how she felt about which way it fell.

She'd sat in bed with a pen and a yellow legal pad. One of
the items she'd written under "Stay" was: "Don't give them the
satisfaction."

Them? Them, the people who whispered, *"Mixed marriage—
it'll never fly."* All those people she watched avert their eyes

quickly, pretending they weren't looking. Rosalie and Jake—if they knew. Which raised another question, the one voiced by perfect strangers who didn't know what the Sam Hill they were talking about, to use one of Jake's expressions, who harumphed, "Well, a Southern girl marrying a black man. *That's* a pretty obvious rebellion, don't you think?" There were people who had suggested to her, to her face, that she had married Jesse as a *statement*. Well, fuck them very much, she thought, if it had been a statement she ought to have told Rosalie and Jake—right?

How easy it was, she thought, to look at other people's lives and see them in terms of yes/no, good/bad, black/white.

Jesse was back now, holding a balloon glass half filled with cognac in one hand, in the other his scotch. He set them both down on the table before her, ever so politely. He still hadn't answered her question: If she'd asked him to stop, would he have stopped?

But while he was in the kitchen he had thrown off his watchful look and exchanged it for one she absolutely hated—righteous indignation, which made his back ramrod straight. His mouth turned down at the corners, yet with a whisper of contempt, as if he smelled something nasty, as if he were Prince Hamlet. Yes, that was it. There was something rotten here, which was certainly not *his* fault, and he was going to weed it out, then rise above it.

But he never pulled it off as tragedy. No, Jesse, she thought, your princely posturing is melodrama, and it stinks.

"I never would have started it, you know," he said now as if he were speaking from some lofty place, a balcony, "if you hadn't wanted me to."

"I *wanted* you to have an affair with Caroline?" Had she?

"Who told me that very first day," he looked down at his watch, "exactly a year ago, that she was attracted to me?"

"Yes. I did. I said that. And it was true, wasn't it, that observation? But that didn't mean I wanted you to go right out and screw her." Emma could hear herself, an angry woman, her voice raised way too loud.

Jesse flared his nostrils as if she had said something unforgivably inelegant.

She pushed on. "Is that not what we're talking about—your screwing Caroline?

He rose from the sofa and leaned against the fireplace, punc-

tuating his speech with gestures of his glass. "Not really. What
we're talking about is *why*. Which you know very well, Emma,
is because *you* didn't want to. You never wanted to be close."
His lip trembled, and his voice shook.

I am standing off and watching this as if I were in another
body, watching myself in the audience, she thought. Go ahead,
Jesse, pull out all the stops.

"You *never* wanted me, never!" He leaned toward her, and
his fist smashed down onto his lovely coffee table. Don't savage
your art, that disconnected part of her thought. The ice in his
glass shivered, his drink slopped.

"Yes, I did."

"When?" Tears poured down his face, into his beard. "When?"

"A long time ago."

"Why did you turn off? How did you get so cold?"

"I didn't *get* cold, Jesse. Not all by myself. Your need, your
never-ending need, wore me out. You say it's because you *want*
me, but I don't think that's it at all. Sex is the way you hold
on to me, control me. Sex is what you use when you're frustrated
with yourself, with Skytop, with whatever the fuck it is that's
keeping you from going back to making art. I can't be *everything* for you, Jesse!"

"I don't want you to be. I just want to feel you close to me.
You've slipped away from me, Emma. You just keep slipping
away."

And as he said those words, Jesse could see Blanche all those
years ago in a shimmery slippery satin dress, jumping into a
golden Cadillac and waving, calling to her children, "I'll be back
in a little while, don't worry." That little while stretched so
long, was endless, measured by the clock of childhood.

And he could hear his father's words, the only words of advice
he'd ever given Jesse: "Only so many fucks in you, Jess. Want
to make sure you get 'em all in. But don't let the women catch
you, boy. You want to stay loose. They want to tie you up."

He'd stayed loose, hadn't he, he'd done what his old man said,
until Emma, and look what had happened. He had let her tie
him up, tie him up in knots, and now *she* was the one who was
always slipping away. Quicksilver. He had reached out for her,
thought he had her, and she was gone, like a firefly.

"Oh, Emma," he cried, and his sobs began. His shoulders shook.

Emma reached out for him. These tears were the genuine article. This was no act, the real part of her said to the part that had been standing off, a witness. This is your husband. This is his pain. And with that the part of her that she always kept inside, protected, the part that had plugged its eyes and ears against Caroline (against Helen, against Rosalie, against Jake, against Jesse, against betrayal and trickery of any kind) opened its mouth and screamed. Then Emma was crying, too.

"Let's try," she whispered into his ear. "Let's stop pretending that we don't care. We do, Jess. I do."

16

————

"I DON'T KNOW WHY you think it has to be a *sex* therapist."

"Because that's where all our problems lay."

"Lie."

"Fucking English teacher."

"Nonfucking English teacher," Emma said sweetly. Too sweetly. "Isn't that it? Isn't that what you want to tell Dr. Quack Quack?"

"*You're* the one who wanted to see someone. Not I."

Well, hell, what else were they supposed to do? Continue crying and yelling at each other? This was California in the seventies. On every street corner people were getting themselves improved, analyzed, actualized. Letting go, talking it out, they said, could solve everyone's problems. They sat in circles, took off their clothes and exposed all their warts and fears before equally imperfect strangers. In this fruit basket of the U.S., human growth had become more popular than any other kind. Who was Emma to fight the tide?

Though she did think about how funny their going to Dr. Ente would seem in West Cypress. You had problems, well, hell, everyone had *something* nasty on his plate. You just bore down and made the best of it. No one questioned maladjustment—or even madness—back home. Like most Southerners, they were almost proud of their quirks and cosseted, rather than confined, their eccentrics. For example, there was old Miss Priscilla Whitmore, who had a thing about money, never touched the stuff, though her family had left her bushel baskets of it. When her dividend checks came each month, her maid took them from the mailbox, opened them and made the deposits. But the bank insisted that Miss Priscilla sign them, so she did, wearing white cotton gloves. Even so, that act called for absolution—washing her hands over and over with Purex straight out of the bottle. After a while, of course, the bleach ate right through the flesh, and it was not unusual to see Miss Priscilla in church after dividend time with red stains seeping into her gloves. People looked away politely and nodded rather than taking her hand. But no one would ever think of recommending that Miss Priscilla see a shrink. Why, that would be rude. Besides which, Emma wasn't sure that there was a shrink within miles of West Cypress.

Of course there were droves of them in California. Right down the hill in Los Gatos was the birthplace of primal scream.

And scream was what Emma thought she was going to do with the Teutonic Dr. Ente, a disciple of Masters and Johnson. She was sorry she'd ever gotten them into this. Drawn swords under the redwoods at dawn was more her style.

"Now that I'm into it, I think Dr. Ente's really okay. Why don't you like him?" Jesse was saying. Their second visit was only two miles and two minutes away.

"Because he's a Nazi. Because he's a big fat slob with food stains on his shirt. How can I talk to anyone like that?"

"Come on, Emma."

"Besides, he doesn't even listen. He talks all the time. You know he'd no good as a therapist. You like him only because he makes it sound like it's all my fault."

"No, just that it's not all *my* fault."

"His office looks like an abortionist's."

"Have you ever been to an abortionist?"

"No. But if he were any good, he could afford a better office."

"This isn't going to work if you don't cooperate. I'll bet you're going to resist the hypnosis."

"And you're hoping he's going to turn me into a nymphomaniac."

"RELAX. Watch the watch."

Watch the watch? What kind of talk was that?

"You're going to become very sleepy."

Actually, she was becoming very antsy. This Dr. Quack Quack who was waving his grandfather's watch in her face was just that.

"Play like you're children," he'd said. "Take baths together. Buy some rubber duckies and paddle around. Then play dress up."

"I have some black lingerie. You want Jesse to wear it or me?"

"Watch the watch. You're not trying."

"That's what Jesse says. Why don't you hypnotize him? Why me?"

"Jesse doesn't have the same kind of problem."

She sat up on his cracked plastic couch. "What kind of problem is that?"

Dr. Ente and Jesse exchanged a look.

"Hey, guys, I can stay home and watch Jesse and his friend Rupert shoot knowing glances for free. I don't need to come here for that." Emma heard Rosalie's voice coming out of her mouth. Well, Rosalie wasn't wrong about everything.

"Emma, Emma. Come, sit here." Dr. Ente patted the chair beside him. "Let's put all our cards on the table. Let's talk."

"So you knew about Jesse's affair for a whole year? Why didn't you do anything about it?"

"I don't know."

"Of course you do. That's no answer."

"I didn't know what I wanted to do. So I let it ride."

"Didn't it make you angry?"

"Of course it made me angry."

"But not angry enough to say anything about it?"

"I guess not."

"Let's try another tack."

"Do you sail, Dr. Ente?"

"What do you mean?"

"Do you sail? You know, boats, water? Tack's a sailing term." Oh, how she'd like, right now, to be out on the *Grits*.

"You're avoiding the issue, Emma."

Jesse rolled his eyes at her. But she knew he was loving this. Ente had been grilling her for the last half hour.

"Now, as I was about to say, let's be specific. You knew when Jesse was going to see Caroline, and you knew, or at least you suspected, where he was going."

"Yes."

"Put yourself in one of those situations. What did you do with your time? Did you sit at home and stare at the walls? Did you cry? Did you talk to friends about it?"

No, I called my lover and we went for a sail and fucked our brains out.

"I tested recipes. I catered dinner parties. I prepared for my classes."

"You could concentrate? You could do all that while your husband was with another woman?"

"What was I supposed to do? Slit my wrists and bleed into the tomato sauce?"

"Emma, Emma. That wit is hiding an enormous amount of hostility. Come, now, did you never want to follow him? To get in your car and see what he was doing? To catch them and . . . let's say, shoot them?"

"Wait a minute." Jesse laughed nervously.

"Be quiet." Dr. Ente frowned at Jesse. "Emma, you never wanted to do any of these things? You never wanted to get back at Jesse in some way, to, let's say for example, have an affair yourself?"

"No."

"So you never had an affair yourself?"

Goddamn this son-of-a-bitch. If she admitted the truth, it would be all over. It was one thing for Jesse to screw around, for her to do so was a completely different matter. "Fucking another man," he'd scream, "when you could have been with me?" She could hear it now. He'd storm out of this office and keep on going. Telling the truth was going to get them exactly the same place this bullshit therapist was getting them, she thought. Nowhere. They were right in West Cypress. Let it lie. Lay. It would work itself out. If it didn't, take it behind the barn and beat the shit out of it.

"No," she said.

"Emma," Dr. Ente shook his head, "I worry about you. I'm afraid you're not at all in touch with your feelings."

"So you haven't seen Caroline in three weeks, since just before you came to me. Right, Jesse?"

"Right."

"And what has been her reaction to this?"

"She's very upset."

"How do you feel about that?"

"It makes me sad. I care a lot for her. She's a very nice woman, and she's very sensitive."

"YOUR nice, sensitive girlfriend called me on the phone a little while ago, Jesse," Emma announced the next afternoon.

"What did she say?"

"She said she was going to kill herself."

17

October 1974

"WHY CAN'T I JUST tell him the truth and have it over with? Why do I keep hanging on?"

"Because it's hard to kiss a marriage goodbye, baby. Believe me, I know. I've done it."

Minor had called the minute Jesse's truck left the driveway. Ah, Minor and his trusty telescope. Could it see through her clothes? Down into her heart? Could he see how much she wanted him (anyone) to rescue her?

"Have you ever thought of doing it again?"

"Doing what?" Minor asked.

"Ending your marriage?"

Two beats passed. Three. "Emma, you know the answer to that."

"Tell me."

"It's the same thing I told you from the beginning. We have good times together. We care about each other. But I'm not leaving Kit. I'm not giving up my son." And then he added in a softer tone, "I'm not what you really want, baby."

"Yes, you are."

"No, I'm not. You know that, Em. Come on. Don't you?"

Three beats passed.

"Yes."

"Sure, now. And I'm always here for you, but not for keeps— and you wouldn't want it any other way."

"Let's don't kid ourselves, kid."

"Right."

She could hear Minor lighting a cigarette. Then he asked, "Do you really think she's going to kill herself?"

"Caroline? I don't know. She sounded really crazy. Jesse says she's manic-depressive. Maybe she forgot to take her medication."

"You never told me that."

"I have a hard time worrying about her problems, Minor. I'm having a tough enough time with my own."

"I'VE been trying to call you for half an hour, Emma. Who were you talking to?"

"Maria. Why? Where are you?"

"At Caroline's."

"That certainly was a quick trip."

"She's taken pills. The ambulance is on the way. I probably won't be home tonight."

HE wasn't home the next night either. Or the one after that.

"Jesse, are you going to stay there and hold her hand for the rest of her life? Shall I send your things?"

"You don't care about anyone except yourself, Emma!" he exploded. "We've destroyed this woman's life and you don't even give a shit!"

THIS time she really was talking to Maria on the phone.

"*We've* destroyed *her* life? Do you know what she did right before her suicide routine? She telephoned Lowie's mother and called Lowie a bitch. So Lowie telephoned Caroline's mother and returned the compliment. *Then* Caroline calls Lowie's boss's wife, some nice fifty-five-year-old woman who's sitting at home playing bridge with her friends, and tells her her husband is having an affair with Lowie. It's gone entirely too far. This poor woman I don't even know has her life in shambles because of us? Because of me and this crazy bitch? *I'd* give her some medication if I could get my hands on her—enough to cool her out forever. I think Dr. Ente was wrong, Maria. I *am* in touch with my feelings and I'm extremely pissed."

JESSE had come home for the night.

"I don't want to hear about how pathetic she is, Jesse. I want you to tell that woman that when she gets out of her phony sickbed she'd better lay off."

"She's been through a lot, Emma. You don't understand how hard this has been for her."

"Hard for *her?* What the hell are we talking about?"

"She loves me."

"Jesus H. Christ! I wish you could hear yourself. It's like you're reciting the Lord's Prayer, like there's something so Godalmighty holy about her love. You tell her that if she makes one more nasty phone call, I'm going to go down there and rip her phone out—her tongue too."

"You leave her out of this!"

"How can I leave her out, Jesse? The woman is smack in the middle of us. She might as well be here, recuperating in our bed."

"You don't know what the fuck you're talking about. I think you've lost your mind."

"You're right, Jesse. I think I'll get out of here for the weekend and see if I can find it. When I finish up at Tony's tonight, I'm not coming home. I'm spending the weekend with Maria and Clifton."

"Tony. Tony Boccia and his goddamned restaurant. That's all I ever hear."

" 'Bye, Jesse. Go stay with your precious Caroline."

AT the bottom of the hill, Emma didn't take the left turn that led down past Los Gatos, through San Jose, up to Berkeley and Maria and Clifton's. She stopped at the pay phone.

"Can we spend the weekend on the *Grits?* . . . Great. . . . I'll meet you at the marina. . . . I know I sound a little frazzled, but I'm all right."

Emma dropped another dime into the phone, dialed Maria's number, and asked her to cover for her. Maria agreed to, but she couldn't promise anything for Clifton. After all, he was *Jesse's* friend.

"I can't tell you how much I appreciate this. . . . I'm okay. Really—I'm upset, but I'll be fine. . . . Of course I don't know exactly what I'm doing. I don't even know approximately what I'm doing. But I'm very very close to figuring it out."

IT was that October weekend that Jesse caught Emma in her lie. When Jesse called, Maria was taking a nap; Clifton answered the phone and hemmed and hawed, but his story didn't fit. And it was *that* Monday morning, when the first rain of the season

came early to the Santa Cruz Mountains, *that* Monday morning
when Emma awoke to the rain's pitter-patter and lay in bed
thinking how much she'd loved summer rain back in West Cypress, *that* Monday morning when Jesse awoke with a magnificent
erection, lifted her out of a tub of soapy water, and made slow
lovely love to her before his rage at the knowledge of her betrayal transformed his passion into rape.

And once that battering was over, *but only with his dick, he
never lifted a hand to you, never, only raised the drawbridge of
his dick,* Emma had heard the click which announced the end
of her indecision and knew it was time to get the hell out of
Dodge.

When she awoke in that motel room in Needles after one day
on the road, *Even Cowgirls Get the Blues,* rather than Jesse, was
lying by her side. Emma slid a look at the book, sat up, stretched
and grimaced.

Ouch! There were sore spots where he'd used her body, spots
that hadn't been called into service in a long time if ever.

But there were no such tender places in her psyche. She
grinned. She was on the road. She was flying.

Halfway through New Mexico, Patsy Cline came on the radio
singing "Your Cheating Heart." Emma closed her eyes and sang
along so long and loud she ran off the road—which was okay.
There was nothing much in New Mexico to run into. It was
West Cypress, *now why was she going to West Cypress?,* that
might prove to be a little bumpy.

Then she had almost conquered Texas, two and a half days
of nothing but miles and miles of miles and miles.

Jake and Rosalie didn't know she was coming. She'd surprise
them, as Rosalie always had done when they visited relatives.

"Of course they'll be home," Rosalie had once answered when
Emma had asked *what if?* "Where else would they be?"

Rosalie would be out in her garden, puttering around with
her fall crop—collards, potatoes, turnip greens.

And what was Jake doing? What he'd always done, sitting
sipping coffee, slowly turning the pages of the paper. Did he
still imagine going to any of the places whose names he read
there, she wondered, to Kenya, Katmandu? Or had both the
years and the tranquilizers which kept away the boogeyman of
hallucination dulled those dreams? She'd have to ask him when
she saw him whether he thought about traveling anymore.

She was in East Texas now, rolling faster and farther, drafting in the zone of no resistance behind eighteen-wheelers, the dinosaurs of the road. The interstate signs flashed by—KILGORE, LONGVIEW, MARSHALL.

This was Texas hill country, then, there, she'd crossed the Louisiana state line. And here was the first exit to Shreveport, thirty miles north of Sweetwell. If she got off the interstate, to whom would she say hello? Only ghosts lived there now, and besides, the hypnotic highway beckoned to her, *Keep going*.

I-20 had no patience for turnoffs and side trips. It did not love old cars, small towns and serendipitous detours. That's what antiquated Highway 80 was for, its meandering two lanes paralleling the straight shot of I-20 in a wavy line.

Emma thought about that. If she got off the interstate now and found that old road, might she meet herself coming the other way, the seventeen-year-old Emma, headed toward Grandma Virgie's funeral and a date with J.D.?

And if she did meet herself traveling into her future, now her past, if she could step back those fourteen years, would she know that Emma Fine? What would she say to that young girl who'd never been away from home, who was at that instant a virgin impatient to give up her prize?

Would she say, Whoa! Stop! Wait! Caution! Look before you leap! If she could do it over again, would she travel all the same roads again?

"You do what you want to do," Minor had said to her that last afternoon floating on the ocean aboard the *Grits*. "If staying with Jesse's what you want, remember that what he is is what he's going to be. And so are you."

"You think so?" She'd run a finger along his face.

He'd kissed her finger. "I'd make it all better for you if I could, baby. But no, I don't think people change. They don't change their basic nature."

Had *she*, she wondered? Was she the same girl who had left West Cypress swearing never to return? If so, why was she now almost there? Just a few minutes more. What solace did she hope to find? Shouldn't she have just gone ahead and boarded a plane early for her appointment at the restaurant in Rome? Wouldn't that make more sense than this, whatever this was?

Then she pulled into Rosalie and Jake's driveway. The carport was empty. Where on earth could they have gone?

18

West Cypress
October 1974

SHE KNOCKED on the side door. It was locked.

"Hello! Is anybody home?"

Nothing. She called again, waited, and had started around the side of the carport to the back when she heard Jake's voice.

"Who is it?" He sounded frightened. The door stayed closed.

"It's me, Daddy, Emma."

"Who?"

"Emma. Emma Rochelle Fine." She laughed then. "Your long-lost daughter. Remember?"

"Emma?" He fumbled with the lock and then the screen and peered out into the bright sunshine of the October day. "Emma, is that you?"

She hugged him then, long and hard. He was so much smaller than he used to be. But his grin was enormous, a black jack-o'lantern hole. Jake hardly ever wore his dentures anymore.

"What are you doing here? Were you coming?" He looked worried then, as if her unexpected visit were something he had known about, something so very important that he had inexplicably forgotten. Or perhaps she wasn't really here; perhaps his hallucinatory terrors had returned.

Emma saw all that in his face and reached out for him again. "No, no, Daddy, I didn't call. I . . ." and then she stumbled. Across three days and almost two thousand miles, and she still hadn't figured out exactly how the rest of that sentence ought to go. "I have a couple of weeks before I leave for Europe and," there it was, "I thought I'd run home and surprise you."

Jake grinned again. She ought to have remembered that he

really didn't care about the particulars. He never did, which was why it was always so easy to make it up as she went along.

At seventeen: *"We were at the drive-in Daddy,"* when she and Bernie had spent four hours at the Cypress Holiday Inn.

At eighteen: *"We're going to the Big Game at LSU,"* when they'd finally sneaked away for a weekend in New Orleans at Bernie's fabled Hotel Monteleone.

And after half a fifth of Jack Daniels had made her sick, as it ought to: *"It must have been that Trenton Inn barbecue."*

"Where's Rosalie?" she asked.

"She and Janey went out to her old place to dig up some fruit trees—or something."

"She never sits still, does she?" Emma laughed.

Jake shook his head. "You know Rosalie. Always doing."

"And yet she's been dying since she was forty."

Jake looked puzzled behind his swimming magnifying lenses.

"You know, Daddy, how she's always talking about how bad she feels, how she's got the rheumatiz, and the next thing you know she's digging postholes or tearing down a wall."

Jake grinned. He stepped backward then. "Come on in the house."

"I will for just a minute, but I'm hungry. Let's run over to The Tavern and get some lunch. I could sure go for an oyster po'boy and a beer."

Jake hesitated. "Rosalie left some chicken."

"Hell, Daddy. I don't come home every day. Let's go celebrate."

"But the chicken, she'll—"

"We'll throw it into the garbage or feed it to the dog."

Jake laughed, and she could see the mischief rising in him. When she was a little girl they had sneaked off every once in a while, as if Rosalie were the Wicked Witch who'd locked them up and said, "Never, never any soft ice cream." Because they had ice cream, didn't they, for sale in the store, though not the creamy kind that came out of a machine in a swirl, was dipped into a vat of melted chocolate. They'd thought those illicit cones from the Tastee Freeze the best stuff in the world.

"Oysters and beer," Emma insisted. "My treat. Let me run in and pee, and we'll go."

Jake was sitting in her car, ready and waiting.

THE beer was cold in frosty bottles. The fried-oyster sandwiches on French bread with mayonnaise and hot sauce tasted exactly the same as when she was sixteen and Bernie had first bought her one. Nothing, Emma thought, nothing in West Cypress ever changes, and in this case she was grateful.

"Good?"

Jake nodded with his mouth full.

Indian summer had lingered on this year, and it was still warm enough to eat outside. There hadn't been much rain here, she thought, watching through the willows the Coupitaw's sluggish flow. She had once read somewhere with surprise that it was one of the prettiest rivers in the country. They were sitting on top of its levee on the Cypress side.

Emma pointed behind her, across River Road to the row of mansions behind a parade of old magnolias. "When I was a very little girl, I used to wish that when I grew up I'd live in one of those houses."

Jake smiled. He wished she did. He wished she lived closer to home.

"I'd watch the ladies get out of their big cars. They wore lots of jewelry and pretty clothes and looked like they smelled good, like they smelled *pink*." She laughed. "Maybe that was why I bought Rosalie that pink toilet water. Do you remember?"

Jake nodded. He remembered. Emma had saved her allowance for weeks to buy Rosalie's birthday present at the five-and-dime store. She'd picked out the bottle all by herself, brought it home and poured its contents into the toilet, then proudly called Rosalie in to see. Rosalie had laughed and laughed and laughed, and then had told everyone who came into the store how Emma had thought the toilet water was for the toilet.

"God, I cried for days, I was so embarrassed. What a literal-minded child I must have been."

Jake leaned back against a tree and listened. Ever since she was a little bit of a thing, so bright and sassy, he'd loved hearing Emma talk even though he could never think of much to say back to her. And now her world was so far away from his, so different, sometimes he didn't even know what she was talking *about,* but that didn't matter. Just the fact that she was here, her low musical voice trilling upward when she was excited, gesturing with her long slender hands, smiling—that was enough.

"I never grew up to be a lady in one of those mansions, did I?" Emma went on. "But you know, I think that their lives must be pretty much as I imagined as a child. Rounds of tea parties and luncheons where they smile all the time and say things like 'Isn't she the sweetest little thing? And doesn't she make the loveliest sandwiches?' "

Her blonde hair glistened in the sunlight. He had always loved her hair. He had been sorry when Rosalie cut it, but now Emma wore it long and curling, falling free as she had when she was a little girl.

"But behind those Junior League smiles, behind those same smiles that they wore at their high-school-sorority initiations, their coming-out parties, their weddings, what kinds of things do you think they hide?"

Jake's attention perked. "What do you mean?"

"Don't you think everybody hides something? *Lots* of things, probably? I mean, nobody's exactly what they seem on the surface."

What the hell are you talking about, Emma? she asked herself. A beer and a half and you're running off at the mouth like you've come home to spill your guts.

Jake thought, Why was she talking about people hiding things? What had he said? He'd said *something* that had triggered her talk about deception, but he couldn't remember what. It must be the alcohol which was making him dizzy. He hadn't had so much as a beer since that night so long ago he'd come home drunk and Rosalie had thrown him out of bed—that night he'd spent in the backyard swing. Jake felt the sweat begin in his armpits, trickle down his sides. Emma knew something. *That's* why she'd come home.

She needed to change the subject, she thought, to rescue herself, because it was getting mighty tempting, it was right there on the tip of her tongue, to spill the beans, to tell her daddy what she'd been thinking about all the way across country, all about Jesse, because he *was* her daddy. That's what daddies were for, no matter how old you were, to listen to your problems, offer you a shoulder to cry on, to pat you on the head and tell you it was all going to be okay. Wasn't it? Especially Southern daddies, that handsome, devil-may-care, Bourbon-flavored rapscallion breed who ruled their roosts without question and bought their darling daughters Coupe de Villes and white tulle debutante gowns even though it meant putting the homestead on the line with a second mortgage.

But her daddy wasn't that kind of daddy, and she wasn't that kind of Southern girl. She hadn't stayed home. She hadn't been dutiful and obedient. She hadn't done any of the things she was supposed to do. So now it was a little late, wasn't it, to try to revert to a type she'd never been?

But wouldn't it be nice if she could? Just now, wouldn't it be lovely to be able to take all her troubles, as if they were a load of dirty laundry she'd brought home from school, and dump them? As if they'd be washed and folded, squeaky clean, in the morning?

But that wasn't going to happen, not in a million years. Not here. So she'd better get on with changing the subject. She did. She switched into what had always been a routine for her visits home—trying to get Jake to tell her more about Helen.

"Daddy," she said lightly, swigging from her beer, "did you ever tell me what it was my momma, Helen, did for a living when she was living in New York?"

There. He knew it. She was easing up on it, but nonetheless closing in.

"She worked in an office. I told you that."

"As a clerk?"

"I'm not sure. I think so."

"I can't believe you never talked about it."

"It was a long time ago, Emma."

"I know, but when you first met, didn't you talk about what you did? You had to talk about something when you went out on dates."

Closer.

"We didn't go out on many dates."

"How long *did* you date before you got married?"

Closer still. He could feel where she was heading, as inexorably as a bullet that had been fired from a gun. Who had told her? Ruth? No, Ruth wouldn't. George? It didn't matter. Maybe she'd just figured it out. Or maybe it *had* been something he'd said. He felt so lightheaded. Hadn't the doctor warned about his medication and alcohol? He'd laughed then. Yet here he was, the irony of it all, a Jew, who, like most, hardly ever touched the stuff, tripped by demon rum.

"Two weeks," he said.

"I know you've told me that before, but I just can't imagine it."

Why not, Emma? she thought then. How long did it take you to decide to move in with Jesse? One night. It happens.

"Why not? I married your stepmother after three days."

"Yes." Emma frowned. "But that was because of me. You didn't marry Helen because of me."

And then there was a silence—a big deep silence that you could have driven twelve eighteen-wheelers through. You could have run both the Coupitaw and the Mississippi through that hole. You could fit Baltimore, West Cypress, Atlanta, New York, California, all of Emma's past and present in that space, and it wouldn't have filled up. And in that silence Emma listened to a bird sing on a branch overhead, and in that moment that was hanging, frozen, still, she thought of herself and J.D., poor dead J.D., together on a blanket beneath a tree, beside the water. And then she saw herself and white-blond Will, making love in the forest, beside a stream, yes, there was, wasn't there, they'd almost rolled into it, that weekend they'd gone to Gatlinburg. She and Minor, rocking on the ocean. Then Jesse, above her, the two of them outside, many times, many places. Then that hanging, frozen moment of time became a tunnel that went back, far back, and Emma saw, as clearly as her hand holding the yet unopened beer bottle in her lap, Helen's face that she'd come to know from the photographs Jake had given her once the secret was out, Helen's blue eyes smiling, her soft brown hair spread out beneath her on a blanket like an aureole, her head twisting and turning as a man pleasured her in the fresh air beside a pond, a lake. And that man wasn't Jake.

"You did." The words flowed from her lips like water, so gently that she wasn't sure she'd said them. "You did marry her because of me, didn't you?"

"No," Jake answered, looking up, looking her dead in the eye, now that like a thunderbolt on this bright cloudless day it came to him that the secret was no longer worth keeping, the secret that had cost him so much. "No, I married her because I loved her."

"But she was pregnant."

"Yes."

Emma turned away, her eyes filled with sudden tears. They

were so hot, those tears, they scalded. She put a finger to her cheek, sure it was boiling.

"I've counted up the months before . . ." she went on breathlessly, for if she said it quickly, maybe it wouldn't hurt. Or it wouldn't be true. Maybe it would just be a story she was telling, an anecdote about someone else's life. *I knew this woman once, and . . .* But it was *her* life, wasn't it? ". . . the months between the story you told me—about getting married at City Hall with her in a dress of pale blue and you in a suit that looked like vanilla ice cream—and my birthday. And I thought, Premature. But I was an awfully big baby for that." Over seven pounds, that certificate had said, the one she'd found in the hall closet in the little suitcase, the same one that had told her about Helen.

Jake just nodded.

"Yet if you got married only two weeks after you met, then . . ." And then, and then, she faltered.

Jake reached over and, in a completely uncharacteristic gesture, took her face in his hand. Then he said it. The words tumbled out.

"Emma, I'm not your father."

Inside her head everything went dead still and bright white. She stood, jumped up, and the beer bottle fell from her lap and rolled down, down, bouncing into the Coupitaw, where it floated, heading south now on a journey of its own.

Emma ran down the levee's other side, across River Road without looking, between two magnolias onto the sidewalk that promenaded before the mansions where in upstairs ballrooms debutantes in long white dresses had come out into the world. She ran in the same direction as her beer bottle floated, and had she been in the position of the bird she'd listened to earlier on the branch above her, she'd have seen that she and the beer bottle ran a head-to-head race, even when it hit a snag for a moment, and at that same instant she hesitated, hearing Jake calling from atop the levee, standing now, "Emma, Emma, stop!"

But she didn't. She ran even faster then, as if he'd yelled, "Keep going, girl, you can do it," as if he were urging her on in the race. She passed the cornerstone of the line of mansions, the glass-enclosed aviary of the local Coca-Cola bottling heir's home. She leaped, again without looking, across the two lanes of the

boulevard that marked the beginning of River Road Park. Tires
screeched. A horn honked. On into the park she ran, past spreading live oaks bearded with Spanish moss. And in her head there
were no thoughts, just a whirligig of shock. She heard her breathing. She heard her footfall. She heard her name, *Emma, Emma,*
though not in Jake's voice.

She had cruised this park at fifteen, part of a carload of giggling
girls. At sixteen, she'd been half of one of the couples she'd been
spying on a year earlier, a parker snuggled in beside Bernie in
his two-tone green Ford, sealed in a liplock.

Emma, Emma, the voice called, and just before she tripped
and fell across the end of a seesaw—a teeter-totter she'd played
on as a child, Jake balanced midway down the end of his side so
that she could lift him, but all the while wishing that she
weren't an only child, wishing that her momma and daddy had
had some more children so she wouldn't feel so alone—just before she tripped and fell flat on her face, sprawled, she realized
that the voice she heard calling her name was her own.

The bottle flowed on down the Coupitaw. It had won. Eventually the bottle would float into the Red, hang a left at the intersection of the Atchafalaya into the Mississippi, past Baton
Rouge, past New Orleans, where Emma and Bernie had spent
that weekend in the Monteleone, past the brewery just on the
other side of the French Quarter levee where it was given birth,
on into the Gulf.

The bottle had gone only about a half mile more of that slow,
low-water journey when Jake finally reached Emma and leaned
over her, brushing gold-and-red leaves out of her hair. She didn't
move. She murmured into the earth, "Why, Daddy?"

"Why what, Missy?" He hadn't called her that since she was
about four.

Why did you marry her? Why didn't you tell me? Why am I
both a motherless and fatherless child?

"Who?" she asked instead.

"I don't know. Helen never told me her lover's name. And I
didn't care. All I knew was that I loved her. I didn't even care
that she didn't love me back at first, though I think she came
to. I didn't care that she tricked me, that she married me because she needed a father for you, because what else was a girl
in trouble to do? I didn't know anything. And I didn't care."

"But who am I?" she screamed then into the fallen leaves and the dirt.

"Why, Emma. You're still Emma Fine, of course."

ON the drive back to the house in West Cypress, Jake said it all over again, as if once he had started talking he couldn't stop. "I love you, Emma, and I loved Helen."

She reached over from the steering wheel and patted his hand, pulling out of herself and into him for a moment because he sounded so pitiful. But she couldn't answer. She couldn't say a word. She just nodded and kept driving slowly. As they approached their house in which she'd never lived, she saw Rosalie's little car in the carport.

And then she found words. "I can't go in," she whispered.

Jake nodded.

Another question occurred to her, and it wasn't why, or who, or what.

"Does she know?"

He shook his head. "No."

Suddenly Emma laughed. She laughed so loud, so strong, from so far deep down inside herself, that she had to pull the car off to the side of the road.

Jake looked at her with frightened eyes. He was afraid she had lost her mind. But he was also afraid that she was going to tell on him, that she was going to tell his secret, now *their* secret.

She gripped his arm. "Well, *I'm* sure as hell not going to spill the beans!"

Jake managed a little embarrassed smile, the same one as when he paid a compliment or when someone complimented him, though in Jake's life those latter occasions had been few and far between.

"Listen," Emma said then, dropped once more to a whisper as if Rosalie could hear them, though she couldn't even *see* them unless she stepped out into the front yard, and she might just do that, any second, she just might. "Listen, Daddy, I'm not going to stop. You get out of the car right here."

"No!"

"I'm all right," she said and smiled to prove that it was so.

"Where are you going?"

Where was she going? Emma Rochelle Fine Tree, no mother, no husband, and now no father, where the hell do you think you're going?

"I'm not sure," she said. "But I'll call you when I get there. I've got to be alone and think about this. You understand, don't you?"

Well, he did, but he wished he didn't.

"Quick now," she said. And then she sounded like herself again. "Go. Git." She reached across him and opened the car door.

Jake got.

19

Driving East Again

EMMA GOT, TOO, right back on the interstate, I-20 headed east, veered over into the left lane, the fast lane, and stayed there. She found herself an eighteen-wheeler convoy and tucked in behind a Peterbilt, sped on past exits to Rayville, Delhi, past the turnoff to Pearl Bank. *Hello, goodbye again, thanks for the memories, J.D.* She was headed for the Mississippi, and an hour and a quarter after she had left West Cypress the tall steel of the Vicksburg Bridge loomed before her. She held her breath.

She'd always done that since the first time she drove across it with Bernie, it sneaking up on them while she was still behind the wheel, and she'd screamed, "No, it's too high, too long, I can't do it."

"Yes, you can, Emma. Just hold your breath."

What seemed like ten minutes later, for the Mississippi is a *wide* river, she'd grinned and gasped, "Goddamn!" And then a flagman had pulled them over. "Double goddamn!" But it wasn't a ticket. The piece of white paper he'd handed her was a postcard, preaddressed to President John F. Kennedy. That must have been about 1962.

"Dear Mr. President," it said. "I want to ask you to cease and desist from your integrationist persecution of the State of Mississippi and to turn your attention to the Communist threat both at our borders and from within."

She still had that postcard somewhere in the bottom of her bureau drawer along with the little notebook with names inscribed in purple ink, photographs of Helen, love letters from Bernie, somewhere back in the mountain home she shared with Jesse Tree.

Jesse! Jesus, he seemed now like part of someone else's life. Emma Rochelle What? Why she hadn't thought about him in . . . she couldn't remember when.

Oh, yes, she could, she'd thought about him just a few hours ago when she was sitting on top of the levee with Jake. Didn't you, Emma? she said to herself. Didn't you think about telling Jake all about Jesse and asking him what you ought to do about the mess you've gotten yourself in, making promises you couldn't keep, saying yes when you should have said no, didn't you? But that seemed like days, weeks, years ago. A lifetime ago, before Jake had said . . . and now that she thought about it, it didn't seem like the telling would have had much to do with Jesse. Somehow, spilling her secret would have been more about Jake, more about closing old wounds, but Jake had beat her to the punch, hadn't he, and opened a gap so wide, wider than the Big Muddy she'd just crossed over—why, the gap between them now had no sides. There was no way to bridge them. How could there be connectors when there was nothing to hang them to? Why, the whole idea of her ever trying to make her family whole was a colossal joke. She had no family. Not Rosalie. And now not Jake. Her mother was long buried with the secret of her father's name. What in the hell *was* her own real name?

Emma looked down at her hands clenched on the steering wheel and realized she had the shakes.

Get hold of yourself, girl. Don't think about it.

I won't, I won't, I won't.

A pickup truck passed her then, and through the window, just before the gun rack, the man driving turned and looked at her and grinned. You're talking to yourself, Emma. You're talking out loud.

The unfamiliar names of Vicksburg streets flashed by her on the interstate.

You're in Mississippi, Emma. Now what?

She pulled off at an exit sign announcing services.

"Fill her up."

"Where you headed?" asked the old man in a blue uniform as he wiped dead bugs off her windshield. He looked down at her license tag and back up at her. "You a long way from home. Where you headed?" he repeated.

"Georgia," she said when she opened her mouth. She listened to the word. It sounded about right.

"You got family there?"

She shrugged, "Used to. My momma was from north of Atlanta. Up near Helen, Tallulah Falls. Tiny place called Meadville. Ever heard of it?"

"Nawh. Cain't say as I have. I'll check your oil since you got
a far piece to go."

That done, he stood by the side of her window, wiping his
hands on a greasy rag. "So you going to visit kin?"

Emma handed him some money. "I don't know. I hope so."

And that was how she decided, since she didn't know who she
was, what she wanted, or what the hell she was doing, to go in
search of her mother, to go to Meadville. It was easier than flipping a coin, and she had to do something, she couldn't just drive
in circles, and she was no good at sitting still. Meadville it is, she
said, Meadville.

She was tempted when she got within spitting distance early
the next morning, having sped across Mississippi, Alabama and
part of the state of Georgia, when she pulled into the little town
of Helen, to just stop. For she'd turned off the main road to
revisit the site where she'd sat shivah for Herman with a bag of
tuna fish and crackers and a brace of Jack Daniels. The motel
where she'd spent that week was still there, but Helen had really
flossed itself up, had tacked pseudo-Swiss carpentry onto the
front of plain Southern houses, full-blown touristique. Well, she
sure as hell wouldn't have come here to mourn her pseudo-daddy
Herman now. Pseudo? Hell, he was as real as any daddy she had.

God Almighty, wasn't life weird? You thought you had the
simple stuff down, like the name of your mother, your father,
your *own* name for that matter, then even *that* slipped sideways.

MEADVILLE is a hamlet perched on a flat space in the north-
Georgia hills, anchored, like many small Southern towns, by a
square. In the center of that square stands a statue to the memory
of the Confederate dead lost in that war that is still referred to
by many locals as the Recent Unpleasantness.

Emma drove around the square a couple of times, reading the
names written on storefronts and attracting the attention of a
trio of old men passing the day on a bench in front of the Piggly
Wiggly grocery store.

"California," one of them said, reading her tags.

"Yep," answered another.

"That girl's a long way from home."

"Might be lost."

"Might be one of them hoopers selling marijuana. Ain't that what they call 'em?"

"Trouble's what I'd call it, young girl being off by herself like that."

"What you think she wants?"

"Guess you can ask her that yourself, Vern. Here she comes."

"Ain't never heard of no one by that name. And I reckon I've lived here most of my life. Helen Kaplan. Nope. No Kaplans." The men exchanged a look. And then the man who'd answered her shoved back his old straw hat. Beneath it his forehead was white. He stared straight at Emma.

"You think maybe that was her married name?" asked the man on his left.

"No, sir. Her married name was Fine, the same as mine. I mean my maiden name."

"You married?" asked the third man.

She had to think about that a second. "Yes, yes, I am."

The man glanced at her left hand. "Don't wear no rings."

"No." Emma shifted her weight from left to right. How did she get herself into these things? She couldn't lie worth spit. Hadn't she gotten caught every time it mattered? What she was best at was omission. Yes, leaving things out was the name of her game.

"They don't wear no wedding rings in California?"

"Well, not everyone does." She flashed him a big smile, hoping that would get her off the hook. But these were mountain folk, not flatlanders, and they were crusty as old billy goats.

"Everybody does around here, what's married. Ain't nobody around here got nothing to hide."

"Now, he's full of it," said the man called Vern. "This rascal's been married for nigh onto forty years. You see any ring on his tough hide?"

Emma looked down at the man's hands, which looked like the roots of an upended tree. They bore a lot of dirt but no gold.

"Tell you what, boys, we ought to stop wasting this nice lady's

time. You want to know anything about Meadville, you ought to
see Miss Carrie."

"Who's she?"

"Miss Carrie?" All three of the men laughed. Among them they
probably had a complete set of teeth. "Miss Carrie is a retired
schoolteacher, sits in the library afternoons now, runs out and
grabs children when they go past, tries to force them to take
books."

"She ever succeed?" Emma asked.

"Yep. I reckon she does about eight or nine times out of ten.
She's fast, Miss Carrie. And hard to argue with, once she's got
her mind made up."

"Where would I find her?"

Vern squinted up at the sun. He didn't wear a watch.

"Well, you could wait until the library opens at one, or you
could go on over to her house."

"I couldn't do that," Emma said.

"Why not?"

"Well, wouldn't that be rude?"

But if she didn't, what was she going to do until then? There
didn't seem to be much happening in Meadville other than sitting out in front of the Piggly Wiggly.

"Maybe I could call her on the phone?"

"Now, why on earth would you want to? She ain't going to
know you no better when you go on over there after you've
wasted a dime. If I was you, I'd just walk down there," the man
gestured down a tree-lined street, the broad-porched houses
spaced far apart, "and knock on her front door."

"LORD have mercy, child. There's nothing I like better than some
company. And I don't get much of it around here."

Emma had already introduced herself and her mission at the
door, but before she was half finished, the tall thin still-pretty
old woman with the snowy cloud of hair piled atop her head had
taken her arm and pulled her inside. Her grasp was strong.
Emma could see what the men might have meant about Miss
Carrie's will being difficult to resist. Had she plopped a book
into Emma's hands, Emma would have sat right down and
read it.

"Can I get you a glass of iced tea?"

"No, ma'am, that's—"

"Don't stand on ceremony, child. If you've just come in from the road, you need something to drink." Miss Carrie was already halfway into the kitchen. Behind her she left the faint scent of lemon verbena.

The living room was filled with a mix of Grand Rapids veneer and Victorian antiques. From her vantage point on a red satin loveseat Emma looked at an inlaid rosewood grandfather clock ticking away in one corner, swinging its brass pendulum. Heavy cream-colored curtains filtered the sun. But the most outstanding feature of the living room was its astounding assemblage of books. They lined the room floor to ceiling in oak bookcases, all of them chockful.

"I see you noticed my books," Miss Carrie said. She carried a silver tray with a green pressed-glass pitcher, two tall glasses and a china sugar bowl.

"I just can't stand it when people sweeten my tea, can you?" Miss Carrie said. "Just assuming that you like it that way. I think a body ought to have a choice."

Emma agreed.

"Well, anyway, *these* are my friends." The old woman gestured at the thousands of volumes around the room. "They were all strangers, like you, when they first came to call. But now I know them by first name, just like I've known all the people of Meadville. Taught them first grade for three generations."

"Three? Goodness, Miss Carrie, I teach in a junior college, but I can't imagine doing it that long. I'm already trying to get out."

"Well, it's different with you younger folks. You pull up stakes and move on. But back in my time if you grew up a maiden lady like I am, well, you did the best you could, and mostly that meant staying put."

"You never wanted to go away from here?"

"Why, where would I go? This is where I grew up."

"You never wanted to see anything else?"

"Oh, child, I don't mean I *never* left. I went to London and Paris and Rome, Venice and Vienna."

Emma's eyes registered surprise.

"Yes. I did. In 1909, my sister and I and two aunts did a grand tour."

"In 1909?"

"Why, yes. I was born in 1889. That makes me eighty-five this past spring; I'll save you the trouble of subtracting. Anyway, it was a wonderful trip, but I'd *seen* it then, don't you know, so I was content to come back home."

"And you never married? But you're still such a lovely woman. I can't imagine." Oh yes you can, Emma. You mean you just can't imagine it in her time.

"Even in those days, it took more than being lovely, thank you, to make it work. I always found that a married woman had to have a certain kind of malleability, a disposition to bend to the will of a man, and I just never had that." Miss Carrie finished her little speech with a lifted chin and pressed lips, as if it was something she'd long ago decided and had repeated many times in the decades since.

"Maybe not all men." Name three exceptions, Emma. Two. Try one.

"No, not all of them. But most of them are like that, too many to make it likely for a headstrong woman like myself to marry."

"Was there never anyone?"

Emma thought then perhaps she shouldn't be so nosy, but Miss Carrie didn't seem to mind.

"Yes, there was one perfectly wonderful man from Asheville." She waved one hand toward her front door. "Up in North Carolina, about fifty miles north. He was from one of the town's first families, and I met him when I was summering with my Aunt Penelope in the summer of 1913. It's cooler up there, you know. Anyway, I met Malcolm that summer, and he courted me all the next year. It was a scandal, what with all those pretty girls in Asheville waiting for Malcolm to decide to settle down, and I was already an old maid of twenty-three, from this little one-horse town no one had ever heard of. But Malcolm didn't care. He rode over all those miles to call on me. " 'I like a woman,' " he said, " 'who has some spunk, who has a mind and knows it.' "

Miss Carrie smiled then and Emma could see the young woman inside her, her cheeks rosy with color. Some spunk, wasn't that what Jesse had loved about her too, until he'd figured out that part of that equation meant that deep down inside she didn't really need him? That she didn't full-time need anyone? No one,

Emma? Then why are you here in the godforsaken north-Georgia hills looking for the momma you've never known?

"What happened to him?"

"He died in the war, the first war. I never met another man who felt the way he did."

They were quiet for a moment. Emma listened to the grand-father clock ticking.

"Now." Miss Carrie sat up straight, with both her blue-veined hands flat on her lap, shell-pink nails pointing straight toward Emma. "That's enough about me. Tell me again whom you've come seeking."

Emma reached into her bag and pulled out the photocopy of her mother's death certificate.

Miss Carrie peered at it closely through her rimless glasses.

"Yes, it does say Meadville. And it does say 1906. Let's see." She figured quickly in her head. "I was seventeen then. I'd just finished my second year of normal school. But I don't remember this name."

"Do you really think you'd remember?"

"If they were here any time at all. This is just a village, Emma. There's not much that can slip by. Unless . . ." She paused and rested her head on her hand as if she were remembering.

"Yes?" Emma tried to keep the hope out of her voice.

"Unless they were just passing through. Could your grand-father have been an itinerant? A traveler? Maybe a circuit preacher?"

"Miss Carrie," Emma laughed, "I doubt it. My grandfather was a Jew."

"Of course! that's it! Maybe he was the Jew!"

"*The* Jew? Miss Carrie, there are *lots* of Jews."

"But not in the South, Emma, you know that. And hardly ever in a wide place in the road like Meadville. Maybe he was the peddler."

"You *do* remember!"

"I do now. He came through about four times a year, selling things from his wagon, things we couldn't get unless we went into Atlanta, which we only did maybe once a year. Toys, dolls, cigars for the men, lace, ready-made dresses." Miss Carrie paused.

"What?" Emma urged her on. "What?"

Miss Carrie smiled, "Oh, I was just thinking, how we heard a rumor once, from somewhere, maybe Miss Lucy's cousin wrote from Elberton, down there where they had Negroes, that he'd let them try the dresses on. So for a while no one would touch the Jew's, Mutt's, dresses."

"Mutt?"

"Here, let me see that certificate again. Look—" she pointed— " 'Emmanuel Kaplan.' Could Mutt have been his nickname?"

Emma nodded. Her heart was pounding in her throat. "Go on."

"Well, anyway, that didn't last long. We couldn't resist his finery just because of what someone said." She smiled. "We decided that that rumor was wrong."

"Did he have a wife?"

"He did at the end. The last time he came through here."

"What was her name?"

"Child, I don't know. I don't remember. I don't even know that I knew then. And I only saw her that once."

"But you did see her?"

"Yes. And I see it now, clear as day. Mutt said that this was his last trip. He was going to be a father. And there was his wife, standing beside the wagon, her dress billowing out in front of her with the child. They were going to end this trip in Atlanta, where he was going to settle down and open a little store."

"And . . ."

"Well, I guess her time was closer on her than they thought. Because the child was born here. My mother, who did some midwiving, was one of the women who saw her through over at Mrs. Simpson's house. I remember Mrs. Simpson talking with my mother about it later in our kitchen. I, being so young, wasn't supposed to hear, but you know how young people are when somebody's hiding something from them. I was all ears. Anyway, she said she'd wondered if Jews were more like everybody else. But helping Mrs. Mutt through the birthing of her baby, she saw that neither one of them had a long tail!"

Both of them laughed.

"But," Miss Carrie continued, "she said, on the other hand, maybe it was just the men."

"And then what happened?"

"Well, as well as I can recall, a week or so after the baby came—"

"It was a girl?"

"Oh, yes, it was a girl, a pretty little girl. Then they left. I guess they went on to Atlanta like they planned. I never heard anything of them again."

"And you never saw them in Atlanta?"

"Oh, child, that's such a big city. It was, to a small-town girl like me, even then. But I bet, Mutt was such a hard-working man, I bet there was a Kaplan's Dry Goods Store."

In Atlanta! Where she'd lived for three years. Right under her very nose.

"You could look there."

"Yes."

"Is that what you're going to do?"

"Keep looking till I find her?"

"Yes, go on searching until you find out what you want to know."

"I don't know that I'll ever know that, Miss Carrie."

The old woman smiled. "I didn't think so. But," she said, rising, "you can think about that tonight. Right now, why don't you come on in the kitchen and help me get supper started. You are going to stay the night?"

"Oh, I couldn't."

"Why on earth not? Are you just being polite, or do you think you'd be bored to tears spending the evening with an old lady?"

"Miss Carrie," Emma laughed, "I'd be delighted."

THE next morning she waved goodbye to Miss Carrie and headed south again. Well, she had to go back through Atlanta anyway, didn't she? That was the easiest route.

To where, Emma? she asked herself as she rolled past Gainesville. What's your final destination? Where's that place you told Jake you were going? Which reminded her, he'd be worried. She had to give him a call.

Final destination—well, she had to get back to California eventually, didn't she? Of course—if for no other reason, she had to go back and pick up her things. Had to pick up her passport. Hell, she had to settle things with Jesse. Then why aren't you driving north toward Chattanooga—back to California, that's the shortest route. No need to go south at all. Unless you're going to Atlanta to search for Mutt, his wife and their daughter, Helen, no need at all.

IT was an absolutely beautiful morning with blue skies, just a little breeze which ruffled her hair as she stood in the phone booth by the side of the fast-food store, one hand in the back pocket of her jeans. A convertible pulled in, full of high-school girls there to grab a quick breakfast. Their laughter was like bright scarves loosed in the air.

"He said what?"

"So what did *you* say?"

Then giggles. Now, *these* were Southern girls, Emma thought. Blonde with lots of white teeth, and wearing identical sweaters. The hardest decision they'd made all year was what color swimsuit to buy to loll in by the pool at the country club.

"Did you finish *Little Foxes?*" one of them asked.

"Yes. Wasn't it great? 'Course by the time old Miz Chapman finishes talking about it, I'll forget how much I liked it."

"Why do you think they always do that?" asked another, and then their voices disappeared with them inside the glass doors.

Well, Emma thought. Well, now.

She dropped a handful of change into the phone. First she called West Cypress. Rosalie answered the phone.

"Hi, howyah doing? . . . Fine. Just called to check in. . . . The weather here in California? Oh, it's fine . . . Daddy's still asleep? Well, tell him hello for me." She hoped he'd understand.

She didn't know for sure she was going to make the second call until she'd already dialed the number from information and it was ringing. What if his wife answered on this Sunday morning?

"Hello?"

"Will?"

"Yes?"

"Will Tucker with the white-blond hair who was waiting to meet me so long ago at State, outside my office?"

"Emma." He didn't say her name as if he was surprised, or excited, but more as if he'd been waiting for her call—for almost ten years.

"Where are you?"

"In a phone booth in Gainesville."

"How long till you'll be here?"

"About an hour."

"I'll be waiting for you at Minnie's."

"They still have great pancakes?"

"Did last week."

WHY, Emma, why? she asked herself, as she threaded her car through Atlanta's labyrinth of similarly named streets, many of them dead ends and half of them called some variant of Peachtree. Why did you call Will? What on earth do you want from him? Don't you have enough on your plate without digging up an old lover who told you to get lost ten years ago, who's married, for Christ's sakes?

But he wasn't. He was still as beautiful as the day she had first spied him at the end of the hall, his hair, silvered blond, glowing under the light. But he wasn't married.

"Emma!" He stood up from the booth in Minnie's, a pink sweater, almost the same shade as the one she was wearing, draped over his shoulders, khakis, loafers. He was more handsome than ever, trim, a monster grin on his face, but no gold on his finger. She'd bumped into him a couple of times after he married, before she ran away to New York. The gold had been there then.

"What on earth are you doing back here? No, wait." He gestured to the waitress, ordered pancakes for them both, crispy bacon on the side. "And keep the coffee coming," he said.

"Mr. Tucker, would you like your own pot?"

"Great idea," he laughed. "Now," and he zeroed his attention in on Emma's face, "tell me everything. Everything from the last time I saw you. Shoot."

She did. She told all, from Atlanta to New York, the trips to Europe, the growing food passion, California, Jesse. When Will pushed her about why she'd left, she added Caroline and Minor. When he asked her what she was doing now in the South, she went all the way back again to Helen, Rosalie, Jake.

When she was through they had long finished the pancakes and the twice-filled coffeepot.

"Let's walk," Will said. It wasn't far to Piedmont Park.

They strolled for a long time in silence, Will's forehead fur-

rowed, one arm thrown across her shoulder. As they passed the
duck pond, she said, "I wonder if those are relatives of those
same ducks I used to feed."

"What?"

"I used to come here and feed them after we split up. I was
crazy. I didn't know what else to do."

He grinned. "So what else is new?"

"Will?"

"What?"

"Did you think I was crazy then?" She hesitated. "Do you
think so now?"

He answered her question with one of his own. "Emma, why
did you call me?"

"I don't know."

"Yes you do. You called me because I told you something a
long time ago that you didn't like but that you knew was true.
And now you want to see if I have any more answers."

"Like what?"

You know what. It hasn't changed, Emma. You cozy up to
people, but only on your terms. You don't really need them.
That's the answer to the puzzle about you, baby. That's the
whole shot."

"I do. I needed you."

"Nawh." He shrugged. "You thought you did. But look how
well you've done without me."

"How *well?* I'm on the verge of divorce!"

"Is that how you measure a whole life? Then I sure as hell
must be a failure."

She could ask it then. "You're divorced?"

"Twice." He waved away the questions he saw in her face.
"You don't want to hear it. All you need to know is that I've discovered that we have a lot in common, you and I, a lot."

"What's that supposed to mean?"

"Means I don't need anybody, either. Been living with my dog
Buster the past two years. I see my son on weekends. The hap-
piest two years of my life."

"I'm not you, Will."

"But yes, you are, my darling. Very close." He pulled her
around to face him, touched her on the cheek. "You are a conundrum, Emma. You are a piece of work. A hey-diddle-diddle. A

kiss-my-ass. In some ways you don't give a flying fuck. You do
what you want to do—probably because you have to. Otherwise
you couldn't breathe. You aren't put together exactly the same as
other people. That's the beauty of you—and the puzzle, the
enigma. You're a contradiction. That same independence that
draws them to you is what pushes them away, 'cause you don't
need them."

"I don't know what you're talking about!" She whirled away
from him, and he pulled her back.

"Oh yes you do. You know that you can walk away from Jesse
just as easily as you've walked away from everybody else in your
life."

"Then why am I having such a hard time doing it?"

"Because you *married* him, which makes a difference, and . . ."
and then he grinned his slow grin, "because he's black. You hate
to give that one up."

"That is *not* true! Jesus, Will, I never thought you were a
racist. You didn't used to be."

"And I'm not now. There was nothing racist about what I just
said, and your reaction was positively knee-jerk. What I mean
is that he fits. It's absolutely typical of you to marry someone
who would stand other people on their ear, sure because he's
talented, sure because he's intelligent, and great, and funny, and
probably has a big dick—Jesus, I don't know what all. But God
Almighty, Emma, wasn't it just the frosting on the cake that he
was black too? Because that made it more exciting? And it was
the goddamned absolute last thing a girl from West Cypress
would do?"

"No!" she shouted. A couple passing turned and stared.

"I'm not saying that you didn't love him. I'm sure you did.
The way you love anybody. Maybe even more. But you didn't
need him, Emma. And there's nothing wrong with that!"

"What do you mean, nothing wrong?" She knew Will. She
remembered this kind of argument from their past. He was up to
some trick. He was going to lead her down a path where she'd
agree to what he was saying, and then he'd cut her legs out from
under her.

"There's absolutely nothing wrong with not needing someone.
It's that need, don't you see, that dependency, that keeps most
people together. Not because they love each other so goddamned

much. It's because they just can't imagine what it would be like
to go on without someone, even if that someone is causing them
an incredible amount of pain. Or when they do leave, they jump
right back into another pot. You don't need that, Emma."

There was pain in her voice. "But I don't want to be alone."

"You never are alone. You weren't before Jesse, remember?
You have friends. You'll always have lovers—if you want them.
And you have work. I don't mean your teaching; you did that
'cause you thought you ought to. But cooking abroad, becoming
a chef! That's it, Emma. You always were the hungriest woman
I'd ever seen in my life. And with your persnickityness, which I
know must extend to your palate, you can't help but be great.
You'll find an Italian lover. A French lover. Oh, Emma, you're
not going to be alone. All that matters anyway is sex and work.
That's what Freud said."

"He said *love* and work, dodo."

"Well, he got that part wrong. What did he know? He was a
repressed homosexual."

"I love your logic, Will."

"And that ain't all." He winked at her and gave her a friendly
pat on the behind. "So, we've settled the Jesse question."

"What do you mean, settled?"

"Have you been listening? You're divorcing him, of course."

"Explain to me exactly why I'm doing that."

Will sat down on a bench and ran his hands across the top of
his lowered head. "Because you don't love him anymore, Emma.
At least not enough to make you stay with him. You've done that
thing. Now you're antsy. You want to move on. Now deny that."

She opened her mouth, then closed it. He was right, she
couldn't.

"You don't need him at all. What you need is to get on about
your business and get your sweet butt over to Europe and start
cooking."

"You better watch out, Will. They're going to arrest you for
practicing psychiatry without a license."

"Psychiatry, hell. I think you left the South, girl, and you lost
your common sense. Got your head full of all that Commie pinko
propaganda. Don't know which way to turn, like a coon up a
tree."

"If you're through talking all that trash, Dr. Tucker, you might as well solve my next problem. I'm sure you must have an opinion about what I ought to do about Rosalie and Jake."

"What's to do? Except to go back and have a decent visit with them. What's the problem?"

"What about the lies they told me all these years? First she, and now he? No, I guess he was first, from the very beginning. He *always* lied to me about being my daddy."

And then, all of a sudden, right in the middle of her joking, her tears began to fall like summer rain. A ball of pain had wadded itself up in her chest, then her throat, and out it came, bouncing. She was crying hard, gasping, shoulders shaking. These weren't like the tears she sometimes shed with Jesse, tears of show, of ought to, obligation. She hadn't cried like this since she was a little girl. This sorrow was the real thing, a sense of loss that laid her waste.

Will stood and watched. Her sobs continued, deeper and louder. Her shoulders shivered. When she choked, he patted her on the back and handed her his handkerchief, but he didn't say a word.

"They lied to me. Rosalie lied to me. Jake lied to me. Aunt Ruth and Uncle George, all of them knew. I *know* they knew. And they never told me the truth. I don't even know my daddy's name," she cried.

"And why do you want to know it?" Will finally said. "Was he such a saint?"

Emma's head jerked up. Mascara ran in black gutters down her face.

"Who the fuck do you think he was, Emma? A playboy millionaire? The president of Harvard? Was he someone just incredibly wonderful, this father of yours who knocked your mother up?"

"Don't?" Her mouth contorted.

"Don't what? Don't speak the truth? You used to tell me about this years ago when we were together, about your mother, your *real* mother, as if she was so great. You never knew her, Emma. You don't know who the hell she was. And all you've learned from Jake is that he loved her enough to go along with it even after he found out that she tricked him into marrying her when she was carrying some other guy's kid. That doesn't make her such a wonderful person, Emma. That's not a nice trick."

"But she . . ."

"But she what? She *died?* People die every day. There's nothing particularly noble about it. It's not as if she did it on purpose for you, like Jesus, that she gave her life so that you could live. It didn't exactly work that way. If she knew that she shouldn't get pregnant because she had a weak heart, then she oughtn't to have been screwing around without being careful enough to keep from getting knocked up."

"Will!" Emma cried. Her guts were turning over. She was going to throw up.

"If you ask me, what was noble was that your father hung in there after he got tricked in the first place, and then whammo! double-tricked because she was dead, and he had you, a two-week-old, on his hands. That wasn't exactly what the man bargained for. What was noble was that Rosalie took you both in."

"Stop!"

"No, I'm not going to stop, because I really think you need to hear this. I absolutely refuse to have you go around like millions of other people, because you're *not* like millions of other people in so many ways, copping out on everything that goes wrong in your life by blaming it all on your parents. 'If only my parents had loved me enough, I wouldn't. . . .' Fuck that. Do you know how much your parents loved you, Emma? *Your* parents, Rosalie and Jake? They went through a lot of shit together. From what you've told me, they didn't even love each other, probably never had sex. They did it for *something,* Emma. I mean, like everybody else, they probably in some ways need one another, but mostly they did it for you, Emma. They stuck because of you."

"I never asked them to." She'd used the same tone at six, with her bottom lip stuck out.

"It doesn't matter. Don't you see that? It doesn't matter what you wanted. What they wanted was to provide a home for you. And they did. They loved you, girl."

"They sure have weird ways of showing it." Emma still wasn't convinced. And if she let herself be, she was going to have to give up a lot.

"Well, the bad news is that they aren't perfect. I know that's hard for you to accept, but they just aren't. Like everybody else, they have ravels and rough edges. They don't always do the right thing. And they may not even be terribly smart, or feeling, or even loving all the time. Some mornings they probably have bad breath. The good news is that they did the best they could. What the fuck did you want from them? Did they abuse you? Did they beat you up? Tie you to the heater? Did they drink? Lock you in a dungeon? Keep you from going to school?"

"You know they didn't."

"Then what did they do that was so awful?"

She whispered, "They didn't know who I was, Will. They still don't. They don't know a thing about me."

"Well, Jesus mothering Christ, Emma. Why's that such big news? When the hell's the last time you ever tried to have a conversation with them? It's not as if you haven't been a little hard-assed secretive yourself."

Emma stayed awake all night thinking about what he'd said.

THE next morning Will asked, "So, today do you want me to help you track down Kaplan's Dry Goods Store? Or do you want to do that alone?"

Emma thought for a long while. Then, "Nope," she finally said.

"Nope what? No help?"

"Nope. I'm giving it up. I'm letting the Kaplans rest in peace, whoever, wherever they are. I thought all night about them, Will, about Rosalie and Jake. I hate to admit ever that you're even the tiniest bit right, but I'm gonna head on back to West Cypress. I guess I need to do some visiting."

"GIVE old Jake and Rosalie a hug for me," he called as she backed out of his driveway.

"You never met them, Will."

"So what? With you for a daughter, they need all the hugs they can get." And then he raced over to the car and opened the door and gave her a big one. "Just kidding," he whispered into her ear. "Another thirty years, Em, you'll be great at it. Hell, you're gonna be the perfect daughter, maybe even before they're dead."

They exchanged a long last embrace.

"Send me postcards from Europe."

She was pulling out again. "What if I decide to come back to Atlanta to open up shop?" she called.

"Great idea! Love to have you back in town. And remember I'll always be behind you, or right next door. But don't start imagining things." He shook a finger at her. "You don't need me full time—any more than I need you. I know you, girl. I know you from before."

"I never loved anybody but you, Will."

"Yeah, sweetheart, and the check is in the mail."

20

West Cypress

EMMA TOOK HER TIME driving the six hundred miles to West Cypress, turned south past Meridian, out of her way, down to New Orleans. She spent a couple of days there eating and walking, walking and eating—stalling. She had crayfish étouffée at the Bon Ton, barbecued shrimp at Manale's, oyster soup at Brennan's, crabmeat Yvonne at Galatoire's.

Might as well pork up, she told herself, before you get to Rosalie's. 'Cause unless some miracle has transpired, there'll be mystery meat and gizzard soup.

Now, Emma, hush your mouth, that's hardly the proper attitude for the returning prodigal daughter, which she was, she thought, sort of. Will's words kept running through her head, over and over again.

From the table next to her, an old man leaned over and tapped her on the shoulder. "Excuse me, if you're through with it, could I borrow your paper?"

Emma started. Atop a frizz of white hair was perched a baseball cap. The man looked like Herman.

"Sure," she said. "I'm finished." She handed the *Times-Picayune* to him. "Take it."

"Thanks." And then he put the paper down. "You live around here?"

"Nope, just visiting." Was the old geezer trying to pick her up?

"On vacation?"

"No. Yes. Well, kind of."

He laughed. "Sounds like you don't know what you're doing."

She laughed, too. "Does, doesn't it? I'm making a big loop.

Touring the Old South. When I finish this," she pointed to the remains of her coffee, "I'm on my way up to West Cypress."

He shook his head. "Heard of it, but don't know it." He wouldn't, for he spoke in the Brooklyn-tinged accent of the native. Northern Louisiana might as well be on another planet to him, the two halves of the state were so far apart in spirit.

"Why should you be going there?"

"It's home." She smiled. "Going to see my momma and daddy."

She chatted with the old man another half an hour. He told her about how he used to be a sailor, shipping in and out of the New Orleans port, after his trips around the world always returning. Jake, she thought, Jake would have loved your life.

"But I always came back," he said. "New Orleans, best place on the earth to be."

"Your family's here?"

"Nawh." He waved a hand in dismissal. "My wife threw me out years ago. Couldn't take all my coming and going. Thought I had a girl in every port." His blue eyes twinkled. Damn, he looked like Herman.

"Did you?"

The old man, whose name was Oscar, just grinned.

"Kids?"

"Two. But they've been long gone. One in Houston, one in San Francisco. I never see them. Your folks are lucky that you're such a good daughter, that you come back home."

EMMA paid her check and stood. It was time to hit the road.

Around Baton Rouge she picked up a radio station that was playing jazz and rhythm and blues. Elvis crooned "One Night with You." Lordy, lordy, didn't he sound good? He didn't look it, though, not in the pictures she'd seen of him lately. All that lean hungriness turned to puffy fat. J.D. had, too, right after he married Maylene. Southern men did that, got married and then took pride in growing bellies, patting them like blue-ribbon watermelons. Why, she'd hardly recognized J.D. in that last photograph with his obituary in the paper. And what about Ricardo Martinez, she wondered then, that sexy Mexican Elvis look-alike, that devil who pretended to be preaching for the Lord, who'd seduced her so at twelve that she'd thrown over her determination to be a Jew (whatever that was) to be baptized in his arms? Were those beautiful brown eyes now buried in pig fat?

Good God! It struck her as she thought about that: If Jake wasn't *really* her daddy, not blood kin anyway, and that other nameless fast-talking, skeedaddling—go on, Emma, say it—worthless son-of-a-bitch was, the one who had left Helen in the lurch, then what if, what if—hell, maybe she was half a Jew again! But no, no, that wasn't right. If her mother was, she was. Oh, hell, Emma, give it up. Just go ahead and be a Southern Baptist—Jew for the rest of your life. It has a certain ring anyway, doesn't it? Then she thought of Will and laughed. He'd say that she'd go out of her way to make something like that up. That she'd do it just to be different, just like . . .

Just like marrying Jesse.

Well, you can run, Miss Emma, but you can't hide. Gotta deal with it *all*, girl. 'Cause anywhere you go it's gonna catch up with you.

Oh, Jesse.

She was pulling into Natchez now, the best route from New Orleans cutting through the southwest corner of Mississippi. Soon she'd cross over the Big Muddy and be back on the Louisiana side.

In a way she'd always wanted Jesse to see all this, the Old South, Natchez, this pretty riverbank town with its antebellum houses that were so gorgeous in the azaleaed springtime when they were filled with visitors taking the tour called the Pilgrimage. He would love the fine woodwork, the elaborate mantelpieces, the hand-carved furniture.

"Sure," he'd say, though, "good work done by slaves' hands." And it was, of course, though some of the furniture was English or French; every brick was laid, every nail hammered by blacks before the Emancipation. And she could imagine what his reaction would be when the tour guide, a Daughter of the Confederacy whose accent would be so thick that even Emma could hardly understand her, pointed out the trapdoor in the master's bedroom floor beneath which lived a slave who was always on call. Or the elaborate fans of peacock feathers she'd seen in many of these homes, suspended over the dining tables. The plantation owners wanted cool breezes when they dined, courtesy of the arm of the little black boy in livery who stood in a corner pulling a

rope. He'd look very much like the statues that so many sub-
urban Southern houses still planted on either side of the driveway, little colored boys in livery, sometimes holding a lamp.

She'd told Jesse about those statues.

"Let's get us a couple for Skytop," he'd said, "and I'll paint
their faces white."

Nope, she'd never been able to convince Jesse that there was
anything in the South that should have been saved from Sher-
man's March. She could never explain to him that, even though
she didn't want to live there anymore, there was a great deal
about the South that she loved.

"Unreconstructed," he'd mumble, teasing her. Though every
once in a while she didn't think he was teasing.

Ah, Jesse. You never should have married a Southern girl.

And then she almost ran off the road.

Now, *there* was a novel idea. Wait a minute, Will, she wanted
to turn around and holler, as if he could hear her across three
and a half states. I didn't do this alone. If, in my marrying Jesse,
his being black was the frosting on the cake, why the hell did he
marry me? Huh? Answer that, Mr. Know-It-All, Mr. Five-Cent
Psychiatrist. Why'd he hitch up with Miss Scarlett?

I don't have time to work this out, she thought then. Just
passed Winnsboro. Before much longer, I'll be in West Cypress.

Why did people marry, anyway? If it weren't race that was
standing between them, there were always a million other things,
though granted, race was a big one. But what about religion,
politics, preference for bedroom temperature, windows open or
closed, peanut butter crunchy or smooth, left or right side, faster,
slower, or not at all? Sometimes she thought it was a miracle that
two people stayed in the same room for more than five minutes
without shooting each other, much less signing on for life.

Well, she had, hadn't she? But she hadn't meant it. Will was
right. *Probably* right.

She flipped an imaginary coin in the air then, as she often did,
to see not which way it landed, but how she felt about it.

Heads, she'd go back to Jesse. Well, sure, they could work it
out. They could both try really hard. They could make more
compromises.

Tails. She exhaled a sigh of relief. It was a little scary. But, oh
Lord, how good it would feel to be free.

Well, she was going to be free anyway, wasn't she? She was going to Europe for at least six months. And Jesse had been pissing in the wind when he said he was coming over after Christmas. He wasn't going anywhere. He was going to rot up there in Skytop.

How quick you are to feel angry at him again, Emma. Can't you remember any of the good times? Can't you give the man a break?

As she drove the last few miles into West Cypress, she did. She looked out at the scenery she'd passed a million times as a girl and recalled loving times with Jesse, her husband, the man whom nobody, nobody in this, her hometown, knew about.

Soon she'd be driving past her Aunt Janey's house, where Aunt Janey still lived with her son Cooter. Emma remembered how she and Jesse used to lie in bed, her telling stories about Cooter and his made-up religion, their almost dying laughing.

She remembered the time she and Jesse had taken a picnic to the amphitheater at Stanford to lie on the grass and listen to the Preservation Hall Band.

She remembered that flight from the Silver Dollar Saloon to Yosemite, their honeymoon suite at the Awahnee.

She remembered the first time they ever made love.

She remembered her eyes in that painting on Skytop's wall.

She remembered Jesse smacking her in the head with the door of that restaurant in Los Gatos and carrying her up the stairs.

Ah, Miss Scarlett, she thought then. What if when you decide that you don't want him, you double back and change your mind? And what if he doesn't give a damn?

But in her heart of hearts she knew it was over. All over but the shouting. Nope. There wasn't even any shouting to do. Will was right. It was time to move on, to drop the Tree from her procession of names and get back to being Emma Fine, Emma Whatsit.

ROSALIE was standing out in the yard when Emma drove up.

"Goodness gracious, sakes alive, you almost scared me to death," she said. "What on earth are you doing here?"

"I thought I'd come visit for a few days. Is that okay?"

"Okay? Why, it's wonderful!" Rosalie's heart was palpitating. "Did you just drive here all the way from California?"

"Well, I sort of mosied my way here. I took my time."

But didn't I just talk with you three or four days ago? Rosalie thought, and then she bit her tongue. Whatever, Emma was here, it didn't matter. "Here, let me help you carry your things in."

"No, that's all right. Let's leave them where they are for a while." Emma glanced around the front yard. "It always looks so pretty," she said. "I wish I had your green thumb."

"It just takes patience," Rosalie said, smiling, pleased with the compliment, breathing a little easier. Oh, how she always wanted to see Emma, lived for it, always had, but somehow things never seemed to go right. *That,* of all the sadnesses she'd known, was the biggest one in her life. "Putting things in the dirt and letting them grow is all I do. Of course, if I don't like what they're doing, I pull them up, try another spot."

"Did you plant that tree?" Emma pointed to the middle of the yard, to a big pin oak.

"I did. I planted it the week we moved in here. That was over ten years ago. It's doing well, isn't it?"

"I don't remember it being that tall."

"Well, it wasn't." Rosalie laughed. "I mean it's grown. Come on around back. I'll show you my winter garden."

But just then Jake came bustling out the side door.

"I thought you were napping," Rosalie cried, "or I would have called you."

"Daddy!" Emma threw her arms around him.

"Emma!"

She whispered into his ear, "I tried to call, but . . ."

He just nodded. He'd worried. He'd cried himself to sleep after Rosalie was snoring, torturing himself with his transgressions. Then, finally, Rosalie said Emma had called, and he'd breathed easier. And now she was here. She'd come home. He stepped back and looked into her face. She winked at him and he dissolved into tears. He thought his heart would burst.

"Why, Jake," Rosalie said, laughing a little, for when had she ever seen such emotion? "You're getting to be just like me, a foolish old woman."

"Yes," he cried then, laughing at the same time, "I guess I am."

They went on a tour of the garden, Jake trailing a little behind, Rosalie pointing out her compost heap, the winter squash, the cabbages, the turnips, the remains of her grapevines.

"I made twenty-two pints of jam," she said. "I thought about making some wine."

"Why, goodness!" Emma said, teasing, pretending to be shocked. "Wine!"

Rosalie laughed. "You can never tell what mischief a woman is going to get into in her old age. I was reading in one of those Sunset gardening books you sent me from California, and it didn't seem like it would be so hard." And then she waited, she waited for Emma to tell her that she didn't know what she was doing, but Emma didn't.

Instead, as if she'd been rehearsing for it earlier, just a little while ago as she'd approached West Cypress trying to remember the good times with Jesse, she remembered an even earlier good time.

"Do you remember when you used to teach in that three-room country school?"

"In Mayhew."

"Yes, and when I was little, before I started school, you used to take me with you sometimes?"

Rosalie nodded. Of course she remembered. She remembered every second of those golden days, Emma's early childhood.

"And out behind the school there were those plum trees. At lunch I'd go out with the big kids and we'd pick plums and eat until we were sick? And you kept saying we ought to save some for jelly, but we never left a one?"

"The school pageant that once?" Rosalie was warming to her own memories of that time. "When we did Tom Thumb? And you were his wife?"

Jake spoke up, "Ro stayed up all one night making your costume. I remember that. It was pink."

"Maybe that's why it's always been my favorite color," Emma laughed. "And when it was really cold, the minute we got there you'd make a fire in the woodstove in the middle of the room? Do you remember that?"

"I'd take cans of chicken soup and put them in a pot on top of that stove and we'd have it for dinner." And then she corrected herself, as Emma had corrected her so many times, "I mean lunch." Lunch was what Emma called dinner, and dinner for supper, and there was no supper in her vocabulary at all.

"Speaking of lunch, or dinner, could I have some?"

"Why, of course," Rosalie said, "let's go on in the house. I've got some okra and some butter beans left over. We ate a while ago. But I'll warm some up."

"And some cornbread?"

"No . . ." Rosalie hesitated.

"That's okay. Later I'll make some."

And on it went like that. It wasn't so hard, she thought. Not hard at all, as long as she kept it light. As long as they just made small talk. Later that evening, after dinner, supper, she started to tell them about her trip to Italy and France.

"Well, I don't know, Emma," Rosalie started. "It seems like an awfully big gamble to be taking."

Emma felt her back start up. "Why?"

"To throw over what you already have for something you don't know about."

"But I do know about cooking. I've been doing it for years now. The catering, working with Tony—"

"Who?"

And suddenly Emma realized, no, of course, they didn't know. She hadn't ever talked about any of that. She'd written, occasionally, a line or two, but how could they know what it was all about?

So she explained. She told them how it had all started the first time she'd gone to France, how she almost felt like she'd lived there in a former life, how familiar everything had tasted. She looked at Jake. He was grinning. And Rosalie listened, nodded, asked a question from time to time.

"Well," she said finally, "I guess you don't have anything to lose. I mean, you can always go back to teaching, can't you, if it doesn't work out."

But it will, it will, don't you see, don't you have any faith in me? Emma started to say, and then she didn't. Because of course Rosalie would want to know that she had a safety net, that she wouldn't starve, that it wouldn't be the way the Depression had been for her all over again.

"Of course," she said. "Of course I could."

IT was shortly after that, when Rosalie left the kitchen, where they'd been sitting around the table, to go to the bathroom, that Emma reached over and squeezed Jake's hand.

"It's okay, Daddy," she whispered so that Rosalie wouldn't
hear. "It's all right."

His eyes filled with quick tears. "I . . . I . . ." he stuttered—
well, part of it was stuttering, and part of it was that he couldn't
find the words.

"I know you did what you thought was right. And it was right,
Daddy. You did the right thing."

"I love you, Emma," he whispered.

"I love you too," she said.

"WELL," said Rosalie a little while later, "I guess we all ought to
be going to bed. It's been a long day."

"You're right," agreed Emma. "And a long road."

"I know that driving's tiring. I'll go and put some covers on
your bed."

"Just leave it. I'll do it. But first there's a phone call I need to
make."

Rosalie's heart sank. She was going to start lining up all her
friends, her escapes out of the house, as always.

"I need to call someone in California," Emma said. "I'll reverse
the charges."

"That's okay," Jake said, without even looking at Rosalie, the
keeper of the purse strings. "Just make your call."

And with that they both headed down the hallway toward the
bedrooms.

Emma looked at the phone on the wall beside the refrigerator.
She hadn't talked to Jesse since she'd left him well over a week
ago. Jesus, it seemed like so much longer. It always did when you
traveled, like you were moving and everything else was standing
still. She smiled then. Was Jesse still standing there in his paisley
robe, waiting for her to come home and make his dinner?

She'd driven halfway across the country and a good piece back.
But California seemed like the end of the world from this vantage point. And so much had transpired in that short time—her
daddy's secret, Miss Carrie and finding out about Mutt and her
grandmother, that they'd been in Atlanta, maybe there were relatives there still. Well, she could go back and find them someday,
if she wanted to, but that didn't seem so important now. And
Will. Gorgeous, too-smart-for-his-own-britches Will. Where did

he get off, thinking he knew so much about her? Was he right? Well, so far it *felt* like he'd been right about her parents—her *parents*, Rosalie and Jake.

But, and then the thought niggled at a corner of her mind, wasn't it weird, wasn't it strange? They *weren't*, really. So who did that make her? Who was she?

Then she heard herself running down River Road, a week or so ago, running from what Jake had told her, calling her own name. *Emma. Emma.* As if she had to say it over and over to hold on. To hold on to her identity.

And then she'd asked him, hadn't she? She'd asked Jake, *"But who am I?"* as if he were one of those daddies, one of those other girls' daddies she'd always admired, the ones who were so sure of themselves, who were so strong, who always had the shoulder to lean on, the answer to every question, she'd cried out to him, lying in the dirt of River Road Park, *"But who am I?"*

And he'd given her the answer, hadn't he, without a moment's hesitation. He didn't stutter. He didn't even have to think. He said, "You're still Emma Fine, of course."

She was, wasn't she? She was the same willful, headstrong, independent, what had Will said, *conundrum, a hey-diddle-diddle, a piece of work?* She grinned then.

It didn't matter, did it? She *was* Emma Rochelle Fine, Southern Baptist–Jew, child of Rosalie and Jake, child of Herman, child of Helen and whoever that slippery devil was (maybe he died, Emma, maybe he fell down a hole, yes, and maybe he was the King of Mesopotamia, what difference?), child of everyone she'd ever known, child of herself—of her own making. And she'd keep on creating herself, wouldn't she, on and on, keep on making herself up as she went along.

But first, first things first, she had to call Jesse. It was time.

She dialed the number and held her breath. And in that breath, and in those four rings, she practiced, running the words through her mind at the speed of light. "I'm flying home tomorrow, Jesse. But just to pack. Just to pick up my things. I'm leaving my car here, because I don't have much time left, and I need to talk to you. I need to explain why I'm not coming back again to stay, why I'm leaving you. After Europe, I'm striking out again on my own. We'll both be better for it, Jess, both of us are better alone."

After the fourth ring he answered, "Hello."

"Jesse," she began.

"This is the residence of Jesse Tree. After the tone, you will have three minutes to leave your message. Thank you and goodbye."

Emma stood there stunned. Jesse's baritone was still ringing in her ears.

And then she laughed. She stood in Rosalie's kitchen and laughed out loud. Jesse didn't need her anymore, either, if he ever had needed her. He didn't even need her to answer the phone.

She left no message, other than her laughter, that deep rejoicing that seemed to burst out of her in these past few days.

"What's so funny?"

Emma jumped. It was Rosalie.

"I made your bed," Rosalie said. And then her curiosity got the better of her, though she knew Emma hated her prying into her business, and she didn't want to ruin the lovely time they'd had so far. She couldn't help herself. "Who *was* that you were laughing with on the phone?"

Well, here it was. She could tell Rosalie something consequential. She could jump over all that small talk and get down to the heart of something. Okay, Will, you talk about my being hard-assed secretive. I can tell her something. I can show those people, who've asked me that question ever since I married Jesse: "A Southern girl marrying a black man. Well, you must have done it out of rebellion. Didn't you do it to show your parents something?" Well, Emma, this is your big chance.

She could say it now, "I have a good-news/bad-news joke for you, Rosalie. The bad news is I'm married to a black man. The good news is I'm getting divorced."

Rosalie was still looking at her, waiting for an answer to her question.

Emma didn't lie. She said, "I was calling Jesse Tree. But he wasn't home."

Rosalie looked at her and nodded. And because the name meant absolutely nothing to her, because she'd never heard it before in her entire life, she smiled and said, "Well, maybe you can try him tomorrow. Maybe then he'll be home."

"I'll do that, Momma," Emma said.

And Rosalie, who hadn't heard Emma say that word in so

many years that she'd given up hope of ever hearing it again, turned and put her arms around Emma.

"It's good to have you home," she said, "even if it's for such a short visit."

"And it's good to be here." Emma hugged her back. "It truly is."

Then Rosalie switched out the light, and both she and her daughter tiptoed out of the dark kitchen—tiptoed so as not to wake the already snoring Jake who was dreaming about sailing on the blue Pacific with his little girl Emma—tiptoed to their bedroom doors, whispered good night and went to bed.